D0481440

The Best of
Nancy Drew®

CLASSIC COLLECTION

Volume 2

The Hidden Staircase
The Ghost of Blackwood Hall
The Thirteenth Pearl

By Carolyn Keene

❖❖❖
Grosset & Dunlap • New York

Acknowledgement is made to Mildred Wirt Benson,
who under the pen name Carolyn Keene, wrote the original
NANCY DREW books.

NANCY DREW MYSTERY STORIES®

The Hidden Staircase

BY CAROLYN KEENE

GROSSET & DUNLAP
Publishers • New York
A member of The Putnam & Grosset Group

Contents

CHAPTER I

The Haunted House

NANCY DREW began peeling off her garden gloves as she ran up the porch steps and into the hall to answer the ringing telephone. She picked it up and said, "Hello!"

"Hi, Nancy! This is Helen." Although Helen Corning was nearly three years older than Nancy, the two girls were close friends.

"Are you tied up on a case?" Helen asked.

"No. What's up? A mystery?"

"Yes—a haunted house."

Nancy sat down on the chair by the telephone. "Tell me more!" the eighteen-year-old detective begged excitedly.

"You've heard me speak of my Aunt Rosemary," Helen began. "Since becoming a widow, she has lived with her mother at Twin Elms, the old family mansion out in Cliffwood. Well, I went to see them yesterday. They said that many strange,

mysterious things have been happening there recently. I told them how good you are at solving
mysteries, and they'd like you to come out to Twin
Elms and help them." Helen paused, out of
breath.

"It certainly sounds intriguing," Nancy replied,
her eyes dancing.

"If you're not busy, Aunt Rosemary and I would
like to come over in about an hour and talk to you
about the ghost."

"I can't wait."

After Nancy had put down the phone, she sat
lost in thought for several minutes. Since solving
The Secret of the Old Clock, she had longed for
another case. Here was her chance!

Attractive, blond-haired Nancy was brought out
of her daydreaming by the sound of the doorbell.
At the same moment the Drews' housekeeper,
Hannah Gruen, came down the front stairs.

"I'll answer it," she offered.

Mrs. Gruen had lived with the Drews since
Nancy was three years old. At that time Mrs.
Drew had passed away and Hannah had become
like a second mother to Nancy. There was a deep
affection between the two, and Nancy confided all
her secrets to the understanding housekeeper.

Mrs. Gruen opened the door and instantly a
man stepped into the hall. He was short, thin,
and rather stooped. Nancy guessed his age to be
about forty.

"Is Mr. Drew at home?" he asked brusquely. "My name is Gomber—Nathan Gomber."

"No, he's not here just now," the housekeeper replied.

The caller looked over Hannah Gruen's shoulder and stared at Nancy. "Are you Nancy Drew?"

"Yes, I am. Is there anything I can do for you?"

The man's shifty gaze moved from Nancy to Hannah. "I've come out of the goodness of my heart to warn you and your father," he said pompously.

"Warn us? About what?" Nancy asked quickly.

Nathan Gomber straightened up importantly and said, "Your father is in great danger, Miss Drew!"

Both Nancy and Hannah Gruen gasped. "You mean this very minute?" the housekeeper questioned.

"All the time," was the startling answer. "I understand you're a pretty bright girl, Miss Drew —that you even solve mysteries. Well, right now I advise you to stick close to your father. Don't leave him for a minute."

Hannah Gruen looked as if she were ready to collapse and suggested that they all go into the living room, sit down, and talk the matter over. When they were seated, Nancy asked Nathan Gomber to explain further.

"The story in a nutshell is this," he began. "You know that your father was brought in to do legal work for the railroad when it was buying property for the new bridge here."

As Nancy nodded, he continued, "Well, a lot of the folks who sold their property think they were gypped."

Nancy's face reddened. "I understood from my father that everyone was well paid."

"That's not true," said Gomber. "Besides, the railroad is in a real mess now. One of the property owners, whose deed and signature they claim to have, says that he never signed the contract of sale."

"What's his name?" Nancy asked.

"Willie Wharton."

Nancy had not heard her father mention this name. She asked Gomber to go on with his story.

"I'm acting as agent for Willie Wharton and several of the land owners who were his neighbors," he said, "and they can make it pretty tough for the railroad. Willie Wharton's signature was never witnessed and the attached certificate of acknowledgment was not notarized. That's good proof the signature was a forgery. Well, if the railroad thinks they're going to get away with this, they're not!"

Nancy frowned. Such a procedure on the part of the property owners meant trouble for her father! She said evenly, "But all Willie Wharton has to do is swear before a notary that he did sign the contract of sale."

Gomber chuckled. "It's not that easy, Miss Drew. Willie Wharton is not available. Some of us have a good idea where he is and we'll produce him at the right time. But that time won't be until the railroad promises to give the sellers more money. Then he'll sign. You see, Willie is a real kind man and he wants to help his friends out whenever he can. Now he's got a chance."

Nancy had taken an instant dislike to Gomber and now it was quadrupled. She judged him to be the kind of person who stays within the boundaries of the law but whose ethics are questionable. This was indeed a tough problem for Mr. Drew!

"Who are the people who are apt to harm my father?" she asked.

"I'm not saying who they are," Nathan Gomber retorted. "You don't seem very appreciative of my coming here to warn you. Fine kind of a daughter you are. You don't care what happens to your father!"

Annoyed by the man's insolence, both Nancy and Mrs. Gruen angrily stood up. The housekeeper, pointing toward the front door, said, "Good day, Mr. Gomber!"

The caller shrugged as he too arose. "Have it your own way, but don't say I didn't warn you!"

He walked to the front door, opened it, and as he went outside, closed it with a tremendous bang.

"Well, of all the insulting people!" Hannah snorted.

Nancy nodded. "But that's not the worst of it, Hannah darling. I think there's more to Gomber's warning than he is telling. It seems to me to imply a threat. And he almost has me convinced. Maybe I should stay close to Dad until he and the other lawyers have straightened out this railroad tangle."

She said this would mean giving up a case she had been asked to take. Hastily Nancy gave Hannah the highlights of her conversation with Helen about the haunted mansion. "Helen and her aunt will be here in a little while to tell us the whole story."

"Oh, maybe things aren't so serious for your father as that horrible man made out," Hannah said encouragingly. "If I were you I'd listen to the details about the haunted house and then decide what you want to do about the mystery."

In a short time a sports car pulled into the winding, tree-shaded driveway of the Drew home. The large brick house was set some distance back from the street.

Helen was at the wheel and stopped just beyond the front entrance. She helped her aunt from the car and they came up the steps together. Mrs. Rosemary Hayes was tall and slender and had graying hair. Her face had a gentle expression but she looked tired.

Helen introduced her aunt to Nancy and to Hannah, and the group went into the living room to sit down. Hannah offered to prepare tea and left the room.

"Oh, Nancy," said Helen, "I do hope you can take Aunt Rosemary and Miss Flora's case." Quickly she explained that Miss Flora was her aunt's mother. "Aunt Rosemary is really my great-aunt and Miss Flora is my great-grandmother. From the time she was a little girl everybody has called her Miss Flora."

"The name may seem odd to people the first time they hear it," Mrs. Hayes remarked, "but we're all so used to it, we never think anything about it."

"Please tell me more about your house," Nancy requested, smiling.

"Mother and I are almost nervous wrecks," Mrs. Hayes replied. "I have urged her to leave Twin Elms, but she won't. You see, Mother has lived there ever since she married my father, Everett Turnbull."

Mrs. Hayes went on to say that all kinds of strange happenings had occurred during the past couple of weeks. They had heard untraceable music, thumps and creaking noises at night, and had seen eerie, indescribable shadows on walls.

"Have you notified the police?" Nancy asked.

"Oh, yes," Mrs. Hayes answered. "But after talking with my mother, they came to the conclusion that most of what she saw and heard could be explained by natural causes. The rest, they said, probably was imagination on her part. You see, she's over eighty years old, and while I know her mind is sound and alert, I'm afraid that the police don't think so."

After a pause Mrs. Hayes went on, "I had almost talked myself into thinking the ghostly noises could be attributed to natural causes, when something else happened."

"What was that?" Nancy questioned eagerly.

"We were robbed! During the night several pieces of old jewelry were taken. I did telephone the police about this and they came to the house for a description of the pieces. But they still would not admit that a 'ghost' visitor had taken them."

Nancy was thoughtful for several seconds before making a comment. Then she said, "Do the police have any idea who the thief might be?"

Aunt Rosemary shook her head. "No. And I'm afraid we might have more burglaries."

Many ideas were running through Nancy's head. One was that the thief apparently had no intention of harming anyone—that his only motive had been burglary. Was he or was he not the person who was "haunting" the house? Or could the strange happenings have some natural explanations, as the police had suggested?

At this moment Hannah returned with a large silver tray on which was a tea service and some dainty sandwiches. She set the tray on a table and asked Nancy to pour the tea. She herself passed the cups of tea and sandwiches to the callers.

As they ate, Helen said, "Aunt Rosemary hasn't told you half the things that have happened. Once Miss Flora thought she saw someone sliding out of a fireplace at midnight, and another time a chair moved from one side of the room to the other while her back was turned. But no one was there!"

"How extraordinary!" Hannah Gruen exclaimed. "I've often read about such things, but I never thought I'd meet anyone who lived in a haunted house."

Helen turned to Nancy and gazed pleadingly at her friend. "You see how much you're needed at Twin Elms? Won't you please go out there with me and solve the mystery of the ghost?"

CHAPTER II

The Mysterious Mishap

SIPPING their tea, Helen Corning and her aunt waited for Nancy's decision. The young sleuth was in a dilemma. She wanted to start at once solving the mystery of the "ghost" of Twin Elms. But Nathan Gomber's warning still rang in her ears and she felt that her first duty was to stay with her father.

At last she spoke. "Mrs. Hayes—" she began.

"Please call me Aunt Rosemary," the caller requested. "All Helen's friends do."

Nancy smiled. "I'd love to. Aunt Rosemary, may I please let you know tonight or tomorrow? I really must speak to my father about the case. And something else came up just this afternoon which may keep me at home for a while at least."

"I understand," Mrs. Hayes answered, trying to conceal her disappointment.

Helen Corning did not take Nancy's announcement so calmly. "Oh, Nancy, you just must come. I'm sure your dad would want you to help us. Can't you postpone the other thing until you get back?"

"I'm afraid not," said Nancy. "I can't tell you all the details, but Dad has been threatened and I feel that I ought to stay close to him."

Hannah Gruen added her fears. "Goodness only knows what they may do to Mr. Drew," she said. "Somebody could come up and hit him on the head, or poison his food in a restaurant, or—"

Helen and her aunt gasped. "It's that bad?" Helen asked, her eyes growing wide.

Nancy explained that she would talk to her father when he returned home. "I hate to disappoint you," she said, "but you can see what a quandary I'm in."

"You poor girl!" said Mrs. Hayes sympathetically. "Now don't you worry about us."

Nancy smiled. "I'll worry whether I come or not," she said. "Anyway, I'll talk to my dad tonight."

The callers left shortly. When the door had closed behind them, Hannah put an arm around Nancy's shoulders. "I'm sure everything will come out all right for everybody," she said. "I'm sorry I talked about those dreadful things that might happen to your father. I let my imagination run away with me, just like they say Miss Flora's does with her."

"You're a great comfort, Hannah dear," said Nancy. "To tell the truth, I have thought of all kinds of horrible things myself." She began to pace the floor. "I wish Dad would get home."

During the next hour she went to the window at least a dozen times, hoping to see her father's car coming up the street. It was not until six o'clock that she heard the crunch of wheels on the driveway and saw Mr. Drew's sedan pull into the garage.

"He's safe!" she cried out to Hannah, who was testing potatoes that were baking in the oven.

In a flash Nancy was out the back door and running to meet her father. "Oh, Dad, I'm so glad to see you!" she exclaimed.

She gave him a tremendous hug and a resounding kiss. He responded affectionately, but gave a little chuckle. "What have I done to rate this extra bit of attention?" he teased. With a wink he added, "I know. Your date for tonight is off and you want me to substitute."

"Oh, Dad," Nancy replied. "Of course my date's not off. But I'm just about to call it off."

"Why?" Mr. Drew questioned. "Isn't Dirk going to stay on your list?"

"It's not that," Nancy replied. "It's because— because you're in terrible danger, Dad. I've been warned not to leave you."

Instead of looking alarmed, the lawyer burst out laughing. "In terrible danger of what? Are you going to make a raid on my wallet?"

"Dad, be serious! I really mean what I'm saying. Nathan Gomber was here and told me that you're in great danger and I'd better stay with you at all times."

The lawyer sobered at once. "That pest again!" he exclaimed. "There are times when I'd like to thrash the man till he begged for mercy!"

Mr. Drew suggested that they postpone their discussion about Nathan Gomber until dinner was over. Then he would tell his daughter the true facts in the case. After they had finished dinner, Hannah insisted upon tidying up alone while father and daughter talked.

"I will admit that there is a bit of a muddle about the railroad bridge," Mr. Drew began. "What happened was that the lawyer who went to get Willie Wharton's signature was very ill at the time. Unfortunately, he failed to have the signature witnessed or have the attached certificate of acknowledgment executed. The poor man passed away a few hours later."

"And the other railroad lawyers failed to notice that the signature hadn't been witnessed or the certificate notarized?" Nancy asked.

"Not right away. The matter did not come to light until the man's widow turned his brief case over to the railroad. The old deed to Wharton's property was there, so the lawyers assumed that the signature on the contract was genuine. The contract for the railroad bridge was awarded and work began. Suddenly Nathan Gomber appeared, saying he represented Willie Wharton and others who had owned property which the railroad had bought on either side of the Muskoka River."

"I understood from Mr. Gomber," said Nancy, "that Willie Wharton is trying to get more money for his neighbors by holding out for a higher price himself."

"That's the story. Personally, I think it's a sharp deal on Gomber's part. The more people he can get money for, the higher his commission," Mr. Drew stated.

"What a mess!" Nancy exclaimed. "And what can be done?"

"To tell the truth, there is little anyone can do until Willie Wharton is found. Gomber knows this, of course, and has probably advised Wharton to stay in hiding until the railroad agrees to give everybody more money."

Nancy had been watching her father intently. Now she saw an expression of eagerness come over his face. He leaned forward in his chair and said, "But I think I'm about to outwit Mr. Nathan Gomber. I've had a tip that Willie Wharton is in Chicago and I'm leaving Monday morning to find out."

Mr. Drew went on, "I believe that Wharton will say he did sign the contract of sale which the railroad company has and will readily consent to having the certificate of acknowledgment notarized.

Then, of course, the railroad won't pay him or any of the other property owners another cent."

"But, Dad, you still haven't convinced me you're not in danger," Nancy reminded him.

"Nancy dear," her father replied, "I feel that I am not in danger. Gomber is nothing but a blowhard. I doubt that he or Willie Wharton or any of the other property owners would resort to violence to keep me from working on this case. He's just trying to scare me into persuading the railroad to accede to his demands."

Nancy looked skeptical. "But don't forget that you're about to go to Chicago and produce the very man Gomber and those property owners don't want around here just now."

"I know." Mr. Drew nodded. "But I still doubt if anyone would use force to keep me from going." Laughingly the lawyer added, "So I won't need you as a bodyguard, Nancy."

His daughter gave a sigh of resignation. "All right, Dad, you know best." She then proceeded to tell her father about the Twin Elms mystery, which she had been asked to solve. "If you approve," Nancy said in conclusion, "I'd like to go over there with Helen."

Mr. Drew had listened with great interest. Now, after a few moments of thought, he smiled. "Go by all means, Nancy. I realize you've been itching to work on a new case—and this sounds like a real challenge. But please be careful."

"Oh, I will, Dad!" Nancy promised, her face lighting up. "Thanks a million." She jumped from her chair, gave her father a kiss, then went to phone Helen the good news. It was arranged that the girls would go to Twin Elms on Monday morning.

Nancy returned to the living room, eager to discuss the mystery further. Her father, however, glanced at his wrist watch. "Say, young lady, you'd better go dress for that date of yours." He winked. "I happen to know that Dirk doesn't like to be kept waiting."

"Especially by any of my mysteries." She laughed and hurried upstairs to change into a dance dress.

Half an hour later Dirk Jackson arrived. Nancy and the red-haired, former high-school tennis champion drove off to pick up another couple and attend an amateur play and dance given by the local Little Theater group.

Nancy thoroughly enjoyed herself and was sorry when the affair ended. With the promise of another date as soon as she returned from Twin Elms, Nancy said good night and waved from her doorway to the departing boy. As she prepared for bed, she thought of the play, the excellent orchestra, how lucky she was to have Dirk for a date, and what fun it had all been. But then her thoughts turned to Helen Corning and her relatives in the haunted house, Twin Elms.

"I can hardly wait for Monday to come," she murmured to herself as she fell asleep.

The following morning she and her father attended church together. Hannah said she was going to a special service that afternoon and therefore would stay at home during the morning.

"I'll have a good dinner waiting for you," she announced, as the Drews left.

After the service was over, Mr. Drew said he would like to drive down to the waterfront and see what progress had been made on the new bridge. "The railroad is going ahead with construction on the far side of the river," he told Nancy.

"Is the Wharton property on this side?" Nancy asked.

"Yes. And I must get to the truth of this mixed-up situation, so that work can be started on this side too."

Mr. Drew wound among the many streets leading down to the Muskoka River, then took the vehicular bridge across. He turned toward the construction area and presently parked his car. As he and Nancy stepped from the sedan, he looked ruefully at her pumps.

"It's going to be rough walking down to the waterfront," he said. "Perhaps you had better wait here."

"Oh, I'll be all right," Nancy assured him. "I'd like to see what's being done."

Various pieces of large machinery stood about on the high ground—a crane, a derrick, and hydraulic shovels. As the Drews walked toward the river, they passed a large truck. It faced the river and stood at the top of an incline just above two of the four enormous concrete piers which had already been built.

"I suppose there will be matching piers on the opposite side," Nancy mused, as she and her father reached the riverbank. They paused in the space between the two huge abutments. Mr. Drew glanced from side to side as if he had heard something. Suddenly Nancy detected a noise behind them.

Turning, she was horrified to see that the big truck was moving toward them. No one was at the wheel and the great vehicle was gathering speed at every moment.

"Dad!" she screamed.

In the brief second of warning, the truck almost seemed to leap toward the water. Nancy and her father, hemmed in by the concrete piers, had no way to escape being run down.

"Dive!" Mr. Drew ordered.

Without hesitation, he and Nancy made running flat dives into the water, and with arms flailing and legs kicking, swam furiously out of harm's way.

The truck thundered into the water and sank

The truck seemed to leap toward them

immediately up to the cab. The Drews turned and came back to the shore.

"Whew! That was a narrow escape!" the lawyer exclaimed, as he helped his daughter retrieve her pumps which had come off in the oozy bank.

"And what sights we are!" Nancy remarked.

"Indeed we are," her father agreed, as they trudged up the incline. "I'd like to get hold of the workman who was careless enough to leave that heavy truck on the slope without the brake on properly."

Nancy was not so sure that the near accident was the fault of a careless workman. Nathan Gomber had warned her that Mr. Drew's life was in danger. The threat might already have been put into action!

CHAPTER III

A Stolen Necklace

"WE'D better get home in a hurry and change our clothes," said Mr. Drew. "And I'll call the contracting company to tell them what happened."

"And notify the police?" Nancy suggested.

She dropped behind her father and gazed over the surrounding ground for telltale footprints. Presently she saw several at the edge of the spot where the truck had stood.

"Dad!" the young sleuth called out. "I may have found a clue to explain how that truck started downhill."

Her father came back and looked at the footprints. They definitely had not been made by a workman's boots.

"You may think me an old worrier, Dad," Nancy spoke up, "but these footprints, made by a man's business shoes, convince me that somebody deliberately tried to injure us with that truck."

The lawyer stared at his daughter. Then he looked down at the ground. From the size of the shoe and the length of the stride one could easily perceive that the wearer of the shoes was not tall. Nancy asked her father if he thought one of the workmen on the project could be responsible.

"I just can't believe anyone associated with the contracting company would want to injure us," Mr. Drew said.

Nancy reminded her father of Nathan Gomber's warning. "It might be one of the property owners, or even Willie Wharton himself."

"Wharton is short and has a small foot," the lawyer conceded. "And I must admit that these look like fresh footprints. As a matter of fact, they show that whoever was here ran off in a hurry. He may have released the brake on the truck, then jumped out and run away."

"Yes," said Nancy. "And that means the attack *was* deliberate."

Mr. Drew did not reply. He continued walking up the hill, lost in thought. Nancy followed and they climbed into the car. They drove home in silence, each puzzling over the strange incident of the runaway truck. Upon reaching the house, they were greeted by a loud exclamation of astonishment.

"My goodness!" Hannah Gruen cried out. "Whatever in the world happened to you?"

They explained hastily, then hurried upstairs

to bathe and change into dry clothes. By the time they reached the first floor again, Hannah had placed sherbet glasses filled with orange and grape-fruit slices on the table. All during the delicious dinner of spring lamb, rice and mushrooms, fresh peas and chocolate angel cake with vanilla ice cream, the conversation revolved around the rail-road bridge mystery and then the haunted Twin Elms mansion.

"I knew things wouldn't be quiet around here for long," Hannah Gruen remarked with a smile. "Tomorrow you'll both be off on big adventures. I certainly wish you both success."

"Thank you, Hannah," said Nancy. She laughed. "I'd better get a good night's sleep. From now on I may be kept awake by ghosts and strange noises."

"I'm a little uneasy about your going to Twin Elms," the housekeeper told her. "Please prom-ise me that you'll be careful."

"Of course," Nancy replied. Turning to her father, she said, "Pretend I've said the same thing to you about being careful."

The lawyer chuckled and pounded his chest. "You know me. I can be pretty tough when the need arises."

Early the next morning Nancy drove her father to the airport in her blue convertible. Just before she kissed him good-by at the turnstile, he said, "I expect to return on Wednesday, Nancy. Suppose

I stop off at Cliffwood and see how you're making out?"

"Wonderful, Dad! I'll be looking for you."

As soon as her father left, Nancy drove directly to Helen Corning's home. The pretty, brunette girl came from the front door of the white cottage, swinging a suitcase. She tossed it into the rear of Nancy's convertible and climbed in.

"I ought to be scared," said Helen. "Goodness only knows what's ahead of us. But right now I'm so happy nothing could upset me."

"What happened?" Nancy asked as she started the car. "Did you inherit a million?"

"Something better than that," Helen replied. "Nancy, I want to tell you a big, big secret. I'm going to be married!"

Nancy slowed the car and pulled to the side of the street. Leaning over to hug her friend, she said, "Why, Helen, how wonderful! Who is he? And tell me all about it. This is rather sudden, isn't it?"

"Yes, it is," Helen confessed. "His name is Jim Archer and he's simply out of this world. I'm a pretty lucky girl. I met him a couple of months ago when he was home on a short vacation. He works for the Tristam Oil Company and has spent two years abroad. Jim will be away a while longer, and then be given a position here in the States."

As Nancy started the car up once more, her eyes

twinkled. "Helen Corning, have you been engaged for two months and didn't tell me?"

Helen shook her head. "Jim and I have been corresponding ever since he left. Last night he telephoned from overseas and asked me to marry him." Helen giggled. "I said yes in a big hurry. Then he asked to speak to Dad. My father gave his consent but insisted that our engagement not be announced until Jim's return to this country."

The two girls discussed all sorts of delightful plans for Helen's wedding and before they knew it they had reached the town of Cliffwood.

"My great-grandmother's estate is about two miles out of town," Helen said. "Go down Main Street and turn right at the fork."

Ten minutes later she pointed out Twin Elms. From the road one could see little of the house. A high stone wall ran along the front of the estate and beyond it were many tall trees. Nancy turned into the driveway which twisted and wound among elms, oaks, and maples.

Presently the old Colonial home came into view. Helen said it had been built in 1785 and had been given its name because of the two elm trees which stood at opposite ends of the long building. They had grown to be giants and their foliage was beautiful. The mansion was of red brick and nearly all the walls were covered with ivy. There was a ten-foot porch with tall white pillars at the huge front door.

"It's charming!" Nancy commented as she pulled up to the porch.

"Wait until you see the grounds," said Helen. "There are several old, old buildings. An ice-house, a smokehouse, a kitchen, and servants' cottages."

"The mansion certainly doesn't look spooky from the outside," Nancy commented.

At that moment the great door opened and Aunt Rosemary came outside. "Hello, girls," she greeted them. "I'm so glad to see you."

Nancy felt the warmness of the welcome but thought that it was tinged with worry. She wondered if another "ghost" incident had taken place at the mansion.

The girls took their suitcases from the car and followed Mrs. Hayes inside. Although the furnishings looked rather worn, they were still very beautiful. The high-ceilinged rooms opened off a center hall and in a quick glance Nancy saw lovely damask draperies, satin-covered sofas and chairs, and on the walls, family portraits in large gilt frames of scrollwork design.

Aunt Rosemary went to the foot of the shabbily carpeted stairway, took hold of the handsome mahogany balustrade, and called, "Mother, the girls are here!"

In a moment a slender, frail-looking woman with snow-white hair started to descend the steps. Her face, though older in appearance than Rosemary's, had the same gentle smile. As Miss Flora reached the foot of the stairs, she held out her hands to both girls.

At once Helen said, "I'd like to present Nancy Drew, Miss Flora."

"I'm so glad you could come, my dear," the elderly woman said. "I know that you're going to solve this mystery which has been bothering Rosemary and me. I'm sorry not to be able to entertain you more auspiciously, but a haunted house hardly lends itself to gaiety."

The dainty, yet stately, Miss Flora swept toward a room which she referred to as the parlor. It was opposite the library. She sat down in a high-backed chair and asked everyone else to be seated.

"Mother," said Aunt Rosemary, "we don't have to be so formal with Nancy and Helen. I'm sure they'll understand that we've just been badly frightened." She turned toward the girls. "Something happened a little while ago that has made us very jittery."

"Yes," Miss Flora said. "A pearl necklace of mine was stolen!"

"You don't mean the lovely one that has been in the family so many years!" Helen cried out.

The two women nodded. Then Miss Flora said, "Oh, I probably was very foolish. It's my own fault. While I was in my room, I took the necklace from the hiding place where I usually keep it. The catch had not worked well the last time I wore the pearls and I wanted to examine it. While I was doing this, Rosemary called to me to come downstairs. The gardener was here and wanted to talk about some work. I put the necklace in my dresser drawer. When I returned ten minutes later the necklace wasn't there!"

"How dreadful!" said Nancy sympathetically. "Had anybody come into the house during that time?"

"Not to our knowledge," Aunt Rosemary replied. "Ever since we've had this ghost visiting us we've kept every door and window on the first floor locked all the time."

Nancy asked if the two women had gone out into the garden to speak to their helper. "Mother did," said Mrs. Hayes. "But I was in the kitchen the entire time. If anyone came in the back door, I certainly would have seen the person."

"Is there a back stairway to the second floor?" Nancy asked.

"Yes," Miss Flora answered. "But there are doors at both top and bottom and we keep them locked. No one could have gone up that way."

"Then anyone who came into the house had to go up by way of the front stairs?"

"Yes." Aunt Rosemary smiled a little. "But if anyone had, I would have noticed. You probably heard how those stairs creak when Mother came down. This can be avoided if you hug the wall, but practically no one knows that."

"May I go upstairs and look around?" Nancy questioned.

"Of course, dear. And I'll show you and Helen to your room," Aunt Rosemary said.

The girls picked up their suitcases and followed the two women up the stairs. Nancy and Helen were given a large, quaint room at the front of the old house over the library. They quickly deposited their luggage, then Miss Flora led the way across the hall to her room, which was directly above the parlor. It was large and very attractive with its canopied mahogany bed and an old-fashioned candlewick spread. The dresser, dressing table, and chairs also were mahogany. Long chintz draperies hung at the windows.

An eerie feeling began to take possession of Nancy. She could almost feel the presence of a ghostly burglar on the premises. Though she tried to shake off the mood, it persisted. Finally she told herself that it was possible the thief was still around. If so, he must be hiding.

Against one wall stood a large walnut wardrobe. Helen saw Nancy gazing at it intently. She went over and whispered, "Do you think there might be someone inside?"

"Who knows?" Nancy replied in a low voice. "Let's find out!"

She walked across the room, and taking hold of the two knobs on the double doors, opened them wide.

CHAPTER IV

Strange Music

THE ANXIOUS group stared inside the wardrobe. No one stood there. Dresses, suits, and coats hung in an orderly row.

Nancy took a step forward and began separating them. Someone, she thought, might be hiding behind the clothes. The others in the room held their breaths as she made a thorough search.

"No one here!" she finally announced, and a sigh of relief escaped the lips of Miss Flora and Aunt Rosemary.

The young sleuth said she would like to make a thorough inspection of all possible hiding places on the second floor. With Helen helping her, they went from room to room, opening wardrobe doors and looking under beds. They did not find the thief.

Nancy suggested that Miss Flora and Aunt Rosemary report the theft to the police, but the older woman shook her head. Mrs. Hayes, although she agreed this might be wise, added softly, "Mother just *might* be mistaken. She's a little forgetful at times about where she puts things."

With this possibility in mind, she and the girls looked in every drawer in the room, under the mattress and pillows, and even in the pockets of Miss Flora's clothes. The pearl necklace was not found. Nancy suggested that she and Helen try to find out how the thief had made his entrance.

Helen led the way outdoors. At once Nancy began to look for footprints. No tracks were visible on the front or back porches, or on any of the walks, which were made of finely crushed stone.

"We'll look in the soft earth beneath the windows," Nancy said. "Maybe the thief climbed in."

"But Aunt Rosemary said all the windows on the first floor are kept locked," Helen objected.

"No doubt," Nancy said. "But I think we should look for footprints just the same."

The girls went from window to window, but there were no footprints beneath any. Finally Nancy stopped and looked thoughtfully at the ivy on the walls.

"Do you think the thief climbed up to the second floor that way?" Helen asked her. "But there'd still be footprints on the ground."

Nancy said that the thief could have carried a plank with him, laid it down, and stepped from the walk to the wall of the house. "Then he could have climbed up the ivy and down again, and gotten back to the walk without leaving any footprints."

Once more Nancy went around the entire house, examining every bit of ivy which wound up from the foundation. Finally she said, "No, the thief didn't get into the house this way."

"Well, he certainly didn't fly in," said Helen. "So *how* did he enter?"

Nancy laughed. "If I could tell you that I'd have the mystery half solved."

She said that she would like to look around the grounds of Twin Elms. "It may give us a clue as to how the thief got into the house."

As they strolled along, Nancy kept a sharp lookout but saw nothing suspicious. At last they came to a half-crumbled brick walk laid out in an interesting crisscross pattern.

"Where does this walk lead?" Nancy asked.

"Well, I guess originally it went over to Riverview Manor, the next property," Helen replied. "I'll show you that mansion later. The first owner was a brother of the man who built this place."

Helen went on to say that Riverview Manor was a duplicate of Twin Elms mansion. The two brothers had been inseparable companions, but their sons who later lived there had had a violent quarrel and had become lifelong enemies.

"Riverview Manor has been sold several times during the years but has been vacant for a long time."

"You mean no one lives there now?" Nancy asked. As Helen nodded, she added with a laugh, "Then maybe that's the ghost's home!"

"In that case he really must be a ghost," said Helen lightly. "There's not a piece of furniture in the house."

The two girls returned to the Twin Elms mansion and reported their lack of success in picking up a clue to the intruder. Nancy, recalling that many Colonial houses had secret entrances and passageways, asked Miss Flora, "Do you know of any secret entrance to your home that the thief could use?"

She said no, and explained that her husband had been a rather reticent person and had passed away when Rosemary was only a baby. "It's just possible he knew of a secret entrance, but did not want to worry me by telling me about it," Mrs. Turnbull said.

Aunt Rosemary, sensing that her mother was becoming alarmed by the questions, suggested that they all have lunch. The two girls went with her to the kitchen and helped prepare a tasty meal of chicken salad, biscuits, and fruit gelatin.

During the meal the conversation covered several subjects, but always came back to the topic of the mystery. They had just finished eating when suddenly Nancy sat straight up in her chair.

"What's the matter?" Helen asked her.

Nancy was staring out the dining-room door toward the stairway in the hall. Then she turned to Miss Flora. "Did you leave a radio on in your bedroom?"

"Why, no."

"Did you, Aunt Rosemary?"

"No. Neither Mother nor I turned our radios on this morning. Why do—" She stopped speaking, for now all of them could distinctly hear music coming from the second floor.

Helen and Nancy were out of their chairs instantly. They dashed into the hall and up the stairway. The music was coming from Miss Flora's room, and when the girls rushed in, they knew indeed that it was from her radio.

Nancy went over to examine the set. It was an old one and did not have a clock attachment with an automatic control.

"Someone came into this room and turned on the radio!" she stated.

A look of alarm came over Helen's face, but she tried to shake off her nervousness and asked, "Nancy, do you think the radio could have been turned on by remote control? I've heard of such things."

Nancy said she doubted this. "I'm afraid, Helen, that the thief has been in the house all the time. He and the ghost are one and the same person. Oh, I wish we had looked before in the cellar and the attic. Maybe it's not too late. Come on!"

Helen, instead of moving from the room, stared at the fireplace. "Nancy," she said, "do you suppose someone is hiding up there?"

Without hesitation she crossed the room, got down on her knees, and tried to look up the chimney. The damper was closed. Reaching her arm up, Helen pulled the handle to open it.

The next moment she cried out, "Ugh!"

"Oh, Helen, you poor thing!" Nancy exclaimed, running to her friend's side.

A shower of soot had come down, covering Helen's hair, face, shoulders, and arms.

"Get me a towel, will you, Nancy?" she requested.

Nancy dashed to the bathroom and grabbed two large towels. She wrapped them around her friend, then went with Helen to help her with a shampoo and general cleanup job. Finally Nancy brought her another sports dress.

"I guess my idea about chimneys wasn't so good," Helen stated ruefully. "And we're probably too late to catch the thief."

Nevertheless, she and Nancy climbed the stairs to the attic and looked behind trunks and boxes to see if anyone were hiding. Next, the girls went to the cellar and inspected the various rooms there. Still there was no sign of the thief who had entered Twin Elms.

After Miss Flora had heard the whole story, she gave a nervous sigh. "It's the ghost—there's no other explanation."

"But why," Aunt Rosemary asked, "has a ghost suddenly started performing here? This house has been occupied since 1785 and no ghost was ever reported haunting the place."

"Well, apparently robbery is the motive," Nancy replied. "But why the thief bothers to frighten you is something I haven't figured out yet."

"The main thing," Helen spoke up, "is to catch him!"

"Oh, if we only could!" Miss Flora said, her voice a bit shaky.

The girls were about to pick up the luncheon dishes from the table, to carry them to the kitchen, when the front door knocker sounded loudly.

"Oh, dear," said Miss Flora, "who can that be? Maybe it's the thief and he's come to harm us!"

Aunt Rosemary put an arm around her mother's shoulders. "Please don't worry," she begged. "I think our caller is probably the man who wants to buy Twin Elms." She turned to Nancy and Helen. "But Mother doesn't want to sell for the low price that he is offering."

Nancy said she would go to the door. She set the dishes down and walked out to the hall. Reaching the great door, she flung it open.

Nathan Gomber stood there!

CHAPTER V

A Puzzling Interview

FOR SEVERAL seconds Nathan Gomber stared at Nancy in disbelief. "You!" he cried out finally.

"You didn't expect to find me here, did you?" she asked coolly.

"I certainly didn't. I thought you'd taken my advice and stayed with your father. Young people today are so hardhearted!" Gomber wagged his head in disgust.

Nancy ignored Gomber's remarks. Shrugging, the man pushed his way into the hall. "I know this. If anything happens to your father, you'll never forgive yourself. But you can't blame Nathan Gomber! I warned you!"

Still Nancy made no reply. She kept looking at him steadily, trying to figure out what was really in his mind. She was convinced it was not solicitude for her father.

Nathan Gomber changed the subject abruptly.

"I'd like to see Mrs. Turnbull and Mrs. Hayes," he said. "Go call them."

Nancy was annoyed by Gomber's crudeness, but she turned around and went down the hall to the dining room.

"We heard every word," Miss Flora said in a whisper. "I shan't see Mr. Gomber. I don't want to sell this house."

Nancy was amazed to hear this. "You mean he's the person who wants to buy it?"

"Yes."

Instantly Nancy was on the alert. Because of the nature of the railroad deal in which Nathan Gomber was involved, she was distrustful of his motives in wanting to buy Twin Elms. It flashed through her mind that perhaps he was trying to buy it at a very low price and planned to sell it off in building lots at a huge profit.

"Suppose I go tell him you don't want to sell," Nancy suggested in a low voice.

But her caution was futile. Hearing footsteps behind her, she turned to see Gomber standing in the doorway.

"Howdy, everybody!" he said.

Miss Flora, Aunt Rosemary, and Helen showed annoyance. It was plain that all of them thought the man completely lacking in good manners.

Aunt Rosemary's jaw was set in a grim line, but she said politely, "Helen, this is Mr. Gomber. Mr. Gomber, my niece, Miss Corning."

"Pleased to meet you," said their caller, extending a hand to shake Helen's.

"Nancy, I guess you've met Mr. Gomber," Aunt Rosemary went on.

"Oh, sure!" Nathan Gomber said with a somewhat raucous laugh. "Nancy and me, we've met!"

"Only once," Nancy said pointedly.

Ignoring her rebuff, he went on, "Nancy Drew is a very strange young lady. Her father's in great danger and I tried to warn her to stick close to him. Instead of that, she's out here visiting you folks."

"Her father's in danger?" Miss Flora said worriedly.

"Dad says he's not," Nancy replied. "And besides, I'm sure my father would know how to take care of any enemies." She looked straight at Nathan Gomber, as if to let him know that the Drews were not easily frightened.

"Well," the caller said, "let's get down to business." He pulled an envelope full of papers from his pocket. "Everything's here—all ready for you to sign, Mrs. Turnbull."

"I don't wish to sell at such a low figure," Miss Flora told him firmly. "In fact, I don't know that I want to sell at all."

Nathan Gomber tossed his head. "You'll sell all right," he prophesied. "I've been talking to some of the folks downtown. Everybody knows this old place is haunted and nobody would give you five cents for it—that is, nobody but me."

As he waited for his words to sink in, Nancy spoke up, "If the house is haunted, why do you want it?"

"Well," Gomber answered, "I guess I'm a gambler at heart. I'd be willing to put some money into this place, even if there is a ghost parading around." He laughed loudly, then went on, "I declare it might be a real pleasure to meet a ghost and get the better of it!"

Nancy thought with disgust, "Nathan Gomber, you're about the most conceited, obnoxious person I've met in a long time."

Suddenly the expression of cunning on the man's face changed completely. An almost wistful look came into his eyes. He sat down on one of the dining-room chairs and rested his chin in his hand.

"I guess you think I'm just a hardheaded business man with no feelings," he said. "The truth is I'm a real softy. I'll tell you why I want this old house so bad. I've always dreamed of owning a Colonial mansion, and having a kinship with early America. You see, my family were poor folks in Europe. Now that I've made a little money, I'd like to have a home like this to roam around in and enjoy its traditions."

Miss Flora seemed to be touched by Gomber's story. "I had no idea you wanted the place so much," she said kindly. "Maybe I ought to give it up. It's really too big for us."

As Aunt Rosemary saw her mother weakening, she said quickly, "You don't have to sell this house, Mother. You know you love it. So far as the ghost is concerned, I'm sure that mystery is going to be cleared up. Then you'd be sorry you had parted with Twin Elms. Please don't say yes!"

As Gomber gave Mrs. Hayes a dark look, Nancy asked him, "Why don't you buy Riverview Manor? It's a duplicate of this place and is for sale. You probably could purchase it at a lower price than you could this one."

"I've seen that place," the man returned. "It's in a bad state. It would cost me a mint of money to fix it up. No sir. I want this place and I'm going to have it!"

This bold remark was too much for Aunt Rosemary. Her eyes blazing, she said, "Mr. Gomber, this interview is at an end. Good-by!"

To Nancy's delight and somewhat to her amusement, Nathan Gomber obeyed the "order" to leave. He seemed to be almost meek as he walked through the hall and let himself out the front door.

"Of all the nerve!" Helen burst out.

"Perhaps we shouldn't be too hard on the man," Miss Flora said timidly. "His story is a pathetic one and I can see how he might want to pretend he had an old American family background."

"I'd like to bet a cooky Mr. Gomber didn't mean one word of what he was saying," Helen remarked.

"Oh dear, I'm so confused," said Miss Flora, her voice trembling. "Let's all sit down in the parlor and talk about it a little more."

The two girls stepped back as Miss Flora, then Aunt Rosemary, left the dining room. They followed to the parlor and sat down together on the recessed couch by the fireplace. Nancy, on a sudden hunch, ran to a front window to see which direction Gomber had taken. To her surprise he was walking down the winding driveway.

"That's strange. Evidently he didn't drive," Nancy told herself. "It's quite a walk into town to get a train or bus to River Heights."

As Nancy mulled over this idea, trying to figure out the answer, she became conscious of creaking sounds. Helen suddenly gave a shriek. Nancy turned quickly.

"Look!" Helen cried, pointing toward the ceiling, and everyone stared upward.

The crystal chandelier had suddenly started swaying from side to side!

"The ghost again!" Miss Flora cried out. She looked as if she were about to faint.

Nancy's eyes quickly swept the room. Nothing else in it was moving, so vibration was not causing the chandelier to sway. As it swung back and forth, a sudden thought came to the young sleuth. Maybe someone in Miss Flora's room above was causing the shaking.

The chandelier suddenly started to sway

"I'm going upstairs to investigate," Nancy told the others.

Racing noiselessly on tiptoe out of the room and through the hall, she began climbing the stairs, hugging the wall so the steps would not creak. As she neared the top, Nancy was sure she heard a door close. Hurrying along the hall, she burst into Miss Flora's bedroom. No one was in sight!

"Maybe this time the ghost couldn't get away and is in that wardrobe!" Nancy thought.

Helen and her relatives had come up the stairs behind Nancy. They reached the bedroom just as she flung open the wardrobe doors. But for the second time she found no one hiding there.

Nancy bit her lip in vexation. The ghost was clever indeed. Where *had* he gone? She had given him no time to go down the hall or run into another room. Yet there was no denying the fact that he had been in Miss Flora's room!

"Tell us why you came up," Helen begged her. Nancy told her theory, but suddenly she realized that maybe she was letting her imagination run wild. It was possible, she admitted to the others, that no one had caused the chandelier to shake.

"There's only one way to find out," she said. "I'll make a test."

Nancy asked Helen to go back to the first floor and watch the chandelier. She would try to make it sway by rocking from side to side on the floor above it.

"If this works, then I'm sure we've picked up a clue to the ghost," she said hopefully.

Helen readily agreed and left the room. When Nancy thought her friend had had time to reach the parlor below, she began to rock hard from side to side on the spot above the chandelier.

She had barely started the test when from the first floor Helen Corning gave a piercing scream!

CHAPTER VI

The Gorilla Face

"SOMETHING has happened to Helen!" Aunt Rosemary cried out fearfully.

Nancy was already racing through the second-floor hallway. Reaching the stairs, she leaped down them two steps at a time. Helen Corning had collapsed in a wing chair in the parlor, her hands over her face.

"Helen! What happened?" Nancy asked, reaching her friend's side.

"Out there! Looking in that window!" Helen pointed to the front window of the parlor next to the hall. "The most horrible face I ever saw!"

"Was it a man's face?" Nancy questioned.

"Oh, I don't know. It looked just like a gorilla!" Helen closed her eyes as if to shut out the memory of the sight.

Nancy did not wait to hear any more. In another second she was at the front door and had yanked it open. Stepping outside, she looked all around. She could see no animal near the house, nor any sign under the window that one had stood there.

Puzzled, the young sleuth hurried down the steps and began a search of the grounds. By this time Helen had collected her wits and come outside. She joined Nancy and together they looked in every outbuilding and behind every clump of bushes on the grounds of Twin Elms. They did not find one footprint or any other evidence to prove that a gorilla or other creature had been on the grounds of the estate.

"I saw it! I know I saw it!" Helen insisted.

"I don't doubt you," Nancy replied.

"Then what explanation is there?" Helen demanded. "You know I never did believe in spooks. But if we have many more of these weird happenings around here, I declare I'm going to start believing in ghosts."

Nancy laughed. "Don't worry, Helen," she said. "There'll be a logical explanation for the face at the window."

The girls walked back to the front door of the mansion. Miss Flora and Aunt Rosemary stood there and immediately insisted upon knowing what had happened. As Helen told them, Nancy once more surveyed the outside of the window at which Helen had seen the terrifying face.

"I have a theory," she spoke up. "Our ghost simply leaned across from the end of the porch and held a mask in front of the window." Nancy stretched her arm out to demonstrate how this was possible.

"So that's why he didn't leave any footprints under the window," Helen said. "But he certainly got away from here fast." She suddenly laughed. "He must be on some ghosts' track team."

Her humor, Nancy was glad to see, relieved the tense situation. She had noticed Miss Flora leaning wearily on her daughter's arm.

"You'd better lie down and rest, Mother," Mrs. Hayes advised.

"I guess I will," Aunt Flora agreed.

It was suggested that the elderly woman use Aunt Rosemary's room, while the others continued the experiment with the chandelier.

Helen and Aunt Rosemary went into the parlor and waited as Nancy ascended the front stairway and went to Miss Flora's bedroom. Once more she began to rock from side to side. Downstairs, Aunt Rosemary and her niece were gazing intently at the ceiling.

"Look!" Helen exclaimed, pointing to the crystal chandelier. "It's moving!" In a moment it swung to the left, then back to the right.

"Nancy has proved that the ghost was up in my mother's room!" Aunt Rosemary said excitedly.

After a few minutes the rocking motion of the chandelier slackened and finally stopped. Nancy came hurrying down the steps.

"Did it work?" she called.

"Yes, it did," Aunt Rosemary replied. "Oh, Nancy, we must have two ghosts!"

"Why do you say that?" Helen asked.

"One rocking the chandelier, the other holding the horrible face up to the window. No one could have gone from Miss Flora's room to the front porch in such a short time. Oh, this complicates everything!"

"It certainly does," Nancy agreed. "The question is, are the two ghosts in cahoots? Or, it's just possible, there is only one. He could have disappeared from Miss Flora's room without our seeing him and somehow hurried to the first floor and let himself out the front door while we were upstairs. I'm convinced there is at least one secret entrance into this house, and maybe more. I think our next step should be to try to find it—or them."

"We'd better wash the luncheon dishes first," Aunt Rosemary suggested.

As she and the girls worked, they discussed the mystery, and Mrs. Hayes revealed that she had talked to her mother about leaving the house, whether or not she sold it.

"I thought we might at least go away for a little vacation, but Mother refuses to leave. She says she intends to remain right here until this ghost business is settled."

Helen smiled. "Nancy, my great-grandmother

is a wonderful woman. She has taught me a lot about courage and perseverance. I hope if I ever reach her age, I'll have half as much."

"Yes, she's an example to all of us," Aunt Rosemary concurred.

Nancy nodded. "I agree. I haven't known your mother long, Aunt Rosemary, but I think she is one of the dearest persons I've ever met."

"If Miss Flora won't leave," said Helen, "I guess that means we all stay."

"That's settled," said Nancy with a smile.

After the dishes were put away, the girls were ready to begin their search for a secret entrance into the mansion.

"Let's start with Miss Flora's room," Helen suggested.

"That's a logical place," Nancy replied, and took the lead up the stairway.

Every inch of the wall, which was paneled in maple halfway to the ceiling, was tapped. No hollow sound came from any section of it to indicate an open space behind. The bureau, dressing table, and bed were pulled away from the walls and Nancy carefully inspected every inch of the paneling for cracks or wide seams to indicate a concealed door.

"Nothing yet," she announced, and then decided to inspect the sides of the fireplace.

The paneled sides and brick front revealed nothing. Next, Nancy looked at the sides and rear of the stone interior. She could see nothing unusual, and the blackened stones did not look as if they had ever been disturbed.

She closed the damper which Helen had left open, and then suggested that the searchers transfer to another room on the second floor. But no trace of any secret entrance to the mansion could be found.

"I think we've had enough investigation for one day," Aunt Rosemary remarked.

Nancy was about to say that she was not tired and would like to continue. But she realized that Mrs. Hayes had made this suggestion because her mother was once more showing signs of fatigue and strain.

Helen, who also realized the situation, said, "Let's have an early supper. I'm starved!"

"I am, too," Nancy replied, laughing gaily.

The mood was contagious and soon Miss Flora seemed to have forgotten about her mansion being haunted. She sat in the kitchen while Aunt Rosemary and the girls cooked the meal.

"*Um,* steak and French fried potatoes, fresh peas, and yummy floating island for dessert," said Helen. "I can hardly wait."

"Fruit cup first," Aunt Rosemary announced, taking a bowl of fruit from the refrigerator.

Soon the group was seated at the table. Tactfully steering the conversation away from the mystery, Nancy asked Miss Flora to tell the group about parties and dances which had been held in the mansion long ago.

The elderly woman smiled in recollection. "I remember one story my husband told me of something that happened when he was a little boy," Miss Flora began. "His parents were holding a masquerade and he was supposed to be in bed fast asleep. His nurse had gone downstairs to talk to some of the servants. The music awakened my husband and he decided it would be great fun to join the guests.

" 'I'll put on a costume myself,' he said to himself. He knew there were some packed in a trunk in the attic." Miss Flora paused. "By the way, girls, I think that sometime while you are here you ought to see them. They're beautiful.

"Well, Everett went to the attic, opened the trunk, and searched until he found a soldier's outfit. It was very fancy—red coat and white trousers. He had quite a struggle getting it on and had to turn the coat sleeves way up. The knee britches came to his ankles, and the hat was so large it came down over his ears."

By this time Miss Flora's audience was laughing and Aunt Rosemary remarked, "My father really must have looked funny. Please go on, Mother."

"Little Everett came down the stairs and mingled with the masqueraders at the dance. For a while he wasn't noticed, then suddenly his mother discovered the queer-looking figure."

"And," Aunt Rosemary interrupted, "quickly put him back to bed, I'm sure."

Miss Flora laughed. "That's where you're wrong. The guests thought the whole thing was such fun that they insisted Everett stay. Some of the women danced with him—he went to dancing school and was an excellent dancer. Then they gave him some strawberries and cream and cake."

Helen remarked, "And then put him to bed."

Again Miss Flora laughed. "The poor little fellow never knew that he had fallen asleep while he was eating, and his father had to carry him upstairs. He was put into his little four-poster, costume and all. Of course his nurse was horrified, and I'm afraid that during the rest of the night the poor woman thought she would lose her position. But she didn't. In fact, she stayed with the family until all the children were grown up."

"Oh, that's a wonderful story!" said Nancy.

She was about to urge Miss Flora to tell another story when the telephone rang. Aunt Rosemary answered it, and then called to Nancy, "It's for you."

Nancy hurried to the hall, grabbed up the phone, and said, "Hello." A moment later she cried out, "Dad! How wonderful to hear from you!"

Mr. Drew said that he had not found Willie Wharton and certain clues seemed to indicate that he was not in Chicago, but in some other city.

"I have a few other matters to take care of that will keep me here until tomorrow night. How are you getting along?"

"I haven't solved the mystery yet," his daughter reported. "We've had some more strange happenings. I'll certainly be glad to see you here at Cliffwood. I know you can help me."

"All right, I'll come. But don't try to meet me. The time is too uncertain, and as a matter of fact, I may find that I'll have to stay here in Chicago."

Mr. Drew said he would come out to the mansion by taxi. Briefly Nancy related her experiences at Twin Elms, and after a little more conversation, hung up. When she rejoined the others at the table, she told them about Mr. Drew's promised visit.

"Oh, I'll be so happy to meet your father," said Miss Flora. "We may need legal advice in this mystery."

There was a pause after this remark, with everyone silent for a few moments. Suddenly each one in the group looked at the others, startled. From somewhere upstairs came the plaintive strains of violin music. Had the radio been turned on again by the ghost?

Nancy dashed from the table to find out.

CHAPTER VII

Frightening Eyes

WITHIN five seconds Nancy had reached the second floor. The violin playing suddenly ceased.

She raced into Miss Flora's room, from which the sounds had seemed to come. The radio was not on. Quickly Nancy felt the instrument to see if it were even slightly warm to prove it had been in use.

"The music wasn't being played on this," she told herself, finding the radio cool.

As Nancy dashed from the room, she almost ran into Helen. "What did you find out?" her friend asked breathlessly.

"Nothing so far," Nancy replied, as she raced into Aunt Rosemary's bedroom to check the bedside radio in there.

This instrument, too, felt cool to the touch.

She and Helen stood in the center of the room, puzzled frowns creasing their foreheads. "There *was* music, wasn't there?" Helen questioned.

"I distinctly heard it," Nancy replied. "But *where* is the person who played the violin? Or put a disk on a record player, or turned on a hidden radio? Helen, I'm positive an intruder comes into this mansion by some secret entrance and tries to frighten us all."

"And succeeds," Helen answered. "It's positively eerie."

"And dangerous," Nancy thought.

"Let's continue our search right after breakfast tomorrow," Helen proposed.

"We will," Nancy responded. "But in the meantime I believe Miss Flora and Aunt Rosemary, to say nothing of ourselves, need some police protection."

"I think you're right," Helen agreed. "Let's go downstairs and suggest it to the others."

The girls returned to the first floor and Nancy told Mrs. Hayes and her mother of the failure to find the cause of the violin playing, and what she had in mind.

"Oh dear, the police will only laugh at us," Miss Flora objected.

"Mother dear," said her daughter, "the captain and his men didn't believe us before because they thought we were imagining things. But Nancy and Helen heard music at two different times and they saw the chandelier rock. I'm sure that Captain Rossland will believe Nancy and send a guard out here."

Nancy smiled at Miss Flora. "I shan't ask the captain to believe in a ghost or even hunt for one. I think all we should request at the moment is that he have a man patrol the grounds here at night. I'm sure that we're perfectly safe while we're all awake, but I must admit I'd feel a little uneasy about going to bed wondering what that ghost may do next."

Mrs. Turnbull finally agreed to the plan and Nancy went to the telephone. Captain Rossland readily agreed to send a man out a little later.

"He'll return each night as long as you need him," the officer stated. "And I'll tell him not to ring the bell to tell you when he comes. If there is anyone who breaks into the mansion by a secret entrance, it would be much better if he does not know a guard is on duty."

"I understand," said Nancy.

When Miss Flora, her daughter, and the two girls went to bed, they were confident they would have a restful night. Nancy felt that if there was no disturbance, then it would indicate that the ghost's means of entry into Twin Elms was directly from the outside. "In which case," she thought, "it will mean he saw the guard and didn't dare come inside the house."

The young sleuth's desire for a good night's sleep was rudely thwarted as she awakened about midnight with a start. Nancy was sure she had heard a noise nearby. But now the house was quiet. Nancy listened intently, then finally got out of bed.

"Perhaps the noise I heard came from outdoors," she told herself.

Tiptoeing to a window, so that she would not awaken Helen, Nancy peered out at the moonlit grounds. Shadows made by tree branches, which swayed in a gentle breeze, moved back and forth across the lawn. The scent from a rose garden in full bloom was wafted to Nancy.

"What a heavenly night!" she thought.

Suddenly Nancy gave a start. A furtive figure had darted from behind a tree toward a clump of bushes. Was he the guard or the ghost? she wondered. As Nancy watched intently to see if she could detect any further movements of the mysterious figure, she heard padding footsteps in the hall. In a moment there was a loud knock on her door.

"Nancy! Wake up! Nancy! Come quick!"

The voice was Miss Flora's, and she sounded extremely frightened. Nancy sped across the room, unlocked her door, and opened it wide. By this time Helen was awake and out of bed.

"What happened?" she asked sleepily.

Aunt Rosemary had come into the hall also. Her mother did not say a word; just started back toward her own bedroom. The others followed, wondering what they would find. Moonlight brightened part of the room, but the area near the hall was dark.

"There! Up there!" Miss Flora pointed to a corner of the room near the hall.

Two burning eyes looked down on the watchers!

Instantly Nancy snapped on the wall light and the group gazed upward at a large brown owl perched on the old-fashioned, ornamental picture molding.

"Oh!" Aunt Rosemary cried out. "How did that bird ever get in here?"

The others did not answer at once. Then Nancy, not wishing to frighten Miss Flora, remarked as casually as she could, "It probably came down the chimney."

"But—" Helen started to say.

Nancy gave her friend a warning wink and Helen did not finish the sentence. Nancy was sure she was going to say that the damper had been closed and the bird could not possibly have flown into the room from the chimney. Turning to Miss Flora, Nancy asked whether or not her bedroom door had been locked.

"Oh, yes," the elderly woman insisted. "I wouldn't leave it unlocked for anything."

Nancy did not comment. Knowing that Miss Flora was a bit forgetful, she thought it quite possible that the door had not been locked. An intruder had entered, let the owl fly to the picture molding, then made just enough noise to awaken the sleeping woman.

To satisfy her own memory about the damper, Nancy went over to the fireplace and looked inside. The damper was closed.

"But if the door to the hall was locked," she reasoned, "then the ghost has some other way of getting into this room. And he escaped the detection of the guard."

"I don't want that owl in here all night," Miss Flora broke into Nancy's reverie. "We'll have to get it out."

"That's not going to be easy," Aunt Rosemary spoke up. "Owls have very sharp claws and beaks and they use them viciously on anybody who tries to disturb them. Mother, you come and sleep in my room the rest of the night. We'll chase the owl out in the morning."

Nancy urged Miss Flora to go with her daughter. "I'll stay here and try getting Mr. Owl out of the house. Have you a pair of old heavy gloves?"

"I have some in my room," Aunt Rosemary replied. "They're thick leather. I use them for gardening."

She brought them to Nancy, who put the gloves on at once. Then she suggested that Aunt Rosemary and her mother leave. Nancy smiled. "Helen and I will take over Operation Owl."

As the door closed behind the two women, Nancy dragged a chair to the corner of the room beneath the bird. She was counting on the fact that the bright overhead light had dulled the owl's vision and she would be able to grab it without too much trouble.

"Helen, will you open one of the screens, please?" she requested. "And wish me luck!"

"Don't let that thing get loose," Helen warned as she unfastened the screen and held it far out.

Nancy reached up and by stretching was just able to grasp the bird. In a lightning movement she had put her two hands around its body and imprisoned its claws. At once the owl began to bob its head and peck at her arms above the gloves. Wincing with pain, she stepped down from the chair and ran across the room.

The bird squirmed, darting its beak in first one direction, then another. But Nancy managed to hold the owl in such a position that most of the pecking missed its goal. She held the bird out the window, released it, and stepped back. Helen closed the screen and quickly fastened it.

"Oh!" Nancy said, gazing ruefully at her wrists which now showed several bloody digs from the owl's beak. "I'm glad that's over."

"And I am too," said Helen. "Let's lock Miss Flora's door from the outside, so that ghost can't bring in any owls to the rest of us."

Suddenly Helen grabbed Nancy's arm. "I just thought of something," she said. "There's supposed to be a police guard outside. Yet the ghost got in here without being seen."

"Either that, or there's a secret entrance to this

mansion which runs underground, probably to one of the outbuildings on the property."

Nancy now told about the furtive figure she had seen dart from behind a tree. "I must find out right away if he was the ghost or the guard. I'll do a little snooping around. It's possible the guard didn't show up." Nancy smiled. "But if he did, and he's any good, he'll find me!"

"All right," said Helen. "But, Nancy, do be careful. You're really taking awful chances to solve the mystery of Twin Elms."

Nancy laughed softly as she walked back to the girls' bedroom. She dressed quickly, then went downstairs, put the back-door key in her pocket, and let herself out of the house. Stealthily she went down the steps and glided to a spot back of some bushes.

Seeing no one around, she came from behind them and ran across the lawn to a large maple tree. She stood among the shadows for several moments, then darted out toward a building which in Colonial times had been used as the kitchen.

Halfway there, she heard a sound behind her and turned. A man stood in the shadows not ten feet away. Quick as a wink one hand flew to a holster on his hip.

"Halt!" he commanded.

CHAPTER VIII

A Startling Plunge

NANCY halted as directed and stood facing the man. "Who are you?" she asked.

"I'm a police guard, miss," the man replied. "Just call me Patrick. And who are you?"

Quickly Nancy explained and then asked to see his identification. He opened his coat, pulled out a leather case, and showed her his shield proving that he was a plain-clothes man. His name was Tom Patrick.

"Have you seen anyone prowling around the grounds?" Nancy asked him.

"Not a soul, miss. This place has been quieter than a cemetery tonight."

When the young sleuth told him about the furtive figure she had seen from the window, the detective laughed. "I believe you saw me," he said. "I guess I'm not so good at hiding as I thought I was."

Nancy laughed lightly. "Anyway, you soon nabbed me," she told him.

The two chatted for several minutes. Tom Patrick told Nancy that people in Cliffwood regarded Mrs. Turnbull as being a little queer. They said that if she thought her house was haunted, it was all in line with the stories of the odd people who had lived there from time to time during the past hundred years or so.

"Would this rumor make the property difficult to sell?" Nancy questioned the detective.

"It certainly would."

Nancy said she thought the whole thing was a shame. "Mrs. Turnbull is one of the loveliest women I've ever met and there's not a thing the matter with her, except that once in a while she is forgetful."

"You don't think that some of these happenings we've heard about are just pure imagination?" Tom Patrick asked.

"No, I don't."

Nancy now told him about the owl in Miss Flora's bedroom. "The door was locked, every screen was fastened, and the damper in the chimney closed. You tell me how the owl got in there."

Tom Patrick's eyes opened wide. "You say this happened only a little while ago?" he queried. When Nancy nodded, he added, "Of course I can't be everywhere on these grounds at once, but I've been round and round the building. I've never stopped walking since I arrived. I don't see how anyone could have gotten inside that mansion without my seeing him."

"I'll tell you my theory," said Nancy. "I believe there's a secret underground entrance from some other place on the grounds. It may be in one of these outbuildings. Anyway, tomorrow morning I'm going on a search for it."

"Well, I wish you luck," Tom Patrick said. "And if anything happens during the night, I'll let you know."

Nancy pointed to a window on the second floor. "That's my room," she said. "If you don't have a chance to use the door knocker, just throw a stone up against the screen to alert me. I'll wake up instantly, I know."

The guard promised to do this and Nancy went back into the mansion. She climbed the stairs and for a second time that night undressed. Helen had already gone back to sleep, so Nancy crawled into the big double bed noiselessly.

The two girls awoke the next morning about the same time and immediately Helen asked for full details of what Nancy had learned outdoors the night before. After hearing how her friend had been stopped by the guard, she shivered.

"You might have been in real danger, Nancy, not knowing who he was. You *must* be more careful. Suppose that man had been the ghost?"

Nancy laughed but made no reply. The girls

went downstairs and started to prepare breakfast. In a few minutes Aunt Rosemary and her mother joined them.

"Did you find out anything more last night?" Mrs. Hayes asked Nancy.

"Only that a police guard named Tom Patrick is on duty," Nancy answered.

As soon as breakfast was over, the young sleuth announced that she was about to investigate all the outbuildings on the estate.

"I'm going to search for an underground passage leading to the mansion. It's just possible that we hear no hollow sounds when we tap the walls, because of double doors or walls where the entrance is."

Aunt Rosemary looked at Nancy intently. "You are a real detective, Nancy. I see now why Helen wanted us to ask you to find our ghost."

Nancy's eyes twinkled. "I may have some instinct for sleuthing," she said, "but unless I can solve this mystery, it won't do any of us much good."

Turning to Helen, she suggested that they put on the old clothes they had brought with them.

Attired in sport shirts and jeans, the girls left the house. Nancy led the way first to the old icehouse. She rolled back the creaking, sliding door and gazed within. The tall, narrow building was about ten feet square. On one side were a series of sliding doors, one above the other.

"I've heard Miss Flora say," Helen spoke up, "that in days gone by huge blocks of ice were cut from the river when it was frozen over and dragged here on a sledge. The blocks were stored here and taken off from the top down through these various sliding doors."

"That story rather rules out the possibility of any underground passage leading from this building," said Nancy. "I presume there was ice in here most of the year."

The floor was covered with dank sawdust, and although Nancy was sure she would find nothing of interest beneath it, still she decided to take a look. Seeing an old, rusted shovel in one corner, she picked it up and began to dig. There was only dirt beneath the sawdust.

"Well, that clue fizzled out," Helen remarked, as she and Nancy started for the next building.

This had once been used as a smokehouse. It, too, had an earthen floor. In one corner was a small fireplace, where smoldering fires of hickory wood had once burned. The smoke had curled up a narrow chimney to the second floor, which was windowless.

"Rows and rows of huge chunks of pork hung up there on hooks to be smoked," Helen explained, "and days later turned into luscious hams and bacon."

There was no indication of a secret opening and Nancy went outside the small, two-story, peak-roofed structure and walked around. Up one side of the brick building and leading to a door above were the remnants of a ladder. Now only the sidepieces which had held the rungs remained.

"Give me a boost, will you, Helen?" Nancy requested. "I want to take a look inside."

Helen squatted on the ground and Nancy climbed to her shoulders. Then Helen, bracing her hands against the wall, straightened up. Nancy opened the half-rotted wooden door.

"No ghost here!" she announced.

Nancy jumped to the ground and started for the servants' quarters. But a thorough inspection of this brick-and-wood structure failed to reveal a clue to a secret passageway.

There was only one outbuilding left to investigate, which Helen said was the old carriage house. This was built of brick and was fairly large. No carriages stood on its wooden floor, but around the walls hung old harnesses and reins. Nancy paused a moment to examine one of the bridles. It was set with two hand-painted medallions of women's portraits.

Suddenly her reflection was interrupted by a scream. Turning, she was just in time to see Helen plunge through a hole in the floor. In a flash Nancy was across the carriage house and looking down into a gaping hole where the rotted floor had given way.

"Helen!" she cried out in alarm.

"I'm all right," came a voice from below. "Nice and soft down here. Please throw me your flash."

Nancy removed the flashlight from the pocket of her jeans and tossed it down.

"I thought maybe I'd discovered something," Helen said. "But this is just a plain old hole. Give me a hand, will you, so I can climb up?"

Nancy lay flat on the floor and with one arm grabbed a supporting beam that stood in the center of the carriage house. Reaching down with the other arm, she assisted Helen in her ascent.

"We'd better watch our step around here," Nancy said as her friend once more stood beside her.

"You're so right," Helen agreed, brushing dirt off her jeans. Helen's plunge had given Nancy an idea that there might be other openings in the floor and that one of them could be an entrance to a subterranean passage. But though she flashed her light over every inch of the carriage-house floor, she could discover nothing suspicious.

"Let's quit!" Helen suggested. "I'm a mess, and besides, I'm hungry."

"All right," Nancy agreed. "Are you game to search the cellar this afternoon?"

"Oh, sure."

After lunch they started to investigate the store-rooms in the cellar. There was a cool stone room where barrels of apples had once been kept. There was another, formerly filled with bags of whole-wheat flour, barley, buckwheat, and oat-meal.

"And everything was grown on the estate," said Helen.

"Oh, it must have been perfectly wonderful," Nancy said. "I wish we could go back in time and see how life was in those days!"

"Maybe if we could, we'd know how to find that ghost," Helen remarked. Nancy thought so too.

As the girls went from room to room in the cellar, Nancy beamed her flashlight over every inch of wall and floor. At times, the young sleuth's pulse would quicken when she thought she had discovered a trap door or secret opening. But each time she had to admit failure—there was no evidence of either one in the cellar.

"This has been a discouraging day," Nancy remarked, sighing. "But I'm not giving up."

Helen felt sorry for her friend. To cheer Nancy, she said with a laugh, "Storeroom after storeroom but no room to store a ghost!"

Nancy had to laugh, and together the two girls ascended the stairway to the kitchen. After changing their clothes, they helped Aunt Rosemary prepare the evening dinner. When the group had eaten and later gathered in the parlor, Nancy reminded the others that she expected her father to arrive the next day.

"Dad didn't want me to bother meeting him,

but I just can't wait to see him. I think I'll meet all the trains from Chicago that stop here."

"I hope your father will stay with us for two or three days," Miss Flora spoke up. "Surely he'll have some ideas about our ghost."

"And good ones, too," Nancy said. "If he's on the early train, he'll have breakfast with us. I'll meet it at eight o'clock."

But later that evening Nancy's plans were suddenly changed. Hannah Gruen telephoned her to say that a man at the telegraph office had called the house a short time before to read a message from Mr. Drew. He had been unavoidably detained and would not arrive Wednesday.

"In the telegram your father said that he will let us know when he will arrive," the housekeeper added.

"I'm disappointed," Nancy remarked, "but I hope this delay means that Dad is on the trail of Willie Wharton!"

"Speaking of Willie Wharton," said Hannah, "I heard something about him today."

"What was that?" Nancy asked.

"That he was seen down by the river right here in River Heights a couple of days ago!"

CHAPTER IX

A Worrisome Delay

"You say Willie Wharton was seen in River Heights down by the river?" Nancy asked unbelievingly.

"Yes," Hannah replied. "I learned it from our postman, Mr. Ritter, who is one of the people that sold property to the railroad. As you know, Nancy, Mr. Ritter is very honest and reliable. Well, he said he'd heard that some of the property owners were trying to horn in on this deal of Willie Wharton's for getting more money. But Mr. Ritter wouldn't have a thing to do with it—calls it a holdup."

"Did Mr. Ritter himself see Willie Wharton?" Nancy asked eagerly.

"No," the housekeeper replied. "One of the other property owners told him Willie was around."

"That man *could* be mistaken," Nancy suggested.

"Of course he might," Hannah agreed. "And I'm inclined to think he is. If your father is staying over in Chicago, it must be because of Willie Wharton."

Nancy did not tell Hannah what was racing through her mind. She said good night cheerfully, but actually she was very much worried.

"Maybe Willie Wharton *was* seen down by the river," she mused. "And maybe Dad was 'unavoidably detained' by an enemy of his in connection with the railroad bridge project. One of the dissatisfied property owners might have followed him to Chicago."

Or, she reflected further, it was not inconceivable that Mr. Drew had found Willie Wharton, only to have Willie hold the lawyer a prisoner.

As Nancy sat lost in anxious thought, Helen came into the hall. "Something the matter?" she asked.

"I don't know," Nancy replied, "but I have a feeling there is. Dad telegraphed to say that he wouldn't be here tomorrow. Instead of wiring, he always phones me or Hannah or his office when he is away and it seems strange that he didn't do so this time."

"You told me a few days ago that your father had been threatened," said Helen. "Are you afraid it has something to do with that?"

"Yes, I am."

"Is there anything I can do?" Helen offered.

"Thank you, Helen, but I think not. There isn't anything I can do either. We'll just have to wait and see what happens. Maybe I'll hear from Dad again."

Nancy looked so downcast that Helen searched her mind to find something which would cheer her friend. Suddenly Helen had an idea and went to speak to Miss Flora and Aunt Rosemary about it.

"I think it's a wonderful plan if Nancy will do it," Aunt Rosemary said.

Helen called Nancy from the hall and proposed that they all go to the attic to look in the big trunk containing the old costumes.

"We might even put them on," Miss Flora proposed, smiling girlishly.

"And you girls could dance the minuet," said Aunt Rosemary enthusiastically. "Mother plays the old spinet very well. Maybe she would play a minuet for you."

"I love your idea," said Nancy. She knew that the three were trying to boost her spirits and she appreciated it. Besides, what they had proposed sounded like fun.

All of them trooped up the creaky attic stairs. In their haste, none of the group had remembered to bring flashlights.

"I'll go downstairs and get a couple," Nancy offered.

"Never mind," Aunt Rosemary spoke up.

"There are some candles and holders right here. We keep them for emergencies."

She lighted two white candles which stood in old-fashioned, saucer-type brass holders and led the way to the costume trunk.

As Helen lifted the heavy lid, Nancy exclaimed in delight, "How beautiful the clothes are!"

She could see silks, satins, and laces at one side. At the other was a folded-up rose velvet robe. She and Helen lifted out the garments and held them up.

"They're really lovelier than our formal dance clothes today," Helen remarked. "Especially the men's!"

Miss Flora smiled. "And a lot more flattering!"

The entire trunk was unpacked, before the group selected what they would wear.

"This pale-green silk gown with the panniers would look lovely on you, Nancy," Miss Flora said. "And I'm sure it's just the right size, too."

Nancy surveyed the tiny waist of the ball gown. "I'll try it on," she said. Then laughingly she added, "But I'll probably have to hold my breath to close it in the middle. My, but the women in olden times certainly had slim waistlines!"

Helen was holding up a man's purple velvet suit. It had knee breeches and the waistcoat had a lace-ruffled front. There were a tricorn hat, long white stockings, and buckled slippers to complete the costume.

"I think I'll wear this and be your partner, Nancy," Helen said.

Taking off her pumps, she slid her feet into the buckled slippers. The others laughed aloud. A man with a foot twice the size of Helen's had once worn the slippers!

"Never mind. I'll stuff the empty space with paper," Helen announced gaily.

Miss Flora and Aunt Rosemary selected gowns for themselves, then opened a good-sized box at the bottom of the trunk. It contained various kinds of wigs worn in Colonial times. All were pure white and fluffy.

Carrying the costumes and wigs, the group descended to their bedrooms, where they changed into the fancy clothes, then went to the first floor. Miss Flora led the way into the room across the hall from the parlor. She said it once had been the drawing room. Later it had become a library, but the old spinet still stood in a corner.

Miss Flora sat down at the instrument and began to play Beethoven's "Minuet." Aunt Rosemary sat down beside her.

Nancy and Helen, dubbed by the latter, Master and Mistress Colonial America, began to dance. They clasped their right hands high in the air, then took two steps backward and made little bows. They circled, then strutted, and even put in a few steps with which no dancers in Colonial times would have been familiar.

Aunt Rosemary giggled and clapped. "I wish President Washington would come to see you," she said, acting out her part in the entertainment. "Mistress Nancy, prithee do an encore and Master Corning, wilt thou accompany thy fair lady?"

The girls could barely keep from giggling. Helen made a low bow to her aunt, her tricorn in her hand, and said, "At your service, my lady. Your every wish is my command!"

The minuet was repeated, then as Miss Flora stopped playing, the girls sat down.

"Oh, that was such fun!" said Nancy. "Some time I'd like to— Listen!" she commanded suddenly.

From outside the house they could hear loud shouting. "Come here! You in the house! Come here!"

Nancy and Helen dashed from their chairs to the front door. Nancy snapped on the porch light and the two girls raced outside.

"Over here!" a man's voice urged.

Nancy and Helen ran down the steps and out onto the lawn. Just ahead of them stood Tom Patrick, the police detective. In a viselike grip he was holding a thin, bent-over man whom the girls judged to be about fifty years of age.

"Is this your ghost?" the guard asked.

His prisoner was struggling to free himself but was unable to get loose. The girls hurried forward to look at the man.

"Is this your ghost?" the police guard asked

"I caught him sneaking along the edge of the grounds," Tom Patrick announced.

"Let me go!" the man cried out angrily. "I'm no ghost. What are you talking about?"

"You may not be a ghost," the detective said, "but you could be the thief who has been robbing this house."

"What!" his prisoner exclaimed. "I'm no thief! I live around here. Anyone will tell you I'm okay."

"What's your name and where do you live?" the detective prodded. He let the man stand up straight but held one of his arms firmly.

"My name's Albert Watson and I live over on Tuttle Road."

"What were you doing on this property?"

Albert Watson said he had been taking a short cut home. His wife had taken their car for the evening.

"I'd been to a friend's house. You can call him and verify what I'm saying. And you can call my wife, too. Maybe she's home now and she'll come and get me."

The guard reminded Albert Watson that he had not revealed why he was sneaking along the ground.

"Well," the prisoner said, "it was because of you. I heard downtown that there was a detective patrolling this place and I didn't want to bump into you. I was afraid of just what did happen."

The man relaxed a little. "I guess you're a pretty good guard at that."

Detective Patrick let go of Albert Watson's arm. "Your story sounds okay, but we'll go in the house and do some telephoning to find out if you're telling the truth."

"You'll find out all right. Why, I'm even a notary public! They don't give a notary's license to dishonest folks!" the trespasser insisted. Then he stared at Nancy and Helen, "What are you doing in those funny clothes?"

"We—are—we were having a little costume party," Helen responded. In the excitement she and Nancy had forgotten what they were wearing!

The two girls started for the house, with the men following. When Mr. Watson and the guard saw Miss Flora and Aunt Rosemary also in costume they gazed at the women in amusement.

Nancy introduced Mr. Watson. Miss Flora said she knew of him, although she had never met the man. Two phone calls by the guard confirmed Watson's story. In a little while his wife arrived at Twin Elms to drive her husband home, and Detective Patrick went back to his guard duty.

Aunt Rosemary then turned out all the lights on the first floor and she, Miss Flora, and the girls went upstairs. Bedroom doors were locked, and everyone hoped there would be no disturbance during the night.

"It was a good day, Nancy," said Helen, yawning, as she climbed into bed.

"Yes, it was," said Nancy. "Of course, I'm a little disappointed that we aren't farther along solving the mystery but maybe by this time tomorrow—" She looked toward Helen who did not answer. She was already sound asleep.

Nancy herself was under the covers a few minutes later. She lay staring at the ceiling, going over the various events of the past two days. As her mind recalled the scene in the attic when they were pulling costumes from the old trunk, she suddenly gave a start.

"That section of wall back of the trunk!" she told herself. "The paneling looked different somehow from the rest of the attic wall. Maybe it's movable and leads to a secret exit! Tomorrow I'll find out!"

CHAPTER X

The Midnight Watch

As soon as the two girls awoke the next morning, Nancy told Helen her plan.

"I'm with you," said Helen. "Oh, I do wish we could solve the mystery of the ghost! I'm afraid that it's beginning to affect Miss Flora's health and yet she won't leave Twin Elms."

"Maybe we can get Aunt Rosemary to keep her in the garden most of the day," Nancy suggested. "It's perfectly beautiful outside. We might even serve lunch under the trees."

"I'm sure they'd love that," said Helen. "As soon as we get downstairs, let's propose it."

Both women liked the suggestion. Aunt Rosemary had guessed their strategy and was appreciative of it.

"I'll wash and dry the dishes," Nancy offered when breakfast was over. "Miss Flora, why don't you and Aunt Rosemary go outside right now and take advantage of this lovely sunshine?"

The frail, elderly woman smiled. There were deep circles under her eyes, indicating that she had had a sleepless night.

"And I'll run the vacuum cleaner around and dust this first floor in less than half an hour," Helen said merrily.

Her relatives caught the spirit of her enthusiasm and Miss Flora remarked, "I wish you girls lived here all the time. Despite our troubles, you have brought a feeling of gaiety back into our lives."

Both girls smiled at the compliment. As soon as the two women had gone outdoors, the girls set to work with a will. At the end of the allotted half hour, the first floor of the mansion was spotless. Nancy and Helen next went to the second floor, quickly made the beds, and tidied the bathrooms.

"And now for that ghost!" said Helen, brandishing her flashlight.

Nancy took her own from a bureau drawer.

"Let's see if we can figure out how to climb these attic stairs without making them creak," Nancy suggested. "Knowing how may come in handy some time."

This presented a real challenge. Every inch of each step was tried before the girls finally worked out a pattern to follow in ascending the stairway noiselessly.

Helen laughed. "This will certainly be a

memory test, Nancy. I'll rehearse our directions. First step, put your foot to the left near the wall. Second step, right center. Third step, against the right wall. I'll need three feet to do that!"

Nancy laughed too. "For myself, I think I'll skip the second step. Let's see. On the fourth and fifth it's all right to step in the center, but on the sixth you hug the left wall, on the seventh, the right wall—"

Helen interrupted. "But if you step on the eighth any place, it will creak. So you skip it."

"Nine, ten, and eleven are okay," Nancy recalled. "But from there to fifteen at the top we're in trouble."

"Let's see if I remember," said Helen. "On twelve, you go left, then right, then right again. How can you do that without a jump and losing your balance and tumbling down?"

"How about skipping fourteen and then stretching as far as you can to reach the top one at the left where it doesn't squeak," Nancy replied. "Let's go!"

She and Helen went back to the second floor and began what was meant to be a silent ascent. But both of them made so many mistakes at first the creaking was terrific. Finally, however, the girls had the silent spots memorized perfectly and went up noiselessly.

Nancy clicked on her flashlight and swung it onto the nearest wood-paneled wall. Helen stared at it, then remarked, "This isn't made of long panels from ceiling to floor. It's built of small pieces."

"That's right," said Nancy. "But see if you don't agree with me that the spot back of the costume trunk near the chimney looks a little different. The grain doesn't match the other wood."

The girls crossed the attic and Nancy beamed her flashlight over the suspected paneling.

"It does look different," Helen said. "This could be a door, I suppose. But there's no knob or other hardware on it." She ran her finger over a section just above the floor, following the cracks at the edge of a four-by-two-and-a-half-foot space.

"If it's a secret door," said Nancy, "the knob is on the other side."

"How are we going to open it?" Helen questioned.

"We might try prying the door open," Nancy proposed. "But first I want to test it."

She tapped the entire panel with her knuckles. A look of disappointment came over her face. "There's certainly no hollow space behind it," she said.

"Let's make sure," said Helen. "Suppose I go downstairs and get a screw driver and hammer? We'll see what happens when we drive the screw driver through this crack."

"Good idea, Helen."

While she was gone, Nancy inspected the rest

of the attic walls and floor. She did not find another spot which seemed suspicious. By this time Helen had returned with the tools. Inserting the screw driver into one of the cracks, she began to pound on the handle of it with the hammer.

Nancy watched hopefully. The screw driver went through the crack very easily but immediately met an obstruction on the other side. Helen pulled the screw driver out. "Nancy, you try your luck."

The young sleuth picked a different spot, but the results were the same. There was no open space behind that portion of the attic wall.

"My hunch wasn't so good," said Nancy.

Helen suggested that they give up and go downstairs. "Anyway, I think the postman will be here soon." She smiled. "I'm expecting a letter from Jim. Mother said she would forward all my mail."

Nancy did not want to give up the search yet. But she nodded in agreement and waved her friend toward the stairs. Then the young detective sat down on the floor and cupped her chin in her hands. As she stared ahead, Nancy noticed that Helen, in her eagerness to meet the postman, had not bothered to go quietly down the attic steps. It sounded as if Helen had picked the squeakiest spot on each step!

Nancy heard Helen go out the front door and suddenly realized that she was in the big mansion all alone. "That may bring the ghost on a visit," she thought. "If he is around, he may think I went outside with Helen! And I may learn where the secret opening is!"

Nancy sat perfectly still, listening intently. Suddenly she flung her head up. Was it her imagination, or did she hear the creak of steps? She was not mistaken. Nancy strained her ears, trying to determine from where the sounds were coming.

"I'm sure they're not from the attic stairs or the main staircase. And not the back stairway. Even if the ghost was in the kitchen and unlocked the door to the second floor, he'd know that the one at the top of the stairs was locked from the other side."

Nancy's heart suddenly gave a leap. She was positive that the creaking sounds were coming from somewhere behind the attic wall!

"A secret staircase!" she thought excitedly. "Maybe the ghost is entering the second floor!"

Nancy waited until the sounds stopped, then she got to her feet, tiptoed noiselessly down the attic steps and looked around. She could hear nothing. Was the ghost standing quietly in one of the bedrooms? Probably Miss Flora's?

Treading so lightly that she did not make a sound, Nancy peered into each room as she reached it. But no one was in any of them.

"Maybe he's on the first floor!" Nancy thought. She descended the main stairway, hugging the wall so she would not make a sound. Reaching the first floor, Nancy peered into the parlor. No one was there. She looked in the library, the dining room, and the kitchen. She saw no one.

"Well, the ghost didn't come into the house after all," Nancy concluded. "He may have intended to, but changed his mind."

She felt more certain than at any time, however, that there was a secret entrance to Twin Elms Mansion from a hidden stairway. But how to find it? Suddenly the young sleuth snapped her fingers. "I know what I'll do! I'll set a trap for that ghost!"

She reflected that he had taken jewelry, but those thefts had stopped. Apparently he was afraid to go to the second floor.

"I wonder if anything is missing from the first floor," she mused. "Maybe he has taken silverware or helped himself to some food."

Going to the back door, Nancy opened it and called to Helen, who was now seated in the garden with Miss Flora and Aunt Rosemary. "What say we start lunch?" she called, not wishing to distress Miss Flora by bringing up the subject of the mystery.

"Okay," said Helen. In a few moments she joined Nancy, who asked if her friend had received a letter.

Helen's eyes sparkled. "I sure did. Oh, Nancy, I can hardly wait for Jim to get home!"

Nancy smiled. "The way you describe him, I can hardly wait to see him myself." Then she told Helen the real reason she had called her into the kitchen. She described the footsteps on what she was sure was a hidden, creaking stairway, then added, "If we discover that food or something else is missing we'll know he's been here again."

Helen offered to inspect the flat silver. "I know approximately how many pieces should be in the buffet drawer," she said.

"And I'll look over the food supplies," Nancy suggested. "I have a pretty good idea what was in the refrigerator and on the pantry shelf."

It was not many minutes before each of the girls discovered articles missing. Helen said that nearly a dozen teaspoons were gone and Nancy figured that several cans of food, some eggs, and a quart of milk had been taken.

"It just seems impossible to catch that thief," Helen said with a sigh.

On a sudden hunch Nancy took down from the wall a memo pad and pencil which hung there. Putting a finger to her lips to indicate that Helen was not to comment, Nancy wrote on the sheet:

"I think the only way to catch the ghost is to trap him. I believe he has one or more microphones hidden some place and that he hears all our plans."

Nancy looked up at Helen, who nodded silently. Nancy continued to write, "I don't want to worry

Miss Flora or Aunt Rosemary, so let's keep our plans a secret. I suggest that we go to bed tonight as usual and carry on a conversation about our plans for tomorrow. But actually we won't take off our clothes. Then about midnight let's tiptoe downstairs to watch. I'll wait in the kitchen. Do you want to stay in the living room?"

Again Helen nodded. Nancy, thinking that they had been quiet too long, and that if there was an eavesdropper nearby he might become suspicious, said aloud, "What would Miss Flora and Aunt Rosemary like for lunch, Helen?"

"Why, uh—" Helen found it hard to transfer to the new subject. "They—uh—both love soup."

"Then I'll make cream of chicken soup," said Nancy. "Hand me a can of chicken and rice, will you? And I'll get the milk."

As Helen was doing this, Nancy lighted a match, held her recently written note over the sink, and set fire to the paper.

Helen smiled. "Nancy thinks of everything," she said to herself.

The girls chatted gaily as they prepared the food and finally carried four trays out to the garden. They did not mention their midnight plan. The day in the garden was proving to be most beneficial to Miss Flora, and the girls were sure she would sleep well that night.

Nancy's plan was followed to the letter. Just

as the grandfather clock in the hall was striking midnight, Nancy arrived in the kitchen and sat down to await developments. Helen was posted in a living-room chair near the hall doorway. Moonlight streamed into both rooms but the girls had taken seats in the shadows.

Helen was mentally rehearsing the further instructions which Nancy had written to her during the afternoon. The young sleuth had suggested that if Helen should see anyone, she was to run to the front door, open it, and yell "Police!" At the same time she was to try to watch where the intruder disappeared.

The minutes ticked by. There was not a sound in the house. Then suddenly Nancy heard the front door open with a bang and Helen's voice yell loudly and clearly:

"Police! Help! Police!"

CHAPTER XI

An Elusive Ghost

By the time Nancy reached the front hall, Tom Patrick, the police guard, had rushed into the house. "Here I am!" he called. "What's the matter?"

Helen led the way into the living room, and switched on the chandelier light.

"That sofa next to the fireplace!" she said in a trembling voice. "It moved! I saw it move!"

"You mean somebody moved it?" the detective asked.

"I—I don't know," Helen replied. "I couldn't see anybody."

Nancy walked over to the old-fashioned sofa, set in the niche alongside the fireplace. Certainly the piece was in place now. If the ghost had moved it, he had returned the sofa to its original position.

"Let's pull it out and see what we can find," Nancy suggested.

She tugged at one end, while the guard pulled the other. It occurred to Nancy that a person who moved it alone would have to be very strong.

"Do you think your ghost came up through a trap door or something?" the detective asked.

Neither of the girls replied. They had previously searched the area, and even now as they looked over every inch of the floor and the three walls surrounding the high sides of the couch, they could detect nothing that looked like an opening.

By this time Helen looked sheepish. "I—I guess I was wrong," she said finally. Turning to the police guard, she said, "I'm sorry to have taken you away from your work."

"Don't feel too badly about it. But I'd better get back to my guard duty," the man said, and left the house.

"Oh, Nancy!" Helen cried out. "I'm so sorry!"

She was about to say more but Nancy put a finger to her lips. They could use the same strategy for trapping the thief at another time. In case the thief might be listening, Nancy did not want to give away their secret.

Nancy felt that after all the uproar the ghost would not appear again that night. She motioned to Helen that they would go quietly upstairs and get some sleep. Hugging the walls of the stairway once more, they ascended noiselessly, tiptoed to their room, and got into bed.

"I'm certainly glad I didn't wake up Miss Flora and Aunt Rosemary," said Helen sleepily as she whispered good night.

Though Nancy had been sure the ghost would not enter the mansion again that night, she discovered in the morning that she had been mistaken. More food had been stolen sometime between midnight and eight o'clock when she and Helen started breakfast. Had the ghost taken it for personal use or only to worry the occupants of Twin Elms?

"I missed my chance this time," Nancy murmured to her friend. "After this, I'd better not trust what that ghost's next move may be!"

At nine o'clock Hannah Gruen telephoned the house. Nancy happened to answer the ring and after the usual greetings was amazed to hear Hannah say, "I'd like to speak to your father."

"Why, Dad isn't here!" Nancy told her. "Don't you remember—the telegram said he wasn't coming?"

"He's not there!" Hannah exclaimed. "Oh, this is bad, Nancy—very bad."

"What do you mean, Hannah?" Nancy asked fearfully.

The housekeeper explained that soon after receiving the telegram on Tuesday evening, Mr. Drew himself had phoned. "He wanted to know if you were still in Cliffwood, Nancy. When I told him yes, he said he would stop off there on his way home Wednesday."

Nancy was frightened, but she asked steadily, "Hannah, did you happen to mention the telegram to him?"

"No, I didn't," the housekeeper replied. "I didn't think it was necessary."

"Hannah darling," said Nancy, almost on the verge of tears, "I'm afraid that telegram was a hoax!"

"A hoax!" Mrs. Gruen cried out.

"Yes. Dad's enemies sent it to keep me from meeting him!"

"Oh, Nancy," Hannah wailed, "you don't suppose those enemies that Mr. Gomber warned you about have waylaid your father and are keeping him prisoner?"

"I'm afraid so," said Nancy. Her knees began to quake and she sank into the chair alongside the telephone table.

"What'll we do?" Hannah asked. "Do you want me to notify the police?"

"Not yet. Let me do a little checking first."

"All right, Nancy. But let me know what happens."

"I will."

Nancy put the phone down, then looked at the various telephone directories which lay on the table. Finding one which contained River

Heights numbers, she looked for the number of the telegraph office and put in a call. She asked the clerk who answered to verify that there had been a telegram from Mr. Drew on Tuesday.

After a few minutes wait, the reply came. "We have no record of such a telegram."

Nancy thanked the clerk and hung up. By this time her hands were shaking with fright. What had happened to her father?

Getting control of herself, Nancy telephoned in turn to the airport, the railroad station, and the bus lines which served Cliffwood. She inquired about any accidents which might have occurred on trips from Chicago the previous day or on Tuesday night. In each case she was told there had been none.

"Oh, what shall I do?" Nancy thought in dismay.

Immediately an idea came to her and she put in a call to the Chicago hotel where her father had registered. Although she thought it unlikely, it was just possible that he had changed his mind again and was still there. But a conversation with the desk clerk dashed this hope.

"No, Mr. Drew is not here. He checked out Tuesday evening. I don't know his plans, but I'll connect you with the head porter. He may be able to help you."

In a few seconds Nancy was asking the porter what he could tell her to help clear up the mystery of her father's disappearance. "All I know, miss, is that your father told me he was taking a sleeper train and getting off somewhere Wednesday morning to meet his daughter."

"Thank you.   Oh, thank you very much," said Nancy.   "You've helped me a great deal."

So her father had taken the train home and probably had reached the Cliffwood station!   Next she must find out what had happened to him after that!

Nancy told Aunt Rosemary and Helen what she had learned, then got in her convertible and drove directly to the Cliffwood station.   There she spoke to the ticket agent.   Unfortunately, he could not identify Mr. Drew from Nancy's description as having been among the passengers who got off either of the two trains arriving from Chicago on Wednesday.

Nancy went to speak to the taximen.   Judging by the line of cabs, she decided that all the drivers who served the station were on hand at the moment.   There had been no outgoing trains for nearly an hour and an incoming express was due in about fifteen minutes.

"I'm in luck," the young detective told herself. "Surely one of these men must have driven Dad."

She went from one to another, but each of them denied having carried a passenger of Mr. Drew's description the day before.

By this time Nancy was in a panic.   She hurried inside the station to a telephone booth and called the local police station. Nancy asked to speak to the captain and in a moment he came on the line.

"Captain Rossland speaking," he said crisply.

Nancy poured out her story. She told of the warning her father had received in River Heights and her fear that some enemy of his was now detaining the lawyer against his will.

"This is very serious, Miss Drew," Captain Rossland stated. "I will put men on the case at once," he said.

As Nancy left the phone booth, a large, gray-haired woman walked up to her. "Pardon me, miss, but I couldn't help overhearing what you said. I believe maybe I can help you."

Nancy was surprised and slightly suspicious. Maybe this woman was connected with the abductors and planned to make Nancy a prisoner too by promising to take her to her father!

"Don't look so frightened," the woman said, smiling. "All I wanted to tell you is that I'm down here at the station every day to take a train to the next town. I'm a nurse and I'm on a case over there right now."

"I see," Nancy said.

"Well, yesterday I was here when the Chicago train came in. I noticed a tall, handsome man—such as you describe your father to be—step off the train. He got into the taxi driven by a man named Harry. I have a feeling that for some rea-

son the cabbie isn't telling the truth.   Let's talk to
him."

Nancy followed the woman, her heart beating
furiously.   She was ready to grab at any straw to
get a clue to her father's whereabouts!

"Hello, Miss Skade," the taximan said.   "How
are you today?"

"Oh, I'm all right," the nurse responded.   "Listen, Harry.   You told this young lady that you
didn't carry any passenger yesterday that looked
like her father.   Now I saw one get into your cab.
What about it?"

Harry hung his head.   "Listen, miss," he said
to Nancy, "I got three kids and I don't want
nothin' to happen to 'em.   See?"

"What do you mean?" Nancy asked, puzzled.

When the man did not reply, Miss Skade said,
"Now look, Harry.   This girl's afraid that her father has been kidnaped.   It's up to you to tell her
all you know."

"Kidnaped!" the taximan shouted.   "Oh, good-
night!   Now I don't know what to do."

Nancy had a sudden thought.   "Has somebody
been threatening you, Harry?" she asked.

The cab driver's eyes nearly popped from his
head.   "Well," he said, "since you've guessed it,
I'd better tell you everything I know."

He went on to say that he had taken a passenger
who fitted Mr. Drew's description toward Twin

Elms where he had said he wanted to go. "Just as we were leaving the station, two other men came up and jumped into my cab. They said they were going a little farther than that and would I take them? Well, about halfway to Twin Elms, one of those men ordered me to pull up to the side of the road and stop. He told me the stranger had blacked out. He and his buddy jumped out of the car and laid the man on the grass."

"How ill was he?" Nancy asked.

"I don't know. He was unconscious. Just then another car came along behind us and stopped. The driver got out and offered to take your father to a hospital. The two men said okay."

Nancy took heart. Maybe her father was in a hospital and had not been abducted at all! But a moment later her hopes were again dashed when Harry said:

"I told those guys I'd be glad to drive the sick man to a hospital, but one of them turned on me, shook his fist, and yelled, 'You just forget everything that's happened or it'll be too bad for you and your kids!' "

"Oh!" Nancy cried out. and for a second everything seemed to swim before her eyes. She clutched the door handle of the taxi for support.

There was no question now but that her father had been drugged, then kidnaped!

CHAPTER XII

The Newspaper Clue

MISS SKADE grabbed Nancy. "Do you feel ill?" the nurse asked quickly.

"Oh, I'll be all right," Nancy replied. "This news has been a great shock to me."

"Is there any way I can help you?" the woman questioned. "I'd be very happy to."

"Thank you, but I guess not," the young sleuth said. Smiling ruefully, she added, "But I must get busy and do something about this."

The nurse suggested that perhaps Mr. Drew was in one of the local hospitals. She gave Nancy the names of the three in town.

"I'll get in touch with them at once," the young detective said. "You've been most kind. And here comes your train, Miss Skade. Good-by and again thanks a million for your help!"

Harry climbed out of his taxi and went to stand at the platform to signal passengers for his cab. Nancy hurried after him, and before the train came in, asked if he would please give her a description of the two men who had been with her father.

"Well, both of them were dark and kind of athletic-looking. Not what I'd call handsome. One of 'em had an upper tooth missing. And the other fellow—his left ear was kind of crinkled, if you know what I mean."

"I understand," said Nancy. "I'll give a description of the two men to the police."

She went back to the telephone booth and called each of the three hospitals, asking if anyone by the name of Carson Drew had been admitted or possibly a patient who was not conscious and had no identification. Only Mercy Hospital had a patient who had been unconscious since the day before. He definitely was not Mr. Drew—he was Chinese!

Sure now that her father was being held in some secret hiding place, Nancy went at once to police headquarters and related the taximan's story.

Captain Rossland looked extremely concerned. "This is alarming, Miss Drew," he said, "but I feel sure we can trace that fellow with the crinkly ear and we'll make him tell us where your father is! I doubt, though, that there is anything you can do. You'd better leave it to the police."

Nancy said nothing. She was reluctant to give up even trying to do something, but she acquiesced.

"In the meantime," said the officer, "I'd advise you to remain at Twin Elms and concentrate on solving the mystery there. From what you tell me about your father, I'm sure he'll be able to get out of the difficulty himself, even before the police find him."

Aloud, Nancy promised to stay on call in case Captain Rossland might need her. But in her own mind the young sleuth determined that if she got any kind of a lead concerning her father, she was most certainly going to follow it up.

Nancy left police headquarters and strolled up the street, deep in thought. "Instead of things getting better, all my problems seem to be getting worse. Maybe I'd better call Hannah."

Since she had been a little girl, Nancy had found solace in talking to Hannah Gruen. The housekeeper had always been able to give her such good advice!

Nancy went into a drugstore and entered one of the telephone booths. She called the Drew home in River Heights and was pleased when Mrs. Gruen answered. The housekeeper was aghast to learn Nancy's news but said she thought Captain Rossland's advice was sound.

"You've given the police the best leads in the world and I believe that's all you can do. But wait—" the housekeeper suddenly said. "If I were you, Nancy, I'd call up those railroad lawyers and tell them exactly what has happened. Your father's disappearance is directly concerned with that bridge project, I'm sure, and the lawyers may have some ideas about where to find him."

"That's a wonderful suggestion, Hannah," said Nancy. "I'll call them right away."

But when the young detective phoned the railroad lawyers, she was disappointed to learn that all the men were out to lunch and none of them would return before two o'clock.

"Oh dear!" Nancy sighed. "Well, I guess I'd better get a snack while waiting for them to come back." But in her worried state she did not feel like eating.

There was a food counter at the rear of the drugstore and Nancy made her way to it. Perching on a high-backed stool, she read the menu over and over. Nothing appealed to her. When the counterman asked her what she wanted, Nancy said frankly she did not know—she was not very hungry.

"Then I recommend our split-pea soup," he told her. "It's homemade and out of this world."

Nancy smiled at him. "I'll take your advice and try it."

The hot soup was delicious. By the time she had finished it, Nancy's spirits had risen considerably.

"And how about some custard pie?" the counterman inquired. "It's just like Mother used to make."

"All right," Nancy answered, smiling at the solicitous young man. The pie was ice cold and proved to be delicious. When Nancy finished eating it, she glanced at her wrist watch. It was only one-thirty. Seeing a rack of magazines, she decided to while away the time reading in her car.

She purchased a magazine of detective stories, one of which proved to be so intriguing that the half hour went by quickly. Promptly at two o'clock Nancy returned to the phone booth and called the offices of the railroad lawyers. The switchboard operator connected her with Mr. Anthony Barradale and Nancy judged from his voice that he was fairly young. Quickly she told her story.

"Mr. Drew being held a prisoner!" Mr. Barradale cried out. "Well, those underhanded property owners are certainly going to great lengths to gain a few dollars."

"The police are working on the case, but I thought perhaps your firm would like to take a hand also," Nancy told the lawyer.

"We certainly will," the young man replied. "I'll speak to our senior partner about it. I know he will want to start work at once on the case."

"Thank you," said Nancy. She gave the address and telephone number of Twin Elms and asked that the lawyers get in touch with her there if any news should break.

"We'll do that," Mr. Barradale promised.

Nancy left the drugstore and walked back to her car. Climbing in, she wondered what her next move ought to be.

"One thing is sure," she thought. "Work is the best antidote for worry. I'll get back to Twin Elms and do some more sleuthing there."

As she drove along, Nancy reflected about the ghost entering Twin Elms mansion by a subterranean passage. Since she had found no sign of one in any of the outbuildings on the estate, it occurred to her that possibly it led from an obscure cave, either natural or man-made. Such a device would be a clever artifice for an architect to use.

Taking a little-used road that ran along one side of the estate, Nancy recalled having seen a long, grassed-over hillock which she had assumed to be an old aqueduct. Perhaps this was actually the hidden entrance to Twin Elms!

She parked her car at the side of the road and took a flashlight from the glove compartment. In anticipation of finding the answer to the riddle, Nancy crossed the field, and as she came closer to the beginning of the huge mound, she could see stones piled up. Getting nearer, she realized that it was indeed the entrance to a rocky cave.

"Well, maybe this time I've found it!" she thought, hurrying forward.

The wind was blowing strongly and tossed her hair about her face. Suddenly a freakish gust swept a newspaper from among the rocks and scattered the pages helter-skelter.

Nancy was more excited than ever. The newspaper meant a human being had been there not too long ago! The front page sailed toward her. As she grabbed it up, she saw to her complete astonishment that the paper was a copy of the *River Heights Gazette*. The date was the Tuesday before.

"Someone interested in River Heights has been here very recently!" the young sleuth said to herself excitedly.

Who was the person? Her father? Gomber? Who?

Wondering if the paper might contain any clue, Nancy dashed around to pick up all the sheets. As she spread them out on the ground, she noticed a hole in the page where classified ads appeared.

"This may be a very good clue!" Nancy thought. "As soon as I get back to the house, I'll call Hannah and have her look up Tuesday's paper to see what was in that ad."

It suddenly occurred to Nancy that the person who had brought the paper to the cave might be inside at this very moment. She must watch her step; he might prove to be an enemy!

"This may be where Dad is being held a prisoner!" Nancy thought wildly.

Flashlight in hand, and her eyes darting intently

about, Nancy proceeded cautiously into the cave. Five feet, ten. She saw no one. Fifteen more. Twenty. Then Nancy met a dead end. The empty cave was almost completely round and had no other opening.

"Oh dear. another failure," Nancy told herself disappointedly, as she retraced her steps. "My only hope now is to learn something important from the ad in the paper."

Nancy walked back across the field. Her eyes were down, as she automatically looked for footprints. But presently she looked up and stared in disbelief.

A man was standing alongside her car, examining it. His back was half turned toward Nancy, so she could not see his face very well. But he had an athletic build and his left ear was definitely crinkly!

CHAPTER XIII

The Crash

THE STRANGER inspecting Nancy's car must have heard her coming. Without turning around, he dodged back of the automobile and started off across the field in the opposite direction.

"He certainly acts suspiciously. He must be the man with the crinkly ear who helped abduct my father!" Nancy thought excitedly.

Quickly she crossed the road and ran after him as fast as she could, hoping to overtake him. But the man had had a good head start. Also, his stride was longer than Nancy's and he could cover more ground in the same amount of time.

The far corner of the irregular-shaped field ended at the road on which Riverview Manor stood. When Nancy reached the highway, she was just in time to see the stranger leap into a parked car and drive off.

The young detective was exasperated. She had

had only a glimpse of the man's profile. If only she could have seen him full face or caught the license number of his car!

"I wonder if he's the one who dropped the newspaper?" she asked herself. "Maybe he's from River Heights!" She surmised that the man himself was not one of the property owners but he might have been hired by Willie Wharton or one of the owners to help abduct Mr. Drew.

"I'd better hurry to a phone and report this," Nancy thought.

She ran all the way back across the field, stepped into her own car, turned it around, and headed for Twin Elms. When Nancy arrived, she sped to the telephone in the hall and dialed Cliffwood Police Headquarters. In a moment she was talking to the captain and gave him her latest information.

"It certainly looks as if you picked up a good clue, Miss Drew," the officer remarked. "I'll send out an alarm immediately to have this man picked up."

"I suppose there is no news of my father," Nancy said.

"I'm afraid not. But a couple of our men talked to the taxi driver Harry and he gave us a pretty good description of the man who came along the road while your father was lying unconscious on the grass—the one who offered to take him to the hospital."

"What did he look like?" Nancy asked.

The officer described the man as being in his early fifties, short, and rather heavy-set. He had shifty pale-blue eyes.

"Well," Nancy replied, "I can think of several men who would fit that description. Did he have any outstanding characteristics?"

"Harry didn't notice anything, except that the fellow's hands didn't look as if he did any kind of physical work. The taximan said they were kind of soft and pudgy."

"Well, that eliminates all the men I know who are short, heavy-set and have pale-blue eyes. None of them has hands like that."

"It'll be a good identifying feature," the police officer remarked. "Well, I guess I'd better get that alarm out."

Nancy said good-by and put down the phone. She waited several seconds for the line to clear, then picked up the instrument again and called Hannah Gruen. Before Nancy lay the sheet of newspaper from which the advertisement had been torn.

"The Drew residence," said a voice on the phone.

"Hello, Hannah. This is Nancy."

"How are you, dear? Any news?" Mrs. Gruen asked quickly.

"I haven't found Dad yet," the young detective replied. "And the police haven't either. But I've picked up a couple of clues."

"Tell me about them," the housekeeper requested excitedly.

Nancy told her about the man with the crinkly ear and said she was sure that the police would soon capture him. "If he'll only talk, we may find out where Dad is being held."

"Oh, I hope so!" Hannah sighed. "Don't get discouraged, Nancy."

At this point Helen came into the hall, and as she passed Nancy on her way to the stairs, smiled at her friend. The young sleuth was about to ask Hannah to get the Drews' Tuesday copy of the *River Heights Gazette* when she heard a cracking noise overhead. Immediately she decided the ghost might be at work again.

"Hannah, I'll call you back later," Nancy said and put down the phone.

She had no sooner done this than Helen screamed, "Nancy, run! The ceiling!" She herself started for the front door.

Nancy, looking up, saw a tremendous crack in the ceiling just above the girls' heads. The next instant the whole ceiling crashed down on them! They were thrown to the floor.

"Oh!" Helen moaned. She was covered with lath and plaster, and had been hit hard on the head. But she managed to call out from under the debris, "Nancy, are you all right?" There was no answer.

The whole ceiling crashed down on them!

The tremendous noise had brought Miss Flora and Aunt Rosemary on a run from the kitchen. They stared in horror at the scene before them. Nancy lay unconscious and Helen seemed too dazed to move.

"Oh my! Oh my!" Miss Flora exclaimed.

She and Aunt Rosemary began stepping over the lath and plaster, which by now had filled the air with dust. They sneezed again and again but made their way forward nevertheless.

Miss Flora, reaching Helen's side, started pulling aside chunks of broken plaster and lath. Finally, she helped her great-granddaughter to her feet.

"Oh, my dear, you're hurt!" she said solicitously.

"I'll—be—all right—in a minute," Helen insisted, choking with the dust. "But Nancy—"

Aunt Rosemary had already reached the unconscious girl. With lightning speed, she threw aside the debris which almost covered Nancy. Whipping a handkerchief from her pocket, she gently laid it over Nancy's face, so that she would not breathe in any more of the dust.

"Helen, do you feel strong enough to help me carry Nancy into the library?" she asked. "I'd like to lay her on the couch there."

"Oh, yes, Aunt Rosemary. Do you think Nancy is badly hurt?" she asked worriedly.

"I hope not."

At this moment Nancy stirred. Then her arm

moved upward and she pulled the handkerchief from her face. She blinked several times as if unable to recall where she was.

"You'll be all right, Nancy," said Aunt Rosemary kindly. "But I don't want you to breathe this dust. Please keep the handkerchief over your nose." She took it from Nancy's hand and once more laid it across the girl's nostrils and mouth.

In a moment Nancy smiled wanly. "I remember now. The ceiling fell down."

"Yes," said Helen. "It knocked you out for a few moments. I hope you're not hurt."

Miss Flora, who was still sneezing violently, insisted that they all get out of the dust at once. She began stepping across the piles of debris, with Helen helping her. When they reached the library door, the elderly woman went inside.

Helen returned to help Nancy. But by this time her friend was standing up, leaning on Aunt Rosemary's arm. She was able to make her way across the hall to the library. Aunt Rosemary suggested calling a doctor, but Nancy said this would not be necessary.

"I'm so thankful you girls weren't seriously hurt," Miss Flora said. "What a dreadful thing this is! Do you think the ghost is responsible?"

Her daughter replied at once. "No, I don't. Mother, you will recall that for some time we have had a leak in the hall whenever it rained. And the last time we had a storm, the whole ceiling was soaked. I think that weakened the plaster and it fell of its own accord."

Miss Flora remarked that a new ceiling would be a heavy expense for them. "Oh dear, more troubles all the time. But I still don't want to part with my home."

Nancy, whose faculties by now were completely restored, said with a hint of a smile, "Well, there's one worry you might not have any more, Miss Flora."

"What's that?"

"Mr. Gomber," said Nancy, "may not be so interested in buying this property when he sees what happened."

"Oh, I don't know," Aunt Rosemary spoke up. "He's pretty persistent."

Nancy said she felt all right now and suggested that she and Helen start cleaning up the hall.

Miss Flora would not hear of this. "Rosemary and I are going to help," she said determinedly.

Cartons were brought from the cellar and one after the other was filled with the debris. After it had all been carried outdoors, mops and dust cloths were brought into use. Within an hour all the gritty plaster dust had been removed.

The weary workers had just finished their job when the telephone rang. Nancy, being closest to the instrument, answered it. Hannah Gruen was calling.

"Nancy! What happened?" she asked. "I've

been waiting over an hour for you to call me back. What's the matter?"

Nancy gave her all the details.

"What's going to happen to you next?" the housekeeper exclaimed.

The young sleuth laughed. "Something good, I hope."

She asked Hannah to look for her copy of the *River Heights Gazette* of the Tuesday before. In a few minutes the housekeeper brought it to the phone and Nancy asked her to turn to page fourteen. "That has the classified ads," she said. "Now tell me what the ad is right in the center of the page."

"Do you mean the one about used cars?"

"That must be it," Nancy replied. "That's not in my paper."

Hannah Gruen said it was an ad for Aken's, a used-car dealer. "He's at 24 Main Street in Hancock."

"And now turn the page and tell me what ad is on the back of it," Nancy requested.

"It's a story about a school picnic," Hannah told her. "Does either one of them help you?"

"Yes, Hannah, I believe you've given me just the information I wanted. This may prove to be valuable. Thanks a lot."

After Nancy had finished the call, she started to dial police headquarters, then changed her mind. The ghost might be hiding somewhere in the house to listen—or if he had installed micro-phones at various points, any conversations could be picked up and recorded on a machine a distance away.

"It would be wiser for me to discuss the whole matter in person with the police, I'm sure," Nancy decided.

Divulging her destination only to Helen, she told the others she was going to drive downtown but would not be gone long.

"You're sure you feel able?" Aunt Rosemary asked her.

"I'm perfectly fine," Nancy insisted.

She set off in the convertible, hopeful that through the clue of the used-car dealer, the police might be able to pick up the name of one of the suspects.

"They can track him down and through the man locate my father!"

CHAPTER XIV

An Urgent Message

"EXCELLENT!" Captain Rossland said after Nancy had told her story. He smiled. "The way you're building up clues, if you were on my force, I'd recommend a citation for you!"

The young sleuth smiled and thanked him. "I must find my father," she said earnestly.

"I'll call Captain McGinnis of the River Heights force at once," the officer told her. "Why don't you sit down here and wait? It shouldn't take long for them to get information from Aken's used-car lot."

Nancy agreed and took a chair in a corner of the captain's office. Presently he called to her.

"I have your answer, Miss Drew."

She jumped up and went over to his desk. The officer told her that Captain McGinnis in River Heights had been most co-operative. He had sent two men at once to Aken's used-car lot. They had just returned with a report.

"Day before yesterday an athletic-looking man with a crinkly ear came there and purchased a car. He showed a driver's license stating that he was Samuel Greenman from Huntsville."

Nancy was excited over the information. "Then it will be easy to pick him up, won't it?" she asked.

"I'm afraid not," Captain Rossland replied. "McGinnis learned from the Huntsville police that although Greenman is supposed to live at the address he gave, he is reported to have been out of town for some time."

"Then no one knows where he is?"

"Not any of his neighbors."

The officer also reported that Samuel Greenman was a person of questionable character. He was wanted on a couple of robbery charges, and police in several states had been alerted to be on the lookout for him.

"Well, if the man I saw at my car is Samuel Greenman, then maybe he's hiding in this area."

Captain Rossland smiled. "Are you going to suggest next that he is the ghost at Twin Elms?"

"Who knows?" Nancy countered.

"In any case," Captain Rossland said, "your idea that he may be hiding out around here is a good one."

Nancy was about to ask the officer another question when his phone rang. A moment later he said, "It's for you, Miss Drew."

The girl detective picked up the receiver and said, "Hello." The caller was Helen Corning and her voice sounded frantic.

"Oh, Nancy, something dreadful has happened here! You must come home at once!"

"What it it?" Nancy cried out, but Helen had already put down the instrument at her end.

Nancy told Captain Rossland of the urgent request and said she must leave at once.

"Let me know if you need the police," the officer called after her.

"Thank you, I will."

Nancy drove to Twin Elms as fast as the law allowed. As she pulled up in front of the house, she was startled to see a doctor's car there. Someone had been taken ill!

Helen met her friend at the front door. "Nancy," she said in a whisper, "Miss Flora may have had a heart attack!"

"How terrible!" Nancy said, shocked. "Tell me all about it."

"Dr. Morrison wants Miss Flora to go to the hospital right away, but she refuses. She says she won't leave here."

Helen said that the physician was still upstairs attending her great-grandmother.

"When did she become ill?" Nancy asked. "Did something in particular bring on the attack?"

Helen nodded. "Yes. It was very frightening. Miss Flora, Aunt Rosemary, and I were in the kitchen talking about supper. They wanted to have a special dish to surprise you, because they knew you were dreadfully upset."

"That was sweet of them," Nancy remarked. "Please go on, Helen."

"Miss Flora became rather tired and Aunt Rosemary suggested that she go upstairs and lie down. She had just started up the stairway, when, for some unknown reason, she turned to look back. There, in the parlor, stood a man!"

"A caller?" Nancy questioned.

"Oh, no!" Helen replied. "Miss Flora said he was an ugly, horrible-looking person. He was unshaven and his hair was kind of long."

"Do you think he was the ghost?" Nancy inquired.

"Miss Flora thought so. Well, she didn't scream. You know, she's really terribly brave. She just decided to go down and meet him herself. And then, what do you think?"

"I could guess any number of things," Nancy replied. "What did happen?"

Helen said that when Mrs. Turnbull had reached the parlor, no one was in it! "And there was no secret door open."

"What did Miss Flora do then?" Nancy asked.
"She fainted."

At this moment a tall, slender, gray-haired man, carrying a physician's bag, walked down the stairs to the front hall. Helen introduced Nancy to him, then asked about the patient.

"Well, fortunately, Miss Flora is going to be all right," said Dr. Morrison. "She is an amazing woman. With complete rest and nothing more to worry her, I believe she will be all right. In fact, she may be able to be up for short periods by this time tomorrow."

"Oh, I'm so relieved," said Helen. "I'm terribly fond of my great-grandmother and I don't want anything to happen to her."

The physician smiled. "I'll do all I can, but you people will have to help."

"How can we do that?" Nancy asked quickly.

The physician said that no one was to talk about the ghost. "Miss Flora says that she saw a man in the parlor and that he must have come in by some secret entrance. Now you know, as well as I do, that such a thing is not plausible."

"But the man couldn't have entered this house any other way," Helen told him quickly. "Every window and door on this first floor is kept locked."

The doctor raised his eyebrows. "You've heard of hallucinations?" he asked.

Nancy and Helen frowned, but remained silent.

They were sure that Miss Flora had not had an hallucination. If she had said there was a man in the parlor, then one had been there!

"Call me if you need me before tomorrow morning," the doctor said as he moved toward the front door. "Otherwise I'll drop in some time before twelve."

After the medic had left, the two girls exchanged glances. Nancy said, "Are you game to search the parlor again?"

"You bet I am," Helen responded. "Shall we start now or wait until after supper?"

Although Nancy was eager to begin at once, she thought that first she should go upstairs and extend her sympathy to Miss Flora. She also felt that a delay in serving her supper while the search went on might upset the ill woman. Helen offered to go into the kitchen at once and start preparing the meal. Nancy nodded and went up the steps.

Miss Flora had been put to bed in her daughter's room to avoid any further scares from the ghost, who seemed to operate in the elderly woman's own room.

"Miss Flora, I'm so sorry you have to stay in bed," said Nancy, walking up and smiling at the patient.

"Well, I am too," Mrs. Turnbull replied. "And I think it's a lot of nonsense. Everybody faints once in a while. If you'd ever seen what I did—that horrible face!"

"Mother!" pleaded Aunt Rosemary, who was seated in a chair on the other side of the bed. "You know what the doctor said."

"Oh, these doctors!" her mother said pettishly. "Anyway, Nancy, I'm sure I saw the ghost. Now you just look for a man who hasn't shaved in goodness knows how long and has an ugly face and kind of longish hair."

It was on the tip of Nancy's tongue to ask for information on the man's height and size, but recalling the doctor's warning, she said nothing about this. Instead, she smiled and taking one of Miss Flora's hands in her own, said:

"Let's not talk any more about this until you're up and well. Then I'll put you on the Drew and Company detective squad!"

The amusing remark made the elderly woman smile and she promised to try getting some rest.

"But first I want something to eat," she demanded. "Do you think you girls can manage alone? I'd like Rosemary to stay here with me."

"Of course we can manage, and we'll bring you exactly what you should have to eat."

Nancy went downstairs and set up a tray for Miss Flora. On it was a cup of steaming chicken bouillon, a thin slice of well-toasted bread, and a saucer of plain gelatin.

A few minutes later Helen took another tray upstairs with a more substantial meal on it for Aunt Rosemary. Then the two girls sat down in the dining room to have their own supper. After finishing it, they quickly washed and dried all the dishes, then started for the parlor.

"Where do you think we should look?" Helen whispered.

During the past half hour Nancy had been going over in her mind what spot in the parlor they might have overlooked—one which could possibly have an opening behind it. She had decided on a large cabinet built into the wall. It contained a beautiful collection of figurines, souvenirs from many places, and knickknacks of various kinds.

"I'm going to look for a hidden spring that may move the cabinet away from the wall," Nancy told Helen in a low voice.

For the first time she noticed that each of the figurines and knickknacks were set in small depressions on the shelves. Nancy wondered excitedly if this had been done so that the figurines would not fall over in case the cabinet were moved.

Eagerly she began to look on the back wall of the interior of the cabinet for a spring. She and Helen together searched every inch of the upper part but found no spring to move the great built-in piece of furniture.

On the lower part of the cabinet were two doors which Nancy had already opened many times. But then she had been looking for a large opening.

Now she was hoping to locate a tiny spring or movable panel.

Helen searched the left side, while Nancy took the right. Suddenly her pulse quickened in anticipation. She had felt a spot slightly higher than the rest.

Nancy ran her fingers back and forth across the area which was about half an inch high and three inches long.

"It may conceal something," she thought, and pushed gently against the wood.

Nancy felt a vibration in the whole cabinet.

"Helen! I've found something!" she whispered hoarsely. "Better stand back!"

Nancy pressed harder. This time the right side of the cabinet began to move forward. Nancy jumped up from her knees and stood back with Helen. Slowly, very slowly, one end of the cabinet began to move into the parlor, the other into an open space behind it.

Helen grabbed Nancy's hand in fright. What were they going to find in the secret passageway?

CHAPTER XV

A New Suspect

THE GREAT crystal chandelier illuminated the narrow passageway behind the cabinet. It was not very long. No one was in it and the place was dusty and filled with cobwebs.

"There's probably an exit at the other end of this," said Nancy. "Let's see where it goes."

"I think I'd better wait here, Nancy," Helen suggested. "This old cabinet might suddenly start to close itself. If it does, I'll yell so you can get out in time."

Nancy laughed. "You're a real pal, Helen."

As Nancy walked along the passageway, she looked carefully at the two walls which lined it. There was no visible exit from either of the solid, plastered walls. The far end, too, was solid, but this wall had been built of wood.

Nancy felt it might have some significance. At the moment she could not figure it out and started to return to the parlor. Halfway along the narrow corridor, she saw a folded piece of paper lying on the floor.

"This may prove something," she told herself eagerly, picking it up.

Just as Nancy stepped back into the parlor, Aunt Rosemary appeared. She stared in astonishment at the opening in the wall and at the cabinet which now stood at right angles to it.

"You found something?" she asked.

"Only this," Nancy replied, and handed Aunt Rosemary the folded paper.

As the girls looked over her shoulder, Mrs. Hayes opened it. "This is an unfinished letter," she commented, then started to decipher the old-fashioned handwriting. "Why, this was written way back in 1785—not long after the house was built."

The note read:

My honorable friend Benjamin:

The disloyalty of two of my servants has just come to my attention. I am afraid they plan to harm the cause of the Colonies. I will have them properly punished. My good fortune in learning about this disloyalty came while I was at my listening post. Every word spoken in the servants' sitting room can be overheard by me.

I will watch for further—

The letter ended at this point. Instantly Helen said, "Listening post?"

"It must be at the end of this passageway," Nancy guessed. "Aunt Rosemary, what room would connect with it?"

"I presume the kitchen," Mrs. Hayes replied. "And it seems to me that I once heard that the present kitchen was a sitting room for the servants long ago. You recall that back in Colonial days food was never cooked in a mansion. It was always prepared in another building and brought in on great trays."

Helen smiled. "With a listening post the poor servants here didn't have a chance for a good chit-chat together. Their conversations were never a secret from their master!"

Nancy and Aunt Rosemary smiled too and nodded, then the young sleuth said, "Let's see if this listening post still works."

It was arranged that Helen would go into the kitchen and start talking. Nancy would stand at the end of the corridor to listen. Aunt Rosemary, who was shown how to work the hidden spring on the cabinet, would act as guard if the great piece of furniture suddenly started to move and close the opening.

"All ready?" Helen asked. She moved out of the room.

When she thought Nancy was at her post, she

began to talk about her forthcoming wedding and asked Nancy to be in the bridal party.

"I can hear Helen very plainly!" Nancy called excitedly to Aunt Rosemary. "The listening post is as good as ever!"

When the test was over, and the cabinet manually closed by Nancy, she and Helen and Aunt Rosemary held a whispered conversation. They all decided that the ghost knew about the passageway and had overheard plans which those in the house were making. Probably this was where the ghost disappeared after Miss Flora spotted him.

"Funny that we seem to do more planning while we're in the kitchen than in any other room," Aunt Rosemary remarked.

Helen said she wondered if this listening post was unique with the owner and architect of Twin Elms mansion.

"No, indeed," Aunt Rosemary told her. "Many old homes where there were servants had such places. Don't forget that our country has been involved in several wars, during which traitors and spies found it easy to get information while posing as servants."

"Very clever," Helen remarked. "And I suppose a lot of the people who were caught never knew how they had been found out."

"No doubt," said Aunt Rosemary.

At that moment they heard Miss Flora's feeble

voice calling from the bedroom and hurried up the steps to be sure that she was all right. They found her smiling, but she complained that she did not like to stay alone so long.

"I won't leave you again tonight, Mother," Aunt Rosemary promised. "I'm going to sleep on the couch in this room so as not to disturb you. Now try to get a little sleep."

The following morning Nancy had a phone call from Hannah Gruen, whose voice sounded very irate. "I've just heard from Mr. Barradale, the railroad lawyer, Nancy. He lost your address and phone number, so he called here. I'm furious at what he had to say. He hinted that your father might be staying away on purpose because he wasn't able to produce Willie Wharton!"

Nancy was angry too. "Why, that's absolutely unfair and untrue," she cried.

"Well, I just wouldn't stand for it if I were you," Hannah Gruen stated flatly. "And that's only half of it."

"You mean he had more to say about Dad?" Nancy questioned quickly.

"No, not that," the housekeeper answered. "He was calling to say that the railroad can't hold up the bridge project any longer. If some new evidence isn't produced by Monday, the railroad will be forced to accede to the demands of Willie Wharton and all those other property owners!"

"Oh, that would be a great blow to Dad!" said

Nancy. "He wouldn't want this to happen. He's sure that the signature on that contract of sale is Willie Wharton's. All he has to do is find him and prove it."

"Everything is such a mess," said Mrs. Gruen. "I was talking to the police just before I called you and they have no leads at all to where your father might be."

"Hannah, this is dreadful!" said Nancy. "I don't know how, but I intend to find Dad—and quickly, too!"

After the conversation between herself and the housekeeper was over, Nancy walked up and down the hall, as she tried to formulate a plan. Something must be done!

Suddenly Nancy went to the front door, opened it, and walked outside. She breathed deeply of the lovely morning air and headed for the rose garden. She let the full beauty of the estate sink into her consciousness, before permitting herself to think further about the knotty problem before her.

Long ago Mr. Drew had taught Nancy that the best way to clear one's brain is to commune with Nature for a time. Nancy went up one walk and down another, listening to the twittering of the birds and now and then the song of the meadow lark. Again she smelled deeply of the roses and the sweet wisteria which hung over a sagging arbor.

Ten minutes later she returned to the house and sat down on the porch steps. Almost at once a mental image of Nathan Gomber came to her as clearly as if the man had been standing in front of her. The young sleuth's mind began to put together the various pieces of the puzzle regarding him and the railroad property.

"Maybe Nathan Gomber is keeping Willie Wharton away!" she said to herself. "Willie may even be a prisoner! And if Gomber is that kind of a person, maybe he engineered the abduction of my father!"

The very thought frightened Nancy. Leaping up, she decided to ask the police to have Nathan Gomber shadowed.

"I'll go down to headquarters and talk to Captain Rossland," she decided. "And I'll ask Helen to go along. The cleaning woman is here, so she can help Aunt Rosemary in case of an emergency."

Without explaining her real purpose in wanting to go downtown, Nancy merely asked Helen to accompany her there for some necessary marketing. The two girls drove off, and on the way to town Nancy gave Helen full details of her latest theories about Nathan Gomber.

Helen was amazed. "And here he was acting so worried about your father's safety!"

When the girls reached police headquarters, they had to wait a few minutes to see Captain Rossland. Nancy fidgeted under the delay. Every moment seemed doubly precious now. But finally the girls were ushered inside and the officer greeted them warmly.

"Another clue, Miss Drew?" he asked with a smile.

Nancy told her story quickly.

"I think you're on the right track," the officer stated. "I'll be very glad to get in touch with your Captain McGinnis in River Heights and relay your message. And I'll notify all the men on my force to be on the lookout for this Nathan Gomber."

"Thank you," said Nancy gratefully. "Every hour that goes by I become more and more worried about my father."

"A break should come soon," the officer told her kindly. "The minute I hear anything I'll let you know."

Nancy thanked him and the girls went on their way. It took every bit of Nancy's stamina not to show her inmost feelings. She rolled the cart through the supermarket almost automatically, picking out needed food items. Her mind would say, "We need more canned peas because the ghost took what we had," and at the meat counter she reflected, "Dad loves thick, juicy steaks."

Finally the marketing was finished and the packages stowed in the rear of the convertible. On the way home, Helen asked Nancy what plans she had for pursuing the mystery.

"To tell the truth, I've been thinking about it continuously, but so far I haven't come up with any new ideas," Nancy answered. "I'm sure, though, that something will pop up."

When the girls were a little distance from the entrance to the Twin Elms estate, they saw a car suddenly pull out of the driveway and make a right turn. The driver leaned out his window and looked back. He wore a smug grin.

"Why, it's Nathan Gomber!" Nancy cried out.

"And did you see that smirk on his face?" Helen asked. "Oh, Nancy, maybe that means he's finally persuaded Miss Flora to sell the property to him!"

"Yes," Nancy replied grimly. "And also, here I've just asked the police to shadow him and I'm the first person to see him!"

With that Nancy put on speed and shot ahead. As she passed the driveway to the estate, Helen asked, "Where are you going?"

"I'm following Nathan Gomber until I catch him!"

CHAPTER XVI

Sold!

"OH, NANCY, I hope we meet a police officer!" said Helen Corning. "If Gomber is a kidnaper, he may try to harm us if we do catch up to him!"

"We'll have to be cautious," Nancy admitted. "But I'm afraid we're not going to meet any policeman. I haven't seen one on these roads in all the time I've been here."

Both girls watched the car ahead of them intently. It was near enough for Nancy to be able to read the license number. She wondered if the car was registered under Gomber's name or someone else's. If it belonged to a friend of his, this fact might lead the police to another suspect.

"Where do you think Gomber's going?" Helen asked presently. "To meet somebody?"

"Perhaps. And he may be on his way back to River Heights."

"Not yet," Helen said, for at that moment Gomber had reached a crossroads and turned sharp right. "That road leads away from River Heights."

"But it does lead past Riverview Manor," Nancy replied tensely as she neared the crossroads.

Turning right, the girls saw Gomber ahead, tearing along at a terrific speed. He passed the vacant mansion. A short distance beyond it he began to turn his car lights off and on.

"What's he doing that for?" Helen queried. "Is he just testing his lights?"

Nancy was not inclined to think so. "I believe he's signaling to someone. Look all around, Helen, and see if you can spot anybody." She herself was driving so fast that she did not dare take her eyes from the road.

Helen gazed right and left, and then turned to gaze through the back window. "I don't see a soul," she reported.

Nancy began to feel uneasy. It was possible that Gomber might have been signaling to someone to follow the girls. "Helen, keep looking out the rear window and see if a car appears and starts to follow us."

"Maybe we ought to give up the chase and just tell the police about Gomber," Helen said a bit fearfully.

But Nancy did not want to do this. "I think it will help us a lot to know where he's heading."

She continued the pursuit and several miles farther on came to the town of Hancock.

"Isn't this where that crinkly-eared fellow lives?" Helen inquired.

"Yes."

"Then it's my guess Gomber is going to see him."

Nancy reminded her friend that the man was reported to be out of town, presumably because he was wanted by the police on a couple of robbery charges.

Though Hancock was small, there was a great deal of traffic on the main street. In the center of town at an intersection, there was a signal light. Gomber shot through the green, but by the time Nancy reached the spot, the light had turned red.

"Oh dear!" she fumed. "Now I'll probably lose him!"

In a few seconds the light changed to green and Nancy again took up her pursuit. But she felt that at this point it was futile. Gomber could have turned down any of a number of side streets, or if he had gone straight through the town he would now be so far ahead of her that it was doubtful she could catch him. Nancy went on, nevertheless, for another three miles. Then, catching no sight of her quarry, she decided to give up the chase.

"I guess it's hopeless, Helen," she said. "I'm going back to Hancock and report everything to the police there. I'll ask them to get in touch with Captain Rossland and Captain McGinnis.

"Oh, I hope they capture Gomber!" Helen

said. "He's such a horrible man! He ought to be put in jail just for his bad manners!"

Smiling, Nancy turned the car and headed back for Hancock. A woman passer-by gave her directions to police headquarters and a few moments later Nancy parked in front of it. The girls went inside the building. Nancy told the officer in charge who they were, then gave him full details of the recent chase.

The officer listened attentively, then said, "I'll telephone your River Heights captain first."

"And please alert your own men and the State Police," Nancy requested.

He nodded. "Don't worry, Miss Drew, I'll follow through from here." He picked up his phone.

Helen urged Nancy to leave immediately. "While you were talking, I kept thinking about Gomber's visit to Twin Elms. I have a feeling something may have happened there. You remember what a self-satisfied look Gomber had on his face when we saw him come out of the driveway."

"You're right," Nancy agreed. "We'd better hurry back there."

It was a long drive back to Twin Elms and the closer the girls go to it, the more worried they became. "Miss Flora was already ill," Helen said tensely, "and Gomber's visit may have made her worse."

On reaching the house, the front door was opened by Aunt Rosemary, who looked pale.

"I'm so glad you've returned," she said. "My mother is much worse. She has had a bad shock. I'm waiting for Dr. Morrison."

Mrs. Hayes' voice was trembling and she found it hard to go on. Nancy said sympathetically, "We know Nathan Gomber was here. We've been chasing his car, but lost it. Did he upset Miss Flora?"

"Yes. I was out of the house about twenty minutes talking with the gardener and didn't happen to see Gomber drive up. The cleaning woman, Lillie, let him in. Of course she didn't know who he was and thought he was all right. When she finally came outside to tell me, I had walked way over to the wisteria arbor at the far end of the grounds.

"In the meantime, Gomber went upstairs. He began talking to Mother about selling the mansion. When she refused, he threatened her, saying that if she did not sign, all kinds of dreadful things would happen to me and to both you girls.

"Poor mother couldn't hold out any longer. At this moment Lillie, who couldn't find me, returned and went upstairs. She actually witnessed Mother's signature on the contract of sale and signed her own name to it. So Gomber has won!"

Aunt Rosemary sank into the chair by the telephone and began to cry. Nancy and Helen put their arms around her, but before either could say a word of comfort, they heard a car drive up in front of the mansion. At once Mrs. Hayes dried her eyes and said, "It must be Dr. Morrison."

Nancy opened the door and admitted the physician. The whole group went upstairs where Miss Flora lay staring at the ceiling like someone in a trance. She was murmuring:

"I shouldn't have signed! I shouldn't have sold Twin Elms!"

Dr. Morrison took the patient's pulse and listened to her heartbeat with a stethoscope. A few moments later he said, "Mrs. Turnbull, won't you please let me take you to the hospital?"

"Not yet," said Miss Flora stubbornly. She smiled wanly. "I know I'm ill. But I'm not going to get better any quicker in the hospital than I am right here. I'll be moving out of Twin Elms soon enough and I want to stay here as long as I can. Oh, why did I ever sign my name to that paper?"

As an expression of defeat came over the physician's face, Nancy moved to the bedside. "Miss Flora," she said gently, "maybe the deal will never go through. In the first place, perhaps we can prove that you signed under coercion. If that doesn't work, you know it takes a long time to have a title search made on property. By then, maybe Gomber will change his mind."

"Oh, I hope you're right," the elderly woman replied, squeezing Nancy's hand affectionately.

The girls left the room, so that Dr. Morrison could examine the patient further and prescribe for her. They decided to say nothing of their morning's adventure to Miss Flora, but at luncheon they gave Aunt Rosemary a full account.

"I'm almost glad you didn't catch Gomber." Mrs. Hayes exclaimed. "He might have harmed you both."

Nancy said she felt sure that the police of one town or the other would soon capture him, and then perhaps many things could be explained. "For one, we can find out why he was turning his lights off and on. I have a hunch he was signaling to someone and that the person was hidden in Riverview Manor!"

"You may be right," Aunt Rosemary replied.

Helen suddenly leaned across the table. "Do you suppose our ghost thief hides out there?"

"I think it's very probable," Nancy answered. "I'd like to do some sleuthing in that old mansion."

"You're not going to break in?" Helen asked, horrified.

Her friend smiled. "No, Helen, I'm not going to evade the law. I'll go to the realtor who is handling the property and ask him to show me the place. Want to come along?"

Helen shivered a little but said she was game. "Let's do it this afternoon."

"Oh dear." Aunt Rosemary gave an anxious

sigh. "I don't know whether or not I should let you. It sounds very dangerous to me."

"If the realtor is with us, we should be safe," Helen spoke up. Her aunt then gave her consent, and added that the realtor, Mr. Dodd, had an office on Main Street.

Conversation ceased for a few moments as the threesome finished luncheon. They had just left the table when they heard a loud thump upstairs.

"Oh, goodness!" Aunt Rosemary cried out. "I hope Mother hasn't fallen!"

She and the girls dashed up the stairs. Miss Flora was in bed, but she was trembling like a leaf in the wind. She pointed a thin, white hand toward the ceiling.

"It was up in the attic! Sombody's there!"

CHAPTER XVII

Through the Trap Door

"LET's find out who's in the attic!" Nancy urged as she ran from the room, Helen at her heels.

"Mother, will you be all right if I leave you a few moments?" Aunt Rosemary asked. "I'd like to go with the girls."

"Of course. Run along."

Nancy and Helen were already on their way to the third floor. They did not bother to go noiselessly, but raced up the center of the creaking stairs. Reaching the attic, they lighted two of the candles and looked around. They saw no one, and began to look behind trunks and pieces of furniture. Nobody was hiding.

"And there's no evidence," said Nancy, "that the alarming thump was caused by a falling box or carton."

"There's only one answer," Helen decided. "The ghost *was* here. But how did he get in?"

The words were scarcely out of her mouth when the group heard a man's spine-chilling laugh. It had not come from downstairs.

"He—he's back of the wall!" Helen gasped fearfully. Nancy agreed, but Aunt Rosemary said, "That laugh could have come from the roof."

Helen looked at her aunt questioningly. "You —you mean that the ghost swings onto the roof from a tree and climbs in here somehow?"

"I think it very likely," her aunt replied. "My father once told my mother that there's a trap door to the roof. I never saw it and I forgot having heard of it until this minute."

Holding their candles high, the girls examined every inch of the peaked, beamed ceiling. The rafters were set close together with wood panels between them.

"I see something that might be a trap door!" Nancy called out presently from near one end of the attic. She showed the others where some short panels formed an almost perfect square.

"But how does it open?" Helen asked. "There's no knob or hook or any kind of gadget to grab hold of."

"It might have been removed, or rusted off," Nancy said.

She asked Helen to help her drag a high wooden box across the floor until it was directly under the suspected section and Nancy stepped up onto it. Focusing her light on the four edges of the panels, the young sleuth finally discovered a piece of metal wedged between two of the planks.

"I think I see a way to open this," Nancy said, "but I'll need some tools."

"I'll get the ones I found before," Helen offered. She hurried downstairs and procured them. Nancy tried one tool after another, but none would work; they were either too wide to fit into the crack or they would not budge the piece of metal either up or down.

Nancy looked down at Aunt Rosemary. "Do you happen to have an old-fashioned buttonhook?" she asked. "That might be just the thing for this job."

"Indeed I have—in fact, Mother has several of them. I'll get one."

Aunt Rosemary was gone only a few minutes. Upon her return, she handed Nancy a long, silver-handled buttonhook inscribed with Mrs. Turnbull's initials. "Mother used this to fasten her high button shoes. She has a smaller matching one for glove buttons. In olden days," she told the girls, "no lady's gloves were the pull-on type. They all had buttons."

Nancy inserted the long buttonhook into the ceiling crack and almost at once was able to grasp the piece of metal and pull it down. Now she began tugging on it. When nothing happened, Helen climbed up on the box beside her friend and helped pull.

Presently there was a groaning, rasping noise and the square section of the ceiling began to move downward. The girls continued to yank on the metal piece and slowly a folded ladder attached to the wood became visible.

"The trap door's up there!" Helen cried gleefully, looking at the roof. "Nancy, you shall have the honor of being the first one to look out."

Nancy smiled. "And, you mean, capture the ghost?"

As the ladder was straightened out, creaking with each pull, and set against the roof, Nancy felt sure, however, that the ghost did not use it. The ladder made entirely too much noise! She also doubted that he was on the roof, but it would do no harm to look. She might pick up a clue of some sort!

"Well, here I go," Nancy said, and started to ascend the rungs.

When she reached the top, Nancy unfastened the trap door and shoved it upward. She poked her head outdoors and looked around. No one was in sight on the roof, but in the center stood a circular wooden lookout. It occurred to Nancy that possibly the ghost might be hiding in it!

She called down to Aunt Rosemary and Helen to look up at the attic ceiling for evidence of an opening into the tower. They returned to Nancy in half a minute to report that they could find no sign of another trap door.

"There probably was one in olden days," said Aunt Rosemary, "but it was closed up."

A sudden daring idea came to the girl detective. "I'm going to crawl over to that lookout and see if anybody's in it!" she told the two below.

Before either of them could object, she started to crawl along the ridgepole above the wooden shingled sides of the deeply slanting roof. Helen had raced up the ladder, and now watched her friend fearfully.

"Be careful, Nancy!" she warned.

Nancy was doing just that. She must keep a perfect balance or tumble down to almost certain death. Halfway to the tower, the daring girl began to feel that she had been foolhardy, but she was determined to reach her goal.

"Only five more feet to go," Nancy told herself presently.

With a sigh of relief, she reached the tower and pulled herself up. It was circular and had openings on each side. She looked in. No "ghost"!

Nancy decided to step inside the opening and examine the floor. She set one foot down, but immediately the boards, rotted from the weather, gave way beneath her.

"It's a good thing I didn't put my whole weight on it," she thought thankfully.

"Do you see anything?" Helen called.

"Not a thing. This floor hasn't been in use for a long time."

"Then the ghost didn't come in by way of the roof," Helen stated.

Nancy nodded in agreement. "The only places left to look are the chimneys," the young sleuth told her friend. "I'll check them."

There were four of these and Nancy crawled to each one in turn. She looked inside but found nothing to suggest that the ghost used any of them for entry.

Balancing herself against the last chimney, Nancy surveyed the countryside around her. What a beautiful and picturesque panorama it was,

she thought! Not far away was a lazy little river, whose waters sparkled in the sunlight. The surrounding fields were green and sprinkled with patches of white daisies.

Nancy looked down on the grounds of Twin Elms and tried in her mind to reconstruct the original landscaping.

"That brick walk to the next property must

have had a lovely boxwood hedge at one time," she said to herself.

Her gaze now turned to Riverview Manor. The grounds there were overgrown with weeds and several shutters were missing from the house. Suddenly Nancy's attention was drawn to one of the uncovered windowpanes. Did she see a light moving inside?

It disappeared a moment later and Nancy could not be sure. Perhaps the sun shining on the glass had created an optical illusion.

"Still, somebody just might be in that house," the young sleuth thought. "The sooner I get over there and see what I can find out, the better! If the ghost is hiding out there, maybe he uses some underground passage from one of the outbuildings on the property."

She crawled cautiously back to the trap door and together the girls closed it. Aunt Rosemary had already gone downstairs to take care of her mother.

Nancy told Helen what she thought she had just seen in the neighboring mansion. "I'll change my clothes right away. Then let's go see Mr. Dodd, the realtor broker for Riverview Manor."

A half hour later the two girls walked into the real-estate office. Mr. Dodd himself was there and Nancy asked him about looking at Riverview Manor.

"I'm sorry, miss," he said, "but the house has just been sold."

Nancy was stunned. She could see all her plans crumbling into nothingness. Then a thought came to her. Perhaps the new owner would not object if she looked around, anyway.

"Would you mind telling me, Mr. Dodd, who purchased Riverview Manor?"

"Not at all," the realtor replied. "A man named Nathan Gomber."

CHAPTER XVIII

A Confession

NANCY DREW'S face wore such a disappointed look that Mr. Dodd, the realtor, said kindly, "Don't take it so hard, miss. I don't think you'd be particularly interested in Riverview Manor. It's really not in very good condition. Besides, you'd need a pile of money to fix that place up."

Without commenting on his statement, Nancy asked, "Couldn't you possibly arrange for me to see the inside of the mansion?"

Mr. Dodd shook his head. "I'm afraid Mr. Gomber wouldn't like that."

Nancy was reluctant to give up. Why, her father might even be a prisoner in that very house! "Of course I can report my suspicion to the police," the young sleuth thought.

She decided to wait until morning. Then, if there was still no news of Mr. Drew, she would pass along the word to Captain Rossland.

Mr. Dodd's telephone rang. As he answered it, Nancy and Helen started to leave his office. But he immediately waved them back.

"The call is from Chief Rossland, Miss Drew," he said. "He phoned Twin Elms and learned you were here. He wants to see you at once."

"Thank you," said Nancy, and the girls left.

They hurried to police headquarters, wondering why the officer wanted to speak to Nancy.

"Oh, if only it's news of Dad," she exclaimed fervently. "But why didn't he get in touch with me himself?"

"I don't want to be a killjoy," Helen spoke up. "But maybe it's not about your father at all. Perhaps they've caught Nathan Gomber."

Nancy parked in front of headquarters and the two girls hurried inside the building. Captain Rossland was expecting them and they were immediately ushered into his office. Nancy introduced Helen Corning.

"I won't keep you in suspense," the officer said, watching Nancy's eager face. "We have arrested Samuel Greenman!"

"The crinkly-eared man?" Helen asked.

"That's right," Captain Rossland replied. "Thanks to your tip about the used car, Miss Drew, our men had no trouble at all locating him."

The officer went on to say, however, that the prisoner refused to confess that he had had anything to do with Mr. Drew's disappearance.

"Furthermore, Harry the taxi driver—we have him here—insists that he cannot positively identify Greenman as one of the passengers in his cab. We believe Harry is scared that Greenman's pals will beat him up or attack members of his family."

"Harry did tell me," Nancy put in, "that his passenger had threatened harm to his family unless he forgot all about what he had seen."

"That proves our theory," Captain Rossland stated with conviction. "Miss Drew, we think you can help the police."

"I'll be glad to. How?"

Captain Rossland smiled. "You may not know it, but you're a very persuasive young lady. I believe that you might be able to get information out of both Harry and Greenman, where we have failed."

After a moment's thought, Nancy replied modestly, "I'll be happy to try, but on one condition." She grinned at the officer. "I must talk to these men alone."

"Request granted." Captain Rossland smiled. He added that he and Helen would wait outside and he would have Harry brought in.

"Good luck," said Helen as she and the captain left the room.

A few moments later Harry walked in alone. "Oh hello, miss," he said to Nancy, barely raising his eyes from the floor.

"Won't you sit down, Harry," Nancy asked, indicating a chair alongside hers. "It was nice of the captain to let me talk to you."

Harry seated himself, but said nothing. He twisted his driver's cap nervously in his hands and kept his gaze downward.

"Harry," Nancy began, "I guess your children would feel terrible if you were kidnaped."

"It would cut 'em to pieces," the cabman stated emphatically.

"Then you know how I feel," Nancy went on. "Not a word from my father for two whole days. If your children knew somebody who'd seen the person who kidnaped you, wouldn't they feel bad if the man wouldn't talk?"

Harry at last raised his eyes and looked straight at Nancy. "I get you, miss. When somethin' comes home to you, it makes all the difference in the world. You win! I *can* identify that scoundrel Greenman, and I will. Call the captain in."

Nancy did not wait a second. She opened the door and summoned the officer.

"Harry has something to tell you," Nancy said to Captain Rossland.

"Yeah," said Harry, "I'm not goin' to hold out any longer. I admit Greenman had me scared, but he's the guy who rode in my cab, then ordered me to keep my mouth shut after that other passenger blacked out."

Captain Rossland looked astounded. It was evident he could hardly believe that Nancy in only a few minutes had persuaded the man to talk!

"And now," Nancy asked, "may I talk to your prisoner?"

"I'll have you taken to his cell," the captain responded, and rang for a guard.

Nancy was led down a corridor, past a row of cells until they came to one where the man with the crinkled ear sat on a cot.

"Greenman," said the guard, "step up here. This is Miss Nancy Drew, daughter of the kidnaped man. She wants to talk to you."

The prisoner shuffled forward, but mumbled, "I ain't goin' to answer no questions."

Nancy waited until the guard had moved off, then she smiled at the prisoner. "We all make mistakes at times," she said. "We're often misled by people who urge us to do things we shouldn't. Maybe you're afraid you'll receive the death sentence for helping to kidnap my father. But if you didn't realize the seriousness of the whole thing, the complaint against you may turn out just to be conspiracy."

To Nancy's astonishment, Greenman suddenly burst out, "You've got me exactly right, miss. I had almost nothing to do with takin' your father away. The guy I was with—*he's* the old-timer. He's got a long prison record. I haven't. Honest, miss, this is my first offense.

"I'll tell you the whole story. I met this guy

only Monday night. He sure sold me a bill of goods. But all I did was see that your pop didn't run away. The old-timer's the one that drugged him."

"Where is my father now?" Nancy interrupted.

"I don't know. Honest I don't," Greenman insisted. "Part of the plan was for somebody to follow the taxi. After a while Mr. Drew was to be given a whiff of somethin'. It didn't have no smell. That's why our taxi driver didn't catch on. And it didn't knock the rest of us out, 'cause you have to put the stuff right under a fellow's nose to make it work."

"And the person who was following in a car and took my father away, who is he?"

"I don't know," the prisoner answered, and Nancy felt that he was telling the truth.

"Did you get any money for doing this?" Nancy asked him.

"A little. Not as much as it was worth, especially if I have to go to prison. The guy who paid us for our work was the one in the car who took your father away."

"Will you describe him?" Nancy requested.

"Sure. Hope the police catch him soon. He's in his early fifties—short and heavy-set, pale, and has kind of watery blue eyes."

Nancy asked the prisoner if he would dictate the same confession for the police and the man nodded. "And I'm awful sorry I caused all this

worry, miss. I hope you find your father soon and
I wish I could help you more. I guess I am a
coward. I'm too scared to tell the name of the
guy who talked me into this whole thing. He's
really a bad actor—no tellin' what'd happen to
me if I gave his name."

The young sleuth felt that she had obtained all
the information she possibly could from the man.
She went back to Captain Rossland, who for the
second time was amazed by the girl's success. He
called a stenographer. Then he said good-by to
Nancy and Helen and went off toward Greenman's
cell.

On the way back to Twin Elms, Helen congratulated her friend. "Now that one of the kid-
napers has been caught, I'm sure that your father
will be found soon, Nancy. Who do you suppose
the man was who took your father from Greenman
and his friend?"

Nancy looked puzzled, then answered, "We
know from his description that he wasn't Gomber.
But, Helen, a hunch of mine is growing stronger
all the time that he's back of this whole thing.
And putting two and two together, I believe it
was Willie Wharton who drove that car.

"And I also believe Wharton's the one who's
been playing ghost, using masks at times—like the
gorilla and the unshaven, long-haired man.

"Somehow he gets into the mansion and listens
to conversations. He heard that I was going to be

asked to solve the mystery at Twin Elms and told Gomber. That's why Gomber came to our home and tried to keep me from coming here by saying I should stick close to Dad."

"That's right," said Helen. "And when he found that didn't work, he had Willie and Greenman and that other man kidnap your dad. He figured it would surely get you away from Twin Elms. He wanted to scare Miss Flora into selling the property, and he thought if you were around you might dissuade her."

"But in that I didn't succeed," said Nancy a bit forlornly. "Besides, they knew Dad could stop those greedy land owners from forcing the railroad to pay them more for their property. That's why I'm sure Gomber and Wharton won't release him until after they get what they want."

Helen laid a hand on Nancy's shoulder. "I'm so terribly sorry about this. What can we do next?"

"Somehow I have a feeling, Helen," her friend replied, "that you and I are going to find Willie Wharton before very long. And if we do, and I find out he really signed that contract of sale, I want certain people to be around."

"Who?" Helen asked, puzzled.

"Mr. Barradale, the lawyer, and Mr. Watson the notary public."

The young sleuth put her thought into action. Knowing that Monday was the deadline set by the railroad, she determined to do her utmost before that time to solve the complicated mystery. Back at Twin Elms, Nancy went to the telephone and put in a call to Mr. Barradale's office. She did not dare mention Gomber's or Willie Wharton's name for fear one or the other of them might be listening. She merely asked the young lawyer if he could possibly come to Cliffwood and bring with him whatever he felt was necessary for him to win his case.

"I think I understand what you really mean to say," he replied. "I take it you can't talk freely. Is that correct?"

"Yes."

"Then I'll ask the questions. You want me to come to the address that you gave us the other day?"

"Yes. About noon."

"And you'd like me to bring along the contract of sale with Willie Wharton's signature?"

"Yes. That will be fine." Nancy thanked him and hung up.

Turning from the telephone, she went to find Helen and said, "There's still lots of daylight. Even though we can't get inside Riverview Manor, we can hunt through the outbuildings over there for the entrance to an underground passage to this house."

"All right," her friend agreed. "But this time you do the searching. I'll be the lookout."

Nancy chose the old smokehouse of Riverview Manor first, since this was closest to the Twin Elms property line. It yielded no clue and she moved on to the carriage house. But neither in this building, nor any of the others, did the girl detective find any indication of entrances to an underground passageway. Finally she gave up and rejoined Helen.

"If there is an opening, it must be from inside Riverview Manor," Nancy stated. "Oh, Helen, it's exasperating not to be able to get in there!"

"I wouldn't go in there now in any case," Helen remarked. "It's way past suppertime and I'm starved. Besides, pretty soon it'll be dark."

The girls returned to Twin Elms and ate supper. A short time later someone banged the front-door knocker. Both girls went to the door. They were amazed to find that the caller was Mr. Dodd, the realtor. He held out a large brass key toward Nancy.

"What's this for?" she asked, mystified.

Mr. Dodd smiled.

"It's the front-door key to Riverview Manor. I've decided that you can look around the mansion tomorrow morning all you please."

CHAPTER XIX

The Hidden Staircase

SEEING the look of delight on Nancy's face, Mr. Dodd laughed. "Do you think that house is haunted as well as this one?" he asked. "I hear you like to solve mysteries."

"Yes, I do." Not wishing to reveal her real purpose to the realtor, the young sleuth also laughed. "Do you think I might find a ghost over there?" she countered.

"Well, I never saw one, but you never can tell," the man responded with a chuckle. He said he would leave the key with Nancy until Saturday evening and then pick it up. "If Mr. Gomber should show up in the meantime, I have a key to the kitchen door that he can use."

Nancy thanked Mr. Dodd and with a grin said she would let him know if she found a ghost at Riverview Manor.

She could hardly wait for the next morning to

arrive. Miss Flora was not told of the girls' plan to visit the neighboring house.

Immediately after breakfast, they set off for Riverview Manor. Aunt Rosemary went with them to the back door and wished the two good luck. "Promise me you won't take any chances," she begged.

"Promise," they said in unison.

With flashlights in their skirt pockets, Nancy and Helen hurried through the garden and into the grounds of Riverview Manor estate.

As they approached the front porch, Helen showed signs of nervousness. "Nancy, what will we do if we meet the ghost?" she asked.

"Just tell him we've found him out," her friend answered determinedly.

Helen said no more and watched as Nancy inserted the enormous brass key in the lock. It turned easily and the girls let themselves into the hall. Architecturally it was the same as Twin Elms mansion, but how different it looked now! The blinds were closed, lending an eerie atmosphere to the dusky interior. Dust lay everywhere, and cobwebs festooned the corners of the ceiling and spindles of the staircase.

"It certainly doesn't look as if anybody lives here," Helen remarked. "Where do we start hunting?"

"I want to take a look in the kitchen," said Nancy.

When they walked into it, Helen gasped. "I guess I was wrong. Someone has been eating here." Eggshells, several empty milk bottles, some chicken bones and pieces of waxed paper cluttered the sink.

Nancy, realizing that Helen was very uneasy, whispered to her with a giggle, "If the ghost lives here, he has a good appetite!"

The young sleuth took out her flashlight and beamed it around the floors and walls of the kitchen. There was no sign of a secret opening. As she went from room to room on the first floor, Helen followed and together they searched every inch of the place for a clue to a concealed door. At last they came to the conclusion there was none.

"You know, it could be in the cellar," Nancy suggested.

"Well, you're not going down there," Helen said firmly. "That is, not without a policeman. It's too dangerous. As for myself, I want to live to get married and not be hit over the head in the dark by that ghost, so Jim won't have a bride!"

Nancy laughed. "You win. But I'll tell you why. At the moment I am more interested in finding my father than in hunting for a secret passageway. He may be a prisoner in one of the rooms upstairs. I'm going to find out."

The door to the back stairway was unlocked and the one at the top stood open. Nancy asked

Helen to stand at the foot of the main staircase, while she herself went up the back steps. "If that ghost is up there and tries to escape, he won't be able to slip out that way," she explained.

Helen took her post in the front hall and Nancy crept up the back steps. No one tried to come down either stairs. Helen now went to the second floor and together she and Nancy began a search of the rooms. They found nothing suspicious. Mr. Drew was not there. There was no sign of a ghost. None of the walls revealed a possible secret opening. But the bedroom which corresponded to Miss Flora's had a clothes closet built in at the end next to the fireplace.

"In Colonial times closets were a rarity," Nancy remarked to Helen. "I wonder if this closet was added at that time and has any special significance."

Quickly she opened one of the large double doors and looked inside. The rear wall was formed of two very wide wooden planks. In the center was a round knob, sunk in the wood.

"This is strange," Nancy remarked excitedly. She pulled on the knob but the wall did not move. Next, she pushed the knob down hard, leaning her full weight against the panel.

Suddenly the wall pushed inward. Nancy lost her balance and disappeared into a gaping hole below!

Helen screamed. "Nancy!"

Trembling with fright, Helen stepped into the closet and beamed her flashlight below. She could see a long flight of stone steps.

"Nancy! Nancy!" Helen called down.

A muffled answer came from below. Helen's heart gave a leap of relief. "Nancy's alive!" she told herself, then called, "Where are you?"

"I've found the secret passageway," came faintly to Helen's ears. "Come on down."

Helen did not hesitate. She wanted to be certain that Nancy was all right. Just as she started down the steps, the door began to close. Helen, in a panic that the girls might be trapped in some subterranean passageway, made a wild grab for the door. Holding it ajar, she removed the sweater she was wearing and wedged it into the opening.

Finding a rail on one side of the stone steps, Helen grasped it and hurried below. Nancy arose from the dank earthen floor to meet her.

"Are you sure you're all right?" Helen asked solicitously.

"I admit I got a good bang," Nancy replied, "but I feel fine now. Let's see where this passageway goes."

The flashlight had been thrown from her hand, but with the aid of Helen's light, she soon found it. Fortunately, it had not been damaged and she turned it on.

The passageway was very narrow and barely high enough for the girls to walk without bending over. The sides were built of crumbling brick and stone.

"This may tumble on us at any moment," Helen said worriedly.

"Oh, I don't believe so," Nancy answered. "It must have been here for a long time."

The subterranean corridor was unpleasantly damp and had an earthy smell. Moisture clung to the walls. They felt clammy and repulsive to the touch.

Presently the passageway began to twist and turn, as if its builders had found obstructions too difficult to dig through.

"Where do you think this leads?" Helen whispered.

"I don't know. I only hope we're not going in circles."

Presently the girls reached another set of stone steps not unlike the ones down which Nancy had tumbled. But these had solid stone sides. By their lights, the girls could see a door at the top with a heavy wooden bar across it.

"Shall we go up?" Helen asked.

Nancy was undecided what to do. The tunnel did not end here but yawned ahead in blackness. Should they follow it before trying to find out what was at the top of the stairs?

She voiced her thoughts aloud, but Helen urged that they climb the stairs. "I'll be frank with you. I'd like to get out of here."

Nancy acceded to her friend's wish and led the way up the steps.

Suddenly both girls froze in their tracks.

A man's voice from the far end of the tunnel commanded, "Stop! You can't go up there!"

CHAPTER XX

Nancy's Victory

THEIR initial fright over, both girls turned and beamed their flashlights toward the foot of the stone stairway. Below them stood a short, unshaven, pudgy man with watery blue eyes.

"You're the ghost!" Helen stammered.

"And you're Mr. Willie Wharton," Nancy added.

Astounded, the man blinked in the glaring lights, then said, "Ye-yes, I am. But how did you know?"

"You live in the old Riverview Manor," Helen went on, "and you've been stealing food and silver and jewelry from Twin Elms!"

"No, no. I'm not a thief!" Willie Wharton cried out. "I took some food and I've been trying to scare the old ladies, so they would sell their property. Sometimes I wore false faces, but I never took any jewelry or silver. Honest I didn't. It must have been Mr. Gomber."

Nancy and Helen were amazed—Willie Wharton, with little urging from them, was confessing more than they had dared to hope.

"Did you know that Nathan Gomber is a thief?" Nancy asked the man.

Wharton shook his head. "I know he's sharp— that's why he's going to get me more money for my property from the railroad."

"Mr. Wharton, did you sign the original contract of sale?" Nancy queried.

"Yes, I did, but Mr. Gomber said that if I disappeared for a while, he'd fix everything up so I'd get more money. He said he had a couple of other jobs which I could help him with. One of them was coming here to play ghost—it was a good place to disappear to. But I wish I had never seen Nathan Gomber or Riverview Manor or Twin Elms or had anything to do with ghosts."

"I'm glad to hear you say that," said Nancy. Then suddenly she asked, "Where's my father?"

Willie Wharton shifted his weight and looked about wildly. "I don't know, really I don't."

"But you kidnaped him in your car," the young sleuth prodded him. "We got a description of you from the taximan."

Several seconds went by before Willie Wharton answered. "I didn't know it was kidnaping. Mr. Gomber said your father was ill and that he was

going to take him to a special doctor. He said
Mr. Drew was coming on a train from Chicago and
was going to meet Mr. Gomber on the road halfway between here and the station. But Gomber
said he couldn't meet him—had other business
to attend to. So I was to follow your father's taxi
and bring him to Riverview Manor."

"Yes, yes, go on," Nancy urged, as Willie Wharton stopped speaking and covered his face with
his hands.

"I didn't expect your father to be unconscious
when I picked him up," Wharton went on. "Well,
those men in the taxi put Mr. Drew in the back
of my car and I brought him here. Mr. Gomber
drove up from the other direction and said he
would take over. He told me to come right here
to Twin Elms and do some ghosting."

"And you have no idea where Mr. Gomber
took my father?" Nancy asked, with a sinking
feeling.

"Nope."

In a few words she pointed out Nathan Gomber's real character to Willie Wharton, hoping
that if the man before her did know anything
about Mr. Drew's whereabouts which he was not
telling, he would confess. But from Wharton's
emphatic answers and sincere offers to be of all
the help he could in finding the missing lawyer,
Nancy concluded that Wharton was not withholding any information.

"How did you find out about this passageway and the secret staircases?" Nancy questioned him.

"Gomber found an old notebook under a heap of rubbish in the attic of Riverview Manor," Wharton answered. "He said it told everything about the secret entrances to the two houses. The passageways, with openings on each floor, were built when the houses were. They were used by the original Turnbulls in bad weather to get from one building to the other. This stairway was for the servants. The other two stairways were for the family. One of these led to Mr. Turnbull's bedroom in this house. The notebook also said that he often secretly entertained government agents and sometimes he had to hurry them out of the parlor and hide them in the passageway when callers came."

"Where does this stairway lead?" Helen spoke up.

"To the attic of Twin Elms." Willie Wharton gave a little chuckle. "I know, Miss Drew, that you almost found the entrance. But the guys that built the place were pretty clever. Every opening has heavy double doors. When you poked that screw driver through the crack, you thought you were hitting another wall but it was really a door."

"Did you play the violin and turn on the radio —and make that thumping noise in the attic— and were you the one who laughed when we were up there?"

"Yes, and I moved the sofa to scare you and I even knew about the listening post. That's how I found out all your plans and could report them to Mr. Gomber."

Suddenly it occurred to Nancy that Nathan Gomber might appear on the scene at any moment. She must get Willie Wharton away and have him swear to his signature before he changed his mind!

"Mr. Wharton, would you please go ahead of us up this stairway and open the doors?" she asked. "And go into Twin Elms with us and talk to Mrs. Turnbull and Mrs. Hayes? I want you to tell them that you've been playing ghost but aren't going to any longer. Miss Flora has been so frightened that she's ill and in bed."

"I'm sorry about that," Willie Wharton replied. "Sure I'll go with you. I never want to see Nathan Gomber again!"

He went ahead of the girls and took down the heavy wooden bar from across the door. He swung it wide, pulled a metal ring in the back of the adjoining door, then quickly stepped downward. The narrow panel opening which Nancy had suspected of leading to the secret stairway now was pulled inward. There was barely room alongside it to go up the top steps and into the attic. To keep Gomber from becoming suspicious if he should arrive, Nancy asked Willie Wharton to close the secret door again.

"Helen," said Nancy, "will you please run downstairs ahead of Mr. Wharton and me and tell Miss Flora and Aunt Rosemary the good news."

She gave Helen a three-minute start, then she and Willie Wharton followed. The amazed women were delighted to have the mystery solved. But there was no time for celebration.

"Mr. Barradale is downstairs to see you, Nancy," Aunt Rosemary announced.

Nancy turned to Willie Wharton. "Will you come down with me, please?"

She introduced both herself and the missing property owner to Mr. Barradale, then went on, "Mr. Wharton says the signature on the contract of sale is his own."

"And you'll swear to that?" the lawyer asked, turning to Willie.

"I sure will. I don't want anything more to do with this underhanded business," Willie Wharton declared.

"I know where I can find a notary public right away," Nancy spoke up. "Do you want me to phone him, Mr. Barradale?" she asked.

"Please do. At once."

Nancy dashed to the telephone and dialed the number of Albert Watson on Tuttle Road. When he answered, she told him the urgency of the situation and he promised to come over at once. Mr. Watson arrived within five minutes, with his notary equipment. Mr. Barradale showed him the contract of sale containing Willie Wharton's name and signature. Attached to it was the certificate of acknowledgment.

Mr. Watson asked Willie Wharton to raise his right hand and swear that he was the person named in the contract of sale. After this was done, the notary public filled in the proper places on the certificate, signed it, stamped the paper, and affixed his seal.

"Well, this is really a wonderful job, Miss Drew," Mr. Barradale praised her.

Nancy smiled, but her happiness at having accomplished a task for her father was dampened by the fact that she still did not know where he was. Mr. Barradale and Willie Wharton also were extremely concerned.

"I'm going to call Captain Rossland and ask him to send some policemen out here at once," Nancy stated. "What better place for Mr. Gomber to hide my father than somewhere along that passageway? How far does it go, Mr. Wharton?"

"Mr. Gomber says it goes all the way to the river, but the end of it is completely stoned up now. I never went any farther than the stairways."

The young lawyer thought Nancy's idea a good one, because if Nathan Gomber should return to Riverview Manor and find that Willie was gone, he would try to escape.

The police promised to come at once. Nancy had just finished talking with Captain Rossland when Helen Corning called from the second floor.

"Nancy, can you come up here? Miss Flora insists upon seeing the hidden staircase."

The young sleuth decided that she would just about have time to do this before the arrival of the police. Excusing herself to Mr. Barradale, she ran up the stairs. Aunt Rosemary had put on a rose-colored dressing gown while attending her mother. To Nancy's amazement, Mrs. Turnbull was fully dressed and wore a white blouse with a high collar and a black skirt.

Nancy and Helen led the way to the attic. There, the girl detective, crouching on her knees, opened the secret door.

"And all these years I never knew it was here!" Miss Flora exclaimed.

"And I doubt that my father did or he would have mentioned it," Aunt Rosemary added.

Nancy closed the secret door and they all went downstairs. She could hear the front-door bell ringing and assumed that it was the police. She and Helen hurried below. Captain Rossland and another officer stood there. They said other men had surrounded Riverview Manor, hoping to catch Nathan Gomber if he did arrive there.

With Willie Wharton leading the way, the girls, Mr. Barradale, and the police trooped to the attic and went down the hidden staircase to the dank passageway below.

"I have a hunch from reading about old passage-ways that there may be one or more rooms off this tunnel," Nancy told Captain Rossland.

There were so many powerful flashlights in play now that the place was almost as bright as daylight. As the group moved along, they suddenly came to a short stairway. Willie Wharton explained that this led to an opening back of the sofa in the parlor. There was still another stone stairway which went up to Miss Flora's bedroom with an opening alongside the fireplace.

The searchers went on. Nancy, who was ahead of the others, discovered a padlocked iron door in the wall. Was it a dungeon? She had heard of such places being used for prisoners in Colonial times.

By this time Captain Rossland had caught up to her. "Do you think your father may be in there?" he asked.

"I'm terribly afraid so," said Nancy, shivering at the thought of what she might find.

The officer found that the lock was very rusty. Pulling from his pocket a penknife with various tool attachments, he soon had the door unlocked and flung it wide. He beamed his light into the blackness beyond. It was indeed a room without windows.

Suddenly Nancy cried out, "Dad!" and sprang ahead.

Lying on blankets on the floor, and covered with others, was Mr. Drew. He was murmuring faintly.

"He's alive!" Nancy exclaimed, kneeling down to pat his face and kiss him.

"He's been drugged," Captain Rossland observed. "I'd say Nathan Gomber has been giving your father just enough food to keep him alive and mixing sleeping powders in with it."

From his trousers pocket the officer brought out a small vial of restorative and held it to Mr. Drew's nose. In a few moments the lawyer shook his head, and a few seconds later, opened his eyes.

"Keep talking to your dad," the captain ordered Nancy.

"Dad! Wake up! You're all right! We've rescued you!"

Within a very short time Mr. Drew realized that his daughter was kneeling beside him. Reaching out his arms from beneath the blankets, he tried to hug her.

"We'll take him upstairs," said Captain Rossland. "Willie, open that secret entrance to the parlor."

"Glad to be of help." Wharton hurried ahead and up the short flight of steps.

In the meantime, the other three men lifted Mr. Drew and carried him along the passageway. By the time they reached the stairway, Willie

Wharton had opened the secret door behind the sofa in the parlor. Mr. Drew was placed on the couch. He blinked, looked around, and then said in astonishment:

"Willie Wharton! How did you get here? Nancy, tell me the whole story."

The lawyer's robust health and sturdy constitution had stood him in good stead. He recovered with amazing rapidity from his ordeal and listened in rapt attention as one after another of those in the room related the events of the past few days.

As the story ended, there was a knock on the front door and another police officer was admitted. He had come to report to Captain Rossland that not only had Nathan Gomber been captured outside of Riverview Manor, and all the loot recovered, but also that the final member of the group who had abducted Mr. Drew had been taken into custody. Gomber had admitted everything, even to having attempted to injure Nancy and her father with the truck at the River Heights' bridge project. He had tried to frighten Miss Flora into selling Twin Elms because he had planned to start a housing project on the two Turnbull properties.

"It's a real victory for you!" Nancy's father praised his daughter proudly.

The young sleuth smiled. Although she was glad it was all over, she could not help but look forward to another mystery to solve. One soon came her way when, quite accidentally, she found herself involved in *The Bungalow Mystery*.

Miss Flora and Aunt Rosemary had come downstairs to meet Mr. Drew. While they were talking to him, the police officer left, taking Willie Wharton with him as a prisoner. Mr. Barradale also said good-by. Nancy and Helen slipped out of the room and went to the kitchen.

"We'll prepare a super-duper lunch to celebrate this occasion!" said Helen happily.

"And we can make all the plans we want," Nancy replied with a grin. "There won't be anyone at the listening post!"

NANCY DREW MYSTERY STORIES®

The Ghost
of
Blackwood Hall

BY CAROLYN KEENE

GROSSET & DUNLAP
Publishers • New York
A member of The Putnam & Grosset Group

Contents

CHAPTER I

A Mysterious Message

"IF I ever try to solve a mystery with a ghost in it, I'll use a smart cat to help me!" Nancy Drew remarked laughingly. "Cats aren't afraid of ghosts. Did you know that, Togo?"

Laying aside the book of exciting ghost stories which she had been reading, the slim, titian-haired girl reached down to pat Togo, her fox terrier. But, as if startled or annoyed by her words, he scrambled up and began to bark.

"Quiet, Togo!" ordered Hannah Gruen, the family housekeeper, from the living-room archway. "What's wrong with you?"

But Togo, hearing the sound of a car door slamming, braced his legs, cocked his head, and barked more excitedly than ever. An automobile had stopped in front of the house, and a middle-aged man was hurrying up the walk.

"It's Mr. Freeman, the jeweler," said Nancy in surprise.

A moment later the doorbell rang sharply, and Nancy hastened to open the door.

"I can't stay long," Mr. Freeman said, speaking rapidly. "I shouldn't have left the jewelry store to come here, only it's important!"

"But Dad isn't at home, Mr. Freeman."

"I came to see you, Nancy. I want you to help an old customer and friend."

The jeweler indicated the parked car. "Mrs. Putney is out there waiting. I tried to get her to talk to the police, but she refused. She won't even tell me all the details of the theft—says there's a good reason why she must keep the matter to herself."

By now, Nancy's curiosity was aroused. "Please bring Mrs. Putney in," she said. "If there is some way I can help her, I certainly will. But if she is unwilling to talk—"

"She'll tell you everything," the jeweler advised in a low voice. "You see, you're a *girl*."

"What has that got to do with it?"

"You'll find out," the jeweler said mysteriously. "Mrs. Putney is a widow. She lives alone and is considered rather odd by her neighbors. I've known her for years, however, and she's a fine woman. She needs our help."

Before Nancy could ask why she needed help, he ran back to the car. After a brief conversation, the woman emerged and the jeweler led her up the walk to the house.

"This is Mrs. Henry Putney, Nancy," Mr. Freeman introduced her, adding, "Nancy Drew is the best amateur detective in River Heights."

From her father, Carson Drew, an outstanding criminal lawyer, Nancy had inherited both courage and keen intelligence. The first case Nancy had worked on with her father was *The Secret of the Old Clock*.

Recently she had solved the mystery of *The Clue in the Old Album*. Although only eighteen years old, Nancy's ability was so well known that anyone in River Heights, who was in trouble, was likely to seek her assistance.

Stepping aside so that the caller might enter the living room, Nancy studied Mrs. Putney curiously. She was a woman well past middle age, and the black of her smartly cut dress accentuated the thinness of her body. Her expression was sad, and in the faded eyes there was a faraway look which made Nancy vaguely uneasy.

Mrs. Gruen greeted the newcomers, chatted a few moments, then tactfully withdrew. Nancy waited eagerly for the callers to reveal the purpose of their visit.

"I shouldn't have come," Mrs. Putney said, nervously twisting a handkerchief. "No one can help me, I'm sure."

"Nancy Drew can," the jeweler declared. Then from a deep pocket of his coat, he withdrew a leather case which bore traces of dried mud.

He opened the case and displayed a sizable collection of rings, necklaces, and pins. He held up a string of pearls to examine.

"Clever imitations, every one!" announced the jeweler. "When Mrs. Putney brought them to me to be cleaned, I advised her to go at once to the police."

"I can't do that," Mrs. Putney replied. "There must be no publicity."

"Suppose you tell me everything," Nancy suggested.

"You promise never to reveal what I am about to tell you?" her visitor asked anxiously.

"Of course, if that is your wish."

Mrs. Putney looked at the jeweler. "I cannot speak in your presence," she said haltingly. "I was warned never to tell any man or woman of this matter."

"That's why I brought you to a *girl detective*," the jeweler said quickly, directing a significant glance at Nancy. "You'll be breaking no confidence in telling Nancy everything. And now I must be getting back to the store."

Bidding them good-by, he left the two together. Satisfied, Mrs. Putney began her story.

"I'm all alone now. My husband died a few months ago," she revealed. "Since then I have had strange premonitions. Shortly after my husband passed away, I had an overpowering feeling the house was to be robbed."

"Clever imitations, every one!" the jeweler announced

"And it was?" inquired Nancy.

"No, but I did a very foolish thing. I gathered all the family jewels, put the collection in this leather case, and buried it."

"Somewhere on your grounds?"

"No, in a secluded clearing in the woods about ten miles from here."

Nancy was amazed that a woman of Mrs. Putney's apparent intelligence should commit such a foolish act. However, she remained silent.

"I decided I'd been unwise, so this morning I went there and dug up the leather case," Mrs. Putney continued. "Then I took the collection to Mr. Freeman to have the pieces cleaned. The moment he saw them he said they were fake."

"Someone stole the real jewelry?"

"Yes, and substituted these copies. I prized my husband's ring above all. It breaks my heart to lose that."

"This is a case for the police," Nancy began, only to have Mrs. Putney cut her short.

"Oh, no! The police must learn nothing about what happened!"

Nancy regarded the woman intently. "Why are you so opposed to talking to anyone except me?" she asked.

"Well, I'm afraid if I call in the police there will be a lot of publicity."

"Is that your real reason, Mrs. Putney?" Nancy was certain that the widow was deliberately withholding the truth. "If I am to help you, I must know everything."

After a pause Mrs. Putney, speaking in a whisper, said, "One night, several weeks ago, my dear husband's spirit came to me. I awoke, or thought I did, and heard a far-off voice. I'm sure it was Henry's. He instructed me to bury the jewels in a place which he described in minute detail and warned me never to reveal to any man or woman that he had told me to do it. Otherwise he would never permit me to hear from him again."

"But he didn't say anything about not telling a girl?" Nancy asked.

"No. That is why I risked coming to you. I need your help desperately. Oh, I hope my coming won't spoil everything!"

Nancy, who did not believe in ghosts or spirits, nevertheless respected Mrs. Putney's belief and was diplomatic in her reply.

"I'm sure that coming to me will not spoil anything," she said. "You must have been robbed by someone who saw you hiding your jewelry, and who knew its value."

"But I told no one my plan."

"I'd like to see the place where you buried the leather case. Why don't we drive out there now in my car?"

"If you like," the widow agreed halfheartedly.

Nancy explained to Mrs. Gruen that she would be gone for an hour or so. Nancy's mother was not living. For many years, the Drew household had been efficiently run by Hannah Gruen, who had been with the family so long that she was regarded as one of them. She loved Nancy as a daughter, and worried a great deal about her whenever the young detective undertook to solve a mystery.

Taking Togo along, Nancy and Mrs. Putney drove through the countryside to the edge of a dense woods which bordered the highway. At Mrs. Putney's direction, Nancy turned down a narrow side road, crossed an old-fashioned covered bridge, and finally parked beneath an arch of thickly interlaced tree limbs.

As the two alighted, a gentle breeze rippled Nancy's hair and stirred the leaves overhead. The rustling in the branches seemed to make Togo uneasy. He pricked up his ears and began to growl.

"Quiet, Togo!" Nancy ordered. "You'd better stay in the car," she added, raising the windows part way. "You might race off into the woods."

"Follow me," Mrs. Putney directed, setting off through a path that curved among the tall trees.

The widow reached a small clearing a few hundred yards from the roadside and halted. Without speaking, she pointed to the center of a grassy place where a section of earth had been dug up.

Nancy glanced around carefully. On all sides, the clearing was shielded by a dense growth of bushes. Quickly she set about inspecting the spot where the leather case had been buried.

The ground was soft, for it had rained hard during the night. If there had been footprints other than those of Mrs. Putney, they had been washed away.

As Nancy straightened up, she heard a car pass along the road. It slowed as if the driver intended to stop, then speeded on.

Nancy continued systematically to search the area for evidence. She was about to abandon the task when her gaze fell upon a scrap of paper which had snagged at the base of a thorny bush. Picking it up, Nancy noticed that it was a page torn from a catalog. On one side was the advertisement:

"BEAUTIFUL LIGHTS, $10.00." On the other, "NO ASSISTANTS."

Doubtful as to the value of the find, Nancy nevertheless slipped the paper into her purse. As she did so, her eyes came to rest upon a long, shiny piece of metal a few feet away.

Before she could pick it up, an agonized scream cut through the silent woods!

CHAPTER II

The First Clue

NANCY whirled around and was relieved to see that Mrs. Putney was safe. The bloodcurdling scream must have come from the road.

"What was that?" The widow was trembling.

"Someone's in trouble!" Nancy exclaimed. "It was a woman's voice!"

Nancy began running in the direction of the road. Mrs. Putney followed as fast as she could.

Out of breath, Nancy reached the place where she had left her convertible. Togo was jumping from seat to seat, barking excitedly.

"Maybe you know something, old boy," Nancy said, and let him out on a leash.

She allowed him to lead her a short distance down the road. He began sniffing the ground, where Nancy noticed some fresh tire prints. Before they reached the first bend in the highway, she heard the muffled roar of a car engine.

"A car must have been parked just out of sight!" she murmured. "Now it's pulling away!"

Though she and Togo ran, the automobile had disappeared by the time they rounded the bend. The dog at this point seemed to lose interest.

"The woman who screamed must have been in the car," Nancy decided. "But who was she? And why did she scream?"

It was too late to attempt pursuit. Thoughtfully Nancy walked back to her own car, where Mrs. Putney anxiously awaited her.

"Did you learn anything, Nancy?"

"Nothing of importance. No one seems to be around here now."

"It was such a horrible scream." Mrs. Putney shivered. "Please, let's leave. I feel so uneasy here—as if unfriendly spirits were watching!"

Nancy suddenly remembered the object in the grass which had drawn her attention just before she had heard the scream. "I'd like to return to the clearing for a minute or two," she said. "Mrs. Putney, why don't you wait here in the car?"

"I believe I will," the widow agreed, quickly getting into the automobile. "But please hurry!"

"I will," Nancy promised.

She started off through the woods with Togo. Though she did not for an instant share Mrs. Putney's belief that "spirits were watching," the woods depressed her.

"I've allowed Mrs. Putney's ghost talk to get on my nerves!" Nancy chided herself.

As she approached the spot where Mrs. Putney had buried the jewelry, Togo began to act strangely. Twice he paused to sniff the air and whine. Once he looked up into Nancy's face as if trying to tell her something, and growled.

"Togo, what is it?" Nancy asked. "One would think—"

She gazed alertly about the clearing. It was deserted, yet every rustle of the leaves seemed to warn her to be careful.

Rather annoyed at her misgivings, Nancy went to the spot where she had been about to pick up the metallic object. Though she looked everywhere, the young detective was unable to find it.

Now more than ever alert, she carefully looked at the ground. In several places the grass had been trampled by herself, Mrs. Putney, or by someone else.

Togo began to sniff and tug at his leash. The dog led her to a depression in the ground which was hidden by bushes. Plainly visible in the soft earth were the prints of a man's shoes.

Stooping down, she examined the footprints thoroughly, measuring them with her hand. Obviously they were fresh. The narrowness of the shoe, and its length, led Nancy to believe that the man who had walked there was tall and thin.

"So that's why I can't find the piece of metal!"

she decided. "He came and picked it up while I was investigating the woman's scream! And probably," Nancy thought ruefully, "she was with him, and her scream was to frighten me away."

Though the trail was indistinct, Nancy could follow the footprints to the shelf of land which overlooked the clearing. The stranger had concealed himself there, watching!

"If he didn't go off in the car, he may not be far from here now," Nancy decided uneasily. "He may be the jewel thief!"

Nancy's attractive face tightened as she realized that danger might be lurking in the forest. She was convinced that the theft of Mrs. Putney's buried treasure was no ordinary affair.

"Only a very clever thief would have taken the trouble to substitute fake pieces of jewelry," she thought. "No doubt it was done to keep Mrs. Putney from discovering her loss and reporting the theft to the police."

Wasting no further time in reflection, Nancy followed the footprints. When the marks were no longer visible, Togo sniffed the ground intelligently, and led her to the road, where he stopped.

"So the man did go off in the car," she sighed.

With Togo trotting along beside her, Nancy returned to her convertible.

"I'm so glad you're back," Mrs. Putney said, greatly relieved. "I was beginning to worry."

En route to River Heights, Nancy said nothing

of her findings, except that she thought the footprints might have been made by the thief. Her companion now seemed only mildly interested, and responded absent-mindedly to questions.

When they came to the city, Mrs. Putney requested that she be dropped off at Mr. Freeman's jewelry store. Reminding her that the case of fake jewelry had been left at the Drew home, Nancy asked what should be done with it.

"I'll get it later," Mrs. Putney decided.

Nancy was pleased to have the case left in her possession, and promptly asked permission to show the jewelry to her father.

"By all means do so," Mrs. Putney said. "Only please be careful not to reveal what I told you about my husband or his instructions."

Nancy promised. After leaving the widow, she drove directly home. When her father arrived from his office, she had the collection spread out on the living-room table in front of her.

"Well, well! What's going on here?" the lawyer exclaimed, pausing to stare. "Have you been robbing jewelry stores lately, Nancy?"

Carson Drew was a tall, distinguished-looking man of middle age, with keen, twinkling blue eyes like those of his daughter. He and his only child were companionable and shared a delightful sense of humor. Nancy sprang up to hug him.

"Dad, I had the most exciting afternoon!"

"Ha! Another mystery!" the lawyer said with a mock groan.

"I think it's going to be a very interesting one. Just look at this fake jewelry!"

Mr. Drew examined the pieces one by one, while Nancy related some of the story.

"One or two facts I can't tell," she said reluctantly. "Mrs. Putney swore me to secrecy."

"I don't like that, Nancy."

"Neither do I, Dad, but in a day or so, she'll change her mind. Meanwhile, I can't pass up a good mystery!"

"I suppose not," her father replied. "The point is, if you're determined to try to help Mrs. Putney, you must be very cautious."

Mr. Drew picked up a jewel-studded pin, studied it a moment, and added, "Whoever made this is a clever craftsman. He must have plotted every move far in advance, for it takes time to make imitations like this."

"Dad, do you suppose a River Heights jeweler made these pieces?"

"Possible. However, I'm sure our jewelers are honest merchants, and if they made the imitations, they did so in good faith."

Nancy replaced the jewelry in the leather case.

"Tomorrow I'll show these pieces to a few of the River Heights stores, and perhaps someone can identify the work."

Soon after breakfast the next morning, Nancy set forth on a tour of jewelry stores. Bigelow Company was the last establishment at which she called, and there luck was with her. Mr. Bigelow, one of the owners, stated positively that the imitations had not been made by his firm, but he gave Nancy a suggestion.

"Look for a man named Howard Brex," the jeweler said. "He was a salesman and former designer for a New Orleans house. Used to sell jewelry to me. Not a bad-looking fellow—tall, dark, slender, and a smooth talker. He was a slippery character, though. Finally went to prison for fraud. Maybe he's been released."

Nancy became excited upon hearing this description of Brex. The footprints in the woods had been those of a tall, slender man!

After thanking Mr. Bigelow for the information, Nancy hurried to her father's office. Perching herself on his desk, she asked him if he had any information about Howard Brex in his files. Ringing for his secretary, the lawyer sent for a certain loose-leaf file and fingered through the B's.

"Brex was released a few months ago from a Louisiana penitentiary with time off for good behavior," Mr. Drew revealed. "You think he may be your thief?"

"Oh, I do," she replied, thrilled at the possibility that she had uncovered a real clue.

The arrival of a client cut short further conversation. Nancy telephoned Mr. Bigelow from the outer office and got the name of Brex's former employer in New Orleans. Then she started for home, a plan of action in mind.

Upon arriving at the Drew house, she was pleasantly surprised to find two friends, Bess Marvin and another girl, George Fayne, on the front porch.

George, her dark hair cut in an attractive short style, was deeply tanned. By contrast, her plump cousin Bess was blonde and fair-complexioned.

"I may have some news for you," Nancy hinted as they entered the house. She left Bess and George in the living room and went to telephone Mrs. Putney. After assuring the widow that her two assistants were girls, Nancy obtained reluctant permission to explain the circumstances of the case to Bess and George.

Rejoining the girls, Nancy said, "How would you two like to go to New Orleans with me?"

CHAPTER III

Tracking a Thief

"NEW ORLEANS!" Bess and George exclaimed.

Nancy smiled at her friends. "I'm working on a new case," she said. "Right now, I'm looking for a tall, dark man."

Bess giggled. "What would Ned say to that?"

Nancy blushed as she replied that the man she was after was probably a thief. Furthermore, the place to start looking for him was New Orleans. She told them the story, saying Brex's former employer should be able to recognize the craftsmanship in any imitation jewelry Brex might have made.

"Dad promised me a trip," Nancy said. "I know he can't go with me now. Tonight I'll ask him if you girls can take his place; that is, if you'd like to go."

"Would we!" exclaimed George.

"While we're investigating this Brex person,

George and I can do some sightseeing," remarked Bess. "New Orleans is such a romantic city!"

A twinkle came into Nancy's eyes. "I'm taking you girls along for protection," she said.

"Oh, we won't desert you." George grinned. "But all work and no play isn't any fun."

That evening Nancy discussed the plan with her father. He readily gave his consent.

Not only might a conference with Howard Brex's former employer bring results, he agreed, but there was a possibility that the suspect might even pawn the stolen articles in his home town.

"It's the most likely place for him to have a fence," declared the lawyer.

As Nancy hurried to the telephone to call her friends, he warned her to be careful in following up the clue in the distant city. To Nancy's delight, George and Bess also received permission to make the trip.

Hannah Gruen helped Nancy pack, while Mr. Drew made plane and hotel reservations. Before leaving, Nancy telephoned to Mrs. Putney to ask permission to take the imitation jewelry to New Orleans.

"I appreciate your efforts," the widow said, "but I'm sure nothing will come of the trip."

"Why do you say that, Mrs. Putney?"

"Last night I had another message from my departed husband. He said the thief who stole my jewelry lost it in a large body of water, and it'll never be recovered!"

Nancy was skeptical of the widow's messages but wisely did not argue with Mrs. Putney. She simply said she would be leaving in the morning with her two friends, and promised to report to the widow immediately upon her return.

The next day the three girls boarded the plane for New Orleans. The day was perfect for flying. An attractive hostess served them a tasty lunch and spent most of her spare time chatting with them.

Once, when the plane stopped briefly to pick up passengers, the girls alighted for a little while to stretch their legs. Upon taking their seats again, they noticed that a dark-haired woman in her late thirties had taken the empty seat next to Bess. She regarded the three intently as they sat down, and smiled in a friendly manner.

"Is this your first plane trip?" she asked Bess.

"No!" Bess replied. Then, not wishing to be rude, she added, "We're going to New Orleans."

"You'll love the city!" the woman declared. "Where are you staying?"

Bess told her. Nancy, seated in front of them, was sorry their hotel had been named. She had wanted to keep their visit to New Orleans as secret as possible. When they reached their hotel George scolded her cousin.

"You'll never learn to be a detective, Bess," she

said severely. "You can't tell who that woman on the plane might be."

Nancy, acting as peacemaker, said, "Let's forget it, girls, and do some sightseeing. It's too late to call on Mr. Johnson, Howard Brex's former boss, today. We'll go there in the morning."

Nancy's friends soon found that she did not intend to spend the time in mere sightseeing. Whenever she came to a jewelry shop, or a pawnshop that was open, she insisted that they go in and look at the jewelry on display.

The trip proved to be pleasurable, if not profitable. Their inquiries led them into many sections of New Orleans. The French Quarter, where the buildings were charming in their elegance of a bygone day, interested them most. Beautiful ironwork, delicately tinted plaster walls, old courtyards, once the center of fashionable Creole family life, fascinated the girls.

On a balcony, a bright-colored parrot chattered at them in friendly fashion. A smiling woman, bearing a basket of flowers, stopped to sell a flower to each girl. On all sides, the visitors saw interesting characters, and heard the soft-spoken dialect which was a blend of French, Cajun, and Gumbo.

Bess sighed contentedly. "If I could only spend a month in this lovely old city!" she said.

"It would be nice," Nancy agreed. "But come on. Here's another shop."

It was the fifteenth they had visited, and even Nancy was becoming weary. She had not seen any trace of the stolen jewelry.

"Let's quit," urged Bess. "I'm starved. Suppose we go to one of those famous restaurants and have oysters baked with garlic, and Creole shrimp, and—"

"And take on five pounds," scoffed George, looking with disfavor at Bess's generous weight.

But the girls ate sensibly and went to bed early. In the morning they accompanied Nancy to the jewelry firm for which Howard Brex had worked. Mr. Johnson, the head of the company, was most cooperative. He studied the imitation jewelry which Nancy showed him, and compared it to some pieces of his own which Brex had made.

"I'd certainly say that all of these were made by the same man," Mr. Johnson declared.

Then he told the girls what he knew of his former salesman. "He was a fine craftsman and made excellent designs," Mr. Johnson said. "Too bad he got into trouble."

"I understand he's been released from prison," Nancy said. "Have you any idea where he is?"

"Not the slightest, but I'll be glad to let you know if I hear anything."

Nancy left both her hotel address and that of her River Heights home. She was in a thoughtful mood as she accompanied her friends on their round of sightseeing and to lunch in a quaint restaurant.

"New Orleans is wonderful!" Bess exclaimed. Counting on her fingers, she added, "We've seen the banana wharf, the market, the garden district, and that old cemetery where all the dead are buried in tombs above the ground."

"That's because this place is below sea level," said George. "Say, do you suppose that guide thought we believed the story about the tomb which is supposed to glow at night with an unearthly light?"

"He said spirits come out and weave back and forth like wisps of fog," said Bess.

"That's just what they are—fog," George declared practically.

"Oh, I don't for a minute believe in ghosts," Bess replied quickly.

"I wish we had time to go to Grand Isle, the haunt of Lafitte and his men," said Nancy.

"Who is he?" Bess asked.

"He was a famous pirate," Nancy replied. "According to tradition, when burying treasure, he always murdered one of his band and left his ghost to guard the hidden loot!"

As the girls left the restaurant and started up the street, Nancy happened to turn around. Emerging from the door of the restaurant was a woman.

"Girls," Nancy said in a whisper, "don't look now, but the woman who was on the plane just came out of our restaurant. I think she was spying on us!"

"Why would she do that?" Bess asked.

"If she follows us, then I'll be convinced she's trying to find out what we're up to in New Orleans," Nancy replied.

To prove her point, the young sleuth turned down one street and up another. The woman did the same.

"I'm going to try something," Nancy said quietly. "Two can play this game."

It was easy for the girls to dodge into three different shops as they rounded another corner. Their pursuer, confused, stood on the sidewalk for several seconds, then turned and walked back in the direction from which she had come. Cautiously Nancy emerged, then Bess and George.

The girls trailed the woman for several blocks. Though there were many pedestrians on the street, they were able to keep their quarry in sight. Apparently she was in a hurry, for she walked quickly, not once slackening her pace. As they rounded a corner, she suddenly disappeared into an alley. Nancy darted forward, just in time to see the woman enter a building.

When she and her friends reached it, Bess was not in favor of continuing the search. Nancy insisted the place was innocent-looking enough, and walked through the open arch. In the distance the girls could hear low singing.

They proceeded down a dimly lighted hall, and in a moment the girls stood beside the door beyond which the singing was coming. A placard on it read: *Church of Eternal Harmony.*

Bess, intrigued, lost her fears and urged that they go inside. Nancy hesitated. At that moment the door opened. A man with long white hair and a beard invited them to enter.

"Our admission is reasonable," he said, smiling. "Only two dollars. If the spirit speaks, your questions will be answered."

Still Nancy hesitated. She realized now that a séance was going on inside. Having no desire to spend two dollars so foolishly, she was about to retreat, when Bess walked boldly into the room beyond. George followed, and Nancy was forced to go along.

After paying admission they seated themselves on a bench near the door. The singing had ceased, and as the girls' eyes grew accustomed to the dim lights, they could see that a number of people sat on benches scattered about the place.

On one wall hung a life-size portrait of a woman swathed in white veils up to her eyes. Long dark hair fell below her shoulders. Every face in the room was upturned, gazing at the portrait.

Presently the white-bearded man announced

that all would have to help summon her spirit.

"Let us sit around this table," he intoned.

Bess stood up to go forward, but Nancy pulled her back to the bench. Several others in the room arose and seated themselves on chairs around an oblong table. The old man took his place at the head of it, his back against the wall, a few feet beyond the portrait.

"Let no one utter a sound," he requested.

Silence fell upon the room. Nancy strained her eyes toward the table, watching intently. The white-bearded man sat perfectly still, looking straight ahead of him. Presently a smile flickered over his face.

"I feel the spirits approaching," he said in a scarcely audible voice.

The words were hardly out of his mouth when three raps were heard. The old man, looking pleased, interpreted the sounds as meaning, "I am here," and invited the participants to ask the spirit for answers to their problems. He explained that one rap would mean Yes, two No, and five would mean that danger lay ahead and the questioner should take every precaution to avoid it.

For several seconds no one spoke. The spirit gave three more sharp raps. Then, shyly, a woman at the table asked:

"Will my child be ill long?"

There came two sharp raps, and the questioner

gave a sigh of relief. Another silence followed. Nancy felt Bess lean forward. Out of the corner of her eye, Nancy had noted that her friend was completely entranced by what was going on. Realizing that Bess was about to ask a question, and fearful she might say something about Mrs. Putney's mystery, Nancy leaned over and whispered into her friend's ear:

"Please don't say anything!"

"Silence!" ordered the old man at the table. "Do you wish to drive away our friendly spirit? Ill luck follows him who disturbs the work of the spirit."

As he spoke, the dim lights faded out. The room was in complete darkness.

Suddenly, on the wall above the portrait, a faint glow appeared. It grew larger, until the whole portrait seemed to be taking form. Bess and George, seated on either side of Nancy, huddled close to her.

Bess nervously clutched her friend's arm until Nancy winced from the pressure. The next moment the three girls gasped.

The portrait had come to life!

The white-bearded man arose from his chair.

"Good people," he said, "Amurah has come to us to speak. But she will answer only the most important questions. Approach no closer, or her lifelike spirit will vanish on the wind."

"Oh, Amurah, tell me, please," implored a young woman from a far corner of the room, "if Thomas comes back to me, shall I marry him?"

Amurah lowered her eyes, then nodded.

"Oh, thank you, thank you," the young woman exclaimed, delight in her voice.

Again Nancy could feel that Bess was about to ask a question. Quietly she laid a finger across the girl's lips. The light around the portrait began to fade.

"Alas, the spirits are leaving us!" the white-bearded medium interpreted.

A few seconds later the lights came on in the room. The old man, arising, made a low bow to the portrait, then announced he regretted that the spirits had not been able to remain long enough to answer the questions of all those present.

"Should you wish further knowledge," he said, "you may seek it from Norman Towner, a photographer, who has a direct connection with the spirit world. From time to time messages appear upon Mr. Towner's photographic plates."

The man ushered his clients from the room, but not before each of them had paused to look at Amurah. George had the temerity to touch the canvas. There was no question but that it was only a portrait. Upon reaching the street, the three girls paused.

"Wasn't it wonderful!" Bess exclaimed, adding

that they should go at once to the studio of Norman Towner.

"Nonsense," George said. "You've already spent two dollars and got nothing for it."

"That's because Nancy wouldn't let me ask a question," Bess argued. "Maybe I'll get an answer when I have my picture taken."

To George's amazement, Nancy encouraged the visit. Not having seen the woman they had followed to the séance, Nancy felt she might have gone to the studio.

By inquiring for directions from pedestrians, the girls arrived at length at a courtyard entered by means of a long passageway. At one side of it a flight of iron stairs led to a carved door which bore the photographer's sign.

"Up we go!" George laughed, starting ahead.

The studio, though old and a bit shabby, was well furnished. The proprietor, a short man with intent dark eyes and an artist's beret cocked over one ear, appeared so unusually eager that the girls wondered if he had many customers.

Nancy inquired the cost of having individual photographs made. The price was reasonable, so the three friends decided upon separate poses.

After the pictures had been taken, the photographer disappeared into the darkroom. Soon he returned with two dripping plates. The pictures on them of George and Bess were excellent. To

Bess's disappointment, however, not a trace of writing appeared on the glass.

"Where is my friend's picture?" inquired George, referring to Nancy.

The photographer returned to the darkroom for it. When Nancy glanced at the wet plate, she inhaled sharply. Just beneath her photograph were the words:

Beware your client's request.

"Spirit writing!" Bess gasped.

"Yes, a message from someone in the other world is warning you not to go on with your work," the photographer said slowly, with emphasis on the word "warning." "Young lady, do not take the warning lightly."

"No, I won't," said Nancy.

She had just glimpsed in the photographer's darkroom the woman they had seen on the plane! The next instant the door closed, and the lights in the studio went out. The room, with its one window heavily curtained, was in complete darkness.

A chill breeze suddenly wafted into the studio. Nancy felt a clammy hand brush across her face and fumble for her throat!

CHAPTER IV

A Strange Adventure

BESS screamed in terror. George, with more presence of mind, groped along the wall until she found a light switch she had noticed earlier. In another moment the room was bright again.

Both girls gasped in horror at what they saw. On the floor, almost at their feet, lay the photographer, unconscious! Bess started toward the man, but checked herself as George demanded:

"Where's Nancy?"

Their friend had vanished from the studio!

In their alarm, the cousins temporarily forgot the photographer. Frantically they ran into the darkroom, then into an adjoining kitchenette.

"Nancy!" George shouted. "Where are you?"

There was no answer.

"Nancy's gone and that photographer isn't regaining consciousness," Bess wailed. "What shall we do?"

"We must call the police," George decided.

Rushing out of the studio and down the iron steps, the girls ran through the deserted courtyard to the street. Fortunately, a policeman was less than half a block away. Hurrying up to him, George and Bess gasped out their story.

Immediately the patrolman accompanied the girls to the studio. As they entered, the photographer stirred slightly and sat up.

"What happened?" he mumbled.

"That's what we want to know," demanded the policeman. "What goes on here?"

"I was showing these girls a plate I'd just developed, when the lights went out. Something struck me on the head. That's all I remember."

"What became of the girl with us?" Bess asked.

The photographer, pulling himself on to a couch, gazed at her coldly and shrugged.

"How should I know?" he retorted.

"And where is the plate with the writing on it?" George suddenly demanded.

"The spirits must have been angry and taken it," the photographer said. "I've known them to do worse things than that."

The policeman appeared to be skeptical. He searched the building thoroughly, but no trace of Nancy or of the missing plate could be found.

Worried over Nancy's safety, and scarcely knowing what to do, Bess and George demanded the arrest of the photographer. The policeman, however, pointed out that they had no evidence against the photographer.

"Now don't you worry, young ladies. Your friend can't be far away. We'll have some detectives on the job right away. But I'll have to ask you to step around to the precinct station and give us a description of Nancy Drew."

Shortly afterward, Bess and George, considerably shaken, returned to their hotel. There, nervously pacing the floor, they debated whether to send a wire to River Heights.

"If Nancy doesn't show up in another half hour, we'd better notify Mr. Drew," Bess quavered. "To tell the truth, I'm so scared—"

"Listen!" George commanded.

Footsteps had sounded in the corridor, and now the door of the suite was opening. The two girls waited tensely. Nancy tottered in. Her hair was disheveled and her clothing wrinkled and soiled. Wearily she threw herself on the bed.

She greeted them with a wan smile. "Hello."

Bess and George ran to her solicitously. "Are you all right? What happened?"

Nancy told them how the hand had clutched at her throat when the lights went out in the studio.

"I tried to scream and couldn't. I was lifted bodily and carried out of the room."

"Where?" George asked.

"I couldn't see. A cold, wet cloth was clapped over my face. I was taken to the basement of a vacant house not far away and left there, bound hand and foot."

"How did you get away?" George questioned.

"I kept working until I was able to wriggle out of the cords. Then I climbed through a window and came straight here."

"Did you get the number of the house?" asked George. "I think we should get a policeman and investigate."

Nancy nodded. "We'll go to the police station as soon as I have a bath and change my clothes."

While Nancy was dressing, the girls discussed their recent experiences. George and Nancy were equally sure the photographer had resorted to trickery in putting the message on the plate.

"He could do it easily," George argued. "Maybe he used a plate which already had been exposed to the printed words."

"I believe there's more to it than that, George," Nancy told her. "I think the woman who spoke to us on the plane figures in it. I saw her at the studio," Nancy disclosed. "I'm convinced the photographer was part of a scheme and only pretended to be knocked unconscious. We must get that plate with the message on it."

"It's gone," said George.

This news added to Nancy's suspicions about the whole adventure. As soon as she was dressed, the girls returned to the police station, and an officer was assigned to accompany them. A careful search was made of the vacant building where Nancy had been imprisoned, but not a clue could be found. Even the cords which had bound her had disappeared.

To their surprise the policeman remarked soberly, "This isn't the first time queer things have happened in this section of the city."

No additional information was gained by calling on the photographer, who maintained his innocence in the affair. Bess and George obtained their pictures, but the man insisted that the plate with the spirit writing had disappeared.

When the girls were in their hotel suite once more, George remarked, "Queer about the warning message—'Beware your client's request.' Do you think it meant Mrs. Putney's case?"

"I'm sure it does. But," Nancy said with a determined smile, "now I'll work even harder to solve the mystery!"

"Nancy," said Bess, "is there anything else we can do down here? I feel we should go home and report to Mrs. Putney."

"Maybe she's had another message!" said George.

"Do you suppose she goes to séances?" Bess asked, "and then later dreams she's hearing her husband talk to her?"

"It's possible," Nancy replied. "But it would be hard to get her to admit it."

Bess and George were glad to leave New Orleans. Nancy's experience had frightened them, and they felt that some sinister motive was back of her temporary abduction. Nancy herself was reluctant to leave.

"I think several people were involved in an effort to get me out of the way so that I couldn't find out too much," she said.

Despite the danger, she thought a further search should be made for the mysterious woman. Yet she agreed there was some justice in the girls' argument that Mrs. Putney should be consulted.

Learning that a plane which stopped at River Heights left within an hour, the girls quickly packed and reached the airport just in time. The trip home was uneventful, but during the flight, Bess revealed that she had a little mystery.

"That's what I wanted to ask Amurah," said Bess. "You remember Mrs. White, who comes to our house once a week to clean? She has a daughter, Lola, who is eighteen. Her mother's terribly worried about her."

Nancy recalled the woman, a very gentle, patient person who had suffered a great deal of misfortune. At present her husband was in a sanatorium, and she was struggling to pay the debts his illness had piled up.

"Where does the mystery come in?" Nancy asked.

It seemed that lately, Lola, ordinarily good-natured and jolly, had become unnaturally subdued. She acted as if she were living in a dream world. Mrs. White said there had been no broken romance, nor had her daughter lost her job.

"In fact," said Bess, "Lola earns good wages at a factory and used to give her mother most of the money. Now she gives her practically nothing but won't say why. Something has happened to her," Bess insisted. "Oh, Nancy, won't you go to see Lola? Maybe she'll tell you what's wrong."

"All right, I will," Nancy promised.

Nancy kept her promise the day after she returned from New Orleans. After calling Mrs. Putney and making an appointment for the following day, she started for Lola White's home, wondering what she would say.

Evidently Bess had told Mrs. White she might expect the visit from Nancy. No sooner had Nancy rapped, than the door was opened by Lola's mother. It was evident that she had been crying.

"Oh, Nancy, I'm so relieved you've come!" she said, her voice trembling. "Lola didn't go to work today. Ever since breakfast she's acted like someone in a trance. Please see if you can do something for her!"

CHAPTER V

The Figure in White

"LOLA dear, Nancy Drew is here to see you," called Mrs. White.

The woman had led the way to the back yard, where her daughter sat motionless, staring into space.

"It is quite useless," sighed Mrs. White. "She will talk to no one."

"Oh, Lola needn't talk," Nancy said in a friendly voice. "I came to take her for a little ride in the country. It's a beautiful day."

"Yes, it is!" Mrs. White agreed. "Lola, wouldn't you like to go for a ride, dear?"

Lola, though looking none too pleased, made no protest. Once in the car, she sat in silence, gazing ahead as if hypnotized.

Nancy pretended to pay no attention as the car sped along the picturesque river road. The prolonged stillness seemed to wear upon Lola, who kept pushing back her long blond hair. Several times she glanced at Nancy. Finally, unable to bear the strain, she asked:

"Why did you bring me out here?"

"To help you if I can." Nancy smiled. "You're worried about something to do with money, aren't you? Is it about your job?"

"Well, sort of," Lola confessed. "It's just that my wages at the factory aren't mine any—" She broke off and gazed forlornly at Nancy.

"Why not tell me everything?" Nancy urged. "Perhaps I can help you."

"No one can. I've pledged to give away almost every cent I earn."

"Whatever induced you to do that, Lola? To whom are you giving the money?"

"I can't tell you," the girl replied, her head low and her voice scarcely above a whisper.

"Do you feel that's fair to your mother? She must need part of your earnings."

"That's what worries me," Lola said miserably. "I've pledged myself and I can't get out of it. I don't dare tell Mother the truth either. Oh, I'm in a mess! I wish I were dead!"

"Now that's silly talk! We'll find a way out of this. If I were you I'd ignore the pledge."

"I don't dare," Lola said fearfully.

Nancy told her that any legitimate organization would not take money to the point of depriving

Mrs. White of needed support. If Lola were paying money to unscrupulous persons, she should have no qualms about breaking the pledge.

"You really think so? If only I dared!"

"I'm sure that your mother would tell you the same thing."

"I guess you're right," Lola admitted. "Maybe I've been foolish."

For another half hour, Nancy talked to the girl in a friendly way, seeking to learn to whom she had pledged her salary. Lola, however, would not reveal the information.

When Nancy finally drove her home, Lola thanked her and promised to follow her advice. The next day Nancy was pleased to hear from Bess that Lola White seemed to be herself again.

"Splendid!" Nancy commented. "I only hope whoever was taking her money will leave her alone now."

As soon as Bess had gone, Nancy hurried to the widow's home. Mrs. Putney herself opened the front door of the big house.

"Oh, I'm so glad you came," she cried excitedly. "While you were gone I remembered something I had forgotten to tell you. In the directions given me by my dear husband as to where I should conceal my jewelry, he mentioned specifically that I was to look for a sign of three twigs placed on the ground and that I should bury the jewel case two steps from the sign in the direction of the big walnut tree. When I reached the clearing I found the three twigs lying crossed on the ground, just as the spirit had directed me."

"Oh, Mrs. Putney, I wish you had told me about this when we were at the spot before!" exclaimed Nancy.

She glanced at her wrist watch. "It's only four o'clock. I'll pick up my friends and drive out now to see if the crossed twigs are still there."

When the girls reached the clearing in the woods, there lay the three crossed twigs. The position seemed too perfect for Nature to have placed them there. Yet Nancy doubted that they were the same ones which Mrs. Putney had seen. Rain and wind would have displaced the others.

"The thief may use this method to communicate with his confederates," Nancy mused. "But why would—"

Her voice trailed off. Through the trees Nancy had seen a flash of white.

"Someone's over there," Bess whispered uneasily.

"Let's try to get closer without being seen!" George urged.

Taking care not to step on dry twigs, the girls entered the woods. Through the bushes, they could see the back of a young woman with long blond hair.

"That almost looks like Lola White!" Nancy exclaimed.

The girl appeared to be reaching high into the crotch of a black walnut tree.

"She's hiding something there!" Nancy whispered excitedly.

The girl suddenly moved off in the opposite direction. Soon she disappeared.

Nancy went quickly to the big walnut. Standing on tiptoe, she reached into a hollow in the trunk of the tree. Triumphantly she pulled out a sealed envelope. The others crowded around her.

The envelope bore no name or address, but on its face was a crude drawing of three crossed twigs!

"Wow!" said George. "The mystery deepens!"

"What's inside?" Bess asked in awe.

"If I had one guess, I'd say money," Nancy replied. "I feel justified in opening it, too, for I'm sure it was meant for the person who stole Mrs. Putney's jewelry."

The other girls agreed. Carefully Nancy slipped her thumb under the flap, gradually peeling it free. Inside was a sheet of paper and ten five-dollar bills.

There was no message but the name "Sadie." So the girl had not been Lola!

"I wonder who the girl was," said George.

"What I want to know is why she left the money here," said Nancy. "We must overtake her and find out!" On second thought she added, "Maybe the thief will come to the tree to get the envelope. I'll stay here. You two go."

"She's hiding something!" Nancy whispered

The cousins darted off, leaving Nancy alone beside the black walnut tree. Carefully Nancy put the envelope back in the hollow, and sat down a little distance away to watch.

As Nancy sat with her back to a tree trunk, she thought she heard the soft pad of steps. She straightened up, listening intently, but heard nothing.

"Probably some animal," Nancy decided.

Nevertheless, she glanced about carefully. Her skin prickled, as if in warning that some stranger might be nearby.

"Nerves!" she told herself.

At that moment Bess and George, unsuccessful in their pursuit of the blond girl, were returning. Coming within view of the big walnut tree, George was astonished to see a strange sight. Though no wind was blowing, a leafless branch of a tree behind the walnut seemed to bend slowly downward.

"Bess, look—" she began, then ended lamely, "Never mind! It's gone now."

"What's gone?" Bess demanded.

"A branch. I guess my eyes tricked me," George admitted.

Hearing the voices of her friends, Nancy quickly arose and came to meet them. Seeing that they were alone, she said in disappointment:

"You weren't able to overtake her?"

"We had miserable luck," Bess admitted. "We didn't even get close enough to see her face."

"We trailed her to the main highway, where she must have hopped a bus," George added.

"I think we should take the money with us," Nancy said. "I'll ask Dad what to do about it."

On tiptoe, Nancy reached into the hollow of the tree. A puzzled expression came over her face.

"The envelope's gone!" she exclaimed.

"It can't be!" insisted Bess.

Nancy groped again and shook her head. "The envelope is gone! But no one was here!"

"I've got an idea," said George. "Maybe someone climbed another tree, crossed over into the big walnut, and then snatched the letter from above!"

"The trees are so close together I suppose it could be done," Nancy admitted doubtfully.

"Wait a minute," George cried out excitedly. Then she told about the slowly bending, leafless branch.

Nancy peered intently up into the old walnut and the maple next to it. "No one there," she observed. "George, you're sure it was a branch and not a fish pole with a hook on the end that was used?" she asked.

"It could have been a pole."

"I understand several things now!" Nancy exclaimed, thinking aloud. "That metal object I saw near here the other day must have been part of a collapsible pole! I'll bet it belonged to the same person who was here today!"

"And the same one who robbed Mrs. Putney!" added Bess.

"George, did the stick bend down out of the tree, or did it come from the direction of the bushes?" Nancy asked.

"I couldn't see well enough to be sure," George replied. "But from where I stood, it appeared to bend down out of a tree behind the walnut."

The three went back to the convertible, agreeing that it might be a good idea to keep a lookout for visitors to the walnut tree. Obviously it was being used as a collection station by someone extracting money from gullible people.

Later, as she drove homeward, Nancy began to wonder whether this might not tie in with Lola White's peculiar actions.

As she turned into her own driveway she noticed a dark-green sports car parked in front. The driver came to meet her.

"Hi, Nancy!" Ned grinned. "Guess I got here a little early."

"I'm late. Been working on a case. Please forgive me."

A week earlier she had accepted Ned Nickerson's invitation to a sundown picnic planned by Emerson College students spending their summer in River Heights.

"I'll be ready in fifteen minutes," she promised.

While Ned waited on the porch, she rushed into the house, showered, and dressed. On her way downstairs, she paused in the kitchen to say good-by to Mrs. Gruen.

"It seems to me you're never home any more," the housekeeper replied. But she added with a smile, "Have a good time and put mystery out of that pretty head for tonight!"

"How could I?" Nancy laughed gaily.

Nancy had not asked Ned where the picnic was to be held. Therefore, she was surprised when she discovered that the spot selected was on the upper Muskoka River, less than a mile from the mysterious walnut tree.

"Want to do me a favor?" she asked Ned.

"Sure thing."

Nancy told him about the money in the walnut tree, its puzzling disappearance, and her suspicion that something sinister was going on.

"And you want to stop and have a look for more envelopes," said Ned. "Okay."

They found nothing in the tree, but the crossed twigs had been removed. Someone had been there! Ned promised to stop at the spot now and then to see if he could learn anything.

They drove on to the picnic spot, where their friends had already gathered. The aroma of broiling hamburgers made them ravenous.

Both Nancy and Ned were favorites among

their friends, and soon everyone was laughing and joking. After all the food had been consumed, some of the young people began to sing. Others went off in canoes.

"Let's go out on the river, Nancy," Ned suggested.

Nancy sat in the bow of the canoe, her paddle lying idle across the gunwales, while Ned paddled smoothly upstream. Moonlight streamed over the treetops and shimmered across the surface of the water. Presently Ned guided the canoe into a cove and let it glide silently toward shore.

"What a night!" he said. "I wish—"

Suddenly Nancy, who was facing the shore, sat bolt upright and uttered a low cry.

"Look over there, Ned!" she exclaimed in a hushed voice. "Am I seeing things?"

The youth, who had been watching the moonlight on the water, turned his head and was startled to see a ghostly white figure wading out into the river from the beach.

"Whew!" Ned caught his breath, nearly dropping his paddle.

As the canoe swung with the current, Nancy got a clear view of the figure in white.

The person wading deeper and deeper into the water was Lola White!

CHAPTER VI

A New Lead

"QUICK, Ned!" Nancy cried, seizing her paddle. "She'll be in over her head in a minute. We must save her!"

Her companion needed no urging. He sent the canoe forward with powerful strokes.

"Lola, stay where you are! Don't move!" Nancy called to her.

The girl did not appear to hear. On she waded, holding her hands in front of her.

As Nancy had feared, the shallow water ended abruptly. The next instant Lola had stepped in over her head. The ducking seemed to bring her out of her trance, and now she began to struggle frantically. If she knew how to swim, she gave no evidence of it.

Fortunately, the canoe was soon alongside her. Quickly Ned eased himself into the water, while Nancy steadied the craft. He seized the struggling and terrified girl, then began to swim toward shore. In a moment they were in shallow water.

Nancy was waiting with the canoe, and the sputtering Lola was lifted into the bottom of the craft. The girl was only half conscious. Nancy bent low over her and caught the words, "the beckoning hand."

"Gosh!" Ned observed uneasily. "She's in a bad way!"

"We must get her home right away," Nancy decided. "And you, too, with those wet clothes."

Paddling as fast as they could, she and Ned started toward the picnic grounds where he had left his car. Midway there, Lola seemed to recover her senses. She sat up and gazed at Nancy as if recognizing her for the first time.

"Lola, why were you wading out into the water?" Nancy asked.

"I can't tell you," Lola answered weakly.

"You said something about a beckoning hand."

"I did?" Lola's eyes opened wide and an expression of horror came over her face.

"You thought someone was calling to you?"

Lola spoke with an effort. "I'm grateful to you for pulling me out of the river. But I can't answer your questions!"

Nancy said no more. Taking off her sweater, she put it around the shivering girl.

Later, when they reached the picnic grounds, she hurried Lola in secret to Ned's car, as the college group made joking remarks to Ned about his bedraggled appearance.

At the White home Nancy and Ned lingered only long enough to be certain that Lola had suffered no ill effects from her immersion.

"Please don't tell anyone what happened," Mrs. White pleaded. "Lola went out this evening without telling me where she was going. I can't imagine why she would go to the river."

"Perhaps to meet someone," Nancy suggested.

"So far as I know, she had no date. Oh, I do so need your help to clear up this mystery, Nancy!"

"I'll do everything I can," Nancy promised.

Upon returning home, the young detective sat for a long while in the Drew library, reflecting upon the events of the evening.

Nancy mused also about the many unrelated incidents that had taken place the past week. Into several of these the mysterious Howard Brex seemed to fit very naturally. Yet of his whereabouts since his release from prison, nothing was known.

Penning a brief note to Mr. Johnson, Brex's former boss in New Orleans, she described the crossed-twig sign, and asked if by chance it had any connection with the suspect and his jewelry designs.

For several days after the letter had been sent, Nancy and her friends kept a fairly close watch on the black walnut tree at the edge of the clearing.

But so far as they could determine, no one visited the tree, either to leave money or to take it away.

"We're wasting time watching this place," Ned commented after the third day. "Whoever it is you're looking for knows you've discovered the walnut-tree cache, and has probably moved to a safer locality."

Nancy was inclined to agree with him. She felt very discouraged, for it seemed that she was making no progress whatever in solving the stolen jewelry mystery. Because she could report no success to Mrs. Putney, she avoided calling upon her.

But a letter from Mr. Johnson, the jewelry manufacturer, brought startling results. He wrote:

The crossed-twig design you described was never used in any work Brex did for us. We have also looked through other jewelers' catalogs, but do not find anything like this design pictured.

However, some time ago, a simple-minded janitor in this office building received from Chicago a letter bearing an insigne of crossed twigs. The man was urged to invest money in stock of the Three Branch Ranch on the promise of doubling his funds. The scheme sounded dishonest, and I persuaded him to ignore it. I would have reported the stock sellers to the authorities, but unfortunately the janitor destroyed the letter before I had a chance to examine it.

Nancy took Mr. Johnson's letter to her father, who read it carefully, then offered a suggestion.

"Why not notify the postal authorities? It's against the law, as you know, to use the mail to promote dishonest schemes."

"Will you do it for me, Dad? Your letterhead is so impressive!"

"All right, I'll dictate a letter to my secretary this afternoon," the lawyer promised.

Nancy decided to write a letter of her own to the Government Information Service to inquire if they had any record of a Three Branch Ranch. Three days later she received a reply. She was told that no such ranch was listed.

"This practically makes it certain the stock scheme is a swindle!" she declared. "The head-quarters of the outfit may be in Chicago, but I'll bet salesmen are working in other places." Yet it was difficult for her to connect Brex, a clever designer of jewelry, with a crooked stock promotion.

Even though she had no conclusive information to convey, Nancy decided to call upon Mrs. Putney to ask a few questions. Just as she was about to leave the house, however, a taxi stopped in front, and the widow herself alighted.

Mrs. Putney looked even more worried than on the previous occasion.

"Poor thing," Nancy said to herself. "I'd like to be able to help her!"

Nancy met Mrs. Putney at the front door, and cordially escorted her into the living room.

"I've come to see you, because you never come to my house," the visitor scolded Nancy mildly.

"I haven't been to see you lately, because I had nothing to report, Mrs. Putney. I intended to call today."

"Then I'll forgive you, my dear. If you were coming, you must have a clue."

"Several of them, I hope. Before I tell you what I suspect, I must ask you a rather personal question, Mrs. Putney. Do you own any stock in the Three Branch Ranch?"

Nancy's question seemed to take the widow completely by surprise.

"What—what do you know about the Three Branch Ranch?" she asked in a voice which quavered with emotion. Her faded eyes reflected stark fear.

CHAPTER VII

Matching Wits

ALARMED, Nancy called to Hannah Gruen, who came in hurriedly from the garden. Then she took Mrs. Putney's arm and led her to a chair.

"I didn't mean to upset you," said Nancy. "Please sit down, and Hannah will bring you a cup of tea."

While Mrs. Gruen was in the kitchen preparing the tea, Mrs. Putney rested quietly.

"How did you discover—about the ranch?" she finally asked in a voice scarcely above a whisper.

Nancy remained silent as the widow slumped back in her chair. When the housekeeper brought her a cup of tea, she sipped it obediently. Presently she declared she felt much better.

"Please forgive me for having distressed you so," begged Nancy.

"On the contrary, I should have told you sooner. Three days ago I had another message from my dear husband. He advised me to invest my money in a good, sound stock. Three Branch Ranch was recommended. That's why I was so startled when you asked me about it, Nancy."

"The message came to you at home?" Nancy inquired.

"No, through a medium. I heard of the woman and attended a séance at her home. It was very satisfying."

"Who is she, and where does she live?"

The question took Mrs. Putney by surprise. "Why, I don't know," she said.

"You don't know!" exclaimed Nancy. "Then how could you attend a séance in her home?"

"I learned of the woman through a friendly note which came in the mail. The message said if I cared to attend the séance, I should meet a car which would call for me that night."

"The car came?"

"Yes. It was driven by a woman who wore a dark veil. During a rather long ride into the country, she never once spoke to me."

"Yet you weren't uneasy or suspicious?"

"It all seemed in keeping with what I had understood to be the general practice in such things. The ride was a long one, and I fell asleep. When I awakened, the car stood in front of a dark house."

"You were taken inside?"

"Yes. The veiled woman escorted me to a room illuminated by only a dim, greenish light. When my eyes became accustomed to it, I saw a white, filmily clad figure lying on a couch. Through this medium, the spirit of my husband spoke to me."

At the recollection, Mrs. Putney began to tremble again.

"Your husband advised you to invest money in the Three Branch Ranch!" Nancy said. "What else did he tell you?"

"That I should listen to no advice from any earthly person, and keep what he told me to myself. Oh, dear!"

"What's the matter?" Nancy asked kindly.

"I've told too much already! I shouldn't have revealed a word of this to anyone!"

The widow arose and in an agitated voice asked Nancy to call a taxi.

"I'll drive you home myself," Nancy offered.

During the ride, the young detective avoided further reference to the subject which so distressed her companion. But as she left the widow at her doorstep, she said casually:

"I suppose you did invest money in Three Branch Ranch?"

"Only a little. I gave what cash I had with me to the medium, who promised to use it to purchase the stock for me."

"I don't like to worry you, Mrs. Putney, but I'm afraid you may lose the money you invested."

"Oh, I couldn't. My husband's judgment on business matters was excellent!"

"I don't question that, Mrs. Putney. But I have evidence which convinces me you were tricked by a group of clever swindlers."

Nancy then told of the letter she had received from the Government Information Service, saying no Three Branch Ranch was listed, and that the postal authorities had been notified.

"Promise me you'll not invest another penny until the outfit can be thoroughly investigated."

"I trust your judgment," the widow said. "I promise."

"And another thing. May I have the note you received telling of the séance?"

"I haven't it. I was requested to return it to the medium as evidence of my good faith."

"Oh, that's a bad break for us," Nancy said in disappointment. "Those fakers think of everything! The letter might have provided a clue!"

"What can we do?"

"Don't admit that you suspect trickery," Nancy advised. "Sooner or later, another séance will be suggested and you will be requested to invest more of your money. Phone me the minute you receive another communication."

"Oh, I will!" Mrs. Putney promised.

After leaving the widow, Nancy began to speculate on how many others in River Heights might have been duped into buying the phony stock. The first one to come into her mind was Lola White. The second was the mysterious Sadie.

"Lola probably signed up for a lot of stock, and is paying the bill little by little, out of her wages," Nancy surmised. "I must see her at once."

Lola was not at her place of employment. Upon being told that the girl had not appeared for work that day because of illness, Nancy drove to the White cottage. Lola was lying in a hammock on the front porch, gazing morosely at the ceiling. She sat up and tried to look cheerful.

"How are you today?" Nancy inquired. "No bad effects from the river?"

"I'm all right, I guess," Lola answered. "Thanks for what you did."

"We were just fortunate to be there when you needed us," replied Nancy. "By the way, do you feel like telling me why you were there?"

"No, I don't," Lola said sullenly.

Nancy did not press the matter. Instead, she asked her if she had ever heard of the Three Branch Ranch. Lola's eyebrows shot up, but she shook her head.

Then Nancy told Lola that her real purpose in coming to call was to ask if she were acquainted with a girl named Sadie.

"Oh, you must mean the one who works at the Save-A-Lot Market," Lola said. "I don't know her last name."

"Thanks a lot, Lola. I'll go to see her." As Nancy went down the porch steps she added, "Keep your chin up, Lola!"

Happy that she had obtained a lead, Nancy climbed into her convertible, waved to Lola, and sped away down the street.

When Nancy inquired at the market whether a girl named Sadie worked there, a tall blonde operating a cash register was pointed out. So busy that she was in no mood to talk, the girl frowned as Nancy paused and spoke to her.

"You're Sadie?" Nancy asked, uncomfortably aware that she was delaying a line of customers.

"Sadie Bond," the girl replied briskly.

"I'm trying to trace a Sadie interested in buying stock in a western ranch," Nancy said, keeping her voice low.

"You've got the wrong girl, miss," Sadie replied. "I don't have money to buy ranches."

Nancy smiled. "Then I guess I'm looking for some other person."

Having drawn a blank, Nancy decided that her next move should be to write an advertisement for the River Heights *Gazette*.

It read:

> *SADIE: If you are blonde and know of a certain walnut tree, a beautiful gift awaits you in return for information. Reply Box 358.*

The second day after the advertisement appeared, Nancy, with Bess and George, went to the *Gazette* office to ask if there had been any replies.

To their astonishment, nearly a dozen letters were handed them.

"Jumping jellyfish!" muttered George. "How many walnut-tree Sadies are there in this town?"

Carrying the replies to a nearby park, the girls divided the letters and sat down to read them. Several were from pranksters, or persons who obviously had no information about the walnut tree but were eager to obtain a free gift.

"Running that ad was a waste of money," Bess sighed, tossing aside her last letter.

Nancy, however, was deeply engrossed in a letter written on the stationery of the Lovelee Cosmetic Company. "Girls, listen to this!" she exclaimed.

" 'I have blond hair. Do you refer to a black walnut tree along the Muskoka River? What is the gift you are offering? Sadie Green.' "

"We must find out more about this girl right away!" Nancy declared.

She telephoned the cosmetic firm and learned that Sadie was the telephone operator. When Nancy spoke about the letter, the girl pleaded with her not to come to the office.

"I'll meet you in the park," Sadie promised. "I'll be there in a few minutes."

The three friends were afraid the girl might not keep her promise. But eventually they saw a young woman with long blond hair approaching.

"I can't stay more than a minute," she said nervously. "The boss would have a fit if he knew I skipped out!"

"Will you answer a few questions?"

"What do you want to know?"

"First, tell me, did you ever hear of the Three Branch Ranch?"

"Never," the girl replied with a blank look.

"Did you leave an envelope with money in the hollow of a tree near the river?" Nancy asked.

The girl moved a step away. "Who are you?" she mumbled. "Detectives? Why do you ask me such a thing?" Before Nancy could reply, she burst out, "I've changed my mind. Keep your present!"

With a frightened look in her eyes, Sadie whirled and ran off through the park.

"That girl is afraid to tell what she knows!" Nancy exclaimed. "But we may learn something by talking to her parents."

Inquiry at the Lovelee personnel department brought forth the information that Sadie lived with an elderly grandfather, Charles Green, on North James Street. The girls went directly there.

Old Mr. Green sat on the front porch in a rocker, reading a newspaper. He laid the paper aside as the girls came up the walk.

"You friends o' my granddaughter Sadie?" he asked in a friendly way. "She ain't here now."

"We're acquaintances of Sadie," Nancy replied, seating herself on the porch railing.

"If you're aimin' to get her to go some place with you, I calculate it won't do no good to ask." The old man sighed. "Sadie's actin' kinda peculiar lately."

"In what way?" Nancy asked with interest.

"Oh, she's snappish-like when I ask her questions," the old man revealed. "She ain't bringin' her money home like she used to, either."

Mr. Green, who seemed eager for companionship, chatted on about Sadie. She was a good girl, he said, but lately he could not figure her out.

From the conversation, Nancy was convinced that the case of Sadie Green was very similar to that of Lola White. After the girls had left the house, Nancy proposed that they drive out to the black walnut.

"I have a plan," she said.

Nancy did not say what it was, but after examining the hollow in the walnut tree, which was empty, she looked all about her. Then she tore a sheet from a notebook in her purse. Using very bad spelling, she printed:

My girl friend told me by leaving a letter hear I can get in touch with a pursen who can give infermation. Please oblige. Yours, Ruby Brown, Genral Delivry, River Heights.

"You hope to trap the man who took the fifty dollars!" George exclaimed admiringly. "But how do you know you'll get an answer? It seems pretty definite that the racketeers aren't using this tree as a post office any longer."

"We'll have to take a chance," said Nancy. "And if there is an answer, someone will have to call for it who answers to the name of 'Ruby Brown.' "

"George and I will," Bess offered eagerly.

Nancy smilingly shook her head. "You're well known as my friends. No, I'll have a stranger call for the letter, so that anyone assigned to watch the post office won't become suspicious."

Nancy arranged with a laundress, who sometimes worked at the Drew home, to inquire for the letter each day.

"Did you get it?" Nancy asked eagerly when Belinda returned the third day.

The good-natured laundress, lips parted in a wide grin, said, "I got it, Miss Nancy!"

Taking the letter, Nancy ran upstairs to her room to open it in private. She gasped when she read the message enclosed, which was:

If you're on the level, Ruby, go to Humphrey's Black Walnut for instructions. If you are a disbeliever, may the wrath of all the Humphreys descend upon you!

CHAPTER VIII

The Ghost at the Organ

REREADING the message several times, Nancy speculated about the Humphreys and their connection with the black walnut tree.

Deciding it best to keep the contents of the message to herself, Nancy went to the River Heights Public Library, hoping to find a book which would throw some light on the Humphreys mentioned in the note. The name sounded vaguely familiar, and it had occurred to her that it might belong to one of the very old families of the county.

Finally Nancy found exactly the book she wanted. Fascinated, she read that a famous old walnut grove along the river once had been known as Humphrey's Woods.

Even more exciting was the information that a duel, fatal to one member of the family, had been fought beneath a certain walnut tree. The tree, known since then as Humphrey's Walnut, was marked with a plaque.

The article went on to say that Blackwood Hall, the family home, was still standing. Built of walnut from the woods surrounding it, the mansion had, in its day, been one of the showplaces along the river. Now the grounds were weed-grown, the old home vacant, and the family gone.

"It seems a pity to neglect a fine old place that way," Nancy thought. "Why would—"

The next sentence aroused her curiosity.

"It is rumored that Jonathan's ghost still inhabits the place!"

Nancy decided she must investigate Blackwood Hall, although she smiled at the thought of any ghost walking there.

But first she would find Humphrey's Walnut. When she returned home, Nancy telephoned Ned, asking if he were free to accompany her, and told him briefly about the letter.

"I'll pick you up in my car in five minutes!" he promised eagerly.

At Nancy's direction, Ned drove as close as he could to the ancient walnut grove by the river. Then they parked the car and started off on foot. They examined each tree for a plaque. It was not until they were deep in the grove that Nancy spied the dull bronze marker with its tragic account of how Jonathan Humphrey had died in a duel while defending his honor beneath the shade of that tree. For fully a minute neither Nancy nor Ned spoke; then Nancy's voice shook off the spell of the place.

"I wonder if anyone will come," said Nancy.

"The note suggested that you were to receive instructions of some kind," Ned remarked.

"Perhaps this tree, also, is used to hold messages. Do you see any hollow in the trunk, Ned?"

The youth, noticing a deep pocket in the crotch of the walnut, ran his hand into it.

"Say, something's crammed in here!" he said excitedly. "Yes, it's a paper!"

"And addressed to Ruby Brown!" Nancy cried, looking at it.

The message was short.

Name the girl friend who suggested you leave that letter.

"Wow!" exclaimed Ned. "Looks as if you've put your foot in it now, Nancy."

Nancy read the message again, then asked Ned to put it back. "Come on!" she urged.

Nancy led the way back to the car and they drove to the walnut tree where she had left her first note signed "Ruby Brown." Again Nancy printed a badly spelled message, asking for instructions on how to find the Humphrey tree.

"That ought to fool him." She chuckled as Ned placed the note in the hollow of the tree. "He'll think poor Ruby is dumb, which is exactly what I want him to think."

"Say, why don't you ask the police to guard the place?"

"Because I'm afraid I'll scare off the man altogether. I want to trap the mastermind behind this thing, not some errand boy."

For the next two days, no mail was received by General Delivery for Ruby Brown. On the third morning, in response to Nancy's telephone call, she learned a letter was at the post office. The laundress went to get it.

"What does our unknown friend write this time?" asked Bess, who had arrived at the Drew home just ahead of the maid. "Does he tell Ruby how to reach the Humphrey Walnut?"

"He says 'Ask Lola White.' "

"Lola!" exclaimed Bess. "That poor girl! Then she *is* involved in that swindler's scheme."

"I've suspected it all along," Nancy admitted. "The fellow is clever. He's suspicious that Ruby Brown is a hoax, but so far I don't think he connects her with me in any way. And it's my job to keep him from finding out."

"What will you do next?" asked Bess. "Talk to Lola?"

"Not right away," Nancy decided. "Unwittingly she might carry the information back to the writer of this note."

"Then what's the next move?"

"Dad says when you're confused—and I admit I am—you should sit back and try to arrange the facts into some kind of order," Nancy replied. "Dad also thinks a change of scenery is a good idea when you're in a mental jam."

"Where shall we go?" asked Bess.

"How would you like to go with me to Blackwood Hall?" asked Nancy. "The book at the library told various stories about this old mansion, which stands within a few miles of River Heights. It's haunted, has a secret tunnel, and is said to house the ghost of one Jonathan Humphrey who lost his life in a duel. Would you like to explore it with me?"

At first Bess insisted that wild horses could not drag her to the deserted mansion. But later, when she learned that Nancy had persuaded George to accompany her, she weakened in her decision.

"I'll go along," she said. "But I'm sure we're headed for trouble."

The trio set off at once, although a summer storm seemed to be brewing. As the girls tramped through the woods along the river, Nancy suddenly stopped short. Below her was the cove where she and Ned had rescued Lola White. The girls were not far from Blackwood Hall now. Could there be any connection between the sinister old place and the strange, hypnotic state in which they had found Lola that night?

Without voicing her thoughts to the others,

Nancy plunged on. At last they came within view of the ancient building. The three-story mansion, where several generations of Humphreys had lived, looked as black as its name, forbidding even by daylight. High weeds and grass choked off any paths that might once have led to the house.

The girls circled the mansion. The wind rattled the shutters and at intervals whistled dismally around the corners of the great structure. An open gate to what had once been a flower garden slammed back and forth, as if moved by an unseen hand.

Nancy walked to the massive front door, expecting to find it securely fastened. To her amazement, as she turned the knob, the door slowly opened on groaning hinges.

"Well, what do you know!" George muttered.

Bess tried to dissuade her friends from going inside, but they paid no attention.

Turning on flashlights, the three girls entered the big hall into which the door opened. The floor was richly carpeted, but Time had played its part in making the carpet worn and gray with mildew.

Velvet draperies, faded and rotted, hung from the windows of an adjoining room. Through the archway, the girls caught a glimpse of a few massive pieces of walnut furniture.

"This looks interesting," Nancy observed. "There's nothing to be afraid of here."

At that moment the front door banged shut behind them. Bess stifled a scream of terror.

"Goose! It was only the wind!" George scolded her. "If you keep this up, you'll give us all a case of the jitters."

"I'm sorry," said Bess, "but it's so spooky."

Just then a sound of sudden, heavy rain told the girls a storm had indeed begun.

Passing through what they took to be a small parlor, the girls found themselves in another long hall, running at right angles to the entrance hall. From it opened a huge room, so dark that their flashlights illuminated only a small section of it.

"Listen!" Nancy whispered suddenly.

As they paused in the doorway, the three distinctly heard the sound of organ music. Bess seized George's arm in a viselike grip.

"W-what's that?" she quavered. "It must be ghost music!"

"It couldn't be—" George began, but the words died in her throat.

At the end of the room a weird, greenish light began to glow. It revealed a small organ.

At the keyboard of the instrument sat a luminous figure.

Bess uttered a terrified shriek which echoed through the ancient house. Instantly the dim light vanished, and the music died away. The long room was in darkness.

Nancy raised her flashlight and ran toward the place where the phantom organist had appeared. Only the old, dust-covered organ remained against the wall.

"It looks as if it hadn't been touched for years," Nancy remarked.

"Oh, Nancy! Let's leave this dreadful place!" Bess wailed from across the room. "The house is haunted! Somebody's ghost does live here!"

Refusing to listen to her friends' pleas to wait, Bess rapidly retreated. A solid slamming of the front door told them she was safely out of the house.

George, keeping her voice low, commented, "To tell the truth, I'm a little nervous, too."

"So am I," admitted Nancy. "This place is haunted all right—not by a specter but by a very live and perhaps dangerous person."

"How did that 'ghost,' or whatever it was, get out of the room so fast? And without passing us?"

"That's what we must find out," Nancy replied, focusing her light on the walls again. "There may be a secret exit that the—"

She ended in midsentence as a girl's piercing scream reached their ears. The cry came from outside the mansion.

"That was Bess!" Nancy exclaimed.

Fearful, the two girls abandoned the search and

raced outdoors. The rain was coming down in torrents, making it difficult to see far ahead.

At first they could not locate Bess anywhere. Then Nancy caught a glimpse of her, huddled among the trees a few yards away. She was trembling violently.

"A man!" Bess chattered as her companions ran up to her. "I saw him!"

"Did you get a good look at him?" Nancy asked.

Bess had been too frightened to do this. But she was sure she must have surprised the person who had come from the direction of the house, for he had turned abruptly and entered the woods.

"Any chance of overtaking him?" Nancy questioned.

"Oh, no!" Bess had no desire either to lead or join an expedition through the woods. "He's gone. He knows his way and we don't. Let's go home, girls. We're wet through, and we'll catch colds."

"I'm going back to the mansion," Nancy announced.

"I'll come along," said George. "We'll hunt again for the hidden exit that the ghost at the organ must have taken!"

Bess reluctantly accompanied her friends. As they reached the massive front door, Nancy noticed that it was closed.

"I'm sure I left it open. The wind must have blown it shut," she remarked.

George tried to open the door. Though she twisted the knob in both directions and pushed hard, the door refused to budge.

"Bolted from inside," George concluded. "The ghost isn't anxious for company."

"I can't get it out of my mind that Blackwood Hall is part of this whole mixed-up mystery," Nancy remarked thoughtfully. "I wish I could get inside again!"

Nancy smiled to herself. Ned was coming to dinner. She would ask him to bring her back to Blackwood Hall that evening. Ghosts were always supposed to perform better at night!

"All right, let's go," she said cheerfully.

Before returning home, Nancy did a few errands, so it was after six o'clock when she reached her own house. Hannah Gruen opened the door excitedly.

"Mrs. Putney has been trying all afternoon to reach you by telephone. She wants to talk to you about something very important."

"I believe Mrs. Putney is going to attend another séance!" Nancy exclaimed.

Nancy hurried to the telephone and called the Putney number, but there was no answer.

"Oh, dear, I hope she won't be taken in again by the faker," Nancy said to herself.

Without the slightest clue as to where to find

Mrs. Putney, Nancy turned her thoughts toward the evening's plan. Ned, upon arriving, fell in eagerly with her idea of going to Blackwood Hall.

"I hope the ghost appears for me too," he said, laughing, when Nancy had told him the story. "Say, how about going there by boat?"

"Wonderful."

After dinner Ned rented a trim little speedboat, and in a short time they reached an abandoned dock some distance from Blackwood Hall. A full moon shone down on the couple as they picked their way through the woods.

"Listen!" Nancy suddenly whispered.

From far away came the sound of chanting.

"It might be a séance!" Nancy said excitedly. "If we hurry, we may get there in time!"

Running ahead of Ned, Nancy paid scant heed to the ground underfoot, and stepped ankle-deep into a quagmire. When she tried to retreat, the mud tugged at her feet. Ned caught her by the arm.

"Stay back, Ned!" she cried out.

The warning came too late. Already Ned had followed her into the quagmire. He, too, tried to extricate himself without success.

"It's quicksand!" Ned cried hoarsely.

Inch by inch, he and Nancy felt themselves sinking lower and lower into the mire!

CHAPTER IX

Another Séance

REALIZING how serious their situation was, Ned urged Nancy to pull herself out of the quagmire by using him as a prop and jumping to firm ground.

"No, don't ask me to do that," Nancy replied. "I might save myself, but you would be pushed so far down, I couldn't possibly get help in time to pull you out."

"If you don't do it, we'll both lose our lives," Ned argued. "Hurry, Nancy! We're sinking fast!"

Nancy refused to listen to his pleas. Instead, she began to shout for help, hoping that some of the chanters would hear her. Ned, too, called loudly until his voice was hoarse.

No one came, and they kept sinking deeper into the quicksand. Soon Nancy was up to her chest.

"I'm afraid there's no help for us," Nancy said despairingly.

The youth scarcely heard her, for just then his feet struck something hard and firm.

"Nancy!" he cried. "I've hit bottom!"

Before she knew what was happening, he grasped her beneath the armpits and tugged hard. The muck gave a loud, sucking sound as it slowly and reluctantly released its hold. A few minutes later Nancy was safe and sound and on dry, firm ground, though she was plastered from heels to head with mud.

"You all right, Ned?"

"I'm okay," he answered.

Nancy scrambled to her feet. Now she must get Ned out! Desperately she looked around for something she could use to rescue him.

"Hold everything, Ned. I'll be back in a jiffy," Nancy called. She had remembered the long painter with which they had moored the motorboat to the dock.

Nancy raced through the darkness to the riverbank. She flicked on the lights of the small speedboat, untied the stout Manila rope which tied it to the pier, and a few minutes later was back at the edge of the quagmire where Ned was patiently waiting. She threw one end of the rope to the boy who calmly tied a noose under his arms. He directed her to toss the other end over the limb of a tree and then pull steadily.

Nancy struggled desperately to pull Ned from the quicksand. As the rope tightened, Ned began slowly but surely to emerge from the mire. Soon he was able to help with his arms and legs, and at last he succeeded in scrambling to safety beside Nancy.

For several minutes neither was able to speak, so exhausted were they from their violent efforts. As the two looked at each other, suddenly both Nancy and Ned began to laugh hysterically.

"If you could only see what you look like!" they exclaimed in the same breath.

Covered with mud and shaken by their unfortunate experience, their one desire was to get into clean clothes. The mystery, they decided, as they started back toward the dock, must wait for another time.

Later, at home once more and in dry clothes, Nancy began to wonder if Mrs. Putney had returned and whether she had been attending another séance. On a chance, she telephoned, but there was no answer. As Nancy reflected on her own adventure, she recalled the sound of chanting she and Ned had heard. Could it have come from Blackwood Hall? she wondered.

Immediately after breakfast the next morning, Nancy called at Mrs. Putney's home. The widow, looking very pale and tired, was wearing a dressing gown.

"I was up very late last night," she explained.

Nancy struggled to pull Ned from the quicksand

Then she added peevishly, "Why didn't you call me yesterday? It seems to me you're always away when I need you," Mrs. Putney grumbled. "Oh, dear! No one seems interested in my affairs—that is, no earthly being."

Nancy, though annoyed by the woman's attitude, was careful to hide her impatience. She realized that Mrs. Putney was a highly nervous individual, upset by the death of her husband, and recent events, and would have to be humored.

The widow remained stubbornly silent about telling where she had been the previous evening. Nancy, following a hunch, remarked:

"By the way, what were you chanting last night just before the séance?"

Mrs. Putney leaned forward in her chair, staring at Nancy as one stupefied. For a moment she looked as if she were going to faint. Then she recovered herself and whispered:

"Nancy Drew, how did you know where I was last evening?"

"Then it's true you were at a séance again last night?"

"Yes, Nancy. I tried to call you yesterday afternoon to let you know that I had been invited to another invocation of the spirits. But I couldn't reach you. *She* took me there again last night."

"She?"

"The woman in the veil," Mrs. Putney explained. "Yesterday afternoon I was instructed by telephone to go to Masonville and have dinner at the Claridge. Afterward, the car would be waiting for me. We drove somewhere into the country," the widow went on. "It seems strange, but I fell asleep again and didn't awaken until it was time to leave the car."

Nancy thought it very strange, indeed. Had the woman been drugged?

"As I opened my eyes, a long, opaque veil was draped over my head. I was led a short distance, where I was told there were several other persons who, like myself, were veiled."

"Did you learn their names?" Nancy interposed eagerly.

"Oh, no. My companion warned that to avoid annoying the spirits, we were not to speak to one another or ask questions."

"Then you all sang?" Nancy prompted as the widow stopped speaking.

"Yes, a woman led us in a prayerful chant," Mrs. Putney continued, her voice growing wistful at the recollection. "After a while we were taken indoors and the spirits came. They spoke to us through the control."

"How can you be certain it wasn't a trick?"

"Because my husband called me Addie. My first name is Adeline, you know, but he always liked Addie better. No one besides my husband ever called me by that name."

"Tricksters easily might have learned of it,"

Nancy pointed out. "The information could have been obtained from neighbors or relatives."

Apparently not listening, Mrs. Putney began to pace the floor nervously. "The spirits advised each of us to contribute money to carry on their earthly mission," she revealed.

"And what is that mission?"

The widow gave Nancy a quick look and replied, "We're supposed to turn money over to the earthly beings who make spiritual communication possible for us. Full instructions will be sent later. I gave them only fifty dollars last night. I felt I had to do that because everyone was giving something."

"A profitable night's work for those people!" Nancy remarked caustically. "You mustn't give another penny."

Mrs. Putney gave Nancy a cold stare. "Everything so far has seemed quite honest to me," she said.

Nancy was dismayed to realize that the widow was fast falling under the spell of the phonies who were trying to fleece her.

"Don't forget your jewelry was stolen," Nancy reminded her.

"I'm sure these people had nothing to do with that, Nancy."

"Mrs. Putney, at any time during the séance did you hear cries for help?"

"Why, no," the woman replied, startled. "Everything was very quiet." Then she added, "When the séance was over, I was taken outside again and helped into the car."

"Still veiled?"

"Oh, yes." A faraway look again came into her eyes. "You know, the trip home was like a dream. To tell the truth, I don't seem to remember anything about it. The next thing I really knew was that it was morning and I was lying on the divan in this very room."

Nancy was greatly disturbed at hearing this. It sounded too much like the strange actions of Lola and Sadie. She asked Mrs. Putney if she had been given anything to eat or drink before leaving the séance. The answer was No. She had noticed no unusual odors, either. Nancy was puzzled; somehow, the mediums must have brought on a kind of hypnotic sleep.

"Please don't ask me to give up the chance to get messages from my dear, departed husband," Mrs. Putney said, forestalling what Nancy was about to request.

Instead, on a sudden inspiration, Nancy told her to continue attending the séances, but asked to be kept informed of what happened. Pleased, Mrs. Putney promised, not realizing that Nancy hoped in this way to get evidence against the group. Then, at the proper moment, she would expose their trickery.

"I'll have to get busy before these people become suspicious and skip," Nancy said to herself as she drove home.

When Nancy told her father about the strange occurrences at Blackwood Hall, he agreed that the place should be thoroughly investigated to find out if fake séances were being carried on there.

"Nancy, I'm afraid to have you go near that place again," the lawyer said. "It sounds dangerous to me. Besides, we have no right to search anyone's property without a warrant. Perhaps your crowd of spirit-invoking fakers have rented the Humphrey mansion."

"But, Dad, everything depends upon it. Won't you go with me, and maybe Ned too?"

On the verge of refusing, Mr. Drew caught the eager, pleading look in his daughter's eyes. Also, he realized that they might very well make important discoveries at Blackwood Hall and the thought intrigued him.

"Tell you what!" he offered impulsively. "If Ned can go with us, we'll start out right after lunch! And I'll take care of the warrant. Captain McGinnis will fix me up."

Nancy ran to the telephone. "With both you and Ned to help me," she said excitedly, "that ghost is as good as trapped now!"

CHAPTER X

The Secret Door

SHORTLY after lunch Nancy arrived at Blackwood Hall with her father and Ned. What Nancy had counted on as a clue to fit into the puzzle, as she had worked it out in her mind, proved to be a disappointment.

"I was so sure there were going to be automobile tracks here," she said. "Mrs. Putney told me she was driven right to the door of the place where the séance was held."

"But here's something interesting," her father called from a spot among the trees.

As Nancy and Ned ran over, he pointed to several deep, narrow tracks and some footprints. The tracks looked as if they had been made by a wheelbarrow, which had been used to make several trips.

"I believe someone was busy moving things out of the house!" Mr. Drew exclaimed. "Anything valuable inside?"

"Furniture," Nancy replied. "Most of it would be too heavy to move by wheelbarrow, though."

"It's more likely the scamps carried away evidence which might incriminate them if found by the police," the lawyer said grimly. "Mediums' trappings, perhaps."

"Wonder if we can get inside," Ned said.

When he attempted to open the door, he found it locked. Thinking it might only be stuck, he and Mr. Drew heaved against the door with all their strength, and suddenly it gave way. The lock was broken.

"Not a very cheerful place," said Ned as the three stepped into the hallway. "This dim light would make anybody think he saw ghosts."

Nancy peered into the adjoining rooms. So far as a hasty glance revealed, none of the furniture had been disturbed. It was possible, of course, that the wheelbarrow tracks had no connection with the fake mediums at all, and perhaps Mrs. Putney's séances in turn had no connection with the ghost of Blackwood Hall!

"Let's separate and see what we can find out, anyway," Nancy proposed.

"All right," Mr. Drew agreed. "But call me, Nancy, if you come upon anything suspicious."

Eager to examine the organ again, Nancy walked along the hall and entered the huge room which was almost in complete darkness. Ned and her father began to search the other rooms.

With scarcely a thought that she was alone, Nancy went directly to the old organ, which stood at an angle across one corner. Laying down her lighted flashlight, she seated herself on the creaking bench and tried to play. No sound came forth.

"Why, that's funny!" Nancy thought, startled. She tried again, pumping the pedals and pressing the keys down firmly. "I certainly didn't dream I heard music coming from this organ! There must be a trick to it somewhere!"

Now deeply interested, Nancy began to examine the instrument inch by inch with her flashlight. There was a small space along the side wall, large enough for a person to squeeze behind. Peering in curiously, she was amazed to see a duplicate set of ivory keys at the rear of the organ!

"Why, the front of the organ is only a sham!"

Eager to investigate, Nancy pushed through the opening. There she found a low door in the wall of the room. "So this is how the ghost vanished so quickly!" she told herself.

Nancy tried the door, which was unlocked. Flashing her light, she saw that a flight of stairs led downward. Cautiously she began to descend. Only after proceeding a short distance along a damp, musty corridor did she regret that she had not summoned her father and Ned.

"They may wonder what's become of me," she thought. "I mustn't be gone long."

Intending to make a speedy inspection, Nancy quickened her steps along the corridor.

"This must be the secret tunnel the book mentioned!" she said to herself.

Soon Nancy came to a heavy walnut door, blocking the passageway. Her light revealed an iron bolt. As she slid it back and pushed the door open, she drew in her breath in sharp surprise. A strange green light on the floor of the room beyond illuminated the back of a ghostly figure standing just ahead of her!

Simultaneously, the flashlight was struck from her hand. It crashed on the floor and went out. The green light also faded away.

Fearful of a trap in the inky darkness, Nancy backed quickly into the corridor, slamming the heavy door and bolting it. Her heart pounding, she felt her way along the tunnel wall. Finally she stumbled up the stairway and through the exit behind the organ.

"Whew, that was a narrow escape!" she thought breathlessly. "I must find Dad and Ned."

Nancy hurried from room to room, upstairs and down, but did not see either of them. She was tempted to call out their names but then thought better of it. Very much concerned, Nancy decided that they must have left the house to investigate the grounds.

As she circled the mansion, the young detective tried to figure out under which room the secret tunnel had been built, and where it led. She noted that there was no outside exit from the cellar as most old houses had. Remembering the length of the musty underground corridor, she could very well believe that the exit was some distance from Blackwood Hall—perhaps in the woods.

When ten minutes or more had elapsed and neither Mr. Drew nor Ned had appeared, a harrowing thought began to disturb Nancy. Maybe the two of them were prisoners in the tunnel room! They might have found the outside entrance to the tunnel and been captured!

Frightened by this possibility, Nancy wondered what to do. Her first instinct was to go to the police. Then she realized that she could not drive the car to get help, because her father had the keys in his pocket. She finally decided that she would have to go back to the underground room at the end of the corridor alone and find out if her father and Ned were being held captive.

Forgetting any thought of safety for herself, she entered the house again. She ran to the organ room and squeezed through the opening to the secret door. There she closed her eyes for several seconds until they became accustomed to the darkness, then carefully she picked her way down the steps and along the passageway.

Reaching the heavy walnut door, she stooped down to look under the bottom for a light beyond. There was nothing but blackness.

Trying not to make any noise, Nancy slid the iron bolt and cautiously opened the door a crack. The place was dark. When nothing happened, Nancy decided to take a chance, and called out:

"Dad! Ned!"

There was no answer. Yet she thought possibly the two men might be lying gagged or unconscious not far away, and she could not see them. Without a light she had no way of finding out.

Nancy listened intently for several seconds, but heard only the sound of her own breathing.

"I'll have to get a light and come back here," she decided finally.

As Nancy was about to leave, she suddenly heard a scraping, creaking sound somewhere overhead.

"Maybe it's Dad or Ned!" Nancy thought excitedly.

Hopefully she hurried to the first floor. Seeing no one there, she climbed the front stairs to the second floor. As she reached the top step, Nancy froze to the spot.

At the far end of the hall, a wraithlike figure was just emerging from the far wall of the hallway!

CHAPTER XI

The Tunnel Room

NANCY uttered no sound. As she watched in the dim light, the ghost flitted noiselessly up a flight of stairs at the end of the hall which evidently led to the top floor.

Without thinking, Nancy started after it on tiptoe. Despite the heavy carpet, a floorboard groaned beneath her weight. Did she fancy that the filmy figure ahead hesitated a moment, then went on?

As she mounted the steps to the third floor Nancy heard another creaking sound. At the top she was just in time to see the white-draped figure again vanish into the wall!

The wall was solidly paneled with black walnut. Though Nancy searched carefully, running her fingers over every inch of the smooth wood panels, she could find no secret door or spring that might release a sliding partition. Returning to the second floor, she examined the panels there also, but without success.

Of one thing Nancy was convinced. The old house harbored more than one sinister character, how many she did not know. There was the figure at the organ, the one who had knocked her flashlight from her hand, the man who had scared Bess almost out of her wits, and now, the apparition she had followed up the stairs. Surely these could not all be one and the same "ghost."

"The one that went up the stairs was a live man or woman, I'm sure of that! But what was he up to?"

Knowing that a further investigation at this time would be worthless, Nancy started once more to look for her father and Ned.

After a futile search of the house and grounds, she decided:

"There's just a chance that they went back to the car and are waiting for me." She hurried down the road.

As she reached the place where the car had been parked, she halted in astonishment.

The automobile was gone!

Before she could examine the rutty road for tire prints, she heard the sound of hurrying footsteps. Whirling, she saw her father and Ned coming out of the woods.

"Nancy, thank heaven you're safe!" Ned exclaimed, hurrying to her side.

"But where's the car?" Nancy demanded.

"The car's been stolen!" Mr. Drew said grimly. "Ned and I heard voices outside and ran to investigate."

"Did you find out who it was?"

"No. But we caught a glimpse of a man streaking through the woods," Ned replied. "He was too far away for us to get a good look at him, and he gave us the slip."

"By the way, here's something I picked up near those wheelbarrow tracks that lead back through the woods," Mr. Drew remarked.

The lawyer handed Nancy a tubular piece of metal which appeared to have been taken from a collapsible rod such as magicians and fake mediums might use.

"Why, this piece is similar to the one I saw in the clearing the other day!" Nancy exclaimed.

"And look what I found on the kitchen stairway!" Ned exclaimed.

From his pocket he drew forth a miniature short-wave radio sending set.

"Does it work?" Mr. Drew asked eagerly.

"I'll see. Messages couldn't be sent very far with it, though."

"Could you tune it to send a message to the River Heights police station or a prowl car?"

Ned made some adjustments on the set, and began sending a request to the police asking that men be dispatched at once to Blackwood Hall. He gave the license number of the missing car and asked that it be rebroadcast over the police radio.

While they waited hopefully for action in response to Ned's call, Nancy related her adventures. She described the underground passageway, the strange appearance and disappearance of the "ghost," and the peculiar scraping sounds she had heard.

"If the police don't show up soon, we'll investigate the ghost room with my flashlight," Mr. Drew declared.

"Look!" Nancy cried out. "There's a car coming up the road."

The three quickly stepped behind some bushes and waited to see if they could identify the occupants of the approaching automobile before revealing their presence. To their relief, it was a State Police car.

"My message must have been relayed to them!" Ned exclaimed. "Swell!"

Two officers alighted, and the trio moved out of hiding to introduce themselves. Upon hearing the full details of what had happened, the troopers offered to make a thorough inspection of Blackwood Hall.

Nancy, Mr. Drew, and Ned accompanied them back to the mansion.

The police looked in every room but found no trace of its recent tenants. When they tackled the secret tunnel, Nancy stayed close behind, eager for a glimpse beyond the walnut door. It proved to be a tiny, empty room with no sign of a mysterious green light, a ghost or a human being. Furthermore, the room had no other exit.

"Is this little room under the house? Or is it located somewhere under the grounds?" Nancy asked one of the officers.

After making various measurements the men announced that it was located under the house, almost beneath the stairwell. It was not connected with the cellar, and no one could hazard a guess as to its original purpose.

"You may have thought you saw a ghost, but don't tell me anyone can get through a locked door," one officer chided the girl.

"I actually did see a figure in white," Nancy insisted quietly. "Something or someone knocked the flashlight from my hand. See, it's over there by the door."

In all fairness, Nancy could not blame the troopers for being a trifle skeptical. She almost began to doubt that she had ever had a frightening adventure in this spot.

Observing Nancy's crestfallen air, Mr. Drew said to the troopers, "Obviously this old house has been used by an unscrupulous gang. When they discovered we were here to check up on them, they moved out their belongings—my car as well."

"Stealing a car is a serious business," one officer commented. "We'll catch the thief, and when we do, we'll find out what has been going on in the old Humphrey house. Meanwhile, we'll have one of our men keep a close watch on this neck of the woods."

"No use sticking around here now," the other trooper added. "Whoever pulled the job has skipped."

"I'm going to keep working on this case until all the pieces in the puzzle can be made to fit together—even the ghosts!" Nancy told her father.

"Here's a bit of evidence," said the lawyer, taking the piece of telescopic rod from his pocket.

One trooper recognized it at once as magicians' or fake mediums' equipment, and asked for it to hand in with his report. Ned turned over the pocket radio sending set which had proved so valuable in bringing the police.

Though the license number of Mr. Drew's car had been broadcast over the police radio, there was no trace of it that night. The following afternoon Mr. Drew was notified that the car had been found abandoned in an adjacent state.

Accompanied by Nancy in her convertible, the lawyer traveled to Lake Jasper just across the state line. His automobile, found on a deserted road, had been towed to a local garage. Nothing had been damaged.

"Some people have no regard for other folks' property," the attendant remarked. "Probably a bunch o' kids helped themselves to your car to go joy riding."

But Nancy and her father were convinced that the car had not been "borrowed" by any joy riders. It had been used by a gangster to transport some unknown objects from Blackwood Hall!

What were the objects, and where had they been taken? Here was one more question to which Nancy must find the answer.

Nancy and her father had just returned home when Bess Marvin came bursting in. "Lola White has been talking wildly about you in her sleep!" Bess said ominously.

"What's so serious about that?" Nancy inquired.

"Lola's mother says she raves about a spirit warning her to have nothing more to do with Nancy Drew! If Lola does, the spirit will bring serious trouble to both of you!"

CHAPTER XII

Nancy's Plan

"Lola believes that a spirit has warned her to have nothing more to do with me, or we'll both be harmed!" Nancy exclaimed.

"That's what she said," Bess answered. "I knew it would worry you."

Her face serious, Nancy started for the telephone. Bess ran after her.

"Are you going to call Mrs. White or Lola," she asked.

"No, I'll go to see them. But first I'm going to call Mrs. Putney." As Nancy looked for the telephone number in the directory, she added, "Members of a sinister ring of racketeers, posing as mediums are convinced that I'm on their trail. To protect themselves, they're having the so-called spirits warn their clients against me!"

"Do you think Mrs. Putney has been warned against you too?" Bess asked.

"We'll soon know." Nancy dialed the widow's number.

"Oh, Mrs. Putney, this is Nancy," the girl began. "I—"

A sharp click told her that Mrs. Putney had hung up. Nancy dialed again. Though the bell rang repeatedly at the other end of the line, there was no response.

"It's no use," she said at last, turning to Bess. "She refuses to talk to me. She must have been warned and is taking the warning seriously."

"What'll you do?"

"Let's go to her home," Nancy proposed. "This matter must be cleared up right away."

As the two girls arrived at the widow's home, they saw her picking flowers in the garden. But when she caught sight of the car, she turned and walked hastily indoors.

The girls went up the porch steps. They knocked and rang the doorbell. Finally they were forced to acknowledge that the woman had no intention of seeing them. Nancy was rather disturbed as she and Bess returned to the car.

"I'm afraid those swindlers have outsmarted us," she commented. "But not for long, I hope!"

She drove at once to the White home. Lola herself opened the door, but upon seeing Nancy, she backed away fearfully.

"You can't come in!" she said in a hoarse voice. "I never want to see you again."

"Lola, someone has poisoned you against me."

"The spirits have told me the truth about you, that's all. You're—you're an enemy of all of us."

Mrs. White, hearing the wild accusation, came to the door.

"Lola, what are you saying?" she said sternly. "Why haven't you invited our friends in?"

"Your friends—not mine!" the girl cried hysterically. "If you insist upon having them here, I'll leave!"

"Lola! How can you be so rude?"

Nancy was sorry to see Mrs. White berate her daughter for an attitude she felt was not entirely the girl's fault.

"I'll leave at once," Nancy said. "It's better that way."

"Indeed you must not," Mrs. White insisted.

"I think perhaps Lola has reached the point where she can work out her own affairs," Nancy said, but with a meaningful glance at Mrs. White, which the latter understood at once.

Nancy and Bess drove away, but pulled up just around the corner.

"I intend to keep watch on Lola," Nancy explained. "She may decide to act upon the suggestion that she straighten out her affairs herself."

"What do you think she'll do?" Bess asked.

"I'm not sure. But if she leaves the house, I'll trail her."

It became unpleasantly warm in the car, and Bess soon grew tired of waiting. Recalling that she had some errands to do, she presently decided to leave her friend.

Time dragged slowly for Nancy, who began to grow weary of the long vigil. Just as she was about to give up, she saw Lola come out of the house and hurry down the street.

Nancy waited until the girl was nearly out of sight before following slowly in the automobile. At the post office Nancy parked her car and followed Lola into the building where she watched her mail a letter.

"I'll bet she's written to those racketeers!" Nancy speculated.

Cruising along at a safe distance behind Lola, Nancy saw her board a bus, and followed it to the end of the line. There Lola waited a few minutes, then hopped an inbound bus, and returned home without having met anyone.

"Either she had an appointment with someone who didn't show up, or else she simply took the ride to think out her problems," Nancy decided.

Of one thing she was fairly certain. The old tree in the woods was no longer being used as a post office. Instead, the racketeers were instructing their clients to use the regular mails.

On a sudden impulse Nancy drove her car back to the post office to make a few inquiries. The clerk might remember a striking blonde like Lola. As she was approaching the General Delivery window, she saw a familiar figure speaking to the clerk. It was the woman that she and the girls had seen on the plane and who had followed them in New Orleans!

Darting behind a convenient pillar, Nancy heard the woman asking whether there were any letters for Mrs. Frank Immer.

The clerk left the window and soon returned shaking his head. The woman thanked him, then left the building. When Nancy was sure the coast was clear she followed. Starting her car, Nancy kept a safe distance behind the woman. A few minutes later she saw her quarry disappear into the Claymore Hotel.

Nancy drove around the hotel once or twice, looking for a place to park. It was some time later that she approached the hotel clerk's desk. Examination of the register revealed no guest by the name of Mrs. Frank Immer, nor had anyone signed in from Louisiana.

"But I saw Mrs. Immer enter here," insisted Nancy. "She wore a large black hat and a blue dress."

The clerk turned to the cashier and asked if he had seen anyone answering the description.

"Maybe you mean Mrs. Frank Egan," the cashier volunteered. "She just checked out."

"How long ago?"

"About ten minutes."

The cashier could not tell Nancy where the woman had gone, for she had left no forwarding address. From a bellhop she learned that Mrs. Egan had directed a taxi to take her to the airport.

"She said something about going to Chicago," the boy recalled.

"Thanks." Nancy smiled.

Determined that Mrs. Egan should not leave the city without at least answering a few questions, Nancy sped to the airport. To her bitter disappointment, as Nancy pulled up, a big airliner took off gracefully from the runway.

"Mrs. Egan probably is aboard!" she groaned.

Nancy checked and confirmed that a woman answering the description had bought a ticket for Chicago, in the name of Mrs. Floyd Pepper.

"My one chance now of having her questioned or trailed is to wire the Chicago police!" Nancy decided. "I'll ask Dad to make the request."

She telephoned to explain matters, and Mr. Drew agreed to send a telegram at once.

Nancy, having done all she could in the matter, returned to the Claymore Hotel with a new plan in mind. She asked for some stationery with the

Claymore letterhead. When she arrived home her father was there.

"Dad, I want to find out if Mrs. Egan has any part in the séances, the stock deals, or the money that used to be put in the walnut tree," said Nancy. "Will you tell me honestly what you think of this plan? I'm going to type notes to Mrs. Putney, Lola White, and Sadie Green."

"Using Mrs. Egan's name?"

"That's the idea. If it doesn't work, then I'll try the name of Immer later. I won't try imitating Mrs. Egan's signature in the hotel register. I'll just type the name."

"But what can you say without giving yourself away?" asked Mr. Drew.

"I'll write that my plans have been changed suddenly," Nancy said. "I'll request them to send all communications to Mrs. Hilda Egan at the Claymore Hotel."

"When she isn't there? And why Hilda? Isn't the name Mrs. Frank Egan?"

"That's how I'll know the answers belong to *me*. I doubt if her clients know her first name, anyway."

Mr. Drew chuckled. "Anyone could tell that you have legal blood in your veins," he said. "But aren't you forgetting one little detail?"

"What's that?" Nancy asked in surprise.

"If Mrs. Putney, Sadie, Lola, or any of the others have ever had any correspondence with Mrs.

Egan, they'll be suspicious of the letters. They may question a typed name instead of one written in her own hand."

"How would it be," said Nancy, "if in the corner of the envelope, I draw the insigne of the Three Branch Ranch!"

"Well, here's hoping," said Mr. Drew a trifle dubiously.

Later that day Nancy wrote the letters, then rushed over to the Claymore and persuaded the hotel clerk, who knew her to be an amateur detective, to agree to turn over to her any replies which might come addressed to Mrs. Hilda Egan.

"Since you say these letters will be in answer to letters you yourself have written, I'll do it," he agreed.

All the next day Nancy waited impatiently for word from the Chicago police in reply to her father's telegram. None came, nor did she receive a call from the clerk at the Claymore Hotel.

"Maybe my idea wasn't so good after all," she thought.

But on the second day, the telephone rang. Nancy's pulse hammered as she recognized the voice of the Claymore Hotel clerk.

"Nancy Drew?"

"Yes. Have you any mail for me?"

"A letter you may want to pick up is here," he said hurriedly.

CHAPTER XIII

Complications

THE letter awaiting Nancy at the Claymore Hotel proved to be from Sadie Green, the girl who worked at the Lovelee Cosmetic Company.

In the communication, which the girl never dreamed would be read by anyone except Mrs. Egan, she revealed she had received a bonus and would gladly donate it to the poor orphans cared for at the Three Branch Home.

". . . In accordance with messages from their deceased parents," the letter ended.

"So that's what they are up to!" Nancy thought grimly. "There's no greater appeal than that of poor, starving orphans! The very idea of trying to rob hard-working girls with such hocus-pocus!"

As soon as Nancy returned home, she promptly typed a reply on the hotel stationery warning Sadie that since certain unscrupulous persons were endeavoring to turn a legitimate charity into a racket, she was to pay no attention to any written or telephoned messages, unless they came from Mrs. Egan herself at the Claymore Hotel.

Nancy's next move was made only after she had again consulted her father. At first he was a little reluctant to consent to the daring plan she proposed, but when she outlined its possibilities, he agreed to help her.

"Write down the address of this shop in Winchester," he said, scribbling it on a paper. "Unless I'm mistaken, you can buy everything you need there."

As a result of Nancy's talk with her father and also with Ned Nickerson, another letter went forward to Sadie Green. The note merely said that the girl would be required to attend an important séance the following night. She was instructed to wait for a car at Cross and Lexington streets.

At the appointed hour, Nancy, heavily veiled, rode beside her father in the front seat of a car borrowed from a friend. In order not to be recognized, Mr. Drew had a felt hat pulled low over his eyes.

"Dad, you look like a second-story man!" Nancy teased him as they parked at the intersection. "Do you think Sadie will show up?"

"I see a blond girl coming now," he replied.

Nancy turned her head slightly and recognized Sadie. Making a slow gesture with her gloved hand, she motioned the girl into the back seat. Mr. Drew promptly pulled away from the curb.

The automobile took a direct route to the vicinity of Blackwood Hall. Nancy covertly watched Sadie from beneath her veil. The girl was very nervous and kept twisting her handkerchief as they approached. But when they got out and started walking, she gave no sign that the area was familiar.

Ned Nickerson had followed in another borrowed automobile which he concealed in a clump of bushes. Then he removed a small suitcase from the trunk, and started off through the woods.

Meanwhile, Nancy and Sadie, with Mr. Drew a little distance behind, approached Blackwood Hall.

"I hope everything goes through as planned," Nancy thought with a twinge of uneasiness. "If Ned is late getting here—"

Just then she saw a faint, greenish light glowing weirdly through the trees directly ahead. At the same moment came a strange, husky chant.

Nancy stepped to one side so that Sadie might precede her on the path. The girl gazed at the green point of light as one hypnotized.

"The spirit speaks!" Nancy intoned.

Simultaneously a luminous hand seemed to appear out of nowhere. It floated, unattached, and reached out as if to touch Sadie.

"My child," intoned an old man's cracked voice, "I am your beloved grandfather on your dear mother's side."

"Not Elias Perkins!" Sadie murmured in awe.

"The spirit of none other, my child. Sadie, I have been watching you and I am worried—most sorely worried. You must give no more money to the Three Branch Ranch or to any cause which my spirit cannot recommend."

"But, Grandfather—"

"Furthermore," continued the cracked voice, taking no note of the interruption, "follow no orders or directions from anyone, unless that person writes or speaks his name backward. Mind this well, Sadie, my child, for it is important."

The voice gradually drifted away as the green light began to grow dim. Soon there was only darkness and deep silence in the woods.

"Oh, Grandfather! Come back! Speak to me again!" Sadie pleaded.

"The séance is concluded," Nancy murmured.

She took Sadie by the arm and led her back to the waiting car. All the way home Sadie remained silent. Only once did she speak and that was to ask "the veiled lady" the meaning of the strange instructions issued by her grandfather.

Nancy spoke slowly and in a low monotone, "You are to reveal no information to anyone and take no orders from anyone unless he spells or speaks his or her name backward."

"I don't understand," Sadie said.

"There are unscrupulous people who seek to

take advantage of you. Your grandfather's spirit is trying to protect you. He has given you a means of identifying the good and the evil. You have been in communication with a Mrs. Egan, have you not?"

The blond girl nodded. And Nancy continued, "Should Mrs. Egan approach you again, saying 'I am Mrs. Egan,' then beware! But should she say 'I am Mrs. Nage,' then you will know that she is to be trusted, even as you trust the spirit of Elias Perkins."

"Oh! I see now what Grandfather meant," Sadie said, and became silent again.

At Cross and Lexington streets, the girl left the car. Nancy and her father drove on home, to find Ned awaiting them.

"How did I do?" the youth demanded in the cracked voice of Elias Perkins as they entered the house together.

Nancy chuckled. "A perfect performance!"

"You don't know the half of it," Ned joked. "I almost messed up the whole show."

As the three enjoyed milk and sandwiches in the Drew kitchen, the young man revealed that he had nearly lost the hand from the end of the rod.

"Next time you want me to perform, buy a better grade of equipment!" He laughed, biting into another ham sandwich.

Ned was referring to the props used during the séance, which Nancy had purchased earlier that day at a store in Winchester. These included a telescopic reaching rod, and the luminous wax hand, as well as a bottle of phosphorus and olive oil, guaranteed to produce a ghostly effect when the cork was removed, which would disappear again at the required moment when it was stoppered.

"When I took the bottle from the suitcase, I nearly dropped it," Ned confessed. "And what's a séance in the dark worth without a spooky light?" he added, laughing.

On the following day, Nancy called at Sadie's home. Sadie was at work, but elderly Mr. Green, eager for companionship, told Nancy everything she wished to know.

"That granddaughter o' mine ain't so foolish as I was afeared," he said promptly. "This morning she says to me 'Grandpa, I've made up my mind to save my money and not give it away to every Tom, Dick, and Harry who asks me for it.' What do you think o' that?"

"Splendid!" Nancy approved. "I hoped Sadie would have a change of heart."

To test Sadie further, Nancy asked Ned the next day to telephone the girl at the Lovelee Cosmetic Company.

"I want to prove a couple of things," she said.

"First of all, I want to find out whether Sadie is really following my instructions, and second, if she knows the name of Howard Brex."

Ned began to laugh. "How would you pronounce Brex backward?"

Nancy smiled too. "Guess you'll have to use his first name. 'Drawoh' is easy."

While Nancy listened on an extension at the Drew home, Ned made the call. He addressed the girl as Eidas instead of Sadie and added, "This is Drawoh speaking."

"My name ain't Eidas, and I don't know what you're talking about," the girl retorted, failing to understand.

Ned quickly asked her to think hard. Suddenly Sadie said:

"Oh, yes, I remember. And what did you say your name is?"

"Drawoh."

After a moment's reflection, the girl said, "I guess I don't know you."

"No," said Ned. "But tell me, have you had any recent communications asking you for money?"

"One came today, but I threw it away," Sadie replied. "I'm not giving any more of my money to those folks. I have to go now."

Sadie hung up.

"Good work, Nancy!" Ned declared as he rejoined her. "Apparently that trick séance brought Sadie to her senses."

"For a few days, anyhow," Nancy agreed. "The job isn't over, though, until these swindlers are behind bars! They still have great influence over Lola and Mrs. Putney and goodness knows how many other people.

"I can easily understand how a person like Sadie would be so gullible, but it's almost unthinkable that Mrs. Putney would fall for that stuff," Ned said.

While the two friends were talking, Hannah Gruen called Nancy to the telephone. The message was from the clerk at the Claymore Hotel. The late-morning mail had brought two more letters addressed to Mrs. Egan.

"Isn't that wonderful, Ned?" Nancy cried. "I'll have to go over to the hotel right away."

"I'll take you there," Ned offered.

He drove Nancy to the hotel and waited in the car while she went inside. The girl was gone several minutes. When she returned, her face was downcast, and she looked very disturbed.

"What's the matter?" Ned demanded. "Didn't you get the letters?"

Nancy shook her head. "The regular clerk went to lunch," she explained. "In his absence, another clerk gave the letters to someone else!"

CHAPTER XIV

The Cabin in the Woods

"A YOUNG woman picked up the letters," Nancy told Ned. "Mrs. Egan must have discovered our scheme and sent a messenger. She was lucky enough, or else she planned it that way, to have the letters called for when my friend was off duty."

"Maybe Mrs. Egan's back in town," Ned suggested.

"Yes, that's possible. The police were never able to trace her. According to word Dad received, she left the plane at one of the stops between here and Chicago."

Ned whistled softly. "Wow! If she's back here, she'll be in your hair, Nancy!"

"She hasn't registered at the Claymore. I found that out. But that doesn't prove she isn't in River Heights. Ned, something's got to break in this case soon. We know that there are several people in the racket and it may be that Brex is the mastermind behind everything. Blackwood Hall evidently had been used as headquarters until we got too interested for their comfort. All of the supernatural hocus-pocus was used not only to fleece gullible victims, but also to scare us off the scent. I feel that there will be a showdown within the next few days."

"Well, I want to be there when that happens, Nancy," said Ned.

Later that day, Nancy called George and Bess and asked them to go with her to Blackwood Hall. The drive to the river road was uneventful. They parked their car some distance away and all three trekked through the walnut woods in the direction of the historic mansion.

"But, Nancy, what *do* you expect to find this time?" asked Bess.

"I realized when I was reviewing the case with Ned today that we never had checked those wheelbarrow tracks from Blackwood Hall. They may lead us to the spot where the gang is now making its headquarters."

The old house looked completely abandoned as the girls approached.

Suddenly George cried, "The wheelbarrow tracks lead away from the house and right into the woods."

For some distance the girls tramped on, stopping now and then to examine footprints where the ground was soft. Suddenly, in the flickering sunlight ahead, they caught sight of a cabin in a clearing among the trees. Approaching cautiously they noted that all the windows were covered with black cloths on the inside. The wheelbarrow tracks led to what obviously was the back door.

"That must be the place!" Nancy whispered excitedly. "See! A road leads right up to the front door just as Mrs. Putney told me!"

Bess began to back away, tugging at George's sleeve. "Let the troopers find out!" she pleaded.

Nancy and George moved stealthily forward without her. After circling and seeing no signs of life around the place, George boldly knocked several times on the front door.

"Deserted," she observed. "We may as well leave."

Nancy gazed curiously at the curving road which led from the cabin. Only a short stretch was visible before it lost itself in the walnut woods.

"Let's follow the road," she proposed. "I'm curious to learn where it comes out."

Bess, however, would have no part of the plan. She pointed out that already they were over a mile from Nancy's car.

"And if we don't get back soon, it may be stolen, just as your father's was," she added.

This remark persuaded Nancy reluctantly to give up her plan. The girls trudged back through the woods to the other road. The car was where they had left it.

"I have an idea!" Nancy declared as they started off. "Why don't we try to drive to the cabin?"

Nancy was convinced that by following the main road they might come to a side lane which would lead them to the cabin. Accordingly, they drove along the. designated highway, carefully scrutinizing the sides for any private road whose entrance might have been camouflaged.

"I see a side road!" Bess suddenly cried out.

Nancy, who had noticed the narrow dirt road at the same instant, turned into it.

"Wait!" George directed. "Another one branches off just a few yards ahead on the highway we were following. That may be the one instead of this."

Uncertain, Nancy stopped the car and idled the engine. Before the girls could decide which road to follow, an automobile sped past on the highway they had left only a moment before. Nancy and the others caught a fleeting glimpse of a heavily veiled woman at the wheel. On the rear seat they thought they saw a reclining figure.

The car turned into the next narrow road, and then disappeared.

"Was that Mrs. Putney on the back seat?" George asked, highly excited.

"I didn't get a good enough look to be sure," Nancy replied. "I got the car license number, though. Let me write it down before I forget."

"Hurry!" George urged as Nancy wrote the

numbers on a pad from her purse. "We have to follow that car!"

"But not too close," Nancy replied. "We'd make them suspicious."

The girls waited three minutes before backing out into the main highway and then turning into the adjacent road. Though the automobile ahead had disappeared, tire prints were plainly visible.

The road twisted through a stretch of woodland. When finally the tire prints turned off into a heavily wooded narrow lane, Nancy was sure they were not far from the cabin. She parked among some trees and they went forward on foot.

"There it is!" whispered Nancy, recognizing the chimney. "Bess, I want you to take my car, drive to River Heights, and look up the name of the owner of the car we just saw. Here's the license number.

"After you've been to the Motor Vehicle Bureau, please phone Mrs. Putney's house. If she answers, we'll know it wasn't she we saw in the car. Then get hold of Dad or Ned, and bring one of them here as fast as you can. We may need help. Got it straight?"

"I—I—g-guess so," Bess answered.

"Hurry back! No telling what may happen while you're away."

The two watched as Nancy's car rounded a bend and was lost to view.

Then Nancy and George walked swiftly through the woods toward the cabin. Approaching the building, Nancy and George were amazed to find that no car was parked on the road in front.

"How do you figure it?" George whispered as the girls crouched behind bushes. "We certainly saw tire marks leading into this road!"

"Yes, but the car that passed may have gone on without stopping. Possibly the driver saw us and changed her plans. Wait here, and watch the cabin while I check the tire marks out at the end of the road."

"All right. But hurry. If anything breaks here, I don't want to be alone."

From the bushes George saw Nancy hurry down the road and out of sight around a bend.

For some time everything was quiet. Suddenly George's attention was drawn to a wisp of smoke from the wide stone chimney.

"There's someone in there, that's sure," she concluded. "Somebody's lighted a fire."

Overpowering curiosity urged George to find out what was going on inside the cabin. She could see nothing through the black-draped windows. Trying to decide whether to wait for Nancy or to make some move of her own, she noticed smoke seeping through the cracks around the door!

"The place must be on fire!" George exclaimed. When still no sound came from inside, she could stand the strain no longer. "I'm going to break in!" she decided.

She flung herself against the locked door, but it scarcely budged. Looking about, she found a rock the size of a baseball. She let it fly at the window nearest the door. The glass splintered and the stone carried with it the black curtain that had covered the window. With a stick she poked out the jagged bits of glass that still clung to the pane. When the smoke had cleared, George stuck her head through the opening.

The one-room interior was deserted, and *there was no fire,* not even in the big stone fireplace! A few wisps of smoke remained. But it did not smell like wood smoke.

"I didn't dream up that smoke," George thought, growing more uneasy all the time. "But the door was locked and I saw no one leave."

Time dragged on, and still Nancy did not return. Finally, after an hour had elapsed, George, alarmed, tramped back to the road where they had taken leave of Bess.

She was about to start for River Heights on foot when the convertible came into view around a bend. Bess pulled alongside.

"Do you know anything about Nancy?" George asked quickly.

"Why, no."

Her cousin related the strange story of the

George hurled a rock at the window

cabin and Nancy's disappearance. Bess, too, was greatly concerned.

"And I didn't bring anyone along, either," she wailed. "Mr. Drew was called out of town unexpectedly, and I couldn't find Ned."

"Just when we need them so desperately! Did you find the car owner's name?"

"Yes, it belongs to Mrs. Putney! But what are we going to do about Nancy?"

"I think Mr. Drew should be notified if we can possibly get word to him. Hannah may know where to reach him by telephone," said George.

The girls made a hurried trip to the Drew home. The housekeeper told them that the lawyer had departed in great haste and was to send word later where he could be reached.

"I really don't know what to do," Hannah Gruen said anxiously. "The Claymore Hotel has been trying to get in touch with Nancy, too. The chief clerk there wants to see her right away. We'd better notify the police. I dislike doing it, though, until we've tried everything else."

No one had paid the slightest attention to Togo, who was lying on his own special rug in the living room. Now, as if understanding the housekeeper's remark, he began to whine.

"What's the matter, old boy?" George asked, stooping to pat the dog. "Are you trying to tell us something about Nancy?"

Togo gave two sharp yips.

"Say! Do you suppose Togo could pick up Nancy's trail and lead us to her?" George asked.

"When she's around the neighborhood, he finds her in a flash," Hannah Gruen said. "Nancy can scarcely go a block without his running after her, if he can get loose."

"Then why don't we give him a chance now?" Bess urged. "Maybe if you get something of Nancy's, a shoe, perhaps, he might pick up the scent—"

"It's worth trying," the housekeeper said, starting for the stairway.

She returned in a few moments with one of Nancy's tennis shoes, and announced she was going along on the search. Taking the eager Togo with them, the group drove back to the spot where Nancy was going to investigate the tire marks. George dropped the shoe in the dust.

"Go find Nancy, Togo!" Bess urged. "Find her!"

Togo whined and sniffed at the shoe. Then, picking it up in his teeth, he ran down the road.

"Oh, he thinks we are playing a game," Mrs. Gruen said in disappointment. "This isn't going to work."

"No, Togo knows what he is doing," George insisted, for in a moment he was back.

Dropping the shoe, the dog began to sniff the

ground excitedly. Then he trotted across the road and into the woods, the others following. Reaching a big walnut tree, he circled it and began to bark.

"But Nancy isn't here!" quavered Bess.

Suddenly the little dog struck off for some underbrush and began barking excitedly.

CHAPTER XV

Two Disappearances

"Togo's found something!" Bess exclaimed, following George, who was parting the bushes that separated them from the dog.

George uttered a startled exclamation as she came upon Nancy stretched out on the ground only a few feet away. Togo was licking his mistress's face as if begging her to regain consciousness.

Just as Hannah Gruen reached the spot, Nancy stirred and sat up. Seeing her dog, she reached over in a dazed sort of way to pat him.

"Hello, Togo," she mumbled. "Who— *How* did you get here? Where am I?" Then, seeing her friends, she smiled wanly.

Observing that she had no serious injuries, they pressed her for an explanation.

"I don't know what happened," Nancy admitted.

On the ground near the spot where the cabin road crossed another dirt road, she had found the familiar Three Branch insigne.

This time, a tiny arrow had been added. Without stopping to summon George, Nancy had hurried along the trail until she came upon another arrow.

A series of arrows had led her deeper into the woods. Finally she had come to a walnut tree nearly as large as the famous Humphrey Walnut.

The tree had a small hollow space in its trunk. It contained no message, however. She had been about to turn back when a piece of paper on the ground had caught her eye. Examination had revealed that it was a half sheet torn from a catalog.

"It matched that scrap of paper I found in the clearing near the Humphrey Walnut," Nancy said.

Obviously the sheet had been ripped from the catalog of a supply house for magicians' equipment. One advertisement offered spirit smoke for sale.

While Nancy had been reading, she had heard footsteps and looked up. Through the woods, some distance up the path, she had seen a young woman approaching. Hastily Nancy stepped back, intending to hide behind the walnut tree.

At that moment something had struck her from behind.

"That's the last I remember," she added ruefully.

"Who would do such a wicked thing?" Mrs. Gruen demanded in horror.

"It's easy to guess," Nancy replied. "The tree must be another place where the members of the gang collect money from their victims. I probably had the bad luck to arrive here at the moment a client was expected.

"You mean the same fellow who had the reaching rod hit you to get you out of the way?" Bess asked. "Oh," she added nervously, "he still may be around!"

"I doubt it," Nancy said. "He probably took the money that girl left, and ran."

"I'm going to inform the police!" Hannah Gruen announced in a determined voice.

Nancy tried to dissuade her, but for once her arguments had no effect. On the way home with the girls, Mrs. Gruen herself stopped at the office of the State Police. She revealed all she knew of the attack upon Nancy.

As a result, troopers searched the woods thoroughly; but, exactly as Nancy had foreseen, not a trace was found of her assailant. However, when they searched the interior of the cabin, they found evidence pointing to the fact that its recent residents were interested in magic.

When they reached home, Mrs. Gruen told Nancy about the telephone call from a clerk at the

Claymore Hotel. She went to see him at once, and was given a letter addressed to Mrs. Egan. It was signed by Mrs. Putney!

The note merely said that the services of Mrs. Egan would no longer be required. The spirit of Mrs. Putney's departed husband was again making visitations to his former home to advise her.

Taking the letter with her, Nancy mulled over the matter for some time.

The next morning, she decided to pay Mrs. Putney a visit, hoping she would be able to see her this time. But Mrs. Putney was not there, and a neighbor in the next house told Nancy she had been gone all morning.

"Doesn't Mrs. Putney ever drive her car?" Nancy asked, seeing it through a garage window.

"Not since her husband died."

"Does she have someone else drive her?"

"Oh, no! She won't let a soul touch the car."

Nancy was puzzled. Someone must have taken the car without Mrs. Putney's permission.

"If that woman we saw in the back seat was Mrs. Putney, maybe she didn't know where she was or what she was doing, any more than poor Lola did when she walked into the river!" Nancy told herself.

Nancy thanked the woman and withdrew. She hurried back to the garage to look for evidence that the car had been used recently. Fortunately the door was not locked. She examined the car carefully. It was covered with a film of dust and the rear axle was mounted on jacks. It had obviously not been driven for some time.

Something else struck Nancy as peculiar. The license plate bore a number that was different from the one registered as Mrs. Putney's.

"Hers must have been stolen and someone else's plate put on her car!" the young detective thought excitedly. "Maybe this number belongs to one of the racketeers and he used Mrs. Putney's to keep people from tracing him!"

Nancy dashed off in her convertible to the Motor Vehicle Bureau office. There she learned that the license on the widow's car had been issued to a Jack Sampson in Winchester, fifty miles from River Heights. But this revelation was mild in comparison with what the clerk told her next.

"Jack Sampson died a few months ago. His car was kept in a public garage. The executor of the estate reported that the license plate had been stolen."

As soon as Nancy recovered from her astonishment, she thanked the clerk for the information. Telephone calls to Winchester brought out the fact that the deceased man's reputation had been above reproach. He could not have been one of the racketeers. Nancy decided that before telling the police where the stolen license plates could be found, she would give Mrs. Putney a chance to tell what she knew about it all.

Hurrying back, she was just in time to see the widow coming up the street with several packages. Nancy hastened to her side and offered to take them. Although Mrs. Putney allowed her to carry them, she did not invite Nancy into the house. Therefore, Nancy told her story of the license plate as they stood on the front porch.

"I wasn't in that car you saw, and you must be mistaken about the license plate," Mrs. Putney told her flatly.

"Come, I'll show you," Nancy urged, leading the way to the garage and opening the door. "Why—why—" she gasped in utter bewilderment.

The correct license number was back on the car!

"You see why I have come to doubt your ability to help me," Mrs. Putney said coldly. "I no longer need your assistance, Nancy. As a matter of fact, I have every expectation of getting my stolen jewelry back very soon. My husband's spirit has been visiting me right here at home as he used to do, and he assures me that everything will turn out satisfactorily."

Leaving Nancy distressed and more concerned than ever, Mrs. Putney walked into the house without even saying good-by. As Nancy started away, she decided that further protection for the widow would have to come from the police.

Next, she drove to police headquarters to see her old friend Captain McGinnis. Nancy explained that she knew someone had appropriated the Putney license plate, and probably would do so again.

"Mrs. Putney has told me some things that make me think someone prowls around there late at night or early in the morning," Nancy told him. "I'm afraid she may be in danger."

Nancy kept to herself the idea that a member of the ring of fake mediums might be playing the role of Mr. Putney's spirit. She had noticed that two windows of Mrs. Putney's bedroom opened onto the roof of a porch. It would be very easy for an agile man to climb up there and perform as the late Mr. Putney.

The officer agreed to keep men on duty to watch the house night and day. Nancy was so hopeful of rapid developments, now, that every time the telephone rang, she was sure it was word that the police had caught one or more of the gang.

But when she had received no word for a whole day, she went to see Captain McGinnis. He told her that plainclothesmen had kept faithful watch of the Putney home, but reported that no one had been found trying to break in; in fact, Captain

McGinnis said he was thinking of taking the detectives off the case because the house was now unoccupied.

"You mean Mrs. Putney has gone away?" Nancy asked incredulously.

"Yes, just this morning," the officer replied. "Bag and baggage. Probably gone on a vacation."

Nancy was amazed to hear this, and also chagrined. She had not expected such a turn of events!

"I'm certain Mrs. Putney isn't on vacation," Nancy told herself grimly. "It's more likely that she received a spirit message advising her to leave.

Recalling the widow's mention of getting back the stolen jewelry, Nancy surmised that Mrs. Putney might have gone off on some ill-advised errand to recover it. Thoroughly discouraged, Nancy had yet another disappointment to face. Scarcely had she reached home, when an urgent telephone call came from Mrs. White.

"Oh, Nancy! The very worst has happened!" the woman revealed tearfully. "Lola's gone!"

"Gone? Where, Mrs. White?"

"I don't know," Lola's mother wailed. "She left a note saying she was leaving home. Oh, Nancy, you must help me find her!"

CHAPTER XVI

A Well-Baited Trap

WORRIED over the news about Lola, Nancy went without delay to see Mrs. White. She learned that the girl had departed very suddenly. Mrs. White was convinced her daughter had been kidnapped or had met with foul play.

"Have no fear on that score," Nancy said reassuringly. She told Mrs. White of her idea that a group of clever thieves might be mesmerizing or threatening their victims in order to get their money. "They're too interested in Lola's earnings to let anything happen to her," she finished.

After telling Mrs. White she was sure her daughter would realize her mistake and return home, Nancy left. She decided to walk in the park and thrash matters out in her own mind. Presently she seated herself on a bench and absently watched two swans in a nearby pond.

She scarcely noticed when a thin woman in

black sat down beside her. But when the stranger took out a handkerchief and wiped away tears, Nancy suddenly became attentive.

"Are you troubled?" she inquired kindly.

"Yes," the woman answered. Eager to confide in someone, she began to pour out her story.

"It's my daughter." The stranger sighed. "She's causing me so much worry. Nellie works and makes good money, but lately all she does is complain she hasn't a penny. She must be frittering it away on worthless amusements."

Nancy listened attentively, made a few queries, and then suggested to the woman that she ask her daughter if she made a practice of leaving money in a certain black walnut tree.

"In a walnut tree!" exclaimed the woman.

"Also, find out if she sends money through the mail, and if so, to whom," Nancy instructed. "Ask her if she ever visits a medium or is helping support orphans at a place called Three Branch Home. Find out if you can whether or not spirits mysteriously appear to her at night."

"My goodness!" the woman cried in amazement. "You must be a policewoman!"

Nancy scribbled her father's unlisted telephone number on a scrap of paper and gave it to the stranger. "If you need help or have any information, call me here at once," she added.

The woman pocketed the telephone number

and quickly rose from the bench. "Thank you, miss. Thank you kindly," she murmured.

Only after the stranger had disappeared, did it occur to Nancy that she might have been unwise in offering advice so freely.

Definitely annoyed at herself, Nancy returned home, where she found a telegram from her father. It said that private detectives working for him in Chicago had traced some of Mrs. Putney's stolen jewelry to a pawnshop there. But the ring belonging to her husband and her pearl necklace were still missing.

Her father's mention of the Putney jewels caused Nancy to wonder anxiously what had become of the widow and of Lola White. Could there be any connection in their simultaneous disappearance? A panicky thought struck the young detective. Perhaps they were being held prisoners at some hideout of the racketeers.

Almost at once Nancy put this idea out of her mind. These people were too clever to resort to kidnapping. Since they knew that Blackwood Hall was under surveillance, it was logical to assume that the gang was operating in new surroundings. If she could discover where Mrs. Putney had gone, then perhaps she would be able to locate the men who were seeking to separate the gullible woman from her money.

From Mrs. Putney's next-door neighbor Nancy

learned that her late husband had owned a hunting lodge on Lake Jasper, across the state line, where he had spent a great deal of time each summer.

So far as anyone knew, his widow had not visited the place since his death. Nancy thought there was a good possibility that Mrs. Putney might be at the lodge now. Moreover, Lake Jasper was the place where Mr. Drew's stolen car had been found!

Hannah Gruen did not entirely approve of Nancy's making a trip to Lake Jasper, preferring that she wait until her father returned. In the end, the housekeeper agreed to the plan but only after the parents of Bess and George had consented to having their daughters accompany Nancy.

"If for any reason you decide to stay more than one night, telephone me at once," Hannah begged.

Taking only light luggage, the girls started off early the next morning. During the drive, Nancy confided to her friends that she suspected Lola had run away from home and did not intend to return.

"Those people who seem to have her in their control have probably found her a job in another town. I must do everything I can to trace her, as soon as I find out about Mrs. Putney."

Lake Jasper was situated in the heart of pine woods country, and was one of a dozen beautiful small lakes in the area. Not knowing Mrs. Putney's address, the girls obtained directions at the post office. They learned that the hunting lodge was at the head of the lake, in an isolated spot.

"No sense going there until we've had lunch," remarked Bess. "It's after one o'clock now, and I'm faint from hunger."

At an attractive tearoom nearby, the girls enjoyed a delicious lake-trout dinner. Later, as they walked toward the car, Nancy suddenly halted.

"Girls," she said, "do my eyes deceive me, or is that Lola White walking ahead of us?"

The person Nancy pointed out was some distance down the street, her back to the three girls.

"It's Lola all right!" Bess agreed. "What do you suppose she's doing at Lake Jasper?"

"My guess is she's here with Mrs. Putney," Nancy replied grimly.

"But I'm sure they don't know each other," Bess said.

"Perhaps the gang arranged for her to come up here with Mrs. Putney," Nancy suggested.

The girls drove half a block ahead of Lola. Satisfied that they had made no mistake in identifying the girl, they alighted and walked directly toward her.

At an intersection the four met. Lola gazed at them, but her face was expressionless. She passed the trio without a sign of recognition.

"Well, of all things!" said Bess as the three

friends halted to stare after Lola. "She certainly was pretending she didn't know us."

"Maybe she didn't," Nancy replied. "Lola acted as she did the time Ned and I found her wading out into the river. I suggest we follow her. Maybe she'll lead us to the Putney Lodge."

The girls waited until Lola was nearly out of sight and then followed in the car. Leaving the village, Lola struck out through the woods. Nancy parked and they continued on foot. A mile from town, near the waterfront, they saw a cabin constructed of peeled logs. An inconspicuous sign tacked to a tree read *Putney Lodge*.

"Your hunch was right, Nancy," Bess whispered as they saw Lola enter by a rear door.

Nancy hesitated. "Seeing Lola here complicates things," she said. "I'm afraid there's more to this than appears on the surface."

Just then Mrs. Putney came out on the porch. The girls remained in hiding. After she went indoors, Nancy said:

"Lola may be completely under the spell of those who have been getting money from Mrs. Putney. They may be using her services here."

"You think Lola, in a hypnotized state, is expected to steal from Mrs. Putney!" Bess gasped.

"Either that, or she may have been instructed to assist a member of the gang. I'd like to do a little scouting around before we let them know we're here."

When the girls reached town, Nancy stopped at the bank. Unfortunately it was closed for the day, but by making inquiries she located the home of the bank's president, Henry Lathrop. Nancy introduced herself and learned that her father once had brought a case to a successful conclusion for Mr. Lathrop.

"And what can I do for you?" the man inquired.

Nancy asked him if Mrs. Henry Putney had a safe-deposit box at the bank in which she might be keeping stocks, bonds, or cash.

"Her husband had a large safe-deposit box, and she has retained it."

Nancy's pulse quickened as she learned Mrs. Putney had spoken to the banker early that morning. The widow had been carrying an unusually large handbag. She had taken her box into a private room and been there some time.

"Something up?" Mr. Lathrop asked.

"I'm afraid so," Nancy answered. "I hope I'm not too late. You see, Mr. Lathrop, a gang of thieves has made away with her jewels, and I suspect that they are now after her inheritance. I've been trying to catch up with these people—"

"If what you say is true, the police should be called in to protect Mrs. Putney," the banker said.

"I agree," Nancy replied. "I have a feeling that the people who are after Mrs. Putney's money may show their hand tonight."

Later, when Nancy related her story to George and Bess, they wanted to know what she was planning.

"A call on the State Police. The next job needs strong men!"

At headquarters Nancy gave the police all the details of the case. The mob was obviously ready to strike and make a quick getaway. It was time that the law stepped in. The young detective made such an impressive presentation of the facts that she was promised that a cordon of troops would be assigned to the lake area that night.

Nancy and her friends obtained a large room at the Lake Jasper Hotel, where the police promised to notify them at once should anything develop. Nancy awoke several times during the night, wondering what might be taking place at the Putney Lodge. She had just opened her eyes again as it was beginning to grow light, when the telephone on the stand by the bed jingled.

Nancy snatched it up. She listened attentively a moment, then turned excitedly to call her friends who were still asleep.

"Girls!" she cried. "The troopers have a prisoner!"

CHAPTER XVII

Breaking a Spell

At headquarters Nancy, Bess, and George learned that a man had been caught entering the Putney Lodge shortly after midnight. He had refused to give his name or answer any questions.

"Will you take a look at the fellow through our peephole and see if you recognize him?" the officer in charge asked. "He's in the center cell."

The three girls were led to a dark inner room. One by one they peered through a sliding wooden window which looked out upon the cell block. None of them had ever seen the prisoner in question, who was pacing the floor nervously.

"Maybe he'll break down this morning," the officer said. "Suppose you come back later."

As they left police headquarters, Nancy proposed that the girls go to the Putney cabin. When they arrived, the lodge showed signs of considerable activity. Mrs. Putney was in the living room, hurriedly packing. She made no effort to hide her displeasure at seeing the three girls.

"How did you know I was here?" she asked.

"It's a long story," Nancy replied. "But please answer one question: Do you still have your stocks and bonds safe in your handbag?"

This question evidently came as a complete surprise. The woman stammered for a moment and then sat down.

"Nancy Drew, I can't face you! You're uncanny. Not a soul in this world knew—"

"Mrs. Putney, please don't be upset," Nancy pleaded. "When you refused to take me into your confidence any longer, and left River Heights, I simply had to use my common sense as any detective would do. I'm trying to protect you against your own generous nature. You have never believed me when I told you that you are the victim of an unscrupulous gang. When I learned that you had opened your safe-deposit box I had to inform the police. It was they who caught your burglar."

The widow finally raised her head. "Yes, my securities are safe. So you—you know about the thief?"

"Very little. Tell me about him."

"It was so upsetting," the widow replied nervously. "My maid and I were sleeping soundly in our bedrooms."

So Lola was working as a maid!

"Suddenly we heard a shot fired," Mrs. Putney went on, "and there was a dreadful commotion. Several State Police officers were pounding on the door. I slipped on a dressing gown and went to see what they wanted. They asked me if I could identify the man they had caught trying to get in through a window."

"Was he anyone you knew?" asked Nancy.

"No, I never saw him before in my life. But I'm frightened. That's why I'm going home."

"And your maid?"

"I haven't told Violet yet."

Nancy quietly revealed that "Violet" was Lola White, that they had met her in the village, and were afraid she was under the influence of the same gang to which the night marauder belonged.

Mrs. Putney became more and more trusting as the conversation progressed. She was ready to admit that she had been foolish to act without advice.

"I suppose you received a spirit message to take your valuables from the bank and hold them until the spirit gave you further instructions," Nancy stated.

"Yes. My late husband contacted me."

"Will you please put them back in your safe-deposit box and not touch them again until—" Nancy hardly knew how to go on to compete with the spirit's advice—"until you have consulted Mr. Lathrop," she ended her request.

"I'll think about it," Mrs. Putney conceded. "Thank you, anyway, for all your help."

Bess spoke up, asking how Lola White happened to be working for her. Mrs. Putney said that the spirit had told her the girl would come to her at the lodge seeking employment and that she was to engage her.

"She had no luggage and told me her name was Violet Gleason," Mrs. Putney added. "She seems very nice, though odd. But if she's acting under some sort of mesmeric spell as you believe, then I don't want her around!"

"Maybe we can bring Lola out of it," Nancy suggested. "Then she'll want to go home, I'm sure. Let's go and talk to her."

Lola was sitting on the dock. As they approached her, she continued to stare at the girls without showing any sign of recognition. She was not unfriendly, however, and Nancy endeavored to bring her out of her trance by mentioning her mother, the school she had attended, a motion-picture house in River Heights, and several other familiar names. Lola merely shook her head in a bewildered way.

"Is her condition permanent?" Bess asked anxiously as the group returned to the lodge.

"I'd like to try one more thing before we take her home," Nancy said. "I don't want Mrs. White to see her this way. Mrs. Putney," she added, turning to the widow, "you will have to help us perform an experiment."

Mrs. Putney agreed to do anything to assist. However, when Nancy explained that her idea was to conduct a fake séance which would bring Lola to her senses, Mrs. Putney hesitated. Finally she said:

"I suppose it's only fair to give it a trial. And I must admit you've been right many times, Nancy. Yes, I'll help you."

While Bess and George stayed with Lola, Nancy and Mrs. Putney went to the village. The widow returned her stocks, bonds, and cash to the bank. Then they drove to Winchester, where Nancy purchased materials needed for the experiment.

At midnight the three girls posted themselves on the side porch of the lodge. Through a window they could see Mrs. Putney and Lola seated in the candle-lighted living room beside a dying log fire, as had been planned.

"Now, if only Mrs. Putney doesn't lose her nerve and give us away!" Nancy said.

"I hope we don't fumble *our* act!" Bess said, nervously adjusting her long veil and gown.

"We won't," replied Nancy. "Shall we start?"

Without showing herself, she flung wide the double doors leading from the porch into the living room. George, out of sight, waved a huge fan.

The resulting gust of wind extinguished the candles and caused the dying embers on the hearth to burst into flames.

George, hidden by darkness, reached in and uncorked a bottle of phosphorus and oil. At once a faint green light glowed spookily in the room.

Working from behind the door, Nancy, by means of a magician's reaching rod, made a large piece of cardboard appear to float in mid-air.

At the same time Bess, the long veil over her face, glided in and seated herself beside the trembling Lola. The girl half arose, then sank back, her eyes riveted on the moving cardboard.

With a quick toss of her wrist, Nancy flung it from the reaching rod, directly at Lola's feet. Plainly visible in glowing phosphorous characters was the Three Branch insigne.

Lola gasped, and even Mrs. Putney, who knew the séance was a fake, recoiled as if from a physical blow. A voice intoned:

"Lola! Lola! Give no more of your money to the orphans. They are not real, and their spirits do not need your help. Lola, do you hear me?"

There followed a moment of complete silence. Then the girl sprang to her feet, muttering:

"Yes, yes, I hear! I will obey!"

She reached out as if to grasp the arm of the figure who was veiled, and then toppled over in a faint. As Bess rejoined the other girls on the porch, Nancy closed the doors. Mrs. Putney flooded the room with light. The séance was at an end.

"Shouldn't we show ourselves now and help bring Lola out of her faint?" Bess asked anxiously as they watched through the window.

"That might give everything away," Nancy said. "I think Mrs. Putney is capable of handling things now. Let's look on from here."

To the relief of the trio, Lola soon revived.

"How are you feeling?" they heard the widow inquire solicitously.

"Sort of funny," the girl answered, rubbing her head. "Where am I?"

"At my lodge, Lola. You are employed here as a maid."

"How can that be?" the bewildered girl asked. "I work in a factory. I must get back to my job! My mother needs my help. I've been giving away too much money."

When Nancy, Bess, and George heard this, they knew the séance had been a success. Not only had Lola regained her normal thought processes, but the idea of refusing to give funds to unworthy causes also had taken firm root.

"Our work here is done," Nancy whispered to her friends. "Let's return to the hotel."

"I'm so relieved for Lola's sake," said George.

The next morning the girls decided to leave Lake Jasper without seeing Mrs. Putney again.

"I'm sure the poor woman is aware now that

she was being cheated by those people," Nancy said. "After she's had time to think matters over, she'll probably call me."

Before leaving Lake Jasper, Nancy went to the police station to see if the prisoner had revealed his identity and admitted his attempted crime.

"No, but we've sent his fingerprints to Washington to find out if he has a record," the officer said.

Nancy asked to look at him again through the peephole. This time, she felt that there was something vaguely familiar about him.

"We know by his accent he's from the South," the police officer told Nancy, "but he won't admit it, nor answer questions about his identity."

The officer turned on a tape recorder and Nancy listened to the prisoner's conversation with a guard. Only when the girls were en route home did it dawn upon Nancy that the man's voice resembled that of the New Orleans photographer!

"Girls!" she exclaimed. "Perhaps he and the prisoner are related! What was that photographer's name? Oh, yes, Towner."

Stopping at a gas station, she telephoned the police station and suggested they try out the name Towner on the prisoner, and mention New Orleans as a possible residence. In a few minutes word came back that the man had denied any connection with either one.

Nancy shrugged. "That photographer naturally

would be connected with this racket under an assumed name," she remarked.

During the drive to River Heights, the girls discussed the mystery from every angle. George and Bess were sure that the whole case soon would be solved and they praised Nancy for what she had done to prevent the gang from fleecing Mrs. Putney.

Nancy, however, pointed out that the original case involving the stolen Putney jewels still remained unsolved.

"The most valuable pieces—the pearl necklace and her husband's ring—haven't been recovered," she said. "Howard Brex, the man I suspected, hasn't been located for questioning yet. Until that has been accomplished, my work isn't done."

Upon her arrival home, pleasant news awaited Nancy. During her absence at Lake Jasper, Mr. Drew had returned.

"I've had a long trip," he remarked, a twinkle in his eye. "Traveling to New Orleans took me several hundred miles out of my way!"

Nancy's eyes opened wide. "New Orleans!" she exclaimed. "Dad, what did you learn?"

Instead of answering, the lawyer handed his daughter a small envelope.

CHAPTER XVIII

Startling Developments

NANCY opened the envelope with great excitement. Inside was a photograph of a thin-lipped, rather arrogant-looking man in his early thirties.

"Who is he?"

"Howard Brex!"

Mr. Drew explained that he had obtained the picture from the New Orleans police. Officers there still were trying to discover where he had gone since his release from prison. Nancy studied the picture and exclaimed suddenly:

"He bears a slight resemblance to the New Orleans photographer! And here's something else, Dad."

Excitedly she related the events that had taken place during his absence. In conclusion, she told about the capture of the Lake Jasper housebreaker, whose voice was very much like that of the photographer.

"Perhaps they're all related!" she speculated.

Mr. Drew offered to wire the New Orleans police for more information.

Then a telephone call confirmed the fact that Mrs. Putney had returned from Lake Jasper. Nancy hurried over to show her the photograph of Howard Brex. The widow received her graciously, but when shown the picture she insisted that she had never seen the man. Nancy had great difficulty in concealing her disappointment.

Upon returning home Nancy telephoned the Lake Jasper police for news of their prisoner. He still refused to talk, but the report from Washington on his fingerprints revealed that he had no criminal record.

No reply came to Mr. Drew's telegram, either that day or the next. But on the second day Nancy received a disturbing letter. It was signed "Mrs. Egan."

Written on cheap paper, the message was brief and threatening. It warned Nancy to give up her sleuthing activities or "suffer the consequences."

Nancy was worried. "This comes of talking to that strange woman in the park!" she thought. "But she certainly didn't look like the kind of person who would serve as a lookout for the gang."

In the hope of seeing the stranger again, Nancy watched the park most of that day. In the late afternoon she saw the woman walking rapidly toward her, carrying several packages.

Nancy stepped behind a bush until the middle-aged woman had passed. Then she followed her to a rooming house.

The woman entered an old-fashioned brick structure. Nancy waited on the stoop for a moment and then rapped on the door, which was opened by the woman she had followed. She greeted Nancy with such evident pleasure that the latter's suspicions vanished.

"Do come in. I lost the telephone number you gave me, and I've been trying for days to find out how to get in touch with you."

Nancy quickly asked a few questions to be sure she was not being misled. The woman was Mrs. Hopkins. Her daughter Nellie, she said, was at work, but should be home soon.

"After talking to you, I asked Nellie those questions you suggested!" Mrs. Hopkins revealed. "She broke down and told me everything!"

Nellie, she added, had disclosed that unknown persons frequently got in contact with her by telephone. Usually it was a woman.

"Each time this stranger called she claimed that she had received a spirit message for Nellie," Mrs. Hopkins continued. "My daughter was asked to give money to the Three Branch Home, the earthly headquarters of the spirits. Orphans are brought there and trained as mediums to carry on the work of maintaining contact with the spiritual world."

"There is no such place as Three Branch Home, Mrs. Hopkins," said Nancy. "It was just a scheme of those thieves to get money for themselves!"

"Nellie realizes that now, I think. Anyhow, she was instructed to leave her contributions on a certain day each week in the hollows of various walnut trees. The places were marked by the Three Branch sign."

"Did she do so, Mrs. Hopkins?"

"The last time Nellie went to the place, she was frightened away. She heard a sound as though someone had been struck, then she heard a moan."

Nancy was convinced that Nellie was the girl she had seen coming toward the big walnut tree where she had been struck unconscious, but she said nothing.

She continued to ask Mrs. Hopkins a few more questions. Nancy did not realize how time had flown by until a young woman, apparently returning from work, entered the room. After Nancy was introduced, Nellie Hopkins grasped the young detective's hand fervently.

"Oh, I never can thank you enough for saving me," she said gratefully. "I don't know why I let myself be taken in by those—those crooked people, except that they said good luck would come to me if I obeyed, and bad luck if I refused."

Nancy replied that she was glad to have been of

service, then she took the picture of Howard Brex from her purse. "Ever see this man?" she asked.

"You don't mean that *he* is a racketeer?" asked Nellie. "I saw him only once. He was tall and slender, and he seemed so nice," she added.

Nellie went on to say that she had met the man in the photograph when she had sat next to him on a bus. She admitted talking to him about her job and her family. She had even told him where she lived. Nellie had never seen him again, and did not even know his name, but she was sure, now, he had used her information to his own advantage. It probably was he who had turned over her address to Mrs. Egan.

Mrs. Hopkins' eyebrows raised, but she did not chide her daughter. The girl would not be so unwise again, she knew.

Nancy went home pleased to know that at last she had found a witness who could place Howard Brex with the group whose activities were connected with the disappearance of Mrs. Putney's jewels. All during the case the tall, thin man, the onetime designer of exquisite jewelry, had figured in her deductions. Just what was the part he played in the mystery? Her father, smiling broadly, opened the door.

"Time you're getting here!" he said teasingly. "I have some news."

"From New Orleans?" she asked eagerly.

"Yes, a wire came this afternoon. Your hunch

was right. The real name of that photographer you saw in New Orleans is Joe Brex. He's the brother of Howard.

"In fact, Howard has two brothers. The other one is John. Their mother was a medium in Alabama, years ago," Mr. Drew continued. "She disappeared after being exposed as a faker."

"But her sons learned her tricks!" Nancy declared. "And maybe she runs that séance place in New Orleans. Oh, Dad, thanks ever so much. We've now placed Howard and Joe Brex as members of our racketeers. I've still got to tie them up with the hocus-pocus that persuaded Mrs. Putney to bury her jewels at the designated spot, and with all of the goings-on at Blackwood Hall. But we're getting places, Dad!"

"The three brothers probably run the extortion racket together, with the woman you saw on the plane to help them," Mr. Drew said grimly.

"We must go back to Lake Jasper and talk to that prisoner tomorrow!" Nancy urged.

During the evening Mr. Drew made a call to the New Orleans police, suggesting they shadow the photographer, Joe Brex, and raid one of the services at the Church of Eternal Harmony.

Nancy's father went on to tell their suspicions concerning Joe's brothers, and to hazard the opinion that the photographer might be in league with them.

"If you can get a lead on whether Joe has been

disposing of any jewelry or other stolen articles, it might be the breaking point in our case."

"We'll see what information we can get for you," the officer told Mr. Drew.

"While I think of it," the lawyer finished, "if you can locate a picture of John Brex, will you send it to me at once?"

"Glad to do it," the officer replied.

The next morning, while Nancy was packing a change of clothes in case she and her father should stay overnight at Lake Jasper, Hannah Gruen brought in a telegram to Mr. Drew. Since he received many such messages, his daughter thought little about this one until she heard him utter an exclamation of surprise in the next room. Running to him, she asked what the wire said.

"Joe Brex recently left New Orleans in a hurry! His whereabouts is not known. The Church of Eternal Harmony was found locked, and the medium gone. The police couldn't locate a picture of John Brex, they say."

Before Nancy could comment, Hannah summoned her to the telephone. "Lake Jasper police calling."

The officer on the wire was brief. "Miss Drew, I'd like your help," he said. "That prisoner who wouldn't talk broke jail last night under very mysterious circumstances! The guard says there was a ghost in his cell!"

CHAPTER XIX

Trapped!

THE story that the Lake Jasper police told Nancy was a startling one.

On the previous night, the cell block had been guarded by an easygoing, elderly man who served as relief during the late hours of the night.

According to his story, he had been making a routine check tour of the cell block, when suddenly a pale-green, ghostly figure appeared to be flitting through the air inside the center cell. A sepulchral voice called him by name and said: "I am the spirit of your dear wife Hattie. Is all well with you? If you will unlock the cell, and come in where I am waiting to speak to you, I will tell you about our Johnny who was drowned and of Allan who was killed in the war."

In fear and trembling, the guard had obeyed. No sooner had he entered the cell when a damp cloth was pressed against his nostrils, and his keys seized from his belt. Just before he lost consciousness he heard the cell door clang shut.

"The same old trick!" exclaimed Nancy.

She told the officer on the telephone the latest information Mr. Drew had received, and their conclusion that the three Brex brothers were responsible for the spirit racket.

"We think your prisoner was John Brex. One of his confederates must have supplied him with the information about the guard. But how could anyone get inside the jail to deliver the spirit paraphernalia to the man in the cell?" asked Nancy.

"Well, a woman came to the office and told us that she understood we were holding an unidentified burglar. She asked if she might visit the prisoner. One of our men took her to the cell and stayed with her in the corridor."

"Was the guard with her all the time she was inside the cell block?" Nancy asked.

"Yes, he was," the officer at the other end of the telephone replied. "Wait a minute," he added quickly. "He left her when she fainted."

"Fainted?" repeated Nancy.

"Well, the woman looked at the prisoner for a long time without a word. Then suddenly she fell to the floor. Our man ran to get some spirits of ammonia. When he got back she was still out, but came around in a jiffy when he applied the smelling salts to her nose."

"There's your answer," said Nancy. "She was a

member of the Brex setup and passed the robe and other things through the bars while the guard was out of the corridor. Where is she now?"

"Gone," replied the officer. "When we took her back to the office she told us that she had thought the man in the cell was her brother she hadn't seen in fifteen years, but decided he wasn't. We had to let her go."

"Well, I think when you catch up with Brex and his fainting visitor you will find them to be confederates," Nancy said.

The officer thanked Nancy for the explanation, and said a nation-wide alarm would be sent out on the escaped prisoner.

"Wherever those gangsters are, I'm sure they didn't have time to take all their loot with them," Nancy remarked to Ned the next afternoon as they sat together in his car in front of the Drew home. "They must have hidden it somewhere around here. Let's try to think where they would be most apt to cache it until things blow over and it becomes safe for them to collect it."

"Some bank vault?" Ned suggested.

"I doubt it. My hunch would be Blackwood Hall."

"But the troopers searched the place."

Nancy reminded him that although the police had been skeptical about her story, she was sure a live "ghost" had come out of one wall and gone through another in the old mansion.

"And those creaking sounds—" Suddenly she snapped her fingers. "There must be some way of getting from the underground room to the upstairs floors without using the stairs."

"Gosh, you could be right! How about hidden stairs between the walls?" Ned asked.

"I'm more inclined to think it may be a secret elevator—one you can operate by pulling ropes to raise and lower it," said Nancy.

"Let's go!" said Ned.

"Wait just a minute while I run into the house. I want to tell Hannah where we're going."

Nancy returned in a moment, and they set out for Blackwood Hall.

"So much about the place hasn't been explained," Nancy said thoughtfully. "Those sliding panels, for instance. They may be entrances to secret rooms as well as to an old elevator!"

In case they should run into trouble, Ned stopped at home and got his short-wave radio sending set.

When they reached Blackwood Hall, Nancy suggested that they separate, and he keep watch outside, in case any of the racketeers should show up. Ned agreed to the plan.

"Yell if you find anything, and I'll come running," he declared.

Nancy took a small tool kit from the car. Once in the house, working inch by inch, she made an inspection by flashlight of the second- and third-floor hallways of the dwelling. There was no evidence of any spring or contrivance that could move the carved walnut panels.

"The panel on the third floor must open from the outside," Nancy said aloud, "for I distinctly saw the "ghost" emerge from the wall on the second floor and disappear *into* the wall in the third-floor hallway. I'll have a look at the basement room and then come back here with a hatchet."

The main part of the basement, entered from the kitchen, revealed nothing to indicate the existence of a hidden elevator.

"If there is one, it must be in that secret room after all," Nancy decided.

Using the hidden door in the organ room, she slowly descended the steps. Her flashlight cut a circular pattern on the cracked walls of the tunnel as she played the light from side to side.

Finally Nancy reached the walnut door. To her amazement it now was bolted on the inner side, but with the tools from the car she managed to let herself in.

All was quiet inside the pitch-dark room. From the doorway, Nancy played her flashlight quickly around the four sides of the room. Satisfied that it was empty, she entered cautiously.

The door behind her creaked softly. Nancy

whirled around. There was no draft, yet the heavy walnut door seemed to move several inches. The door must be improperly hung, she thought.

Then, inch by inch, she began to inspect the paneled walls. At the far end of the room, she came upon a section which she found, upon minute examination, was not in a true line with the rest of the woodwork.

"This may be something!" Nancy thought, her pulse pounding.

She tugged and pushed at the paneling. Suddenly it began to move. It slid back all the way to reveal, just as Nancy had expected, a small, old-fashioned elevator, consisting of a wooden platform suspended on ropes, with another rope extending through a hole in the floor.

But her first thrill of discovery gave way to a cry of horror. Facing her in the elevator were two men—Howard Brex and his brother John, the escaped prisoner from Lake Jasper!

Confronted by the pair, Nancy backed away and tried to flee through the walnut doorway. Howard Brex seized her arm while the other man, holding a flashlight, blocked the exit.

"No, you don't!" Howard warned. "You've made enough trouble for us."

"I'm not afraid of you or your brother!" Nancy stated defiantly. "The police will be here any minute."

"Yes?" the man mocked. "If you're depending

"Nancy Drew, you've made enough trouble!" Howard
Brex rasped

on your boy friend to rescue you, guess again. We'll take care of him as soon as we dispose of you."

Nancy was dismayed to hear that the man knew Ned was awaiting her outside. She realized that if she screamed for help, it would only draw him into the trap.

"What do you plan to do with me?" she demanded.

"We'll take care of you, so you'll never bother us again," Howard Brex replied as he shoved her roughly toward the elevator. "Fact is, we've decided, since you have such a fondness for ghosts, to let you spend the remainder of your life with the ghost of Blackwood Hall!"

"You had plenty of warning," Howard went on. "But would you mind your own business? No! Not even after I knocked you out in the woods one day when you were spying on one of my clients."

Nancy knew she must keep them talking. As soon as Ned became concerned about her long absence he would radio for help. "So you admit you've cheated innocent people with your fake séances," she remarked.

"Sure, and don't think it isn't a good racket!" John Brex boasted.

"How many people have you fleeced?"

"So many that we'll be able to take a long vacation," his brother bragged.

"You sold some of Mrs. Putney's jewelry. But you still have her most valuable pieces!" Nancy accused him.

"Sure," Howard agreed. "We'll wait until the hubbub dies down. We'll sell the necklace and her husband's ring after we skip the country."

"You climbed along the roof outside of Mrs. Putney's bedroom window at night and spoke to her as if you were her husband's spirit," Nancy went on accusingly.

"You're a smart kid," John Brex mocked.

"You do know a lot," said Howard. "Even more than I thought. Well, the sooner we get this job over with, John, the better for us."

"I suppose your mother helped with the racket," Nancy remarked, hoping to gain time. "She ran those fake séances in New Orleans, and pretended to be the portrait of Amurah coming to life."

"It was a good trick," Howard said boastfully.

"She had a double wall built in the house so she could hide there?" Nancy asked.

"Sure, and she did the rapping back there, too."

"Was the old man at the Church of Eternal Harmony your brother Joe?"

"Yes, in disguise. The whole family's in the racket. John's wife has been helping us, and her friend, too."

"The friend is the one who drives the car, isn't she?" Nancy queried.

"Wouldn't you like to know?" John sneered.

"And she hypnotizes people?"

"No!" growled Howard. "She just gives them a whiff that makes them drowsy. *I* do the hypnotizing. Whenever any of my clients get out of line, I produce the beckoning hand."

"One of your luminous wax hands," declared Nancy. "And you must be a ventriloquist as well. Lola White nearly lost her life walking into the river because you hypnotized her," she accused him.

"That was your fault," the man replied. "You came snooping around here before I had a chance to get her out of it."

"Did you do your hypnotizing near the walnut trees that were used as hiding places for money and letters?" Nancy asked. "Or at the cabin where you held the fake séances?"

"Both places."

"I imagine the Three Branch symbol represented you three clever brothers."

"That'll be enough from you, young lady," snarled John. "I'm getting fed up with this dame's wisecracks, Howie!"

"You even played the organ," Nancy said coolly, turning to Howard. "And when you didn't have to use the dummy ghost, you dressed like one yourself."

John interrupted roughly, "This has gone far enough."

Before Nancy could ask another question, the men thrust her into the elevator. Her flashlight and car tools were taken from her.

"Nancy Drew, you're about to take your last ride!" Howard told her brutally. "In a few moments, young lady, you will join the ghost of Blackwood Hall!"

CHAPTER XX

A Hidden Discovery

THE secret panel closed in Nancy's face. A few moments later she felt the rope beside her moving and the lift began to rise slowly upward with a creaking, groaning sound.

What were John and Howard Brex going to do now? Move out their loot? Capture Ned?

With a jerk, the elevator suddenly halted. Nancy tugged at the rope. It would not move!

At the same moment, Nancy saw a faint, greenish glow arising from one corner of her prison. Presently she became aware of an unpleasant odor rapidly growing stronger. Then Nancy understood.

"Those fiends uncorked a bottle of phosphorus and oil in this elevator, and they've probably added a deadly sleeping potion for me to inhale," she thought, breaking out in cold perspiration. "That's what they meant by saying that in a few moments I would join the ghost of Blackwood Hall. They meant Jonathan Humphrey, who died in the duel. I'll die at Blackwood Hall too!"

For an instant Nancy nearly gave way to panic. Then reason reasserted itself.

From her pocket she took a handkerchief. Covering her nose and mouth with it, she groped about frantically on the floor of the dark elevator. Guided by the greenish glow, she found a small bottle in one corner.

Already weak and dizzy, Nancy had no time to search further for the stopper. Instead, she pulled off her suit jacket and jammed part of the sleeve into the opening of the bottle.

Immediately the light was extinguished. But Nancy by now felt so drowsy that she was forced to sit down.

Sleep overcame her. She had no idea of how much later it was when she awoke. But now she felt stronger. The sickening odor was gone. She could think clearly.

She pounded against the wooden sides of the elevator shaft. Three of the walls seemed to be as solid as stone. Only the fourth seemed thin. Could this be the panel of the third-floor hallway?

The old house was as still as death itself. Nancy was certain Howard and John Brex had fled, and no doubt they had captured Ned too. As time dragged on and still no one came, she became convinced that her friend had met with disaster.

"I told Hannah that Ned and I were coming here," Nancy thought. "She'll be worried about our long absence and send help."

Then a harrowing thought came to her. Maybe her friends had come and gone while she was asleep! By the luminous hands of her wrist watch, Nancy knew she had been in the elevator over two hours.

"It's no use!" she despaired. Then instantly she added, "I *mustn't* give up hope!"

Nancy sat down again on the floor, trying to figure out some means of escape. But scarcely had she closed her eyes to concentrate than she became aware of sounds.

Pressing an ear against the crack between the elevator floor and the wall, Nancy listened intently. With a thrill of joy she recognized Bess's high-pitched voice. Then she heard others speaking: her father, Hannah Gruen, and George Fayne.

Nancy began to shout and pound on the elevator door. Attracted by the noise, her friends came running up the stairway. Nancy kept shouting directions, until finally they were able to locate the wall panel behind which she was imprisoned.

"Nancy!" her father called. "Are you all right?"

"Yes, Dad, but I'm in an elevator and can't get out. I can't even move it."

"We'll soon find a way. If we can't open this panel, we'll tear the wall down!"

"Is Ned safe?" Nancy asked anxiously.

"Haven't seen him," her father replied. "Hannah got worried after you'd been gone so long, and told us you had come here. Ned isn't with you?"

"No," Nancy replied in a discouraged voice, then added, "Please go down to the ghost room and see if you can find out how to move this elevator."

Several minutes passed, then Mr. Drew reported no success.

"It's a very old-fashioned hand type and works by pulling a rope," he said. "Evidently they have locked the wheel over which the rope passes at the top. Well, here goes the wall!"

Nancy heard a thud, then the sound of splintering wood. A moment later light beamed through a small hole.

"Hand me the flashlight," said Nancy. "Maybe I can find out how the panel opens."

In a few moments Nancy located a lock. Releasing it, she pushed up the section of wall and tumbled into her father's arms.

"Thank goodness you're safe!" Hannah cried, hugging her in turn. "When you didn't come home, I knew something had happened!"

"Bless you, Hannah, for bringing help!" Nancy exclaimed.

From the yard came the sharp yipping of a dog. "Why, that sounds like Togo!" Nancy exclaimed.

"We left him in the car," her father explained. "Something must have excited him."

Hastening downstairs, the party reached the front porch just as several state troopers, surrounding two women and two men, emerged from the woods. Nancy was overjoyed to see Ned leading the procession!

"They've captured Howard and John Brex!" she cried. "And that first woman with them—she's the one we met on the plane. The other must be the veiled chauffeur!"

Ned ran to Nancy's side. Breathlessly he explained that upon seeing the two men leaving Blackwood Hall, he had hurriedly summoned state troopers by means of the short-wave set.

"Then I trailed the Brex brothers and kept sending my location to the police. What a chase!"

"You did a swell job, fellow," complimented one of the troopers. "We sure had a hard time trying to keep up with you."

"We caught the men and the women at a little hotel down the river," Ned added. "They were packing their duds, intending to make a getaway."

"Good work, Ned!" Nancy congratulated him. "This practically winds up the case, except for capturing Joe Brex."

"Don't worry about that," Mr. Drew interposed. "The police will run him in before forty-eight hours have elapsed."

The four prisoners refused to talk when confronted by Nancy and her party. Though they would not admit that they had any loot hidden at Blackwood Hall or elsewhere, their arrogance was completely gone. Howard Brex looked completely crestfallen when Nancy repeated to the troopers all the damaging evidence he had boastfully revealed to her a few hours earlier.

When Ned heard how they had put her in the elevator to die, he was filled with remorse. Having no idea anything more had happened than Nancy had smoked out the gangsters, he had felt it all right to leave her and go after them.

"I'll never do that again!" he vowed.

Tearfully, John Brex's wife, the woman they had seen on the plane, admitted her identity. She acknowledged having trailed the three girls to New Orleans after learning that Mrs. Putney had engaged Nancy to find the stolen jewelry. When they threw her off the scent, and she saw them coming out of the Church of Eternal Harmony and heading for the photographer's, she hastened to warn Joe. John happened to be there, and the three concocted the scheme of putting the warning on the plate and carrying Nancy away in a car to an empty house in order to frighten her off the case.

Mrs. Brex's friend also admitted her guilt. She had adopted clever disguises for the sole purpose of deceiving Nancy, as well as the people the group sought to cheat. It was she who had picked up the Egan letters at the hotel.

"Don't say another word!" John shouted. "You've said too much already!"

Here George interrupted to address Howard Brex. "After you had abandoned having séances at Blackwood Hall and moved your equipment by wheelbarrow to the cabin, we tracked you there and found smoke—acrid smoke, not wood smoke, coming out the chimney and from under the door."

Howard sneered. "Had you guessing, eh? All I was doing was trying out a new brand of spirit powder. I ducked out a back window when I heard someone trying to break into the place."

After the prisoners were taken off to jail, Nancy suggested that a trooper remain at Blackwood Hall with her and the others to investigate the paneled walls of the rambling old house.

"I want you all to take an elevator ride with me!" Nancy said gaily, "and see if we can locate the gangsters' loot."

The wall panel on the third floor still stood open. Nancy swung a flashlight around the elevator. In a moment she found what she was looking for: the mechanism to run the car. It was high up in the shaft under the roof. An iron bar was thrust through the wooden wheel over which the rope ran.

In a moment the wheel again was free. Using the rope, Nancy lowered the elevator platform to the level of the second floor. There she examined carefully each wall of the elevator shaft. To her joy she located the spring that operated the panel from the inside. It rolled back exposing the second-floor hall.

Then she turned her attention to the opposite wall of the elevator shaft. It, too, seemed to be a panel, and she went over every inch of it for a catch. When she found it, she pressed the release and the panel slid noiselessly upward.

"A secret room!" she cried.

The others crowded around her. Before them stood a manikin dressed in flimsy white, as well as reaching rods, bottles of phosphorus, oil, and several books on hypnotism.

Besides these, the searchers found box upon box of envelopes stuffed with bills. But most important was a notebook containing the names and addresses of people who had been swindled by the spirit racket.

"This money will help repay all those people who have been robbed," Nancy declared.

Under the eaves Nancy came upon a large chest which proved to contain a complete set of craftsmen's tools such as a jeweler would use—Howard Brex's outfit.

"I suppose those clever imitations which Mr. Freeman detected when Mrs. Putney took them to be cleaned were fashioned right here in Black-wood Hall," Mr. Drew said thoughtfully.

"But where are Mrs. Putney's missing gems?" Nancy asked.

"Right here in this envelope!" George spoke up. "Now your work on the case is really complete." Turning to the officer, she said, "Nancy got into this thing trying to trace Mrs. Putney's stolen jewelry. Whoever would have thought that all this could happen before the thieves were caught?"

The following day, events occurred very rapidly. Joe Brex and his mother were arrested in Chicago. Joe acknowledged he had built up a good business in spirit photography.

He and the others finally confessed their full part in the sordid Three Branch swindle, and admitted that they first cajoled, then threatened their victims when they did not yield to the suggestions of the spirits. The men also admitted having stolen Mr. Drew's car to move out some of their props.

To celebrate the successful conclusion of the mystery, Hannah Gruen planned a surprise dinner and invited all of Nancy's closest friends, and also Mrs. Putney.

"Oh, my dear," the widow said, tears in her eyes, "I was so unfair to you in my thoughts. At times I felt you lacked all understanding of my case. But you've made me realize how utterly stupid I was to be fooled into thinking my husband's spirit was giving me messages. Now, dear, I know you won't accept money as a reward for the work you have done in my behalf, but I hope you will take as an expression of my everlasting gratitude this cameo ring which belonged to my husband's mother. It is one of the jewels you helped me to recover."

"Oh, Mrs. Putney, I couldn't," protested Nancy.

"Nonsense," Mrs. Putney interrupted. "I have no one to inherit my lovely things when I go. I want you to have it as a memento of a case you solved in which many innocent people were saved from serious loss."

"You are very generous, Mrs. Putney. I would love to wear it. I enjoyed every moment I was working on the mystery—except the quagmire and the elevator incident," Nancy declared. "Dad," she said, turning to Mr. Drew, "I would never have done it without all the help you gave me."

"Ridiculous," Mr. Drew objected.

"I'll bet you could tackle your next case single-handed," Mrs. Putney insisted.

That exciting mystery, *The Clue of the Leaning Chimney,* was to come as a baffling surprise to the girl detective.

"Say," said George, laughing, "we learned enough about magicians' tricks to go into the ghost business ourselves. How about fitting up a studio at Blackwood Hall and running séances?"

Bess shivered. "No, thanks. We've just learned that it never pays to flimflam the public."

"Anyway, it's much more fun to catch the people who try to do the flimflamming!" Nancy said, smiling.

NANCY DREW MYSTERY STORIES®

The Thirteenth Pearl

BY CAROLYN KEENE

GROSSET & DUNLAP
Publishers • New York
A member of The Putnam & Grosset Group

Contents

CHAPTER I

Mr. Moto

"How would you girls like a drink of pearl powder?" Nancy Drew asked her friends Bess and George. "It's calcium and is guaranteed to cure anything that's wrong with you."

The two girls laughed, sure that Nancy was joking. The attractive, blue-eyed, strawberry blond sleuth shook her head.

"I'm not kidding. It's true."

Bess, a slightly overweight blond who, like the others, was eighteen years old, made a face. "You know how I like to eat, but powder made from pearls!"

George, to whom food meant little, was a slender athletic-looking brunette. "So far as I know, there's nothing wrong with me, so I'll pass."

"Well, Nancy," Bess urged, "tell us what the joke is."

Once more Nancy insisted that pearl powder had been used extensively as a cure-all. "In ancient Japan and other Asiatic and Oriental countries, it was very popular. Nowadays physicians prescribe other medications, but pearl powder can still be purchased in certain pharmacies."

George stopped smiling and looked intently at her friend. "My guess is that you've started working on a new mystery, and it has something to do with pearls. Am I right?"

"Yes," Nancy replied. "There's a Japanese jeweler in town who's a specialist in repairing fine old pieces of jewelry. His name is Mr. Moto. Recently he came to my Dad asking for help on a mystery."

Bess spoke up. "But your dad isn't a detective. He's a lawyer."

"True," Nancy agreed, "but in this case, a fantastic theft took place. Mr. Moto didn't want to go to the police because, if the loss became known, he feared it might cause international complications."

George took a deep breath. "I'm hooked. Tell us more."

Nancy told the girls that a large firm with offices all over the world might be involved.

Bess interrupted. "Is this very confidential?"

"Very," Nancy replied. She went on to say that her father was unable to help with the case at the present time and had told Mr. Moto that Nancy was an amateur detective. Mr. Drew had suggested that the three girls start working on the mystery until he could take over.

"What did Mr. Moto say?" Bess asked.

"He agreed."

"Great!" George exclaimed. "When shall we begin?"

"Right now," Nancy replied. "I'll tell Hannah where we're going." She was referring to the Drews' lovely housekeeper, who had acted as a mother to Nancy since she was three years old and her own mother had passed away. At the moment Hannah Gruen was in the kitchen baking a lemon meringue pie, which happened to be Mr. Drew's favorite dessert.

Minutes later the girls drove off in Nancy's sleek blue car to the center of River Heights. As they turned into a side street looking for the jewelry shop, Bess suddenly said, "Oh, there it is. But what's happening?"

Nancy and George gazed at the front door of the shop. A young Asiatic man was racing from the store with a pearl necklace dangling from one hand.

"I'll bet he's a thief!" George cried out. "Let's nab him!"

But by the time Nancy stopped her car at the curb across from the jeweler's, the young man had jumped into an automobile and sped off in the opposite direction. Unfortunately, the car had

"I'll bet he's a thief!" George cried out.

been too far away for Nancy and the others to glimpse the number on the license plate.

"Oh dear!" Bess said with a sigh. "There was our chance to be heroines, and we lost it!"

Nancy was eager to see if Mr. Moto was all right and hurried across the street into the shop. Bess and George followed. No one was inside, but in a few moments an elderly, kind-looking Japanese man came from a rear room.

He smiled and bowed to the girls. "May I assist you?" he asked.

Nancy spoke quickly. "We just saw a young man run from your shop with a pearl necklace in his hand. Did he buy it?"

"No. I have been in the back room. I did not see or hear anyone."

He looked into a display case, then clasped his hands in dismay. "It is gone! A very expensive necklace!"

Nancy, Bess, and George described the young man as best as they could. Mr. Moto did not recognize him.

"He was a thief, indeed!" the jeweler lamented.

The girls expressed their sympathy, and Nancy asked Mr. Moto if he was going to call the police. The rather frail-looking jeweler shook his head. "Not now. I have a bigger problem on my mind."

"I know," Nancy said and introduced herself and the other girls. "You came to see my father about the theft of an unusual piece of jewelry. He told you that until he is free, we would work on your case."

Mr. Moto frowned. The girls assumed that he was thinking, "What do they know about solving mysteries?"

Bess spoke up at once and glibly told how many cases Nancy had successfully concluded. "And sometimes George and I helped her," she added.

Mr. Moto stroked his chin. "Ah, so. Then I will tell you about my trouble. But you must promise to keep this matter to yourselves."

Each girl said she would honor his secret.

"I have a client named Mrs. Tanya Rossmeyer," the jeweler began. "She is a very wealthy lady and owns a great deal of expensive jewelry. Her most precious piece is a necklace of pearls. There are twelve on each side of a very large one, which has the luster of the moon. The strand is made of natural, not cultured pearls."

"It must be worth a fortune!" Bess burst out.

"It is," Mr. Moto agreed. "I believe there is no other one like it in the world."

Nancy asked him about the theft.

"Someone entered my shop and opened the safe," Mr. Moto replied. "He cut off the thirteenth pearl from the rest of the strand. Mrs. Rossmeyer will be very angry and sue me for a lot of money. I will lose my insurance and will be forced to close my shop!"

The three girls were surprised that the burglar had cut only one pearl from the necklace. How much easier it would have been to steal the whole thing!

Nancy said, "Would you let us see the part of the necklace that you still have?"

The jeweler obligingly opened the safe, which was built into the counter and was well-hidden from view.

Nancy thought, "A casual customer would not realize this is a safe. The thief must have been somebody who knows about it, besides being an expert safe-cracker."

Mr. Moto twirled the dials of the lock left and right, then opened the heavy door. Inside were many small drawers. He pulled one out and reached in for the pearl necklace.

"You see where—" he began, then stared at the strand before him. Finally he cried out, "This is not Mrs. Rossmeyer's necklace! The thief substituted this one! These are smaller than Mrs. Rossmeyer's pearls. Oh—she—"

The jeweler suddenly put a hand in his pocket, then fainted, sinking to the floor. The girls ran behind the counter. Nancy and Bess picked him up and carried him to the back room.

"George, shut the front door and lock it!" Nancy called out.

After putting Mr. Moto on a couch, she felt in his pocket where he had put his hand, and she discovered a small bottle of heart tablets. Quickly she placed one under the man's tongue.

"Don't you think we should call a doctor?" Bess asked worriedly.

Nancy thought that Mr. Moto probably had attacks like this from time to time and carried the special pills for that reason. "If he doesn't revive in a few minutes, then we'd better call an ambulance."

George had locked the front door and had gone behind the counter. She restored the pearl necklace to the safe and closed the heavy door. Then she twirled the knob back and forth and tried the handle. The safe was locked.

By this time Mr. Moto had recovered in the back room but was glad to lie on the couch. He insisted he did not need a doctor but asked the girls not to leave him for a while.

George reported that she had locked everything, and he thanked her. "You are most kind," he said. "When I first noticed that the thirteenth pearl was gone, I was so excited that I did not examine the rest of the necklace. Now I know the substitute is not nearly as valuable as the stolen one. Oh, oh! What shall I do?"

Nancy suggested that Mr. Moto lie still until he felt completely well. He agreed and used this time to tell them the full story of what he suspected had happened.

"I believe the thief who was here is working

for an international organization called World Wide Gems, Incorporated, which deals in old and rare jewelry. Recently it has been hinted in the trade that an underworld organization has infiltrated World Wide Gems. This does not mean that the whole company is dishonest, but it is felt that certain employees are not above stealing. No one dares accuse World Wide Gems, since it might stir up real trouble and even cause bloodshed at the hands of the powerful underworld group."

"But why did the thief leave the substitute necklace?" George asked, puzzled.

"Probably he did not want to leave that compartment in my safe empty. With the other necklace in it, I might not have noticed the loss for a while," Mr. Moto replied.

"Where is World Wide Gems located?" Nancy inquired.

"They have branches in many big cities all over the world," Mr. Moto replied. "You can see that an investigation of them would cause many problems."

"Yes, it would," came the stern voice of an unseen man. "You'd better forget the whole thing if you value your life!"

Mr. Moto and the girls were startled. Nancy and her friends jumped up and ran to the back door from where the voice had seemed to originate. No one was there! Puzzled, they searched the premises inside and out, but in vain. It was as if a ghost had spoken.

Bess shivered. "This is positively spooky!"

CHAPTER II

Hidden Camera

THE three girls rejoined Mr. Moto, who had turned very pale. Nancy was afraid he might have another attack. She suggested that he stay on the couch while the girls made a further search for the person who had spoken.

He agreed but said he did not want to close the shop. "With these losses I cannot afford to prevent customers from coming in," he explained worriedly.

Bess offered to work in the store for him. "I would enjoy selling somebody a diamond engagement ring or a wedding ring," she said, her eyes twinkling.

The jeweler smiled faintly. "Some time ago I had a special camera put in to take pictures of anyone who seemed suspicious. This neighborhood is not as high-class as it used to be, and sometimes I have dishonest people coming in."

He got up and showed Bess where the camera was located in a corner of the ceiling. It pointed directly toward the counter.

"There is a button under the counter," he said. "If you press it, the camera will take a picture instantly and develop it. See, here it is."

Bess nodded, sat down on a high stool behind the counter, and gazed at the display before her. Mr. Moto went to lie down again, and when Bess looked at him a few minutes later, he was sound asleep. She smiled and returned to the shop.

Meanwhile, Nancy and George had gone to hunt for the source of the voice. They could find no shoe prints of the eavesdropper and no noticeable fingerprints.

George walked up the driveway between Moto's shop and the next store and questioned pedestrians on the street. None had seen anyone entering or leaving the alleyway. Then she asked people if a man had lingered near the jewelry shop. In each case, the answer was no.

Nancy inquired in apartments above the stores. Most of the tenants were apparently out because they did not answer their doorbells. The few who were home had seen nothing.

She returned to the rear of the jewelry shop. When Nancy looked up, she noticed a young woman leaning out of a window.

Nancy called up to her, "Did you by any chance see a man loitering around Mr. Moto's place?"

"When?" the woman asked.

"Oh, a little while ago, about twenty minutes," the young sleuth replied.

"Yes. A fellow was standing by the back door. He spoke to someone inside."

"He must be the one," Nancy said. "What did he look like?"

The neighbor said she could not see him too well from upstairs. "He was rather short and stocky, had very black hair, and wore a gray suit. I'm afraid that's all I can tell you."

"It's a wonderful identification." Nancy smiled. "By the way, was he of Asiatic origin?"

The woman shook her head. "I couldn't see his face, but I don't think he was." She asked if something was wrong.

Nancy replied that the man had called into the shop, then disappeared. This answer seemed to satisfy the woman, and Nancy was glad she did not have to go into further details.

The young sleuth now turned up the driveway and met George in the street. "Any luck?" she asked.

"None," George replied. "How about you?"

Nancy told her about the clue she had just picked up. Then the girls began questioning passers-by, but no one had seen the mysterious stranger. The two sleuths were about to give up when they saw a woman with a large package walking toward a parked sedan.

To Nancy's inquiry, she answered, "Yes, a man fitting that description ran up the alleyway just as I parked my car."

"Did you see his face?" George inquired. "Can you tell us what nationality he was?"

The woman smiled. "He appeared to be of Italian descent."

Nancy and George were thrilled by this additional information. Now they had something to work on!

"Did you see where the man went?" George asked as she helped the woman put her package into the car.

"Yes. He jumped into a black sedan that somebody else was driving, and they sped off in a hurry."

"Thank you very much," Nancy said. "We're trying to locate this man, and your information will help."

Before the stranger could become inquisitive, the girls turned and walked to the rear of the shop again, letting themselves in through the back door.

Meanwhile, Bess had had an adventure of her own. A rather large, mannish-looking woman with an abundance of blond hair exaggeratedly coiffed had briskly walked into the store. She came up to the counter and said in a harsh voice, "Please give me Mrs. Rossmeyer's address in Europe."

Bess did not like her customer. She seemed hard and cruel. "I don't know the address," the girl replied.

"Oh, come now," the woman said. "If you work here, you certainly must know what address Mrs. Rossmeyer left with Mr. Moto. She's in Europe somewhere. I'm a friend of hers and am going abroad. I want to look her up."

"I'm really sorry," Bess replied, "but I truly don't know it. Why don't you come back some other time and talk to Mr. Moto?"

The stranger was annoyed. "Where is Mr. Moto? Get him. He'll give it to me."

Bess was beginning to worry. The woman did not look or act like a nice person, and she felt that giving her any further information might not be in the best interest of either Mrs. Rossmeyer or Mr. Moto.

She said, "Please come back another day, perhaps tomorrow."

"But I must have the address today!" the woman insisted.

Bess was not sure she knew how to handle the situation. Finally she said, "I'll tell Mr. Moto you were here. What's your name?"

The stranger grew red in the face with anger. "That's none of your business!"

"She's not honest," Bess thought frantically. "She's trying to hide something!" With trembling fingers, the girl reached under the counter and pushed the button that operated the camera on the ceiling.

Trying hard to conceal her nervousness, Bess said, "If you won't leave your name, what shall I tell Mr. Moto?"

"Never mind. But you'll be sorry for your stubbornness, you silly girl!"

With this, the woman turned and hurried out the door. For a moment, Bess stared after her, shocked and surprised. Then she sank down on the stool, trembling.

Just then Nancy and George returned. Having found Mr. Moto sleeping, they tiptoed through the back room into the shop.

"Oh, am I ever glad to see you!" Bess said, her voice shaking.

"What's the matter?" George asked, alarmed.

Bess poured out her story. When she told about taking the woman's photograph, Nancy said, "Good for you! Maybe the police can identify this person. From what you say, I doubt that she's really a friend of Mrs. Rossmeyer's."

The other girls agreed. Bess looked toward the camera. "Who's going to climb up there and get the picture?"

George seemed the most likely candidate. But try as she would, she was unable to reach the camera. At this moment Mr. Moto walked into the shop. He looked refreshed, and color had come back to his face. He gazed up at George, who was stepping on one shelf and trying to reach another.

"What—what are you doing?" he asked in a puzzled voice.

"Bess took a picture of a woman who claimed to be a friend of Mrs. Rossmeyer's. How do you get it?"

Mr. Moto smiled. "I will bring a ladder." He disappeared into the back room and, in a few seconds, returned with a tall, narrow ladder. It had a hook at the end that fitted over the shelf beneath the camera.

"Push that lever on the right," he directed. "The picture will come out the front."

George did this, and a photo appeared. She pulled it out, then descended the ladder. She laid the snapshot on the counter, and they all gazed at it.

"It's an excellent likeness," Bess remarked.

Mr. Moto said, "I do not recognize the woman. You say that she claimed to be a friend of Mrs. Rossmeyer's?"

"Yes," Bess replied, and explained what had happened. "But I don't believe she was telling the truth. She was horrid."

"I do not like this," Mr. Moto said, visibly disturbed.

Nancy asked the jeweler to tell them more about Mrs. Rossmeyer.

"She is a widow," he began, "and travels in European high society. She is not sociable with River Heights people. She has a personal maid, an Asiatic who travels with her. When Mrs. Rossmeyer is at home, her maid does all the shopping, cooking, and so on. There are no other servants."

Nancy felt that Mr. Moto considered the woman a little strange but was too polite to say so.

"I have never seen Mrs. Rossmeyer," he went on. "I only spoke to her over the telephone. The maid brought in the necklace."

"Mr. Moto, would you mind if we take this photograph to the police? It might be a clue to the thief who took Mrs. Rossmeyer's necklace."

Mr. Moto nodded. "But do not say anything about the stolen strand of pearls. I am permitting you to take this picture to the police because Mrs. Rossmeyer's life may be in danger."

As the girls were ready to leave, they extracted a promise from him that he would close up his shop and go home soon.

He smiled. "You are so thoughtful. I appreciate all of this. I believe you will be able to solve my mystery."

"We certainly hope so," Nancy said.

At headquarters it did not take Chief McGinnis long to identify the woman in the photograph.

"Her name is Rosina Caputti," he said, "and

she's the wife of an underworld character known as Benny the Slippery One Caputti."

"What's his specialty?" Nancy asked.

"According to the report, he's a jewel thief."

"Oh!" Bess burst out. It seemed as if she was about to say more, but nudges from Nancy and George made her keep quiet. The three girls wondered if Caputti and his wife were connected with World Wide Gems, Inc.

While Chief McGinnis answered a phone call, Nancy whispered to Bess, "You did a great job today. I think we picked up a very good clue to the mystery!"

CHAPTER III

Sudden Flight

WHEN Chief McGinnis finished his phone call, he looked at Nancy and grinned. "Young lady," he said, "are you getting mixed up with underworld characters?"

The girl smiled back. "Not if I can help it," she replied. "But if there's one for me to catch, you know I'll certainly go after him!"

"Well, watch your step," the officer advised. "The Caputti's are suspected of having committed a number of crimes, but nothing could ever be proved against them."

"I don't want to see that Rosina Caputti again!" Bess declared. "She has a horrible expression on her face, and her eyes bored right through me in Mr. Moto's shop."

Nancy remarked, "You said Caputti is a jewel thief. Does he specialize in pearls?"

"Yes, although he'll take along anything that's handy," the chief replied. "Why do you ask?"

"Because that's what Mr. Moto works with primarily," Nancy replied. "I'd like to find out more about pearls."

"You should call on Professor Joji Mise," Chief McGinnis told her. "He is Japanese and has lived in this country a long time teaching Japanese art. He's a most interesting person, and I'm sure he can give you lots of information about pearls and the customs of his country. Tell the professor I suggested you get in touch with him."

The girls thanked Chief McGinnis and left headquarters.

"Let's call on Professor Mise this afternoon," Nancy suggested as they climbed back into her car. "We can have lunch at my house first."

Bess and George agreed. Later, when they were about to leave the Drew home, Nancy's dog Togo, a frisky bull terrier, barked and whined.

"He wants to come along," said Nancy. "Listen, old fellow, if I take you, will you behave?"

Togo wagged his tail vigorously, which meant that he was promising to be good on the trip. He jumped into the passenger seat in the front, so Bess and George climbed into the rear. When they reached the Mise house, Nancy left Togo in the car and opened the four windows part way for air.

The girls found Professor Mise at home. He

proved to be charming, and his wife a lovely, dainty lady. He considered the police chief a good friend and a very fine officer.

Nancy asked the professor about his native country, and he began to describe Japan, its customs, and some of its history. As he was talking, a large, beautiful tortoise-shell-colored cat wandered into the room, jumped up on the sofa, and settled down to go to sleep.

"What a beautiful animal!" Nancy remarked.

Professor Mise told her that it was a *mike-neko*. "They are a great rarity, and among Japanese fishermen there's a superstition that these cats can make accurate weather forecasts. Japanese sailors often have one or more aboard their vessels. It is even said that they are a charm against shipwreck."

"How interesting!" said Bess, who owned a cat, but admitted it was not as beautiful as this one. Then she requested that the professor tell them something about the history of pearls. "They're only found in the waters of Asia, aren't they?" she asked.

"Oh, no. Pearl oysters live in many parts of the world," the professor replied. "Did you know that even American Indians prized pearls and wore strands of them?"

The girls shook their heads, and their host continued. "Not every tribe did, mostly the ones along the seashore. Indians in Virginia, for instance, liked necklaces, beads, and sometimes even anklets made from pearls."

George spoke up. "How did you find out about this?"

The professor said that it was reported in old documents by white settlers of the 17th century. "Even in Ohio," he went on, "which is not on the ocean, skeletons with pearls in their mouths were found dating back to the era of mound builders."

George raised her eyebrows. "In their mouths?"

"I suppose the Indians believed that the healing propensities of the pearl would be beneficial for the dead person's journey to the happy hunting grounds. You know that the pearl was used for medicinal purposes when that science was still in its infancy. In India, for instance, people used to insert one or more pearls in the wounds of injured warriors to help them heal."

"Do pearls last forever?" Bess asked.

"I do not know about forever, but one pearl found in a Japanese storehouse was a thousand years old. After the dust had been removed, it turned out that the pearl had retained its original luster."

"How marvelous!" Bess exclaimed.

Just then Nancy heard Togo barking. She looked out the window in time to see him leap from the car. He ran to the house and whined to be allowed to come in.

Nancy went to the front door to chastise her pet, but the dog had other ideas. He scooted past her into the living room, where he heard voices. Suddenly he spied the cat on the sofa. He shot across the room and barked furiously at the animal.

The *mike-neko* stood up and arched its back. Togo put his paws on the couch and yapped at the cat. Frightened, it jumped onto a table, knocking over a beautiful Japanese vase. Nancy made a dive for her pet and grabbed him by the collar.

"You naughty, naughty dog!" she exclaimed and took him back to the car. This time she closed the windows a little more so he could not get out again.

She returned to the house and apologized for Togo's actions. "I'm dreadfully sorry about the vase," she said. "May I have it mended or replace it? I would feel much better about this."

Mrs. Mise had taken hold of her cat. She turned to Nancy. "You are not responsible for this mishap. I would not think of permitting you to buy us another one."

Although Nancy was very insistent, her host and hostess would not give in. To help the girl over her embarrassment, the professor went on talking about Japan and pearls.

He mentioned that for thousands of years, people knew only of natural pearls found in oysters. "Then came the industry of pearl culture," he said. "Today it is one of the biggest businesses in Japan. You really should visit that group of beautiful islands and see one of the culture farms."

"Just how are cultured pearls made?" George asked.

"As far as the oyster is concerned, the same way as 'natural' pearls. It happens when a small foreign object gets inside the shell, like a grain of sand, for instance.

"In the pearl beds, man helps this process by inserting a sphere ranging in diameter from two to ten millimeters. These nuclei come from the shell of freshwater bivalves and are polished prior to their use."

"I'll bet the oyster doesn't like that one bit!" Bess declared.

"True. It annoys the oyster so much that it gives off a fluid called nacre. This coats the offending object and hardens. The result is a pearl."

"Then cultured pearls are really not imitations," George said.

"Oh, no. Today that is practically all you can buy because few natural pearls are fished any more. But in ancient times, divers searched the deep water for the oysters. They risked their health, and many times their lives, hunting for pearls, which only royalty and aristocrats were allowed to wear."

"How mean!" Bess said. "That seems very unfair."

Her cousin George could not resist teasing her. "Why Bess, I always thought you wanted to be a queen!"

Bess made a face, but did not comment.

Professor Mise said, "My brother and his wife live just outside Tokyo. If you are ever in Japan, you must look them up. You would be welcome at their home, and my brother, who is retired from government work, would take you to one of the culture farms."

George smiled. "Is it a Japanese custom to invite people to your brother's home?"

The Mises laughed. "In a way, yes," the professor replied. "But we invite only people we like."

"Such a trip would be very exciting," Nancy said. "But right now I can't leave here because I'm working on a case for Mr. Moto, the jeweler."

"Oh, I know Mr. Moto well," the professor said. "A very nice man."

The girls and the Mises talked for a while longer about pearls and Japan, then Nancy and her friends stood up to say good-by.

"Please visit us again soon," Mrs. Mise said. "We will be glad to tell you more about our country."

The girls promised to do so, then thanked their hosts and left.

The following morning, Nancy suggested going to Mr. Moto's shop again. Perhaps he had heard from Mrs. Rossmeyer or had another idea as to who might have stolen her necklace.

When the girls walked through the door, they were surprised to see a stranger standing behind the counter. Nancy inquired about Mr. Moto and was told that the jeweler had left very hurriedly for Japan.

"My name is Kikichi," the man explained. "I am a friend. Mr. Moto asked me to take care of his shop while he is away. May I help you?"

"Did Mr. Moto say *why* he was leaving?" Nancy asked.

"No. He did not."

"Does he have any relatives in Japan?" George asked. "Perhaps it was a family emergency?"

"I do not know. He did not say."

Nancy wondered if by chance the jeweler had received a lead to Mrs. Rossmeyer's stolen necklace and had gone to retrieve it. But why had he not called her?

All three girls felt that Mr. Moto's sudden disappearance was quite strange. Was Mr. Kikichi telling the truth, or was he covering up a secret or foul play?

To verify his story, the girls began looking around the shop, admiring the various art objects. They called back and forth to Mr. Kikichi asking questions and receiving answers.

Nancy drifted toward the back room where Mr. Moto had lain down to sleep the previous day. She wanted to look inside for clues.

As she came closer, Mr. Kikichi called out, "This way. Don't go back there! Come this way!"

Nancy pretended not to hear him and hurried into the room despite his orders. She stopped short in amazement. The place was a shambles!

CHAPTER IV

Rising Sun Insignia

NANCY stared at the disheveled room for a moment, shocked and surprised. Then she retreated silently, waved to Bess and George, and hurried to the front door. With a quick good-by to Mr. Kikichi, who looked angry, the girls left Moto's shop.

Outside, Nancy told what she had seen. "Let's walk around the place. Perhaps we can pick up a clue as to what happened," she suggested.

Two cars were parked in the driveway to the right, and several tire tracks led to the street. Nancy examined them closely. An unusual one caught her eye.

"It has a Rising Sun insignia," she thought. "I wonder whether those tires came from Japan." She checked the tires of the two parked autos, but neither had treads with a Rising Sun mark.

The young sleuth showed Bess and George what she had found. "The tracks are still clear. I wonder if the person whose car made them knows Mr. Moto and gave him a ride?"

She followed the tracks down the driveway until they ended in the street. Here there were so many criss-crossing marks that it was impossible to tell which way the car with the Rising Sun tires had gone.

Disappointed, Nancy returned to the shop. She asked Mr. Kikichi if he knew anyone who owned a car with Japanese tires. He shook his head. "No. Why?"

She did not answer. Instead she said, "Mr. Moto was gone by the time you arrived here this morning?"

"Yes."

"And the back room was a mess when you came?"

"Yes."

"Don't you think that's rather unusual? Mr. Moto was a very neat man. He never would have left his place looking like that."

"You mean," said Mr. Kikichi, "that you suspect foul play? If so, why would Mr. Moto have telephoned me about his plans?"

Nancy said she did not know, but possibly something had happened to him afterwards.

"When did he call you?" she inquired.

"Yesterday. I had just finished dinner."

"I'll go outside and ask people in the area if they saw anyone here last night or very early this morning," Nancy told him.

Bess and George, meanwhile, had walked up and down the street, waiting for Nancy. When she did not reappear, they continued searching for clues.

By this time, Nancy had left Mr. Moto's shop through the back door, trying to find someone to ask about the jeweler. She noticed the neighbor from upstairs to whom she had spoken the day before. The woman was about to cross the street.

Nancy hurried toward her and asked if she had been aware of any disturbance in Mr. Moto's place the previous night.

"No," the neighbor replied. She added with a laugh, "Once my husband goes to sleep, I can't hear anything but his snoring. Why, is something wrong?"

"I don't know," the young sleuth replied. "Mr. Moto left very suddenly for Japan."

"That's strange," said the woman, who introduced herself as Mrs. Rooney. "I was speaking to him just the other day and asked him if he had any intention of visiting his homeland. He said no, not for a while. He was going to wait until he retired in a few years."

"Does he have any family in Japan?" Nancy asked.

"Yes, a brother, Tetsuo, who lives in Tokyo.

Mr. Moto told me about him many times. He's a widower and has visited the United States twice."

Nancy thanked Mrs. Rooney and went to look for Bess and George. She found them a few minutes later.

George held a pair of men's Japanese sandals in her hands.

"Where did you get these?" Nancy asked.

"We found them under a bush next to the driveway," George said.

"I wonder if they belong to Mr. Moto," Bess said.

Nancy examined the leather sandals. "They are quite large," she said. "And Mr. Moto is a small man."

"Let's ask Mr. Kikichi," George declared. "They might belong to him, even though he's not a tall person, either."

The girls went back into the shop and showed their find to Mr. Moto's friend. "Oh, no," he said. "These do not belong to me, and they would not fit Mr. Moto. Not many Japanese have large feet like this!"

A customer walked in at that moment, and Mr. Kikichi went to help her. Bess, George, and Nancy walked outside again.

"What are you going to do with those sandals?" Bess asked Nancy.

"I'm holding on to them for a while," Nancy said. "I have a hunch they might be a clue." She put them in her car, then told her friends what she had learned from Mrs. Rooney.

"I don't believe Mr. Moto went to Japan to visit his brother without planning this ahead," George said after hearing the story.

Nancy nodded. "I'm afraid he may have been kidnapped!"

Bess and George agreed. "The fact that he didn't call Nancy or her father after he had asked them for help just a day or so before is very suspicious," George declared.

"That, and the messed up room," Bess added. "Do you think we should tell Chief McGinnis about this, Nancy?"

"Yes, but first I'll get in touch with Dad. Maybe he'll have an idea."

Bess sighed. "This is becoming too much for me. Stolen jewels, missing persons, a possible kidnapping! I want no part of it."

"For the time being, you'll get your wish," George said, glancing at her watch. "We promised your mother we would take her shopping. Did you forget?"

"I'll drive you home," Nancy offered.

"Oh, no. We'll walk," Bess said. "It isn't far. You go back to your sleuthing so you'll be all finished when we see you later."

Nancy grinned. "I doubt that I'll be that lucky."

As the girls walked off, she decided to talk to

Mr. Kikichi again. "He must be wondering what we were doing there and why we asked so many questions," she thought.

When she entered the shop, he emerged from the back room. "I was locking the rear door," he announced. "What do you wish?"

"I wanted to tell you that I'm trying to find a clue to who might have come in here last night and wrecked Mr. Moto's room," Nancy explained to him.

"I see," said Mr. Kikichi. He looked at her but made no comment except to say that he would straighten up the room when he had a chance.

Nancy promised she would be in touch with him in case she heard from Mr. Moto, then left.

She drove to her father's office and told him what she had seen.

"It certainly appears suspicious," he agreed. "It's possible there was foul play, and Mr. Moto was taken to Japan by force. I'll get in touch with the airlines and see what I can find out. If they have no record of his leaving, I'll contact other likely airports. I'll also check on Mr. Kikichi and notify the police."

Nancy said good-by to her father, but did not go home. Instead, she decided to follow up the clue of the Rising Sun tire. She went to a large garage and asked the manager if people in town used tires with that symbol.

"No," the man replied. "I know of only one person in River Heights who does. I guess he imports them from Japan."

"Is he American or Japanese?" Nancy asked with increasing enthusiasm.

"Oh, he's Japanese, but he lives in this country. For some time now he has had a home on the outskirts of town. I understand he travels to Japan a lot, though."

Nancy was elated. "Do you know his name?"

"Yes. Mr. Kampura."

Nancy thanked the man and went to a public telephone booth to consult the directory. To her disappointment, Mr. Kampura was not listed.

The young sleuth drove back to her father's office and told him what she had found out. Mr. Drew called Chief McGinnis and asked if he knew Mr. Kampura.

"Not personally," the officer replied. "But I understand he has rented a place outside of town."

"What business is he in?" the lawyer inquired.

"He's in the wholesale jewelry business. I believe he works for World Wide Gems, Inc. If you want to contact him, you'd better hurry. He's leaving the United States on Thursday."

Nancy had overheard the conversation. "You know, Dad," she said excitedly, "it appears as if all our leads point to Japan!"

Her father smiled. "You're right. Especially since I've found out that the World Wide Gems headquarters are in Tokyo!"

"Oh, Dad—"

"I know. You want to go there—"

"Yes! On the same flight that Mr. Kampura is taking!"

"Let me think about this for a moment." Mr. Drew went outside to speak to his secretary, then returned, smiling. "I just checked on a few things. I have several business clients in Tokyo, and it might not be a bad idea to see them personally. We could—"

"Oh, Dad, you're wonderful!" Nancy jumped up and gave her father a big hug. "Perhaps Professor Mise could call his brother and tell him we're coming!"

"Good idea. You get in touch with him, and I'll take care of the reservations. Then you'd better pack your wardrobe, and lay out some things for me that you think I might need."

Excited, Nancy drove home and told Hannah Gruen about the proposed trip.

"My, my," said Hannah. "You certainly do get around solving mysteries. This latest one is in beautiful Japan?"

Nancy laughed. "I don't know whether I'll find the solution there, but it's where all my clues lead to. I'm really worried about Mr. Moto."

The kindly housekeeper said she was glad Nancy and her father were leaving. "With underworld characters here who might have harmed Mr. Moto, I think it's a good idea that you're going out of town."

Nancy phoned Professor Mise to tell him the news. A half hour later he called back and said he had telephoned his brother and that Toshio Mise and his wife would be happy to have the Drews as guests in their home, and they would pick them up at the airport.

Nancy passed the message on to her father when he came home.

"That's extremely nice of the Mises," he said. "I hope we'll be able to repay them somehow for their hospitality."

"Have you any news on Mr. Moto?" Nancy inquired hopefully.

"He didn't fly out of any of the coastal airports, at least not under his own name. But if he was kidnapped and taken to Japan, I'm sure his abductors provided a fake passport."

"Which would make it even harder for us," Nancy said. "Oh, I do hope we find out what happened to him."

When Nancy and her father reached the airport in New York on Thursday, he said, "How do you propose to identify Mr. Kampura? There might be many Japanese on board our plane."

A sudden idea came to Nancy. "Let's have him paged and wait near the check-in counter. When he shows up, we can see what he looks like."

Her father agreed, stepped up to the desk, and put in the request. Then he and Nancy walked out of sight, but watched the counter carefully from a distance.

Soon a Japanese man arrived to answer the call. He was about six feet tall, slender, and had a severe, square-jawed face. He reminded Nancy of Genghis Khan's cruel raiders of ancient times.

Mr. Drew turned to his daughter and whispered, "Nancy, don't ever tangle with him!"

The Drews hurried away before Kampura could learn that the call was a fake. "Dad," Nancy said, "remember I told you about the sandals Bess and George found in Mr. Moto's driveway?"

"Yes."

"They were rather large for a Japanese man, yet they were made in Japan."

"Many sandals are."

"But these were not the kind usually sold in our country."

"I see what you mean. You think they might belong to Mr. Kampura because he's very tall?"

"Yes! Between the sandals and the tire tracks with the Rising Sun insignia, I'm convinced Mr. Kampura was in Mr. Moto's shop recently!"

"I'm inclined to agree," Mr. Drew said.

Just then a message came over the loudspeaker.

"Will Mr. Campbell Drewry please go to the nearest phone?"

Nancy's father winked at her and headed for a booth. The girl was puzzled. Slowly she followed her father and watched him pick up the receiver. Why had he answered the call?

Suddenly an idea came to Nancy. She recalled that Campbell was her father's middle name, which he never used.

"Clever!" she thought to herself, a smile spreading across her face. "Dad must have instructed his office to use that name in case they had a message for him before he left. This way he could not be identified," Nancy thought. "I wonder what the message is?"

CHAPTER V

Shocking News

"MR. DREWRY" reported to Nancy that his secretary, Miss Hanson, had checked with various other airlines that Mr. Moto might have taken to Japan.

"None of them had any record of a flight booked in his name," he said. "I also got word on Mr. Kikichi. As far as she could ascertain, he's in the United States legally, and there were never any charges against him."

"Thank you for your report, Mr. Campbell Drewry," Nancy said with an impish grin as they walked toward the boarding gate. Mr. Drew squeezed his daughter's left arm affectionately.

"You're welcome. And now we'd better go. Our flight is ready."

The Drews followed a group of passengers onto the large jet and took their seats. Nancy was intrigued by the dainty hostesses in native kimonos. Before the first meal was served, the young women brought in steaming hot towels for the passengers to wash their hands with. When the trays of food were set before them, the Drews looked at them, wondering how they would enjoy the exotic dishes.

Nancy remarked politely, "Isn't that an attractive color arrangement?" The tray contained a bouquet of green parsley in a small vase. Next to it was a tiny platter with pinkish raw fish. White boiled rice and a dish of broiled eel were alongside it. A pot of green tea was served, and dessert consisted of a combination of fresh apricots and peaches.

Mr. Kampura was seated at the very front of the plane near the exit door. Once Mr. Drew walked up close to him and talked to the hostess, but he kept his eyes on the Japanese man all the while. Kampura was speaking to the man sitting next to him, but their conversation was unintelligible to the lawyer.

When they arrived at their destination many hours later, Mr. Kampura was the first to get off the plane. Nancy and her father tried to follow him, but with most of the passengers standing in the aisle, it was impossible.

The Drews claimed their baggage and walked out into the lobby. They noticed a Japanese couple who were waiting near an exit. The man looked so much like Professor Mise in River Heights that Nancy and her father felt he must be his brother.

The Americans walked up to the couple.

"Pardon me, but are you Mr. and Mrs. Mise?" Nancy asked.

The man smiled. "Ah, yes. And you are Mr. Drew and Miss Nancy Drew?"

"Yes, we are," the lawyer replied. "We're delighted that you speak English. Unfortunately, we have never learned your language."

The couple bowed low to the visitors, and Mr. Mise said, "You make us very happy by visiting us. Perhaps you will pick up some Japanese phrases while you are here."

"I'd like to," said Nancy.

Mr. Mise took her suitcase, and the Drews followed their hosts outside to a waiting car. Nancy could not resist taking a peek at the tires. They did not have the Rising Sun insignia on them.

As Mr. Mise drove through the city, Nancy and her father commented how much it resembled an American metropolis, despite the sprinkling of one-story brown wooden houses, which served as a small reminder of "Old Japan." Most of the people wore Western dress, and the streets were literally teeming with the city's ten million inhabitants.

Mr. Mise came to an open area with a large

marketplace and stopped the car. "Would you like to get out and walk around?" he asked. "This is one of our flower markets. We Japanese like our gardens to be all green because we think it induces tranquility and rest. But we enjoy flowers in the house."

Part of the area was filled with chrysanthemums of every conceivable color and size. These flowers were not yet in full season, and apparently they had been forced.

Mr. Drew spoke up. "May I purchase some for you, Mrs. Mise?"

The woman smiled and bowed. Later Nancy learned that it was considered bad manners for a Japanese to refuse a gift, which was called a *presento.*

Yellow chrysanthemums were bought, then the journey proceeded to the Mises' home, which was several miles out of town. It proved to be a beautiful place and was entirely concealed from the road by trees and bushes. A gardener on a step ladder was pulling needles from a pine tree.

Mrs. Mise explained why. "Japanese do not care for bushy gardens. We like to be able to look through the foliage, so a certain number of needles are pulled out."

They rode to the house. Mrs. Mise, Nancy, and Mr. Drew alighted, while Mr. Mise took the car to the garage. The house was designed in true Japanese style, with sliding panels for walls.

The panels could be opened easily to give more space.

Mrs. Mise said with a smile, "We do not sit on the floor to eat, as many of our countrymen do. We prefer the type of table and chair that you have in your country."

Nancy asked if the couple slept on the floor, as was the custom, and was told that in their second floor bedrooms there was American furniture. Mrs. Mise led the Drews to their rooms, and while the visitors were unpacking clothes, she arranged the chrysanthemums in a typical Japanese pattern. At the top of the bouquet was one flower, surrounded by leaves. Below it was another, and near the rim of the vase was a third. The arrangement was very artistic.

When Nancy and her father came downstairs and noticed the beautiful bouquet, Mrs. Mise explained that the top flower represented Heaven, the middle one Man, and the lowest one Earth.

At dinner, which was served by a dainty young woman in Japanese costume, conversation turned to the main reason for the Drews' visit. The stolen necklace was not mentioned, but Mrs. Rossmeyer was. The Mises had heard of her through the press, but had never seen the woman.

"We are interested in an organization called World Wide Gems," Mr. Drew told them. "Do you happen to know a Mr. Kampura, who is connected with the company?"

Mr. Mise said, "I have met the man but do not know him well. World Wide Gems has its main office in Tokyo, but the many salesmen are scattered throughout the world."

Nancy asked, "Would it be possible for us to meet Mr. Kampura?"

Mr. Mise thought this could be arranged. He would telephone in the morning to find out.

Now the Drews told the Mises about the missing jeweler, Mr. Moto. "We heard from his friend, Mr. Kikichi, that he had gone to Japan," Nancy explained. "But none of the airlines we asked had issued a ticket to him. We think he might have been kidnapped."

"Oh, no!" Mrs. Mise said. "What are you going to do?"

"He has a brother in Tokyo," Nancy said, "Tetsuo Moto. I would like to find out if Tetsuo has heard from him."

Mr. Mise brought out a telephone directory to find Tetsuo's number. There was a listing, but when he called up, he was told that the number had been disconnected because the man had moved.

"Shall I get in touch with the police and explain the situation?" Mr. Mise asked. "Perhaps they can trace Tetsuo Moto for you."

"That would be a good idea," Mr. Drew said, and the host put in the call.

"The officers will let me know if they can find

him," he reported after a short conversation. "And now it is late. Any time you wish to go to bed, do tell us. We want you to feel at home while you are here. Please do not hesitate to ask us for anything you may desire."

Mr. Drew said, "You are very thoughtful. Nancy and I are tired and would appreciate getting some sleep. Once more I want to thank you for inviting us here."

Nancy spoke up. "Your brother, the professor, and his wife are wonderful people. I can see that you are exactly like them."

Everyone said good-night and went to his room. The following morning when Nancy came to breakfast she found an envelope alongside her plate. Her name was printed on it in large, bold letters. Inside was a single sheet of writing paper containing the following equation:

$$4 + 9 = 13$$

Puzzled, Nancy handed the note to Mr. Mise and asked if he knew what it meant.

A worried expression spread over his face. "Four is *shi* in Japanese, which also stands for death. Nine is *ku,* which translates to suffering in pain. Thirteen has no double meaning."

"It does to me," Nancy said slowly. "I'm sure it refers to the thirteenth pearl."

"I do not understand," Mr. Mise said. "What is the thirteenth pearl?"

"Danger!" Mr. Drew said tensely, then told the Mises about Mrs. Rossmeyer's stolen necklace.

When he finished, their host frowned. "Do you think the stolen thirteenth pearl has been brought to this country?"

"That's what we're trying to find out. We believe that Mr. Kampura might be mixed up in this somehow, and we are here to investigate."

Mrs. Mise had a suggestion. "When you go to Mr. Kampura's office, Nancy should dress like a Japanese girl. Then she will not be recognized if someone is following you."

Mr. Mise thought this was a wise idea. He also felt that he should go with Nancy, while Mr. Drew and his wife should leave later and take a different route.

An appointment with Mr. Kampura had been made for 11:00 o'clock. This left plenty of time for Mrs. Mise to disguise Nancy. The woman said she had been a dancer and knew all about make-up.

"I am sure I can make you look like a Japanese girl."

First she rubbed white salve on Nancy's face and covered it with powder to lighten her suntanned skin. Then she darkened and upturned Nancy's eyebrows and put a black wig on her head. It had a tiny lotus blossom on one side. She was given a rosebud-type mouth.

Finally Mrs. Mise brought out a pretty but

subdued kimono, an obi, a pair of white stockings, and sandals. When the young detective was ready, she went downstairs. Her father and Mr. Mise were astounded at the change in her appearance.

"It's a perfect disguise!" Mr. Mise marveled. "I would never recognize you."

Mr. Drew joked about his lovely little Japanese daughter. Then she and Mr. Mise set off in his car. They arrived at the offices of World Wide Gems about ten minutes earlier than Mr. Drew and Mrs. Mise.

Mr. Kampura had a very attractive office furnished partly in Japanese and partly in Western style. Nancy bowed low when she was introduced, but on purpose her name was so slurred that no one could understand it.

Just then a man walked into the room and stopped short when he saw the visitors. "So sorry to interrupt," he said with a smile. "I was not aware that you had guests."

Mr. Kampura seemed uncomfortable at the interruption. "This is Mr. Taro, the president of our organization," he introduced the pleasant-looking Japanese man. "May I present—"

But Mr. Taro, not wishing to disturb the meeting, had already turned and slipped out the door. Nancy breathed a muted sigh of relief, since she did not want her name repeated.

"Nancy, it's a perfect disguise!" Mr. Mise exclaimed.

"What can I do for you?" Mr. Kampura asked, impatience showing in his voice.

"I will be brief," Mr. Drew replied, realizing that Mr. Kampura did not wish his callers to stay long. "I am a lawyer in the United States, and it is important that I find Mrs. Tanya Rossmeyer. I understand she is probably in this country buying jewelry."

Mr. Kampura said nothing, so Mr. Drew went on, "It is essential that I discuss a legal matter with her. I have been told that she has purchased a good bit of jewelry from your company. Can you tell me where she is?"

There was a long pause, then Mr. Kampura said, "Yes, I know of Mrs. Rossmeyer. She was a client of ours. But I believe she was in Europe recently and met a tragic death!"

CHAPTER VI

Conked Out!

FOR several moments after Mr. Kampura's shocking announcement about Mrs. Rossmeyer, there was silence. Nancy and her father looked at each other, then at the Mises.

Finally Mr. Drew asked, "Are you sure of your information? We heard nothing about this in our country."

Mr. Kampura rose from his chair and said, "I have no details. Her death was discussed at a jeweler's conference. As you know, she was a lover of gems and, therefore, was well known to the trade."

"In a company as large and successful as yours," Mr. Drew said, "I suppose you have a good deal of thievery."

"Oh, no, not at all," Mr. Kampura replied. "We have very tight security and little loss." Impatiently, he stepped from behind his desk and went toward the door. The Drews and the Mises realized that he did not wish to prolong the meeting, and they followed him.

"I'm from a rather small town in the United States," Mr. Drew said. "However, a Japanese man lives there who is an expert on gems. His name is Moto. Do you know him?"

"No," Mr. Kampura replied, "I have never heard of him."

He opened the door, and the visitors thanked him, said good-by, and left. No remarks were exchanged as they went down in the elevator and out the building.

When they were seated once more in the Mises' car, Mrs. Mise spoke up. "Nancy, I am sure that Mr. Kampura did not discover your disguise. I am very glad."

"So am I," Nancy remarked. "I have a hunch that Mr. Kampura was not telling the truth about either Mrs. Rossmeyer or Mr. Moto. Let's try to find out about Mrs. Rossmeyer through other sources."

Mr. Mise directed them to a Tokyo newspaper office that published an English edition. They looked through file copies for any notices of the socialite's death. There was nothing, and the group drove home.

Mr. Drew made various overseas telephone calls but could not verify the report that Mr.

Kampura had given them. Finally Nancy had an idea.

"Dad, you remember Renee Marcel who attended school with me? She was from Paris and now is a society reporter for a paper there. Why don't I get in touch with her? Surely if Mrs. Rossmeyer died, Renee would know about it."

"Good thinking. Phone Renee and see what she can find out."

Nancy put in the call and surprised her friend. The two girls chatted about personal matters for a few moments, then Nancy asked about Mrs. Rossmeyer.

"Hold the line," Renee answered. "I will make a quick search." She was gone no more than two minutes. "Nancy," she said upon her return, "this story is not true. Night before last, Mrs. Rossmeyer gave a large dinner party in Paris. I'll try to get in touch with her and let you know more details if I can."

Nancy gave Renee the Mises' telephone number and waited for an answer. It came after lunch.

"I learned that Mrs. Rossmeyer is in good health," Renee reported. "She told a friend that for personal reasons she was going into hiding for a short time."

"Have you any idea where?" Nancy asked.

Renee said that one source had mentioned Japan, another the United States. Later that day, the girl phoned again. She had spoken to the porter in Mrs. Rossmeyer's hotel. He had heard her say the previous day that she was heading for the airport to fly to Japan to the Mikomoto Pearl Farm. It was her expectation to make some large purchases.

Nancy was elated about the news. "Could we go there soon and verify the report?" she asked Mr. Mise.

"It is a long way from here," he said. "But a friend of mine runs a seaplane that he charters to groups. Let me call him and see when the next flight is."

After a short phone conversation, their host hung up with a smile. "The plane is leaving for the pearl farm early tomorrow morning."

"Wonderful!" Nancy exclaimed. "We're in luck!"

Conversation now turned from Mrs. Rossmeyer to Mr. Kampura. Had he lied intentionally to throw the Drews off the scent? Was Mrs. Rossmeyer in some way connected with World Wide Gems? Was he trying to protect her? And why had he denied knowing Mr. Moto? Had they not been his tire tracks that showed the Rising Sun insignia in the rear of the jewelry shop?

Nancy mentioned that she felt it was probably wise to contact the police at this point. "They may have records on World Wide Gems, Mr. Kampura, and Mrs. Rossmeyer."

Mr. Mise said he would take Nancy to headquarters but suggested that perhaps she would like to remove her Japanese disguise.

"I'll be happy to," Nancy said.

It took her nearly half an hour to restore her skin to the American look, to lighten the blackened eyebrows, and to change into her own clothes. Then she and Mr. Mise set off. He knew the chief of police personally and explained their case, translating for Nancy what he learned.

"It is not generally known, but World Wide Gems is under surveillance in several countries," the chief told them. "As you heard in the United States, the organization as a whole is not suspected of any wrongdoing, but certain members are thought to have connections with underworld characters. The police are watching carefully."

"Is Mr. Kampura under suspicion?" Nancy asked.

"Not so far. Why?"

"Because we think that he visited Mr. Moto's jewelry shop in River Heights just before the jeweler disappeared without a trace. But Mr. Kampura denied knowing Mr. Moto. He also told us Mrs. Rossmeyer had a fatal accident, which does not seem to be true."

The chief nodded thoughtfully. "We will try to find out more about Mr. Kampura."

Nancy asked the chief about Mr. Moto, but as far as he knew, the man had not come to Japan.

"I'm afraid he was kidnapped," Nancy said. "It

seems strange that Mr. Kikichi, whom he left in charge of his shop, had not heard anything from his friend after he left."

"It is possible," the officer said, "that Mr. Moto, for some reason of his own, disappeared in a hurry, and therefore left his room in a shambles. Has anyone investigated the possibility that he might have gone into hiding?"

Nancy admitted that they had not thought of this. "But why should he?" she asked. "He has had the shop in River Heights for many years and is highly respected."

"Even the finest people can have enemies," the officer said with a smile. "They might be connected with business, or family, or even friends."

"But Mr. Moto is such a nice man. I can't imagine his having any personal enemies. I'm sure that if something happened to him, it was because of the thievery going on in his business."

The chief promised to let her know if any leads to Mr. Moto's disappearance turned up, and Nancy and Mr. Mise thanked him, then left.

After their visit to police headquarters, there was still enough time for the Drews to do some shopping and to go to Mr. Tetsuo Moto's former residence to see if they could learn a clue from the neighbors.

Mr. Mise picked up Mr. Drew, who had visited a business associate during his daughter's trip to police headquarters, then he drove the Drews to the Ginza, Tokyo's main shopping street. Nancy's first purchase was a lovely pearl necklace for Hannah Gruen. The salesman showed them matching earrings and suggested that the lucky receiver of the necklace could surely use earrings to go with it.

Mr. Drew smiled. "All right, we'll take them for Hannah, too."

Pretty pins of pearls intertwined with enameled leaves were selected for Bess and George. Nancy's gift to Ned Nickerson was a pearl stick pin, and she bought cufflinks for Burt and Dave with money the girls had given her. The Drews concluded their shopping with a lovely pearl and silver bracelet for Mr. Drew's sister, Eloise.

While they were waiting for the articles to be gift-wrapped, Nancy wandered around the store looking at pictures on the walls. Suddenly she stopped in front of an oil painting of a queen. She was wearing a necklace with a huge pinkish pearl in the middle and smaller-sized white ones on both sides of it.

"I wonder if this is like Mrs. Rossmeyer's," Nancy thought and looked at the date of the picture. It was a hundred years old.

"This type of necklace must have been popular with royalty in those days," the girl mused.

Just then Mr. Mise said he would bring the car to the door. After he left, the Drews examined various art objects that were displayed throughout the shop. They saw a vase that was very similar to the one belonging to Professor Mise and his wife in River Heights, which Togo had inadvertently broken.

"Let's buy it and have it sent to them!" Nancy urged her father. He agreed. When the transaction was taken care of, they walked out of the shop and climbed into Mr. Mise's car.

He drove them to the street where Mr. Moto's brother had lived. They found the small apartment building facing one of the many streams that crisscrossed the city.

"Suppose we question the neighbors first," Nancy suggested. "I'll go with Mrs. Mise and Dad with Mr. Mise, so we each have a translator."

"Good idea," Mr. Drew agreed. "We'll meet out here when we're finished."

It was more than an hour before the four assembled in the street again. Their search had been unsuccessful. A number of people had known Tetsuo Moto, but could tell the Drews no more than that he had moved to the country. Next, the group went to all neighborhood stores and questioned the owners, but again in vain. There was no trace of the jeweler's brother!

"We'll just have to rely on the police to track him down," Mr. Drew said to Nancy, who was very disappointed. "I'll call them again tonight."

She nodded. "Even though I believe Mr. Moto was kidnapped, I was still hoping to pick up some

information from his brother, Tetsuo. Well—"
she sighed, "maybe we'll find a clue elsewhere."

Early the following morning the Mises and the
Drews set out for a visit to a pearl farm. They
drove to the dock where the seaplane was an-
chored and joined a group of people for the take-
off. The journey was pleasant and the scenery
interesting, with woods and mountains in the
background.

"Tell me something about pearl farms," Nancy
begged Mr. Mise.

"I will be glad to," he said. "You see, there are
two kinds of beds, those in which the oysters are
raised until they are large enough to be used in
pearl culture, and those in which they are kept
after insertion of the nucleus."

"Today we'll see one of the latter kind, won't
we?" Nancy asked.

"That is right. They must be in an area where
nutritious plankton is plentiful and where the
currents can flow freely around the oyster," Mr.
Mise went on, "but they shouldn't be near mouths
of rivers that pump pollution into the sea."

"Should the water be a certain temperature?"

"Oh, yes. The oysters tolerate a range between
fifty and seventy-seven degrees Fahrenheit. Since
the farm waters reach temperatures below fifty
degrees in the winter, the rafts and baskets must
be moved farther south. To people in the culture

region, these caravans that are pulled by boats are a familiar sight."

Nancy laughed. "I wonder if the oysters enjoy the trip."

"I suppose we will never know," Mr. Mise said with a chuckle.

"How about depth?" Nancy asked. "Does that influence the production of nacre?"

"Definitely. In shallow water, more layers develop, but they tend to be of inferior quality."

"What is considered shallow?"

"About seven to ten feet. You see, when water temperatures are between fifty-nine and seventy-seven degrees in the summer, increased nacre production is encouraged. But in the winter, the oysters are lowered to a depth of about seventeen to twenty feet. This insures a lovely pink color and better quality."

"How old are the oysters when they are injected with the nucleus?" Nancy inquired.

"About two years."

After a long flight, the pilot's voice sounded over the intercom. He announced that they would be landing soon. He spoke first in English, then in Japanese.

Suddenly the seaplane began to lurch.

"What's happening?" Nancy asked apprehensively, looking at her father.

"I don't know," Mr. Drew replied. "I can't imagine—"

The craft lurched again, and the smooth hum of the engines seemed to change. The passengers were tossed about, and a woman screamed. An engine conked out, then the other. Nancy and her father grabbed each other's hands. Were they about to crash?

CHAPTER VII

Chase in the Park

THERE were tense and fearful moments as the plane descended at a quick rate toward the sea. All passengers were strapped in and put their heads in their laps, awaiting the crash.

But the pilot was skillful. He managed to touch the water lightly, then lifted the craft so it bounced along the shoreline like a stone being tossed across the water.

He finally managed to land safely, and no one was injured. Relieved, the passengers aboard began to talk excitedly.

Mr. and Mrs. Mise congratulated Nancy and her father for having remained so calm. "I can see that you are experienced travelers," Mr. Mise said as the seaplane floated tranquilly to a dock.

"Good thing we didn't crash," Mr. Drew said, "or the pearl-making oysters here would have gotten a dreadful scare!"

The others laughed, then Mr. Mise asked the pilot what had gone wrong and translated the answer.

"He feels that someone tampered with the engines. After a complete examination, he will let us know."

Mr. Drew said he would appreciate this, as his group intended to fly back to Tokyo that same day. "Meanwhile, we'll tour the pearl farm."

A guide took the visitors offshore in a boat, showing them the long bamboo rafts that contained the oyster beds.

"The oysters hang from the rafts in wire-mesh or plastic baskets," he explained. "They feed on plankton and must be cleaned from time to time. We have a crew here that inspects the beds daily. The men must keep an eye on worn or broken ropes and inspect the oysters for disease."

"Who injects the nuclei?" a white-haired Englishman asked.

"That's done by young ladies called *tamaire-san*. Freely translated, that means *Miss Pearl-pusher*," the guard replied with a smile. "The girls open the oysters carefully with a special tool. After the operation, the oysters are allowed to rest for a while in quiet waters about seventeen feet deep."

"It must be quite a shock to their systems," Nancy declared.

"It is, and many eject the nucleus. We have

x-ray equipment that tells us which oysters do, and we do not bother raising those."

"I see some floating buoys way out there," Nancy remarked. "What are they for?"

"Those are experimental glass fiber buoys, roughly one foot in diameter, which will eventually replace wooden or bamboo rafts because they are more durable and economical," the guide replied.

"When are the pearls ready for harvesting?" Mr. Drew inquired.

"They are 'beached' after about two to three years. This takes place in the arid winter when the pearl-sac cells have stopped secreting nacre, and the top layer is completely crystallized."

"I'll bet that's an exciting occasion," Nancy remarked.

"Yes, indeed. The oysters are opened one by one with small knives, and out come pearls in many sizes and different qualities. About twenty percent cannot be used at all, and truly precious pearls are quite rare."

"Can you produce a bigger pearl by inserting a larger nucleus?" a blond woman asked.

"Yes, but that is risky financially because large nuclei kill many oysters."

"I feel sorry for the poor oysters," Nancy said. "For two to three years they are irritated by the foreign object inside them."

"True," the guide admitted. "But then, nature

does the same thing. Man does not harm the oyster any more than nature does."

When their tour was over, Nancy and her father spoke to the manager of the pearl farm and asked if Mrs. Tanya Rossmeyer had visited the Mikimoto Farm.

"No," he said, "and we have not heard from her. However, I will be glad to call you if Mrs. Rossmeyer should visit us."

The Drews thanked the man and gave him the Mises' phone number, then joined the rest of the group for the return flight.

The trip back to Tokyo was uneventful, and they reached the Mises' home in the evening. On the doorstep lay a note addressed to Nancy Drew.

She opened it quickly and held her breath. The familiar $4 + 9 = 13$ equation was the only message. Nancy showed it to the others, then said to her father, "It's not fair to put the Mises in any danger. I think you and I should leave here."

"You mean, go back to the United States?" her father asked.

Before Nancy could reply, both Mr. and Mrs. Mise spoke up. They insisted that their guests stay with them. They were not afraid, and besides, they felt that they could give the Drews some protection.

"Anyway, the person who is sending these threats may forget the whole affair if we do not take him seriously. Meanwhile, I suggest that we get away from the house for more sightseeing," Mr. Mise said.

Nancy and her father did not feel this way about it, but did not object to the idea.

"What do you recommend?" Mr. Drew asked.

"A trip to the famous Nara Park," Mr. Mise said. "It is a lovely place to visit and is full of interesting things to see."

Mrs. Mise smiled. "Nancy, you will love the little deer that come out of the woods and greet tourists."

"Isn't that quite a distance from here?" Nancy inquired.

"Yes, about an hour's flight," Mr. Mise replied. "I will make the reservations right away."

Next morning they drove to the airport and departed for Nara. The town had been Japan's capital in the 8th century, preceding Kyoto and Tokyo. The visitors enjoyed the sights before continuing to the famous park, which was a spectacularly beautiful place. People crowded the entrance and chuckled at the small deer that clustered around them, bowing their heads in welcome.

"Aren't they darling?" Nancy exclaimed. She patted several of the animals, who were very friendly, then followed the Mises on a walk along the paths that meandered among the trees.

They finally came to an enormous statue of

Buddha and gazed at it in awe. The benign figure had its right hand raised as if blessing a congregation. Mr. Drew remarked that it must weigh an enormous amount.

"Five hundred tons," Mr. Mise said. "The total height is seventy-one and a half feet. The Buddha itself is fifty-three feet tall, and the face alone is sixteen feet in height."

"That really is tremendous," Nancy remarked. "When was it cast?"

"In the year seven hundred and forty-nine A.D. It contains several metals, but the outside is bronze."

Nancy asked her host about the main tenets of Buddhism and its great teacher Guatama Buddha.

Mrs. Mise replied, "That suffering is inherent in life, and that one can be liberated from it by mental and moral self-purification."

Nancy thought this over, then said, "If a person could do that, he would be perfect."

"That is true," Mr. Mise said. "Many Buddhist priests try to attain this goal and deny themselves most of the pleasures of life. We, who are not priests, also try to accept pain and to live moral and upright lives."

Nancy smiled. "You are such kind, helpful people. I am sure you're succeeding beautifully."

The couple seemed embarrassed by the compliment and changed the subject. Nancy, meanwhile, had noticed how many people were taking photographs. Most of them were Japanese, but there was a sprinkling of visitors from countries all over the world.

Suddenly she saw a man who was snapping *her* picture. She stared at him and realized that he was short, had black hair, a hard face, and was wearing a gray suit. He looked to be of Italian descent. Could he possibly be Benny the Slippery One Caputti?

When the man became aware that she had spotted him, he turned and hurried around the statue. Nancy took off after him, her camera ready to snap his picture.

By the time she reached the rear of the great monument, the fugitive was running away at a fast clip. Nancy pursued him and was closing the distance between them, when suddenly a guard stepped up and stopped her.

"Please! You must not pursue an innocent man in this holy park!" he said.

Nancy was amazed. What made the guard think that the fleeing man was innocent? Certainly the fact that he was racing away made him highly suspect!

She said, "I don't think that man is innocent. I believe he's wanted by the police!"

Suddenly Nancy realized that the guard had spoken English without the slightest accent, and that he did not look Japanese. Was he a friend of

Caputti's and had he borrowed or stolen the Japanese guard's uniform?

The girl decided to pay no attention to him and started to hurry off. He grabbed her by the shoulders. "Don't you dare run away!" he hissed at her.

CHAPTER VIII

Nancy Accused

NANCY had to make up her mind in a hurry whether to try to get away from the man or turn the tables on him and prove that he had helped a criminal escape.

In the distance she saw her father running in her direction. He had called another guard, who was hurrying along with him.

By the time Nancy's adversary realized that he was about to be caught, he let go of her and started to run. But the girl grabbed his wrist and held on tightly. Tug as he would, he could not get away before Mr. Drew and the other guard had caught up.

"What's going on here?" the lawyer demanded.

Before the suspect could answer, the guard who had accompanied Mr. Drew spoke up. "This man is not one of us!" He turned to the impostor. "Who are you?"

The man did not reply, so Nancy told her story and her suspicion that he was in league with a man who was wanted by numerous United States authorities.

"I will take him into custody and hold him until he talks," the legitimate guard declared.

He asked the impostor where he had obtained the uniform. The suspect stared defiantly, but said nothing.

Nancy tried to catch him by surprise. "Where did Benny Caputti go?" she asked him.

The prisoner jumped and blinked, indicating that the girl had touched upon a vital subject. Still he did not talk.

"It is against the law to impersonate an officer," the guard declared. "You will have to come with me!"

Suddenly the suspect cried out, "Why don't you arrest this girl? She molested a visitor, trying to photograph him against his will. See her camera? She was bothering people with it."

Nancy and her father were startled, but Nancy said calmly, "He's trying to twist things around. The fellow who fled, and who I believe is in league with this man, took *my* photograph. That's why I chased him."

The guard nodded and handcuffed the prisoner. "I understand. Just give me your names and addresses in case the police want to contact you."

The Drews did, but before leaving Nara, they went to headquarters and told the full story. They suggested that the chief get in touch with United States Authorities regarding Caputti and the suspect, who evidently acted as a bodyguard for Benny the Slippery One. The officer thanked them for the information and promised to look into the matter.

When the Drews and the Mises reached home late next afternoon, they found Haruka, the delightful maid whom the family employed, had arranged a special dinner. The reason was that it was Mrs. Mise's birthday!

Haruka had made paper bird and flower decorations using the famous Oregami method. She had hung them in various parts of the dining room. On the table she had put live flowers of various colors interspersed with green vines. In one corner of the room, the maid had placed a huge jardiniere and filled it with lavender wisteria that gently drooped over the sides.

Haruka served a delicious dinner that included strips of fish with rice and fried vegetables. Warm sake, a wine made from rice, was served with the meal. Dessert consisted of a flat piece of plain cake in which the center was scooped out and had been replaced with half of a large, ripe peach. Over it she had poured a hot, pink peach sauce, and she had decorated around the edge with scattered peach leaves.

Everyone enjoyed the delicious meal, and they each proposed toasts to wish Mrs. Mise a happy birthday. When dinner was over, Haruka brought in a large cage with hundreds of gorgeous butterflies in it. She announced that this was her personal gift to Mrs. Mise. She had recently been on vacation and had collected them herself.

"They are beautiful!" Mrs. Mise told her, then translated for the Drews.

"You know my love for the colors blue and yellow," she continued. "How exquisite these butterflies are."

Everyone stood up to look at the fluttering creatures. Nancy liked a particular one that had various shades of blue from light to dark from its center to the wing tips. Mr. Drew's favorite was a reddish brown butterfly with black spots on its wings.

After the excitement about the gift had subsided, Mr. Mise gave his wife his *presento*. It was a high comb studded with pearls for his wife's hair.

"How beautiful!" Nancy exclaimed.

"My husband is a most kind man," Mrs. Mise said. "This is a lovely way to remind me of this birthday."

Nancy and her father were sorry they had not known about the special occasion and did not have a gift for their hostess.

Suddenly Nancy laughed. "Dad," she said, "we brought *presentos* for the Mises from the United States. In all the excitement about villains we completely forgot!" She asked to be excused, went upstairs, and got the gifts from her suitcase. She brought them down and handed a package to each of their friends.

Mr. Mise's *presento* was a new type of fountain pen. After thanking the Drews, he said that he was delighted to own one of them, since they had not yet reached the Japanese market.

His wife's gift was a dainty lace handkerchief. It had been made by a nun who was an expert at needlecraft. She had learned the art in Belgium. Mrs. Mise was thrilled with the *presento*.

Further conversation was interrupted by the ringing of the telephone. Haruka answered and said that it was for Mr. Drew and Miss Nancy. When Mr. Drew said hello, there was a click on the line, and it went dead.

Nancy and her father looked at each other. Was this a hoax, or was Mr. Caputti trying to find out whether the Drews had returned to the Mises' home?

The lawyer asked Haruka if she had any idea from where the call had come.

"It was from overseas, sir," she said. "I am so sorry you were interrupted."

A few minutes went by and the phone rang again. This time Mr. Drew answered it himself.

"Is this the Mise home?" a man asked.

"Yes."

"Am I speaking with Mr. Drew?"

"Yes."

"This is Professor Joji Mise in River Heights," the caller identified himself.

"I'm glad to hear from you," Mr. Drew said. "Did you just call a few minutes ago and were interrupted?"

"Yes. I had to try again. Unfortunately, I have bad news for you."

Nancy, who stood close enough to the receiver to overhear the conversation, felt a chill going down her spine. Instantly she thought of Mr. Moto and Mr. Kikichi.

"I have just learned," the professor went on, "that burglars broke into Mr. Moto's shop. Chief McGinnis asked me to tell you about it. They took everything in the place."

"That is, indeed, bad news," Mr. Drew remarked. "What about Mr. Kikichi?"

"He was beaten unconscious and taken to the hospital. But he is all right now."

"Are there any clues to the burglars?" Mr. Drew inquired.

"Yes, the police think that Benny Caputti and his wife were responsible. Further investigation revealed that they might have fled to Japan. We thought you should know this."

Mr. Drew told the professor of their trip to Nara. "My daughter believes she spotted Mr. Caputti but was stopped from pursuing him by a fake guard." He gave the details of the event, and the professor suggested that the Drews try to locate the couple.

"We'll do our best," Mr. Drew promised. "I suppose the River Heights police are working on this, but we may find some good leads here."

"Fine. I will report this to the chief. And now I would like to say hello to my brother and his wife."

As Mr. Drew said good-by to the professor and handed the phone to Mr. Mise, Nancy felt frustrated. Not only had they failed to find Mr. Moto, but now all his property had been stolen! While she and her father discussed the case, she did not know that a good lead would turn up soon. The Mises joined them a few minutes later, but their conversation was interrupted again when the phone rang a third time.

The call was for Nancy. It proved to be from the chief of the Tokyo police force. "We are holding a woman here who has been using a phony passport," the officer told her. "She resembles the description you gave us of a suspect the other day. Is it possible for you to come here to identify her?"

CHAPTER IX

Identification

WHEN Nancy arrived at Tokyo police headquarters with her father and Mr. Mise, she was taken at once to a brightly lighted room. In the center of it stood a tall, three-sectioned Japanese screen. The young sleuth was told to sit down in a comfortable chair behind it.

To her amazement, she found that she could look through the screen but was not visible to anyone on the other side.

The chief explained that this was a rather recent invention. "Similar screens are being installed in many homes, where it is desirable for the owner to be able to look outside but not to be observed by curious passersby.

He told the young sleuth that presently a woman would walk across the room. Nancy was to observe her carefully and decide if she could identify her.

"She will not give us her name or tell us where she is from," the officer explained. "But she matched the description of the woman you gave us the other day in connection with Mrs. Rossmeyer, so we thought you might be able to help us."

He left the room and she waited eagerly for the suspect to appear. In a few minutes, the door opened again. A woman came in, looking around for anyone watching her. Seeing no one, she walked toward a door on the other side. Nancy had no doubt in her mind that she was indeed Rosina Caputti!

The young detective had a wild desire to dash from behind the screen, confront Rosina, and try to get a confession from her. She wanted to ask questions about Mr. Moto and World Wide Gems. However, she knew that this would be hopeless. Mrs. Caputti would deny everything and refuse to talk.

The woman reached the far side of the room and was about to go out the door, when she apparently changed her mind. With an evil glint in her eyes, she made a beeline for the screen behind which Nancy was sitting. The young sleuth wondered what to do. Should she play a cat and mouse game and dodge to the front of the screen? She had only a fraction of a second to decide. Having identified Mrs. Caputti, she decided to stand her ground.

The next instant, the suspect hurried around to the back. She stopped short and stared at Nancy balefully.

"You little vixen!" she shouted, grabbing the girl by her hair.

Nancy wrenched the woman's hands away and exclaimed, "Leave me alone! It won't do you any good to harm me. You're Rosina Caputti, and you're likely to stay in prison!"

The commotion brought the chief back into the room. "What is going on?" he shouted.

Mrs. Caputti said, "This little busybody was spying on me. I won't have it! Why did you tell me to walk across this room?"

Nancy answered the question. "So I would be able to identify you."

At this Mrs. Caputti screamed and tried to get her hands on the girl again. "I never saw you in my life!"

Nancy, who was athletic and strong, pinned the woman's hands behind her, while the chief called out in Japanese, apparently for help. Another officer appeared instantly. The two men wrestled with Mrs. Caputti, who was fighting them like a tigress. Finally she was hustled away, and the chief returned to Nancy.

"The woman is definitely Rosina Caputti," the girl told him.

"Thank you very much," he said, bowing. "I

"You little vixen!" the woman shouted at Nancy.

did not know she would act like this, but I am glad you were able to identify her."

He and Nancy walked into his office, where Mr. Drew and Mr. Mise were waiting.

Nancy's father asked, "What was all that screaming about?"

The young detective gave him the details, then smiled. "I'm glad the chief rescued me. Mrs. Caputti is much larger than I. I'm not sure I would have won the battle!"

The officer grinned. "I would say you are very strong and agile yourself."

Nancy and her father thanked the chief and said good-by. He replied, *"Sayonara."*

When the three reached home, they found Mrs. Mise upset. Nancy sensed this at once and asked, "While we were gone, did something unpleasant happen?"

Mrs. Mise nodded and replied, "A man, who would not give his name, phoned several times asking for Mr. Drew and Nancy Drew."

"What did you tell him?"

Mrs. Mise smiled. "I said that no one by that name was here. And you were not. You were at the police station."

Her husband said that was very clever, and she went on, "The man made threatening remarks, but would not say who he was. Finally he became angry and said, 'I will not phone again, but tell Mr. Drew and that daughter of his that four plus nine still equals thirteen!' "

"It sounds as if he is getting desperate," Mr. Drew commented.

"And scared," Nancy added. "Maybe this unknown speaker planned to steal the thirteenth pearl, but somebody else got there first. He thinks we know who it was and is trying to find out."

Mr. Drew thought this was a shrewd guess. "Perhaps he's one of the underworld characters, but is being double-crossed by another member."

Nancy knew Mrs. Mise was convinced that she and her father were in grave danger, but their hostess did not express her thoughts aloud. Instead, she said, "I think this evening we should forget all about this mystery and have a good time. If my husband wishes to do so, I suggest that we all go to the Kabuki Theater."

Nancy and her father were delighted with this idea. They had an early supper, then drove to the huge theater. When they took their seats, the Drews were amazed that many people were eating or walking down the aisles, even though the first play had already begun. To Nancy this seemed very rude.

Mr. Mise read her thoughts. "These plays are very old," he said, "and from childhood on people get to know them. Many Japanese can recite them almost line for line, so by eating or walking around, they really do not miss any part of the play with its exquisite poetic lines."

"Why are men in women's parts?" Nancy inquired.

"This goes back to the seventeenth century when the government forbade female actors and dancers on stage. The men, as you can see, are heavily made-up and whitened to resemble women."

"And they speak in falsetto voices," Nancy added, then turned her attention to the play again.

She noticed that when a husband and wife returned to their home, the man walked up to the door, took his sandals off with the toes heading toward the door, and walked in. His wife paused, turned around, and removed her shoes, leaving them pointing outward.

Nancy did not mention this until they were on their way home. Then she asked what it meant.

Mrs. Mise told her that in ancient Japanese custom, the man was the sole owner of his house. Everyone else was a guest, even his wife. For this reason, she had to point her sandals outward, which was the proper position to leave.

The Drews' evening had been most enjoyable. Before going to bed, Mrs. Mise offered their American friends tea. She appeared a few minutes later with a large tray. On it were the necessary utensils: a pot of steaming hot water, pottery tea bowls, a tea container, and a bamboo whisk and dipper. There was also a plate of delicious little bean and sugar cakes.

"Tea was brought to Japan from China in the eighth century," explained Mrs. Mise while she spooned the green powder into the bowls. "It was found to have consoling, calming, and soothing powers, and the masters of the Zen religion made a ritual out of its drinking."

She spooned in just enough water to cover the bottom of the bowls. Then she whirled the wisk between her hands to make the mixture frothy before handing the bowls to the Drews.

"This is the manner in which tea is prepared during the tea ceremony," Mrs. Mise went on. "Everyone sits on the floor on the backs of his heels, with toes crossed and knees together, and all bow low each time before eating or drinking. The hostess has carefully learned the skills of the ceremony in the form sanctified by a great tea master, and her movements are very precise."

They drank the thick, opaque liquid.

"This is good," Nancy said, "but it is slightly bitter."

Mrs. Mise smiled. "The tea ceremony involves deep, true friendship. It is said that love of all humanity is in the tea, not in coffee or any other drink, only in Japanese green tea."

"It is also guaranteed to help you sleep, in case you have any trouble," Mr. Mise added.

But Nancy had no problem falling asleep. She had had a full and exciting day. She did not know how long she had been in bed when she heard her name called softly.

At first the girl was too sleepy to pay attention, but after "Nancy, Nancy, Nancy!" was repeated several times, she became wide awake.

"Who are you?" she asked.

There was no answer to her question, but the speaker demanded, "Have the prisoner released from jail and go home!"

CHAPTER X

Night Scare

WITH the threat ringing in her ears, Nancy jumped out of bed. The voice had come from outside, so she ran to the window and was just in time to see a man reaching the bottom of a tree. Evidently he had climbed it in order to call into Nancy's room.

She ordered him to stop, but knew it was useless. Quickly she grabbed her flashlight and pointed it toward the intruder. By now he was rushing toward some bushes. The light revealed that he was short, had thick, shiny black hair and wore a gray suit!

This was the description Mrs. Rooney had given of the man whom she had seen running from Mr. Moto's store! Could he be Benny Caputti?

Nancy concluded that the incident should be

reported to the police, and that a guard should be posted at the house if the Drews were to remain there.

She put on her robe and slippers and went to her father's room. When he was fully awake, Nancy told him what had happened. He was greatly disturbed, realizing that the man who had climbed the tree might have entered Nancy's room and harmed her!

"I like your idea of a guard," he told his daughter. "In the morning we'll talk it over with the Mises. Actually, I'm embarrassed staying here and putting them through all this trouble. We should offer to move at once."

Mr. Drew went to the telephone and called police headquarters. He reported that a man had been roaming around the Mise property who matched Caputti's description. The officer on duty promised to look out for the suspect.

Nancy finally went back to bed but found it hard to sleep, even though she had closed her window and pulled down the bamboo shade. Finally she dozed off and dreamed about climbing up and down trees after Benny the Slippery One Caputti, but never catching him. She slept later than usual, but no one disturbed the weary detective. When Nancy finally came to breakfast, her father and the Mises were already eating.

Nancy bowed low, which seemed to please her hosts, and said good morning. Mr. Drew had already told the Mises what had happened the evening before. "I mentioned, Nancy, that you and I felt we should leave and not put our kind friends to any more trouble. They wouldn't listen to my proposition. I guess I'm losing my ability to sell an idea."

"That is not the reason!" Mrs. Mise objected. "We are very interested in the case and want to do all we can to help you solve it. That is why we insist you remain here."

Mr. Mise changed the subject by showing the Drews the morning paper. For the benefit of his guests, he had thoughtfully bought an English edition. He pointed to a headline which read:

Daring Robbery in Jewelry Store
Only One Valuable Piece Stolen!

The article said that the theft was most unusual. Although the shop had a burglar alarm system, it had not been set off, and the police were at a loss to explain why. Also, they were puzzled by the fact that the only article taken was a necklace containing 25 pearls. The center pearl was very large and on each side of it were 12 smaller ones.

"That sounds like Mrs. Rossmeyer's!" Nancy exclaimed.

"It does, indeed," Mr. Drew agreed. "What do you think happened?"

"Benny the Slippery One comes to mind," she

replied. "I don't know how he got his nickname, but it could mean that he knows how to turn off burglar alarms and slip in and out of jewelry stores unnoticed."

"You are talking about the same man who climbed the tree last night and called into your room?" Mrs. Mise asked.

"Yes."

"But how could he do two things at the same time?"

"Does the article mention what time the robbery took place, Nancy?" Mr. Drew asked.

"It could have been any time after closing yesterday. When the store's custodian arrived at five-thirty this morning, he discovered that the alarm had been turned off. Thinking this strange, he called the owner of the shop. The man came immediately and discovered that the valuable necklace was missing. He phoned the police and they, in turn, gave the item to the newspaper just before it went to press."

"So Benny had plenty of time for the burglary, either before or after he climbed the tree," Nancy said. "I certainly wish I could find out if that necklace was Mrs. Rossmeyer's."

"Possibly World Wide Gems sold it to that jewelry store," Mr. Drew added, "and then Benny or someone working for him went to get it back."

"To make more money by reselling it!" Mrs. Mise added. "What a racket!"

Just then the telephone rang. Hannah Gruen was calling and said that Mr. Drew should phone his office as soon as it was open. "Meanwhile, I'll talk to Nancy," she added.

The young sleuth was delighted with what Hannah had to tell her. Ned Nickerson, Burt Eddleton, and Dave Evans were coming to River Heights to visit Nancy, George, and Bess. They wanted to know how soon Nancy would be home.

"I told them I thought in about a week," Hannah remarked.

"I'll certainly be there by then," Nancy agreed. "Dad and I hope to wind up the mystery soon." She told Hannah what happened since the Drews had arrived in Japan.

When she came to the part about Caputti climbing the tree and calling into her room, the motherly housekeeper gasped. "Oh, Nancy dear, please watch your step!" she begged.

"Don't worry, Hannah," Nancy replied. "I'm doing my best. This is a very puzzling case."

After good-by's had been said, Nancy wondered what to do next. An idea came to her. She said to her father, "Let's go outdoors and see if we can find any clues to the man who was here last night."

The two excused themselves and walked into the garden. Near the bushes through which the suspect had gone were footprints!

"These are strange," Nancy said. "It's not a

complete impression, just the ball of the foot. We can't deduce much from this, but let's see where the prints lead."

"The fugitive must have been running very fast because only the forward part of the foot is showing," Mr. Drew commented. "He was literally on his toes. Nancy, what can you tell from these prints?"

"That the man is short. He takes short steps but doesn't leap. I'd say he's an excellent runner. This may be another reason for his nickname, Benny the Slippery One, if he, indeed, was the intruder."

The Drews followed the shoe prints until they ended in the street, where it was impossible to trace them any further.

Nancy and her father returned to where they had started their search and examined the area between the bushes and the tree. Here the ground was firmer and no prints were visible. The Drews looked carefully at the bark of the tree, thinking its roughness might have snagged something from the man's clothing.

Soon Nancy detected a few thin, wooly, gray threads. "Dad! These could be from Benny's suit!" she exclaimed.

"You're right," Mr. Drew replied after examining the evidence closely. "I'm sure the police would like to see them."

Carefully Nancy deposited the find in her

pocketbook. "I wonder why he has such a liking for gray suits," she mused, then began to search around the tree.

A few seconds later, the girl sleuth cried out, "Oh, Dad, I've found another good clue!"

CHAPTER XI

A Detective Assists

MR. DREW hurried over to see what Nancy had discovered. She had picked up something from the ground directly under the tree.

"What is it?" he asked.

She held out her hand. In it lay a United States 25-cent piece. "I'm sure that man who climbed the tree dropped this. It implies that he's from our country!"

"You're right," her father agreed.

"Well, we have a fair description of him. He's not very tall, has black hair, wears a gray suit of lightweight wool, and is probably an American. Do you think that's enough for the police to go on?"

"It's a bit sketchy, but it sounds like Benny the Slippery One," her father replied.

When they returned to the house to report their clue, they noticed a man walking up the driveway toward them. They waited for him. He was Japanese but spoke perfect English. He introduced himself as Mr. Natsuke and explained that his name meant ornamental button. "My ancestors made them and thus received the family name."

Nancy's eyes twinkled. "If I should forget your name, you won't mind if I call you Mr. Button?"

Mr. Natsuke grinned and said that he was the private detective who had come to watch the Mise house during the daytime. Later he would be relieved by a nightshift man. He carried a radio, over which he could receive messages from headquarters.

Nancy asked him if he could also talk to the chief. "Yes, indeed," Mr. Natsuke replied. "Have you a message for him?"

"Yes, I do," Nancy replied and showed him the American quarter and the shreds of cloth she had discovered in the tree.

"We have already told the chief what the suspect looks like, and I'm sure he would be interested in this bit of evidence from his clothes."

The detective promised to call headquarters at once and take the threads with him when he returned there in the evening.

Nancy and her father thanked him and went

into the house. Mrs. Mise was waiting to give them an invitation. "My husband and I are going to a wedding this afternoon. The parents of the bride have graciously invited you to come. I think you would be interested in watching a Japanese wedding."

The Drews were happy to accept and asked what they should wear.

Mrs. Mise said that she would lend Nancy a pretty kimono and flowers for her hair. Mr. Drew had brought a white summer suit with him, which would be appropriate.

Nancy turned to her father. "We will have to get the bride and groom a *presento*," she said, and asked if he could go with her to a store where silver pieces were sold.

Mr. Drew nodded, even though Mrs. Mise declared this was not necessary. The Drews insisted, however, so she directed them to a shop within walking distance. Before Nancy and her father left, Mrs. Mise announced that she had a hairdresser's appointment in an hour.

"I believe you would find it interesting to come along," she said to Nancy. "The beauty salon is in the basement of a hotel, and they specialize in getting brides ready for their weddings."

"Perhaps I can get my hair shampooed and set," the girl said. "Then I won't feel that I'm being too inquisitive when I watch a bride prepare."

Mrs. Mise offered to make an appointment for

her and asked the Drews to please be back within an hour.

When Nancy and her father reached the shop, she could not refrain from talking to the manager about the strange jewel theft the night before.

"It was most unfortunate," he commented. "We think we have very tight security, but then, one never knows."

The Drews purchased a filigreed silver basket for the bride. The saleswoman told them such baskets were used by Japanese families to hold tea biscuits and little cakes with fruit. Nancy suggested to her father that they send a bud vase to the bride's parents. Both matters were taken care of, and the saleswoman promised that the gifts would be delivered before the wedding.

Nancy and her father reached home just in time for her to go with Mrs. Mise to the beauty parlor. On the way, the young sleuth kept looking out the rear window. She was sure that a car was following close behind!

"I don't want to frighten you, Mrs. Mise," she said, "but I think the man in back of us might try to harm us. Could you suddenly turn and lose him?"

Mrs. Mise was startled. Then she smiled. "I am not what you call a racing driver, but I think I can get rid of the man."

At the next corner, she made a quick left turn through a yellow light. By the time her pursuer reached the intersection, the signal had changed to red, and traffic prevented him from following. Mrs. Mise made a few more turns to throw off the man completely.

"Good for you!" Nancy said. "You might take up auto racing."

Mrs. Mise smiled merrily. When they reached the hotel in which the hairdresser was located, a uniformed attendant took the car, and Mrs. Mise and Nancy walked into the lobby. They rode an elevator to the beauty salon in the basement. Mrs. Mise announced herself and introduced Nancy. Both were shown to chairs. Nancy noticed that near her a bride was being prepared for her wedding. The young detective marveled at the process.

First, the girl's hair was tied on top of her head in a little knot. She wore a low-cut, sleeveless gown, and the operator rubbed cold cream all over her face, neck, shoulders, back and arms. After a few minutes, the cream was wiped off and white powder was dubbed generously over it with a puff. The same operation was repeated after a little while, and Nancy assumed that the process would continue until the bride-to-be had flesh the color of snow. The American girl was particularly interested in the fact that the back of the bride's neck received special attention.

Mrs. Mise, whose hair had been washed already, reached over and said, "Japanese consider the back of the neck and upper shoulders to be more beautiful than the front of the neck and the chest. That is why it must be pure white."

Nancy nodded. Just then her own attendant arrived and shampooed her hair. Nancy's hair was already combed before the process of whitening the bride was finished.

As the beautician set Nancy's hair in loose pin curls, a dainty batiste slip was pulled cautiously over the bride's head and shoulders. Then she was told to lean back so that her eyebrows could be dyed coal black.

While Nancy was left alone under the dryer, she could give the bride her undivided attention. The operator put pink lipstick on the Japanese girl in three applications. After each one, she brushed it daintily so that the lips finally became like a perfect rosebud. Nancy had to admit that while the girl looked very artificial, she was startlingly beautiful.

After the make-up had been completed, the operator brought in the exquisite bridal kimono and adjusted it properly. At that moment a messenger arrived with a large box containing the wig and hair ornaments. It was gently lifted out and set over the bride's hair.

The headgear was a combination wig and hat that had no crown. A white band went completely around it, and fastened to the band were many combs and pins containing danglers of all sorts.

Once more Mrs. Mise leaned over and explained to Nancy that these were symbols. "They indicate a long, happy life, lovely children, and enough money to be comfortable. The white cloth is called a *tsuno-hakushi*. Translated, that means a horn-concealer. It serves as insurance to the future husband that his bride will try not to show any horns of jealousy."

Nancy grinned as Mrs. Mise got back under her dryer. It was not until both had their hair combed out that they felt free to talk.

Suddenly Mrs. Mise said, "Nancy, didn't you mention a Mrs. Rossmeyer from your country who might be in Japan?"

"Yes. Why?"

Mrs. Mise replied, "I just overheard the girl at the desk say that Mrs. Rossmeyer had called to cancel her appointment."

The information excited Nancy. "Mrs. Mise, please ask the girl if Mrs. Rossmeyer is staying at this hotel."

The Japanese woman smiled and went to the desk. When she returned, her answer was, "Yes, Mrs. Rossmeyer is staying here."

"I must see her at once!" Nancy exclaimed.

"I will wait here while you hurry upstairs and speak to the room clerk." Mrs. Mise said. "Find out which room the woman is staying in."

Nancy nodded and went up the steps to the

lobby. After a short wait, she was able to get the clerk's attention.

"I would like to call on Mrs. Rossmeyer," Nancy said.

CHAPTER XII

Suspicious Taxi Driver

"I'M SORRY, miss, but Mrs. Rossmeyer checked out a few minutes ago," the clerk said.

"Did she say where she was going?" Nancy asked.

He shook his head. "Is it important that you find out?"

"Yes, it is. Very important. Is there any way I can get this information?"

The obliging clerk asked his assistant to take over, then came from behind the desk. With Nancy at his side, he inquired at the travel agency in the hotel and asked several porters and the maid who took care of Mrs. Rossmeyer's room.

His efforts were in vain, until a porter, just coming in from outside, told him that the socialite had departed for the airport.

Nancy thanked the kind clerk, then telephoned the Mise home. The maid answered and said that both Mr. Drew and Mr. Mise had gone into the city on business.

"Then may I speak to the man who is guarding the house?" Nancy asked.

When Mr. Natuske came to the phone, she told him what she had learned about Mrs. Rossmeyer's departure.

"Do you know where Mr. Mise has gone?" Nancy asked him.

"Yes, to his bank."

Nancy requested its name, then made a call. She was able to catch Mr. Mise and told him about Mrs. Rossmeyer. "Could you get in touch with the airport authorities and find out where she's going?"

Mr. Mise promised to do so at once.

Nancy returned to the beauty salon. She and Mrs. Mise paid their bills, then left the hotel. On the way home, Nancy told her companion what she had learned from the clerk, and that Mr. Mise would follow the trail.

When they arrived at the house, Nancy went to talk further with Mr. Natsuke. She asked him if anything had happened since she had spoken to him on the phone.

"Yes," he replied. "I saw a man sneaking around the house and taking pictures of both the first and second floors. Unfortunately, I could not get to him in time. He spotted me and ran like a deer."

"What did he look like?" Nancy asked.

"He was Japanese, of medium height, and wore a dark business suit. I got in touch with headquarters and reported it."

Nancy remarked that the people who had been spying on the Mise property now obviously realized that it was being guarded. "I hope none of them will return!"

Mr. Natsuke agreed whole-heartedly.

Nancy had just entered the house when Mr. Mise returned. Eagerly she asked him if he had any luck chasing Mrs. Rossmeyer.

"Yes and no," the Japanese replied. "I was told by the airline that she and her maid departed for Rome. But just before leaving, there had been a commotion in the terminal building."

"A commotion?" Nancy asked in surprise.

Mr. Mise nodded. "When the police rushed up, they learned that Mrs. Rossmeyer had been robbed of two strands of pearls and a valuable ruby and pearl pin!"

"How dreadful!" Nancy exclaimed, then asked if the authorities had obtained any clues to the thieves.

"Perhaps," Mr. Mise replied. "Mrs. Rossmeyer said she suspected the driver of a private taxi that had picked her up at the hotel. She had used him several times before while in Japan and had always found him honest. But now he is a prime suspect because he was the only person near her during the trip to the airport. He took her bags and assisted her from the cab. The theft could have happened then."

"Did the police get his name and address?" Nancy asked.

Mr. Mise said Mrs. Rossmeyer had given it to them. "He is Joe Slate, a Japanese, although he was born in the United States. He drives Americans who speak only English."

"Did the authorities get in touch with him?"

"They called his home, and there was no answer. When they went to his house, they found that he had disappeared. He lived in a furnished apartment, and all his belongings were gone."

Nancy wondered if he could be a member of the Caputti gang, since it specialized in jewel robberies. She asked Mr. Mise if immigration and customs officials had been consulted.

"I do not know, but I will contact both of them," he said.

Mr. Mise spent some time on the telephone. When he returned to Nancy, he said, "Neither immigration nor customs has any record of a Joe Slate."

Nancy wondered if any fellow cabbies might have some information on him and suggested that Mr. Mise speak to the police again and ask for an inquiry of all taxi drivers in Toyko, public or private.

An hour later came a preliminary report. No one who had been questioned so far had any idea where Joe Slate had gone.

"He slipped through our fingers," Nancy said, disappointed.

"Well, there are still a few drivers who have not been questioned yet. And a policeman is stationed across the street from Slate's apartment in case he should come back. If a clue should turn up, the police will call us."

Just then Mr. Drew arrived. He had visited another client, then called on a Tokyo lawyer who was an acquaintance of his. "I did some sleuthing of my own," he said, "and asked this man about Rosina Caputti."

"Oh, good!" Nancy said. "What did he tell you?"

"She's still in jail because the passport she was using had been stolen from a woman she resembles. Fortunately, it's now in the possession of its owner. But Mrs. Caputti still refuses to tell why she was using a false passport to enter the country."

"That's no news," Nancy said.

"The news is coming now," Mr. Drew said with a smile. "Mrs. Caputti had a caller in jail. He gave his name as Joe Slate."

"Joe Slate!" Nancy exclaimed. "That's the

name of Mrs. Rossmeyer's private taxi driver who is suspected of having robbed her!"

She told her father the story and asked if he had obtained a description of Joe Slate.

"He's Japanese, medium height, and speaks English without an accent," Mr. Drew replied.

"He sounds like the same man who drove Mrs. Rossmeyer!" Nancy declared.

Mr. Drew frowned. "This is very puzzling. You say Slate has disappeared? He had told Mrs. Caputti that he would get a lawyer for her. So far no one has come."

"How long ago did he visit her?"

"I believe just yesterday."

At this moment Mrs. Mise walked up to them. "I do not mean to interrupt," she said politely, "but we must dress for the reception if we do not wish to be late."

Nancy and her father excused themselves and went off to change their clothes. When they appeared a little while later, Mr. Drew declared that he had never seen his daughter look prettier.

Nancy's eyes twinkled. "You mean I might have made a good Japanese girl?"

He grinned back at her. "You certainly would have made a good Japanese detective!"

Mr. and Mrs. Mise looked charming in their outfits, but Nancy could not help but think how distinguished her father looked in his white, formal dress.

"The ceremony will be attended only by close

members of the family," Mrs. Mise told Nancy on the way to the hotel where the reception was to be held.

"I'm sorry," Nancy said. "I would have loved to have seen it."

"I can tell you a little about the ceremony," Mrs. Mise said. "Most weddings take place, as we Japanese say, 'before the Shinto Gods.' Sometimes this is only a scroll with the name of a God hanging in front of the couple as they exchange their vows, but mostly a Shinto priest presides. He must exorcise any evil influences that the couple might be exposed to, and does this with a shake of the streamers attached to a wand."

"And then they drink the ceremonial drink?" Nancy asked. "I've heard about that."

"Yes. That is the most important part of the ceremony. Both bride and groom must take the ritual drink, three times, then another three times, then another—nine times in all. After this the bride removes her headgear, signifying that she has left her family. There are no rings or other tokens exchanged at a Japanese wedding."

"I heard that in the olden days the groom was not allowed to see the bride's face until after the wedding," Nancy spoke up.

"That is true. It was feared that if he saw it, he might not wish to marry her. The removal of the hat is still the symbolic gesture of showing her face."

When they reached the reception, they found the newlyweds seated at the head of a long table, while the bride's and groom's families were on opposite sides.

"You see the elderly man next to the couple?" Mrs. Mise said to Nancy. "He is the sponsor of the wedding. In this case, he is a senior member of the accounting firm for whom the groom works."

Just then the man stood up and spoke in Japanese. "He's presenting the couple to the party," Mrs. Mise explained. "He tells about their families and their achievements."

After the speech, various guests sang short songs, some of which, Mrs. Mise said, were from plays.

As the festivities proceeded, guests mingled and spoke to the young couple and their parents. Nancy noticed the many jewels the women were wearing. There were not only pearls in abundance, but diamonds, rubies, sapphires, emeralds, and semiprecious stones. All of them were gorgeous. Most of the women wore fancy head-combs.

Nancy thought, "What a wonderful place for a thief like Benny the Slippery One to operate!"

After wishing the bride and groom great happiness in their married life and thanking the newlyweds' parents for inviting them, the Drews followed the Mises toward a table with dainty refreshments.

They had been there only a few minutes when

one of the hotel's messenger boys walked up to Mr. Mise. He handed him a letter and spoke in Japanese.

After he left, Mr. Mise opened the envelope. Inside was another one addressed to Nancy. A bit nervous about what its contents might be, she took out the message. It read:

$4 + 9 = 13$. *Your time is getting short!*

CHAPTER XIII

The Party Thief

MRS. MISE was very upset, and she was on the verge of tears. "This is so bad," she said, "so very bad."

Nancy patted the woman's hands. "Let's try not to take this warning too seriously. I think that whoever has been writing these notes is a coward. If not, he would have done something more drastic by this time."

Mr. Drew knew that Nancy was trying to make their hostess feel better. He doubted, however, that Nancy could take the matter so lightly.

He was right. Secretly Nancy was greatly worried. She had a feeling that her adversary desperately wanted to frighten her. Nancy asked Mr. Mise if he would try to find the porter who had brought him the note. "I'll go with you," she added.

Together they hurried to the lobby of the hotel and walked past the porters who were seated on a bench in a little niche.

Mr. Mise shook his head. "I don't see the young man here," he declared. "Maybe he was from another hotel."

Nancy asked, "Did he wear the same uniform as these men?"

Mr. Mise nodded. "That means he could not be from another hotel." Suddenly a smile crossed his face. "Here he comes now!"

A young man was walking out of an elevator. Mr. Mise and Nancy went up to him, and the two Japanese conversed for a few minutes. Then Mr. Mise translated for Nancy.

"The porter says that a little boy arrived with the note, then left the hotel. He does not know whether the child came from the street or whether he is staying at the hotel."

"In other words, someone probably gave him a tip to bring the note to the porter, so the real sender couldn't be traced," Nancy reasoned. "Very clever."

"Whom do you suspect the sender is?" Mr. Mise asked.

"Benny Caputti. He either followed us or happened to see us here. If the latter is true, he was in the hotel. In either case, he might still be here!"

"And you would like to find him," Mr. Mise said with a smile. "But it is a large place, and you cannot search the rooms!"

"I know," Nancy said. "But Benny would be where the jewelry is—"

"Which is at the reception!" Mr. Mise completed her sentence.

"Right. Let's go back there and tell Dad."

When Mr. Drew and Mrs. Mise heard about what had happened, they offered to look around for a man who matched Caputti's description. Nancy and her father went off together. The Mises walked in a different direction.

Presently Nancy noticed a short, black-haired man who, although he was not dressed in a gray suit, was obviously American or European like Caputti. He was walking quietly among the guests, when Mr. Mise appeared on the scene and took her arm.

"Nancy, I would like you to meet Mr. Shopwell. He is president of an American bank in Tokyo."

Nancy managed to hide her surprise and shook hands with Mr. Shopwell. How glad she was that she had said nothing!

The Drews and Mr. Mise spoke to the bank president for a while, then continued their sleuthing. Nancy saw another man some distance away who was dressed in black dinner clothes and fit the description of Benny the Slippery One. Suddenly she stopped short and grabbed her father's arm.

"Look!" she said. "That man! He's snipping a pearl necklace right off that woman's neck!"

The young detective and her father made their way through the crowd to close in on the thief, who had slipped the necklace into his right pants pocket.

He was walking away from the woman with quick steps. When Nancy and her father caught up to him, they each took an arm.

"We saw you steal that woman's necklace!" Nancy accused him.

"That is a lie!" the thief cried out.

"You can't deny it," Mr. Drew said. "The necklace is in your right pants pocket!"

The suspect stepped a few paces away. "You are wrong!" he insisted, still backing up further. "You are wrong. I'll prove it to you!" With that he turned the pocket inside out.

Several coins fell to the floor, but that was all. The pearl necklace was not among them!

Nancy and her father were stunned. It seemed like the work of a magician. The Drews had to agree that the necklace was indeed not there and apologized as the man angrily pushed the pocket back into its place. Then he picked up his coins from the floor.

"But I saw you take it!" Nancy insisted. "I'm

"He's slipping a pearl necklace off that woman's neck!"
Nancy said.

sure I saw you take it. But if I was wrong, I'm sorry."

The man nodded and turned to leave. The Drews walked away quickly before there might be a scene.

"I can't understand what happened," Mr. Drew said tensely. "We both watched him take that necklace!"

"I have an idea," Nancy spoke up. "Maybe there was a hole in his pocket, the pearls fell to the floor, and were picked up by an accomplice! Remember, there were a few people between us and that man, so we might not have seen the necklace drop."

"You're right," her father agreed. "Let's go back to the spot and see what we can learn."

By the time they reached the area where the theft had occurred, the owner had discovered her loss. She was Japanese, and began exclaiming in bitter tones in her language. The Drews did not understand what she was saying but noticed another guest hurrying up to her. She was an American who apparently understood some Japanese. However, she spoke to the woman in English. "I saw a necklace on the floor a few minutes ago. A Japanese woman picked it up, slipped it into her purse, and walked off. I assumed it belonged to her."

Mr. Drew whispered to his daughter, "You were right about the hole in the thief's pocket.

And the woman who picked up the necklace was indeed an accomplice."

Nancy was annoyed at herself for letting the thief slip through her fingers so easily. Why had she not looked for a hole in his pocket when he turned it inside out?

She spoke to the guest who had watched the person pick up the pearls from the floor. "Would you recognize her if you saw her again?"

"I believe I would," the American replied. "She wore a very pretty kimono and carried a matching handbag."

"Would you mind pointing her out to me?"

When the woman hesitated, Nancy added, "I'm trying to catch a thief, and I believe he's at this party."

The American consented, while Mr. Drew asked other guests if any of their jewelry was missing. Suddenly there was a hubbub as one woman after another discovered that their gems had been stolen. Bracelets, necklaces, pins, and hair ornaments were gone. A valuable ruby and diamond necklace was reported by a friend of the bride to have been stolen.

Mr. Mise notified the police, and a number of officers arrived in a few minutes to search for the thief. All guests cooperated and permitted themselves to be searched.

A young officer asked Nancy for her purse. She smiled.

"I don't have one with me," she said. "I put my comb into the bottom of my kimono sleeve as I understand Japanese women often do."

"Then I must examine your sleeves," the officer said.

He found nothing in the left one, then reached into the right. To Nancy's horror he pulled out a gorgeous ruby and diamond necklace!

CHAPTER XIV

The Trap

NANCY was so shocked at seeing the beautiful necklace taken from her sleeve that for a moment she was speechless.

Her father came to her defense. "This is ridiculous. My daughter certainly does not own that and did not take it from anyone."

The officer asked how she could explain its presence in her sleeve. "You had better come up with a good story, or I will have to take you to headquarters!" he said sternly.

"I have already spoken to the chief about a case I'm working on involving stolen jewelry," Nancy said.

The officer raised his eyebrows in amazement.

"It started in the United States," the girl detective went on. "A valuable necklace was stolen from a jeweler in my hometown just before the jeweler mysteriously disappeared. My father and

I came here to investigate because several leads pointed to Japan. We hope to locate the stolen piece and also the thief."

"Is it *this* necklace?" the officer asked.

"No. But I saw a very suspicious man take a string of pearls from a woman. When I accused him, he denied it. Since he didn't have it on his person, we couldn't prove it, and he left. Then other people complained about having their jewelry stolen. I know he framed me before slipping out so I could not pursue him any longer!"

Nancy gave more details of the case, and the young officer did not know how to proceed. Since evidence was found on her person, could he legally let her go?

By this time Mr. and Mrs. Mise had come up to Nancy and her father and asked what the trouble was. They knew the officer. As soon as they heard what had happened, both vouched for Nancy, saying the accusation was unjust.

The policeman finally agreed to release Nancy into the Mises' custody if they would guarantee her appearance in court if she were called. Mr. Mise promised.

The commotion over the jewelry thefts had ruined the wedding reception. Nancy and her father went to find the bride and groom and their parents, but all of them had left.

"I certainly feel sorry for them," Nancy declared. "It should have been such a happy occasion. To have something like this happen will be an unfortunate memory for them."

Mr. Drew and the Mises agreed.

"I see they have opened the doors once more," Mr. Mise said. "I suppose they did not find the thief and his accomplice. Evidently they escaped before the doors were closed. We may as well go home ourselves now."

He kept in close touch with the police for the next few hours, but learned nothing helpful. Had the reception thieves left the country, or was Caputti still in Japan?

Mrs. Mise remarked, "As long as Mrs. Caputti is in jail, I doubt that her husband would leave town."

"He might," Mr. Drew said. "Benny's a very cruel man."

The following morning Nancy asked Mr. Mise if he would take her and her father back to the World Wide Gems offices to talk to Mr. Kampura about the case. He was not in, and the only person available was Mr. Hashi, the local manager.

When questioned by the Drews about the various jewel thefts, he said he knew nothing about them. Nancy asked him if he was aware that World Wide Gems was under suspicion.

"Oh, no! We are a reputable organization!" he replied. "Where did you hear such a rumor?"

Nancy gave no details but thought she detected a frown on the man's face. Other than that, he showed no sign of being disturbed. Instead, he insisted on the fine reputation of the company and that it was considered the finest jewelry wholesaler in the world.

"That must be of great satisfaction to you and the other executives," Nancy said. "Actually we were told that the president and other top officials are not directly involved."

Mr. Hashi was annoyed. He took this remark as an inference that *he* might be under suspicion, not being a top official himself.

"If you are implying that I am dishonest, I wish to inform you that my integrity has never been questioned. Now I must say good-by to you," he said coldly.

He arose, then bowed stiffly and held this position until the callers had left his office. As they were walking down the hallway, the visitors came face to face with Mr. Taro, the president of the company. He wished them a pleasant morning and kept on going.

Nancy stopped him. "Mr. Taro," she said, "we came to ask if any jewelry has been offered to you by a Mr. Caputti or a Mr. Slate."

"No, neither one of them has been here," the man replied. "In fact, recently no one has come to me with anything valuable to sell."

"Thank you," Nancy said, and her group continued toward the elevator.

Suddenly her father turned around and hurried back to Mr. Taro. "Pardon me," he said to the president, "but it is important for me as a lawyer to know whether you, as head of this company, are aware of the fact that World Wide Gems is presently under suspicion of underhanded dealings."

Mr. Taro laughed. "It is impossible. You heard a rumor that is absolutely not true." With that, he hurried on.

Mr. Drew joined Nancy and Mr. Mise in front of the elevator. Before it arrived, a young Japanese woman, who evidently worked for World Wide Gems, approached them.

"Follow me," she said to Nancy in a low voice. "I can tell you something important!"

Nancy signaled to her father to watch where they were going in case of foul play, then walked quickly after the woman to a ladies restroom.

When the door was closed behind them, the stranger said, "I cannot stay away from my desk very long or my boss will be suspicious. I am Mr. Taro's secretary, and I am worried about him. He is an honest man, but recently he has become suspicious of certain officials in the company. He is afraid that they are carrying on some dishonest schemes in regard to the purchase of jewelry."

Nancy nodded. "He probably didn't want to admit it to us. How did you find out about it?"

"I overheard a conversation on his private telephone line. I do not know to whom he was speaking, but the other person said, "Yes, I received a warning note that said four plus nine equals thirteen."

Nancy was startled. The look on her face prompted the young woman to ask whether she knew what it meant.

"I have an idea it stands for danger," Nancy replied, but did not mention having received several similar warnings.

"I know you are a detective," the Japanese woman went on. "I spent some time in your country and read about you. When I overheard your name today, I felt I could trust you. I am so worried about Mr. Taro. Perhaps you can help him. He is a wonderful person, and I do not wish to have any harm come to him."

"I'm glad you told me," Nancy said. "I'll do my best."

"Thank you," the girl said. "Now I must go."

She opened the door and hurried out quickly. Nancy waited several seconds before following her, so that no one in the hallway would suspect that they had been talking. Then she joined her father and Mr. Mise again. They all went down and walked into the street.

When they arrived home Nancy told her story so that Mrs. Mise could hear it, too. When she was finished, everyone was shocked.

"This is a most complicated affair," Mrs. Mise said. "Those jewel thieves are dreadful people!"

"I have a feeling that top officials at World Wide Gems who are not involved with the underworld might be in grave danger. They must have found out certain things and are now being threatened."

"And the criminals would stop at nothing to gain their ends," Mr. Mise added. "I am so worried about both of you."

The Drews did not feel comfortable either, but said that they had been in precarious situations before and never quit when they were hot on the trail of wrongdoers.

"I'd like very much to see a list of all people working for World Wide Gems," she added.

Mr. Mise jumped up from his chair. "It just occurred to me that I have one. I own a small amount of stock in the company. A list came with the annual report. However, it gives only the names of officers."

"That's enough to start with," Nancy said, and he went to get it. Nancy and her father read the names of the many vice presidents.

Suddenly the girl exclaimed, "Look! I can't believe it!"

"Don't tell me Mr. Caputti is an executive of World Wide Gems," her father teased.

"No, but wait until you hear who is! *Mrs. Tanya Rossmeyer!*"

Mr. Drew stared at her. "You're kidding!" I had no idea that she was active in any business."

"She certainly doesn't act like a business woman," Nancy added, "traveling from one place to another without telling anyone her schedule."

"That's true," her father agreed. "On the other hand, with her love and knowledge of gems, she would be qualified."

"She had some quite valuable jewelry stolen," Nancy mused. "Perhaps she was allowing herself to be robbed by a confederate of the company as a cover up! Dad, Mrs. Rossmeyer could be in league with the thieves at World Wide Gems!"

Mrs. Mise had sat down in one corner and started to read the morning paper. Suddenly she cried out, "Here is an amazing article!"

"What does it say?" Nancy asked.

"It is a report from Rome that states that Mrs. Tanya Rossmeyer, while attending a dinner, was robbed of a priceless necklace!"

CHAPTER XV

Phony Papers

"WHAT else does the newspaper article say?" Nancy asked Mrs. Mise.

The Japanese woman continued to read, then translated. "The police have been unable to locate Mrs. Rossmeyer since the theft. Newsmen and friends have not heard from her either."

Mrs. Mise went on reading. "It was conjectured that Mrs. Rossmeyer might have left for the United States. Police and friends have said that oftentimes, on a whim, she would pack up, leave wherever she was, and not tell anyone where she was going. Then suddenly she would turn up in a different country."

"She might have gone home to River Heights," Nancy speculated. "One thing we have never asked about is the companion who is said to travel with her. Was she with Mrs. Rossmeyer? Is she mixed up in the jewel racket?"

Mr. Mise spoke up. "Would you like me to call the newspaper and ask if they have any information about the woman?"

"Please do," Nancy replied.

Mr. Mise went to the phone. He returned in a short time to say that when last seen, Mrs. Rossmeyer's companion was with her. "Would you like to go to headquarters and talk to the chief?"

"Yes," Nancy and her father replied together.

The chief had little to add to the newspaper story, but while his visitors waited, he made a long distance call to the chief of police in Rome. Then he reported that an investigation had been made, and anyone who might have any information on the jewel theft or the whereabouts of Mrs. Rossmeyer had been questioned thoroughly.

"One person overheard the two women talking about returning to the United States," he added. "But someone else had heard them mention that they would go to Paris. Where they went, nobody knows."

Nancy asked him what he knew about World Wide Gem's recent business dealings. When Nancy told of her theory regarding Mrs. Rossmeyer, the chief nodded.

"We do not feel that she is involved in any dishonest dealings," he said. "All the information we have collected indicates that Mrs. Rossmeyer is not really active as an officer of World Wide

Gems. It was advantageous for them to use her name, which is synonymous with fine jewelry and good advertising. But we are still investigating all angles."

The telephone rang, and the chief answered. After a brief conversation he hung up and said, "I just had a message from Interpol. Someone in your hometown claims to have seen the missing Mr. Moto in the back seat of an automobile. The police strongly suspect that he never left River Heights!"

Nancy and her father looked at each other. "I had almost come to the same conclusion," she said.

After thanking the chief, they drove back to the Mise home. Mrs. Mise had a message for Mr. Drew. His office had called and indicated that it was important for him to return home as soon as possible.

"In view of what we just heard at headquarters," Mr. Drew said to Nancy, "I don't think it would be worthwhile for you to stay, either. Both Mr. Moto and Mrs. Rossmeyer are obviously not in Japan, and I don't believe you can do any more to locate Mr. Caputti than the police can."

Nancy agreed. She felt it was more important to follow the clue to Mr. Moto, who, she was convinced now, was being held against his will by someone in his hometown. Also, in the back of her mind was the statement from Bess and George that Ned, Burt, and Dave were coming to visit the girls in River Heights.

"Maybe they can help us hunt," she thought.

The Drews told their hosts that they were planning to leave the following day.

"Oh, we must have a farewell party," Mrs. Mise said at once.

"That's very sweet of you," Nancy said, "but it is not necessary. Anyway, we are not giving you enough time to plan anything."

Mrs. Mise said, "Perhaps, as you say, there is not enough time to invite friends, but I suggest that we go to Mr. Mise's club this evening. It has a very fine restaurant, and I think you will enjoy the food there."

The club proved to be not only an excellent place to eat, but it was filled with many interesting art objects. A lovely Japanese girl named Lei greeted them. She wore a beautiful flowered satin kimono with a contrasting obi. She had a very fetching high hair-do accented by combs. Lei showed them several charming old pictures of Japanese life as it was hundreds of years ago.

Mr. Drew was particularly interested in pictures of old-time Japanese fishermen using the cormorant bird to make their catch. They held the bird like a kite on a string. When the cormorant swooped down to the water and scooped up a fish in its bill, the fisherman would quickly pull it in and take the catch!

"The poor cormorant!" Nancy said. "He worked so hard for nothing."

Their guide smiled. "I venture to say that the fishermen allowed the birds to have their fill after they did their job."

Next to the pictures, Lei showed them jeweled crowns, which she said had been worn by royal children in various countries. She pointed to one, which she said was Russian.

"Long ago girls usually married young in that country. The brides were shaved in order to accommodate the crown jewels they would wear," she explained.

While the group was eating, the headwaiter told Mr. Mise that he had read about the disappearance of Mrs. Tanya Rossmeyer.

"She is a member of our club," he remarked. "I hope nothing has happened to her. She was here only a short while ago."

"Did she by any chance mention to you where she was going after her visit to Rome?" Mr. Drew inquired.

"No. I have no idea. She frequently travels from place to place."

When the group arrived home, Nancy and her father packed. They were booked to fly to the United States the following evening.

"It's high time we get back and take up our work," the lawyer said.

"I can hardly wait," Nancy added.

After breakfast, the young detective said she would like to go to the jail and try to talk to Mrs. Caputti.

"Maybe if I tell her I know a lot about the jewel thefts, she may break down and confess," Nancy reasoned.

"I doubt it," her father said, "but I suppose it's worth a try."

Mrs. Mise offered to go along, and when the two arrived, they asked to see the warden. After introducing themselves, they inquired whether it would be possible to speak to Mrs. Caputti.

The warden smiled. "So sorry," he said. "Her lawyer came here with certain papers and she was released."

"Released!" Nancy exclaimed. She was stunned. "But I'm sure there must be some mistake. Mrs. Caputti's husband is wanted in the United States, and we believe she works with him in committing jewel robberies!"

The warden shrugged. "I am certain you must be wrong. I told you, her lawyer came here with the papers."

"What did he look like?" Nancy asked.

"He was tall for a Japanese, and powerfully built. Rather stern faced, I would say."

The truth dawned on the girl detective. "What was his name?"

"Mr. Kampura!"

CHAPTER XVI

Mysterious Invitation

"OH NO!" Nancy exclaimed in dismay.

The warden stared at her. "What is wrong?"

"Mr. Kampura is suspected of dishonest dealings. I'm sure he forged those papers. Will you please check them and verify the signature?"

By now the warden felt uncomfortable. "Of course. I will get them from my file," he said, and left. A few minutes later he returned with a folder. "The documents were signed by Judge Hiawasa. I shall call him at once and confirm his signature."

He phoned the judge's chambers and apparently found him in. After a brief conversation in Japanese, the warden hung up. His face ashen white. "You were right. Judge Hiawasa never is-

sued an order for the release of the woman prisoner. Oh, what have I done!"

"You let a known criminal out of jail," Nancy
said. "But it was not your fault," she added,
realizing the man's distress. "I'm sure the forgery
was an excellent one."

The warden promised to get in touch with
higher authorities at once. He thanked Nancy
and Mrs. Mise for their help, and both said they
were glad to have been of some service to him.

Nevertheless, they were worried about Mrs.
Caputti being free and spoke about it on the way
home. "I suppose now she'll join her husband,"
Nancy said, "and perhaps they will leave the
country together, if he has not already gone."

When Mrs. Mise and Nancy reached home, the
girl detective packed her bags. Then their hosts
drove the Drews to the airport and said good-by.

"Be sure to let us know how you progress with
the case," Mr. Mise said.

"Indeed we will," Nancy replied. "We never
can thank you enough for your help in trying to
solve this international case."

In the airport Nancy and her father looked
carefully for the Caputtis. There was no sign of
them, and finally Nancy and her father boarded
their plane.

When they reached River Heights the next
day and walked into their own house, Hannah

was overjoyed to see them. After she and Nancy exchanged hugs, Mrs. Gruen said she had worried every minute during the Drews' absence.

"Any special reason?" Nancy's father asked her.

The housekeeper said that several phone calls had come for them. When she told the persons that the Drews were not at home, they had left various messages.

"I've written them all down for you to look at later. Some of them were warnings of one sort or another. Several of the callers demanded to know how to get in touch with you. Of course, I did not tell them, and while I didn't say so, my answers inferred that you were only out of town temporarily."

"Good for you!" Mr. Drew praised her. "You probably saved us a lot of trouble."

When Nancy walked into the dining room, she was amazed to see the table set for a number of people.

"Who's coming?" she asked.

Hannah Gruen smiled. "Three guesses."

Nancy counted the number of places, then said, "Bess, George, Ned, Burt, and Dave."

"Correct."

Before the guests arrived, Nancy unpacked her clothes and the gifts she had brought. Hurrying downstairs, she put the boxes at the places where each recipient would sit, and she attached cards.

All the guests arrived in a little while. Bess said, "Oh, Nancy, I'm so happy you're home safe and sound," and hugged her.

George was eager to hear about Nancy's adventures. "And don't leave out a word!" she commanded.

Burt and Dave, both strong, sturdy football players, greeted the Drews enthusiastically, saying they were envious of their exciting trip. Ned, more handsome than the others, had brown eyes, wavy dark hair, and a ready smile. He gave Nancy an affectionate embrace.

"It's sure great to have you back," he said.

The dinner was filled with fun and excitement, and the guests were thrilled with their presents. Hannah, Bess, and George put on their necklaces, while Ned fastened his stickpin to his necktie. Burt and Dave were surprised to receive anything, but Nancy explained that their gifts were actually from Bess and George, who had given her money to buy souvenirs for their friends.

"They're neat!" all the recipients exclaimed, and Hannah hurried to the mirror to admire her matching necklace and earrings.

"And now tell us about your trip and what sleuthing you did in Japan," George begged.

Nancy and her father kept their audience spellbound for some time. Bess actually shivered at the episode of the man calling into her bedroom at the Mises', and again at the frame-up when the necklace was found in Nancy's kimono sleeve.

"I'm afraid we didn't accomplish as much as we had hoped," the young sleuth said. "We think, however, that we will be able to continue our work from here."

When Nancy finished her account, Mr. Drew turned to Bess and George. "Suppose you tell us what you've been doing during our absence."

George smiled. "We watched Mr. Moto's shop whenever we could to see if Mr. Kikichi would do anything suspicious."

"Did he?" Nancy asked eagerly.

"No. Not a thing. But one day on the way home we saw Mr. Moto in the back seat of a car. At least we think it was Mr. Moto. He seemed to be asleep. Perhaps he was drugged."

"George, that's a wonderful clue!" Nancy exclaimed. "We heard it from the Tokyo police chief but had no idea that it came from you!"

"We reported it to Chief McGinnis," Bess took up the story. "He promised to pass the information on to you."

"We tried to follow the car," George said, "but lost it in traffic."

"Did you get the license number?" Mr. Drew asked.

"Yes," Bess replied. "The police checked it out and found that the car was stolen. It was discovered the following day in a supermarket parking lot."

"Too bad," Nancy said.

As the group at the table was eating dessert, the telephone rang. Nancy, being nearest the hall door, jumped up and answered it.

"Is this Miss Nancy Drew?" a man's voice asked.

"Yes."

"I am a friend of Mr. Moto's. As you know, he's planning to go to Japan. Mrs. Rossmeyer is home now and is giving a surprise farewell party for him. She would like very much to have you come."

"Mr. Moto is still in this country?" Nancy asked, pretending to be surprised.

"Yes. The party will be tomorrow night at her home at eight o'clock. Please bring an escort if you wish. When you arrive, say to the doorman, 'Twelve and thirteen'."

Nancy, frowning, walked back to the table and sat down. "I was just invited to a surprise party and told to bring an escort," she explained to her friends.

"Who called?" Bess inquired.

"A friend of Mr. Moto's!"

"You're kidding!" Ned burst out. "Did he give his name?"

"No. He said the party would be held by Mrs.

Rossmeyer as a send-off for Mr. Moto, who is going to Japan."

"Then Mrs. Rossmeyer is home?" Mr. Drew asked.

"Apparently."

Hannah Gruen shook her head. "This is very strange. Mrs. Rossmeyer plans a party. There are no formal invitations, Mr. Moto appears mysteriously at Mrs. Rossmeyer's, and you're invited. She doesn't even know you! Something's fishy. I don't believe you should go."

"Hannah is probably right," Mr. Drew agreed. "What else did the man say, Nancy?"

"That was it, except he told me to introduce myself and my escort by the numbers twelve and thirteen."

"That does it!" Hannah cried out. "It's a trap! Nancy, I am afraid you are in great danger if you accept!"

"But if I don't, I might miss a wonderful chance to solve the mystery!" Nancy objected. "And if Ned comes with me and we're careful, I'm sure we can avoid falling into any trap. Ned, are you game to go?"

"I wouldn't miss it for the world," he replied. He flexed the muscles in his arms. "Bring on your crooks."

Everybody laughed, then Bess asked, "If Mr. Moto was responsible for losing Mrs. Rossmeyer's valuable necklace with the thirteenth pearl, why should she be giving a farewell party for him?"

Still puzzled, the group sat around the table for a long while. Then Bess and George said they should leave. Burt and Dave went with them. After Nancy had helped Hannah tidy up, the housekeeper and Mr. Drew said they were going to retire.

Nancy and Ned stayed in the living room for some time discussing what they might expect at Mrs. Rossmeyer's party. Nancy smiled. "I suppose I'll have to dress up."

"I brought party clothes myself," Ned announced. "One never knows what a guest of yours may be expected to do, or where he might be asked to go, so I came prepared with all sorts of clothes."

The house was very quiet, with Togo asleep in the kitchen. The couple sat in semidarkness. Not a sound came from outdoors, until suddenly there were footsteps and a commotion near the front door.

Nancy and Ned jumped up to see what it was. Ned took hold of Nancy's arm. "Don't open the door," he warned. "You have been in so much trouble, and this might be more of it."

A man's voice outside shouted, "Open up or we'll break down the door!"

Nancy and Ned did not move. The warning

was not repeated. Instead, there was a splintering crash, and the front door burst open. A huge vicious dog bounded inside, directly at the couple!

CHAPTER XVII

Pounds of Jewelry

BEFORE the police dog could attack Nancy and Ned, they bounded into the living room, jumped over the back of a sofa that stood cater-cornered to the wall, and dropped to the floor.

The furious animal jumped onto the sofa and snarled at them. He did not pounce on the couple, however, apparently afraid of being caught in the narrow enclosure.

"Help! Help!" Nancy and Ned shouted at the top of their lungs.

Suddenly the man at the front door called out, "This is your last warning!"

The big dog, meanwhile, had jumped off the sofa and tried to crawl underneath it in order to get at Nancy and Ned. He succeeded only partway, but kept snarling at the trapped couple.

"Help!" Nancy cried out again. "But be careful! There's a vicious dog in here!"

Just then her father came running down the stairway in his bathrobe and slippers. He carried a stout cane. As Mr. Drew reached the last step, the stranger, who stood in the doorway, commanded, "Don't interfere!"

Nancy's father paid no attention. He turned on the ceiling light in the living room and approached the sofa. At the same moment, Hannah Gruen appeared from the kitchen, also wearing a bathrobe and slippers. In one hand she held a broom, in the other a bucket of water.

Nancy suddenly remembered her pet. Frantically she called out, "Where's Togo?"

"Up in your room waiting for you," Hannah replied. "I shut the door, so he can't get out."

The unfriendly German shepherd had started to back out from under the couch. Hannah whacked him with the broom, and as soon as the dog's head appeared, she threw the bucket of water into his face.

The animal yelped in pain from the whacks, and his owner whistled for him. Willingly, the defeated attacker ran from the house. Ned pushed the sofa forward and hurried after him to the door. The visitors had already left in a car.

The lock had been broken, but with Mr. Drew's help, Ned managed to nail it shut. Then they pushed the sofa back into place.

In the meantime, Nancy had emerged from her hiding place and thanked Hannah for taking care of Togo, who was barking wildly upstairs.

"Shouldn't we report this to the police?" Nancy asked her father. "The dog might be a clue to who the stranger was."

"Yes, that's a good idea. Call right away."

Nancy spoke to the officer on duty and asked if he had a record of large German shepherds owned by the residents of River Heights.

"Yes, we do have a list from the license bureau. I'll phone each owner and find out where his dog has been," he promised. Twenty minutes later he called back. "Every German shepherd in town was indoors during the time when the vicious dog entered your home," he reported.

Nancy thanked the officer and decided that "the voice" and the vicious dog had come from out of town. She mentioned this to her father, and she remarked, "The stranger certainly is well-protected."

Late the next afternoon she and Ned dressed for Moto's farewell party. Since Nancy did not know where Mrs. Rossmeyer's house was, she decided to call Mr. Kikichi.

"Mrs. Rossmeyer is at home?" he inquired, amazed.

"I guess so," Nancy replied. "She invited me

to come and see her. Have you heard from Mr. Moto?"

"No."

This answer puzzled Nancy, but she did not tell Mr. Kikichi that the party was supposed to be in his friend's honor. She got directions and thanked the man.

On the way to Mrs. Rossmeyer's, Nancy and Ned discussed the situation. "It's over my head," Ned confessed. "Tell me your thoughts."

"There is a possibility Mr. Moto has not been kidnapped, but instead has chosen to go into hiding," Nancy said, but she did not sound convincing.

"But if this is so, why hasn't Mr. Kikichi been invited to the party?" Ned asked.

"Not only that," Nancy said, "But just before Mr. Moto disappeared, he told us that he had never met Mrs. Rossmeyer. If the party is really in his honor, she must have been introduced to him after that."

Ned added, "And perhaps he told her about you. That's why you were invited."

"Could be," Nancy agreed thoughtfully. "But I still think all this is very strange."

"I do, too," Ned said. "And so does your father. He gave me a bunch of keys in case Mrs. Rossmeyer is in league with the crooks and tries to lock us up in her estate." He pulled out two rings with master keys on them. "You take one, and I'll take the other. Your Dad felt they might come in handy."

"Good idea." Nancy smiled and put the key ring into her evening bag. "Dad thinks of everything to protect me." She smiled at her companion. "And you do pretty well yourself at the same job." She quickly added, to cover any embarrassment he might feel, "I'm suspicious of those numbers we were told to use for identification. I wonder what it's about."

"I'm with you."

"Suppose I say 'number twelve and escort' to the doorman? I'd like to avoid thirteen."

"That's a good idea," Ned agreed. "And please stay close to me. Together we'll be safer if any funny business is going on."

It was almost dark when they reached the road to which Mr. Kikichi had directed them. It was narrow, rutted, and looked like a lane through the woods, rather than the entrance to an elegant estate.

As they drove along, Ned remarked, "Mrs. Rossmeyer must like privacy, unless Kikichi is sending us in the wrong direction."

Just then, however, the house came into view. Many cars were parked near the brightly lighted entrance.

"He didn't." Nancy chuckled. "And there's really a party going on. Now I feel better."

"So do I," Ned said as he positioned his car in

such a fashion that they could make a quick get-away if necessary. Then the couple walked up to the house.

They could see people through the windows and paused to look at them. About half were American, the other half Asiatic. All wore evening clothes, but many of the outfits were so outlandish that Ned whispered, "They're dressed as if they were going to a Halloween party."

"And look at the jewelry! There must be tons of it!" Nancy said.

She was astonished at the gems the women were wearing. After studying necklaces, Nancy suddenly realized that so far as she could judge from the distance, every one contained twenty-five pearls. Like Mrs. Rossmeyer's stolen piece, there was a large center pearl with twelve smaller ones on each side.

The center pearl differed with each necklace. Some were white, others gray, many were blue, a few were rose-colored, and three of them were black.

Nancy pointed out her discovery to Ned. "There certainly must be some significance to that," she said in a barely audible voice.

"Perhaps we shouldn't go in," Ned suggested. "How about reporting the party to the police? By the way, the man who called you said it was a surprise. Well, I'd say it is!"

Nancy nodded but insisted they go in. "I have

a feeling we're on the verge of making a big discovery, and I don't want to back out now."

He finally agreed, and the two went up a few steps to a large, open veranda. From there they walked to the front door. It was opened by a man in a red velvet uniform. He looked at the couple and put out an arm as if to stop them.

To allay any suspicion on his part, Nancy smiled and said, "I am number twelve and this is my escort."

The doorman stared at her, and she and Ned held their breaths, wondering what would happen next.

CHAPTER XVIII

The Weird Ceremony

THE doorman at Mrs. Rossmeyer's home did not question Nancy and Ned. They went into a large hall, and from there into the living room where a reception line had formed. Mrs. Rossmeyer was heavily covered with jewelry from head to toe.

Nancy was amazed that she wore no necklace, however. Her white satin dress was covered with gems that sparkled in the artificial light. Even its standing collar and long sleeves were embroidered with numerous pearls, diamonds, rubies, and emeralds.

"She's decked out like a Christmas tree," Ned whispered to Nancy.

The young sleuth suppressed a smile and stared at the woman. She did not look at all like Nancy had pictured her. She was very thin, had prominent cheek bones, and a determined-looking chin. Her hair was straw-colored, and there was an overabundance of rouge on her cheeks.

"I expected her to be beautiful," Nancy said to Ned in a low, disappointed tone.

He grunted almost inaudibly. "She lets her gems make up for her looks!"

Nancy glanced along the receiving line and around the room. She did not see Mr. Moto, the jeweler. "I wonder where he is," the young sleuth thought.

In a few minutes, she and Ned moved up to the head of the receiving line, where Mrs. Rossmeyer was shaking hands with various guests, kissing some, and whispering into one woman's ear.

When Nancy reached the hostess, the girl said, "We appreciate your invitation. Your party is wonderful."

On the spur of the moment she decided not to use her right name. "I'm Nan Drewry," she added, "and this is my friend, Edward Nickson."

Mrs. Rossmeyer stared hard at them but made no comment. She turned to the Japanese man on her left. "I would like you to meet Mr. Moto," she said.

Startled, Nancy shook hands with him and asked, "By any chance are you related to Mr. Moto, the jeweler from River Heights?"

"No, I am not," was the answer.

Ned shook hands with the slightly built man,

but asked no further question. "I hope you enjoy your trip to Japan," he said.

"I am sure I will," Mr. Moto replied, and the couple moved on.

They mingled with the crowd, but realized that they knew no one, and none of the guests spoke to them. So their conversation was confined to admiring the gorgeous paintings, rugs, and tapestries with which the mansion was furnished.

As they walked back into the center hall, Nancy and Ned heard a strange noise upstairs. Curious, they went to the second floor. In one of the beautifully furnished bedrooms, an elderly American woman, dressed in evening attire and wearing a lot of pearl jewelry, was seated on the side of a bed. She rocked back and forth rhythmically, muttering to herself.

She paid no attention when Nancy and Ned walked through the open door. Wondering if the woman were ill and needed help, Nancy went closer. The old lady was mumbling in a singsong voice.

Ned grabbed Nancy's arm. "She's nuts!" he whispered. "If I were you, I wouldn't get too near her. You never can tell what people like that will do. She may attack you!"

Nancy heeded Ned's warning but listened carefully to the muttering. Finally she managed to distinguish a few words. "Sacred nacre, moon, high tides."

The woman was not only rocking, but rolling her eyes from one side to the other. She repeated the same words over and over and added, "Full moon, beautiful shell, lovely pink."

Nancy whispered to Ned, "These terms were used in ancient times in the pearl cults." Quickly she explained a little about this to him then added, "Maybe this woman belongs to a modern pearl-worshipping cult!"

Ned looked disgusted. "She belongs in a funny farm!"

Nancy hardly paid attention to what he was saying. She wondered if the woman was in a trance, or for some reason, was she acting? The stranger finally stopped muttering and began to moan, her voice rising and falling.

Ned said, "I can't stand any more of this. It's driving me off my rocker!"

Nancy consented to leave. When they walked out of the bedroom, an American man in evening clothes came up to them. He smiled and said, "Mrs. Rossmeyer would like to see you in her private quarters."

Ned hesitated, looking at Nancy. He felt they might be walking into a trap. Nancy nodded almost imperceptably, then started to follow the man. Ned went along reluctantly.

The stranger led them down the long hallway to a door. He clicked on a wall light, then opened the door. Nancy and Ned saw a narrow corridor in front of them. Did this lead to Mrs. Ross-meyer's private quarters?

The young couple entered the corridor and the door behind them locked itself. Their guide suddenly began to sprint toward a door at the far end of the narrow hall. Before Nancy or Ned could catch him, he had slipped through the door and pushed it shut.

Ned tried to open it, but the door was locked. Then the light in the hallway went out and they stood in total darkness! Together they groped their way to the other door. It, too, was locked.

Nancy and Ned were trapped!

For a moment the young people stood motionless, thoughts racing through their minds. Suddenly Nancy grabbed her friend's arm. "Ned—the keys!" she whispered. "Let's try all those keys Dad gave us."

"That's the best idea you've had all night," Ned murmured and pulled out his key ring. As silently as possible, he tried one key after another. None of them fit!

After he had fumbled with the last one, he sighed. "That's it. Now let me have yours, and hope we have better luck!"

Nancy handed him her set, and patiently the young man tried again. Finally one of the keys went into the keyhole. Ned maneuvered it carefully, gritting his teeth. Tensely he turned it, but the key stuck! Ned jiggled it back and forth and then turned it again. This time it worked! He opened the door a crack.

"Wow!" he said, wiping his wet forehead in relief.

The young people tiptoed out into the larger hallway. No one was in sight, but weird-sounding Asiatic music drifted from the first floor. The couple listened for a moment. There were no other sounds.

"What's going on?" Ned asked.

"I don't know, but I mean to find out!" Nancy replied with determination. "It's evident that whatever is taking place, Mrs. Rossmeyer and Mr. Moto didn't want us to see it!"

Carefully Nancy and Ned made their way to the stairs. They saw that no one was in the downstairs hall. Apparently all the guests had assembled in the living room.

The young sleuth stood in silence for a few moments, then motioned for Ned to follow her. Cautiously the two sneaked down the steps to the first landing. From this vantage point they could see everything clearly. Both gasped!

Ned whispered, "I can't believe it!"

In the center of the living room a small red velvet and gold throne had been set up. Mrs. Rossmeyer was seated on it, a pearl tiara on her head. The electric lights had been turned out, and hundreds of candles illuminated the strange scene.

The guests had put on long, white ceremonial robes over their evening clothes and formed a long line. They began marching around Mrs. Rossmeyer. As each one approached her, he or she bowed and then kneeled.

"What do you think this means?" Ned asked Nancy, a puzzled look on his face.

"It's some kind of weird cult," Nancy replied. "I think I know what it is. Tell you later."

Behind the woman seated on the throne stood a Japanese man. He held up a large, purple velvet banner with a beautiful open pink shell painted on it. Attached to one corner was a huge white pearl.

The thought flashed through Nancy's mind, "Could this be the thirteenth pearl stolen from Mr. Moto's shop?"

After the last guest had paid obeisance to Mrs. Rossmeyer, everyone began to dance to the weird music. The performers moaned and cried and rolled their eyes as the woman on the bed had done.

"This is crazy!" Ned declared. "We must call the police!"

Nancy nodded. "Let's get out of here. I hope no one sees us."

The two young people tiptoed down the stairs as fast as they could. Nancy held her breath and kept her eyes on the open living room door, hoping no one would notice them going past.

No one did, and when they reached the front door, the uniformed man was not in sight. Nancy and Ned breathed sighs of relief and slipped quietly out into the darkness.

They ran to Ned's car, and he started it. As he drove along the rutted lane, Nancy put a hand on his right arm.

"Ned, before we notify the police, let's go to the newspaper office!"

CHAPTER XIX

The Thirteenth Pearl

"THE newspaper office?" Ned asked, puzzled.

"Yes," Nancy replied. "I believe that the real Mrs. Rossmeyer is still in Europe and that the one who was at the party is an impostor!"

Ned was amazed. "You mean she just borrowed the house?"

"Yes," Nancy replied.

"I didn't realize that you had never seen a picture of Tanya Rossmeyer," Ned commented.

"Unfortunately I haven't, but the Gazette must have plenty of them."

When they arrived at the newspaper office, a young man at the front counter asked, "You wish to place an ad? It's too late for the morning paper. That has just been put to bed."

Nancy and Ned looked puzzled, and he explained, "That means the forms have been locked in place and the paper put on the press."

Nancy spoke up. "We didn't come about an ad. There may be a big story breaking for you people. May I see some photographs of Mrs. Tanya Rossmeyer?"

The young man, who said to call him Jim, went to an inner room to look through the files. A few minutes later he came back with a folder containing several photographs of the well-known socialite.

"Here she is," Jim said. "I hear the woman's loaded." He grinned. "That means she has a lot of money."

Nancy ignored his facetiousness. After she and Ned had looked at three different photographs of the striking brunette who appeared to be in her late thirties, they were convinced that the woman at the party had indeed been an impostor.

Ned thanked Jim, and the young couple left. When they were outside, Ned remarked, "So that 'goddess' was just a cheap fake!"

"Yes." Suddenly Nancy thought of something else and turned back to the newspaper office. "I wonder if there were any recent articles telling exactly where the real Mrs. Rossmeyer is," she said.

Jim was surprised to see them again. "Did you bring the big story you promised?" he asked.

Nancy smiled. "Not yet. I'd like a little help

first. Will you check recent papers to see if there have been any recent articles about Mrs. Rossmeyer?"

Jim went off and came back with a copy of the morning paper. "Maybe there's something in here," he said.

Nancy and Ned turned the pages and ran their fingers down the various columns. Suddenly Ned stopped.

"Look at this!" he said, and he began to read aloud:

> *Mrs. Tanya Rossmeyer of River Heights*
> *is giving a dinner party on Tuesday for*
> *Count and Countess Sorrentino.*

Nancy interrupted. "Tuesday! That's today! Where is the item from?"

"Paris," Ned replied.

"That settles it. Mrs. Rossmeyer is in Paris and not in River Heights."

"Is that the big story?" Jim asked.

Once more Nancy smiled enigmatically. "No. But I believe you will have it very soon."

Before the young man could ask further questions, Nancy and Ned raced from the newspaper office. Their next stop was police headquarters. They burst inside and told the officer on duty that a fake Mrs. Rossmeyer had "borrowed" the socialite's home and was having a big and very strange party there.

"What!" the officer said. "I'll get some men with squad cars to investigate at once."

Nancy suggested that the policeman follow her and Ned. "We've just come from the estate and know exactly where it is," she added.

While the men were assembling, Nancy told the officer that she suspected the group who was at the estate were jewel thieves. "They've probably robbed Mrs. Rossmeyer's house. Would you get in touch with my father and Chief McGinnis? I'm sure they'll want to come along."

When the young sleuth and her companion reached the Rossmeyer mansion, they found to their dismay that it was in darkness. The last car of guests was just pulling away. It was not coming toward them, but going out a back service road.

"Let's follow it!" Nancy urged Ned.

"Okay. But we'd better not get too close or the driver will become suspicious."

The chase led beyond the borders of River Heights, and Nancy was worried. Would the police go back now and perhaps notify the State Troopers to continue the hunt?

Nancy said nothing to Ned, but she wished she had brought her own car with its CB radio. Ned had driven his car to her home, and she had seen no reason to make a switch.

After they had traveled a good many miles, the driver ahead turned into a wooded area. The dirt road twisted and turned until it finally led to an encampment. The main house seemed to be a converted barn. For safety, Ned parked some distance away.

He and Nancy jumped out and quietly but quickly hurried forward. They encountered no one, since the people ahead of them had already gone inside. Cautiously the young people went up to the nearest window and peered in.

They recognized many of the people who had been at the party. They were standing around, still in their ceremonial robes, but the scene was not solemn. The cultists were talking and laughing loudly. One of them put on a record, and they began to dance singly or in couples, going through strange gyrations.

Presently two men walked near the window, which was partially open. They were Mr. Kampura and Benny the Slippery One Caputti!

Nancy and Ned dodged out of sight but remained close enough to listen. Benny Caputti laughed raucously. "We certainly pulled that one off all right. Good thing those kids didn't see us and Rosina!"

"That's right," Kampura said. "Praise to the pearl and the lovely moon goddess."

"Say, we brought so much food back, we'd better feed Moto," Benny said.

Kampura chuckled. "Which one?"

"Not our Moto, of course. The sneaky little jeweler who caught on to us and is now sitting in the dungeon!"

"We certainly have to decide what we'll do with him soon. I still think we should have gotten rid of him right away."

Nancy and Ned looked at each other. Mr. Moto the jeweler was the prisoner of the cult people! But where was he, in the house, or one of the other buildings? They wondered if the thieves had harmed him.

Kampura and Caputti were joined by a third man who snickered. "It's a good thing we locked up that girl and her boyfriend. The nerve of them to crash the party!"

The three men moved away from the window, and Nancy whispered to Ned, "They don't even know we've escaped!"

"And they don't know we were invited," Ned added. "I wonder who called you." Nancy admitted she had no idea.

At that moment two other men passed the window and stopped near it. One of them said, "We can't leave that girl and her boyfriend in the hallway forever. Early tomorrow morning, you go back and quietly unlock the doors."

His companion grinned. "And give them some pearl soup!"

Both men laughed uproariously but were interrupted by the "goddess." She reprimanded them for their hilarity and suggested that everyone go to bed.

"There is work to be done in the morning," she declared. "I have a new list of jewelry stores for you to work on."

The woman clapped her hands. Everyone fell silent, and she commanded the cult members to retire to their rooms. Within minutes everyone had left, and the lights were turned out.

Nancy and Ned wondered where the police were. Had the River Heights men forgotten to notify them. Or had the replacements not been able to follow Ned's car?

"Are you game to go inside the house and see if we can find a telephone to notify the police?" Nancy asked.

"Yes. Let's see if we can locate a door that isn't locked."

Not far from where they were standing was an open door. Nancy and Ned tiptoed inside. Before them was a flight of steps with another door at the top. Ned opened it, and they found themselves in a kitchen. It was in darkness, but a small flashlight Nancy pulled from her pocket illuminated their way to another door. It swung open noiselessly, and the two sleuths went into an elegantly furnished dining room.

No telephone was in evidence. Nancy thought, "Perhaps 'Mrs. Rossmeyer' keeps it hidden."

The two young people proceeded through

another door and this time stood stock-still, gaping in astonishment. They were in a small room with a large glass case in the middle of it. It stood on a pedestal, and in the center, swathed in purple velvet, was the form of a woman's neck and shoulders. A light in the top of the case shone on an exquisite pearl necklace draped over the form. Nancy counted the pearls. There were twelve on each side of a huge, magnificent center one with a slightly pinkish cast!

Nancy and Ned were stunned. Was this the one stolen from the real Mrs. Rossmeyer? Was it the one her companion had brought to Mr. Moto for repairs?

In front of the glass case, three figures in white hooded robes were kneeling on the floor. They remained in that position and gave no indication that they had seen or heard the young people. Every few seconds they glanced up at the necklace with adoring eyes.

Nancy put her lips to Ned's ear. "We *must* get the police!"

The two retraced their steps through the dining room and kitchen and went outside.

"Maybe the officers lost us and couldn't find this place," Ned suggested. "Why don't we walk up the road and wave them down?"

Nancy agreed, and they started off. As they hurried along the dirt road, they were suddenly stopped by two men who appeared from the bushes and blocked their way like huge, looming shadows!

Nancy and Ned stood frozen to the spot. Before they had a chance to think, they were tackled by the two men. As the young couple fought desperately, they smelled a strong, sweet odor coming from cloths that their attackers had shoved in their faces. Nancy and Ned blacked out!

CHAPTER XX

The Captive's Story

SOME time later, Nancy revived. She was lying on a hard, cold floor in total darkness.

Relieved that she was neither bound nor gagged, she sat up. "Ned?" she called out. "Ned, are you here?"

Ned tried to clear his head of the confusion resulting from his ordeal. "I'm here," he replied. "Where are you?"

Nancy felt in her pocket for the flashlight. Fortunately it had not been taken from her. She played the beam around. "I think we're in a barn," she said, "and—"

A low groan interrupted her. It came from a prone figure lying near Nancy. The young people rushed up to the bound and gagged victim, and Nancy shone her light on him.

"Mr. Moto!" she cried out in dismay.

167

Quickly Nancy and Ned unbound the jeweler and removed the cloth from his mouth. "Are you all right?" Nancy asked anxiously.

"Much better now that the gag is off," the man replied. As Nancy and Ned raised him to a sitting position, a smile crossed his face. "Miss Drew!" he exclaimed. "How did you find me? And who is this young man?"

"This is my friend Ned Nickerson. But before we tell you anything more, we must get away from here."

"How did you come in here?" Mr. Moto asked. "I was asleep and didn't hear anyone enter."

"We were taken prisoners," Nancy replied ruefully, "and gassed."

"Oh, dear!" Mr. Moto cried out. "Then we will not be able to leave. The big doors are padlocked on the outside."

Ned, who had gone to investigate, came to the same conclusion. "He's right, Nancy. There's no way to get these open."

"We'll figure out something," Nancy said, trying to sound calm. "In the meantime, Mr. Moto, tell us what happened to you."

"I found out about the cult and the jewel thieves, so they kidnapped me. Mr. Kampura did it. He left his sandals by mistake and was quite worried that they would be found."

"We did find them," Nancy said. "And we

suspected they belonged to him, but we couldn't prove it."

Mr. Moto nodded. "In order to avoid any suspicion," he went on, "they made me call my friend Mr. Kikichi and ask him to take over the store while I was supposedly in Japan."

"Then Mr. Kikichi is innocent after all!" Ned exclaimed.

"Of course he is," Mr. Moto said. "Do you know if he's all right?"

"Yes," Nancy replied. "I'm afraid he was hurt when your store was burglarized after your disappearance, but he's fine now."

"Oh, dear, oh—" Mr. Moto clasped his hands in despair and turned white. Nancy was afraid he might have another attack, but she and Ned managed to calm the jeweler.

"Please don't worry," Nancy told him. "Mr. Kikichi has recovered completely, and I'm sure we're close to solving this mystery, and you will be able to recover your losses."

"Tell us what happened to you after you were brought here," Ned urged.

"They held me in this barn and only unbound me long enough so I could eat and get some exercise. When I talked to you on the telephone, Miss Drew—"

"It was *you* who called and invited me to Mrs. Rossmeyer's party?" Nancy asked, very surprised.

"Yes, it was. The man who comes in here to watch me while I'm eating was called away on an emergency for a few minutes. I know there is a phone in the covered box over in that corner, so I used it."

"That was clever and very courageous," Nancy said admiringly.

"But why didn't you tell Nancy you were a prisoner?" Ned inquired.

"I was afraid that someone might overhear me on an extension. I am sure there are many phones in the complex here. That is why I disguised my voice and did not ask for help directly or tell you to go to the police. I thought you would catch on and try to rescue me."

"But how did you know about the party?" Nancy asked.

"I overheard two men say they were using Mrs. Rossmeyer's house for a big ceremonial celebration. They expected an honored guest whose name happens to be Moto, too. He was on his way to Japan."

"We met him," Nancy said.

"He is a close friend of the woman who calls herself Mrs. Rossmeyer," Mr. Moto went on, "and works as a liaison between this country and Japan. The fake Mrs. Rossmeyer is an expert jewel thief and organizes those who do the stealing for the Caputti gang."

"Are all the cult members thieves?" Ned asked.

"Not all. Only a select group. The others are dedicated pearl cultists."

"We must get out of here!" Nancy said after a moment of silence. "Can't we break down the door, Ned?"

"That would make so much noise we'd attract their attention, and they'd come running," he objected. "We'll have to think of something else."

At this moment they heard a loud commotion at the main house. Through a crack in the door, they could see lights flashing and orders being issued.

"The police have arrived!" Nancy exclaimed, relieved.

"If you're right," Ned said, "then we may as well try to break down the door!"

He looked around for a pole or another heavy article they could use as a battering ram. He found several new wooden fence rails and picked one up. It was very heavy. Ned took hold of the front end, Nancy grabbed the middle, and Mr. Moto insisted upon holding the rear.

Wham! The barn doors shivered but did not break. The three retreated a little, then ran forward into the wooden barrier again. This time there was a splintering crash.

"Once more!" Ned urged.

They went back farther, then rushed ahead

and with great force, rammed the door. The lock broke away, and the doors flew open.

The prisoners dashed out. Lights from cars and lanterns proved that the police had surrounded the house. Cultists in slippers and bathrobes were running from several exits, screaming and calling on the pearl goddess.

Nancy, Ned, and Mr. Moto hurried toward the house. The jeweler panted. "Crazy thieves!"

They found the place bustling with police. Many of the cultists had already been rounded up, including Mr. Kampura, Benny the Slippery One Caputti, and the "pearl goddess." She was being questioned along with the other Mr. Moto.

The officer in charge told her that all of them were under arrest, but the woman argued violently. In an arrogant manner she kept proclaiming her innocence, insisting that the cult was only interested in tranquility. Suddenly she noticed Mr. Moto, the jeweler, and blanched.

He cried out angrily, "I accuse you of kidnapping me and holding me prisoner, and of impersonating Mrs. Rossmeyer!"

The woman stared at him, speechless.

Nancy stepped forward. "You had me and my escort locked in Mrs. Rossmeyer's home tonight!"

Before the woman had a chance to reply, there was loud barking outside, then a policeman came in, desperately trying to contain a fierce German shepherd that bounded up to Mr. Caputti, pulling the officer along.

"That's the vicious dog that almost attacked us at my home after his owner broke the door down!" Nancy cried out. "And you were the one who sent me those warning notes in Tokyo!" She pointed at Benny the Slippery One, who glared at her in silence.

Two more prisoners were brought in, a heavy-set blond woman who struggled fiercely and a young Japanese man.

"Rosina Caputti!" Nancy exclaimed. "She managed to get out of the Tokyo prison with the help of Mr. Kampura and a number of forged documents! And that man next to her stole a pearl necklace from Mr. Moto's shop and made his getaway just when my girl friends and I arrived."

The officer in charge looked at Nancy admiringly. "You seem to know more about these people than we do. Would you be willing to testify against them?"

"Yes, indeed," Nancy replied.

Mr. Moto spoke up. "While you are busy rounding up these criminals, I would like permission to search this house. I am sure I can identify many stolen pieces of jewelry. From conversations I overheard, I know where some of their hiding places are."

"Go ahead," the officer told him, and Mr. Moto,

Nancy, and Ned started off. The girl sleuth first led Mr. Moto to the room where the priceless necklace was displayed in the glass case.

Excitedly he rushed up and examined the piece. "It is the one, the very one, that was stolen from me! The one Mrs. Rossmeyer left in my care!"

Mr. Moto took the lid off the glass case and reached in. With almost loving hands he lifted the necklace from the figure, gazed at it, and dropped it into his pocket.

"I am so thankful to get it back," he said, "and Nancy Drew deserves full credit for finding this."

Nancy blushed at the praise. "I had plenty of help—my girl friends, my father, and Ned, to say nothing of Professor Mise and his wonderful relatives in Tokyo."

"You went to Tokyo?"

"Yes. My father and I stayed with the professor's brother and his wife. While I was there, I tried to find your brother, Tetsuo, because I thought he might be able to tell me where you were. But he had moved, and none of the neighbors knew his new address."

"How did you know I had a brother? You are an incredible detective."

"Mrs. Rooney, your neighbor, told me."

Mr. Moto smiled. "She is a nice lady. I talk to her often. And you are right. Tetsuo moved to a small town near Kyoto. In a way, I am glad you did not find him. He knew nothing about my problems, of course, and if he had any idea of my disappearance, I am sure he would have been very worried."

Nancy nodded. "So it all turned out for the best. Now we'd better continue searching this house."

In their hunt, the trio found most of the pieces that had been stolen from Mr. Moto's shop while Nancy and her father were in Japan.

"This proves that the cultists were responsible for that robbery," Nancy said, "and for harming Mr. Kikichi."

Mr. Moto pulled open a secret drawer in a desk that he had heard Kampura mention to another member of the cult, and he pulled out many strings of pearls. Each one had a thirteenth pearl in the middle!

"Look how beautiful they are!" Mr. Moto said. "All different hues. I wonder where these came from?"

"There have been many thefts, especially in Japan," Nancy said. "I'm sure the pieces can eventually be identified and returned to their rightful owners."

Her next find was a diamond and ruby necklace. "That's like the one that was slipped into my kimono sleeve to make me look like a thief!" she said.

"Where did that happen?" Mr. Moto asked, taken aback.

"At a wedding in Tokyo."

The jeweler threw up his hands. "It is true that World Wide Gems have dishonest people working in every country!"

"I'm afraid so," Nancy answered. "No doubt this will come out at the trial."

"I wonder who the leader of the group is," Nancy mused.

"Mr. Kampura. I overheard someone say this. He has confederates all over the world who are giving World Wide Gems a bad name."

"What about the real Mrs. Rossmeyer?" Nancy asked. "She's on the board of directors of that company, you know."

"I was not aware of that. But I do know she is a fine, honest lady. Just before she left for Europe, Mrs. Rossmeyer had me appraise a lot of her jewelry. They are among the pieces we found."

At this moment Mr. Drew and Chief McGinnis walked into the room. The lawyer grabbed his daughter affectionately.

"Thank goodness you're safe!" he said. Then his eyes fell on the jeweler. "Mr. Moto!" he exclaimed. "I'm so glad to see you. Where have you been?"

"Tied up in the barn. Nancy and Ned saved me from a terrible fate," Mr. Moto replied. "I must make charges against my kidnappers and the other jewel thieves. Will you represent me?"

The lawyer said he would be very glad to do so. Together the men walked into the room where the "pearl goddess" was still arguing with police about her innocence.

Mr. Drew said to her, "How do you explain your connection with World Wide Gems, Inc.?"

At first the woman would not admit anything, but finally, seeing that her protests were useless, she broke down and told the full story.

The heads of World Wide Gems, Inc. were honest men, but many of those under them in various countries were committing thefts under the supervision of Mr. Kampura. They also employed groups of thieves, and they used the cultist organization to cover up the operation and their encampment as a place to hide their loot.

After all the guilty parties had been taken away by the police, Nancy and Ned drove off in his car to return to River Heights.

"Nancy, you did a great job," he praised her as he drove down the wooded lane.

She merely smiled and said, "You were a terrific help, Ned." She paused a moment, then said, "Do you think we'll ever get another mystery to solve?"

Ned chuckled. "It's just like you to say that, Nancy. It seems to me that you have had quite a few mysteries to solve since *The Secret of the Old Clock.*"

Mr. Drew had offered to take Mr. Moto to his home. On the way, the Japanese jeweler said to him, "I think you have the most wonderful daughter in the world!"